I0831356

All characters and situations in this book
with the exception of locales, historical figures
and events are fictitious. Any resemblance to
actual persons living or dead is purely coincidental.

ISBN-13: 9780615663555
First Edition

A sincere thank you to

Serigo Toscanno at Fresno County Homicide,

Steve Dugas at LaTech Aviation,

Jimmy Liuzza at Antoine's,

The friendly staff at Lincoln Parish Library,

Ricky Johnson at Anadarka,

and Laurian Garner for her enduring patience.

For my children

Patrick, Alissa, and Lina

BEHIND THE IVY

The Falling Reign

by

Edward P. Cummings

PART I

The Legend Unfolds

One

AN UNPLEASANT rolling of his stomach, more so the winding road than the destination, Nathan Lewis can't take it anymore—the Louisiana forest closing in on him. "Excuse me," he spoke with a sense of urgency, tapping the driver's shoulder, "… can you pull over? I'd like to sit up front if you don't mind."

Pulling to the side of the road, the young driver, nineteen-year-old Nick Adams, said it was no problem. "Happens out here all the time," he assured Nathan, never witnessing or having been carsick himself.

A sturdy frame just shy of six-feet, forty-one years old and in good health, Nathan got out of the cab with little effort. He has a rugged look about him: unruly hair down to his collar; dark afternoon stubble; and a thin, pinkish scar bordering his left brow. Women who are preoccupied with his blue eyes overlook the scar. Those that don't, romanticize on how he got it.

Lightheaded, Nathan breathed in the stale air, a quick stretch before sliding into the front seat. "You're not lost, are you," he asked.

"No, this is the right road," answered Adams, consulting his roadmap. “It’s the number that’s wrong.”

Somewhat concerned, Nathan pulls out a telegram, reading aloud for the third time the address at the end of the message.

“I’m pretty sure the eighty-two-hundreds are in Ouachita Parish,” said Adams. “Though every now an’ then one ‘ill show up halfway ‘cross the State.” Folding the map in disgust, Adams returned to the road—careful with the accelerator.

Clutching the telegram, Nathan said to him earnestly, “Well, it’s good to have a map regardless … is it not?”

Each bend more sullen than the one before, the further they drive the closer the trees seem to huddle together. A gloomy, repressive corridor, mile after mile the road engulfs Nathan’s dwindling space; his breath erratic and Adams asking if he’s okay.

“I’ll get over it, once we’re out of these miserable woods.”

No way of knowing the next curve to be the last, the sun appears on a most welcome stretch of road; a once majestic now withering mansion looming in the background.

The estate is surrounded by a wall of stone and mortar. A narrow, asphalt drive leading to the mansion, Adams pulls alongside a rickety mailbox just outside.

“I can’t make out the name,” said Nathan, leaning out the window, “… go ahead and drive up.”

The narrow drive, riddled with weed infested cracks and giant potholes, Adams renders the estate as deserted; his despondent gaze certain of it. “You’re sure about this … this being the right place and all?”

Stepping from the cab, Nathan confirms they have the right house. The flight from Pittsburgh and long drive from the airport, he’s inclined to stretch his legs. Lingering around the cab, stalling more than stretching, after a minute or so Nathan confronts the mansion—his father’s buried past as he sees it.

In stolid wonder, an invidious memory takes hold. What took place on Thursday, two days ago, Nathan recalls he must have been at lunch when the tragedy occurred. The shocking news was given to him that night, but even more shocking, Western Union showed up bright and early the next morning.

A wary Adams pops the trunk, unloading two large bags and a carryon. "This may be the right house," he said, looking around, "… but what if nobody's home?"

Nathan read the telegram to himself once more, folding it in half, running his thumb across the crease. "No, there's someone here," he said. "I'm certain of it."

Adams took charge of Nathan's luggage, making his way toward the house.

"You don't have to do that," said Nathan. Submissive for two days, people not letting him do for himself, Nathan advocates it's time to be productive again. Placing a value on the young man's company, though they were lost for nearly an hour, it was good to talk to someone who didn't offer you their deepest sympathies. Rendering the fare, Nathan a very generous man, he told Adams to keep the change.

The young man, a long drive ahead, got in his cab and sped away; a premonition coming to Nathan as he stood there all alone. Entwined with a summer's leaf floating across the driveway, Nathan had a funny feeling a journey of his own would soon take flight.

An enormous lawn, the ambulant leaf succumbs to a grand fountain—lodging at the base of an eight-foot Conquistador. The ironclad figure points his spear toward the heavens, his granite eyes peering over the wall in a chiseled trance, appearing as though he's plotting to conquer the world.

With the leaf no longer free, *a ward of the soldier*, Nathan empathizes completely, turning to and confronting the house where his father grew up.

A morbid sight of better looking days, the mansion is covered in a ragged blanket of ivy. Bare vines overwhelm the porch and Nathan takes a deep breath, making his way up the concrete steps.

The pillars and walls are ripe with mold, and the only thing amiss, as Nathan can see, are the security bars over the windows and doors—all having a fresh coat of paint.

Grabbing the one remaining doorknocker, Nathan sent a thunderous jolt throughout the mansion. The echo quickly subsides and he hears the faint sound of footsteps descending a staircase. In a brief period of time, somewhere between the bottom of the stairs and the front door, the footsteps are no longer there and everything is quiet.

Leaning forward, his ear between the iron bars, Nathan is startled by an arousing click, the inner door then cracking open and a suspicious eye peeking through.

"Hello," inquired Nathan, tilting his head at the eye. "I'm looking for my grandmother, Margaret Lewis."

The door creaked ever so warily, a tense moment as the sparse opening bears the silhouette of a thin but shapely figure.

"I'm sure this is the right address," attested Nathan, scanning the telegram with his finger. "2641 Parish Road 82 … *14?*"

The door inhaled a summer's breath, its opening wide enough to show Nathan the seasoned features of a woman he once met as a child. A pair of deep-green eyes studied his face, promptly surveying him from top to bottom. Leaning her silver head forward, the woman spoke softly with a cognitive tone. "Your name is Nathan … is it not?"

What she said gave Nathan a chill. Quite often he'll ask a question in the same backward manner—the intonation word for word. *Dialectic grammar*, thought Nathan, his father's idiom confirming his relationship to the old woman.

Removing a ring of keys from her apron, a long-sleeve

blouse and comfortable slacks underneath, the old woman unfurls the bars separating them. Her eyes move back and forth across the lawn. Satisfied with what she sees, or does not see, the old woman grabbed Nathan by the wrist, pulling him inside and shutting the door. "Sorry about that," she readily apologized.

"No harm done," Nathan pardoned the old woman, baffled by her strong grip.

"Now," said the old woman, smiling for the first time, "… let me get a good look at my grandson." The old woman stepped into the foyer between a pair of winding staircases and grand balcony. "*Nathaniel Alexander Lewis*," she emphatically declares. "You've grown into a handsome man. Your hair is a bit long, but it suits you. You've always been a defiant one. And I see you have a scar… *how odd*."

Nathan's reaction is subtle, the only bright spot on his haggard face.

"You have my father's smile. I remember that about him. He always smiled when I was around." A sorrowful look came about the old woman and she paused for a moment. "I was beginning to worry about you, wondering if you received my telegram. Sorry about the last minute booking. There were no first-class seats available. It must have been uncomfortable for you. My goodness. *Where are my manners!* After all you've been through, would you like to sit down?"

"Yes, but I'd like to bring my bags in first."

Nathan leaned toward the door and the old woman put a hand on his shoulder. She looked worried. "I have someone who'll tend to that."

"Is everything all right?"

"Up until Thursday, everything was fine."

Adams popped his favorite cassette into the player, Stevie Ray Vaughan resonating from the speakers. Tapping the steering wheel like a small drum, a limousine fast approaching, Adams slows down, hugging the shoulder.

A native of Shreveport, though Adams has seen his share of limousines, he's never seen one this far from the highway. With the exception of the windshield and front windows, Adams glancing at the chauffeur, the rest of the windows are blackened.

Keeping an eye on the vehicle in his rear-view mirror, the woods swallowing the image, Adams wonders where the limousine is heading, the cassette then switching tracks and the song *Crossfire* playing.

On Parish Road 230, the limousine comes to a sudden stop and two men invade the grassy shoulder. The dark skinned warriors, one much older than the other of eighteen, are wearing nothing but a leather pouch around their neck and loincloth over their genitals. Both are barefoot with solemn streaks of paint covering their cheeks. Their heads are banded in olive and ruby colored cloth; the knotted strands dangling in the back alongside their long, barbed hair. They are both tall, strong looking men, each one possessing a bamboo tube and carousel of tiny darts lodged in a wooden armlet.

A man whose upper arm is wreathed with a leafy tattoo hands them a bottle of water with Latin markings. The warriors take a drink, listening to the man speaking in their native tongue. "Toncha! Umbogwa domtaloa mogui-ia! Quickly I say. Now go!"

The two warriors rush into the woods, loincloths and hair flopping back and forth. The man with the leafy tattoo shut the door, instructing the chauffeur, Raymond, to head for Shreveport.

The shrewish and frail inhabitants of the forest are unaware of the warriors, both men remarkably silent along the briery path they take. The afternoon sun is brutal and beads of sweat clothe each warrior, creating tributaries that soak their loincloths and wet the ground. A stone wall appears from out of nowhere and the warriors quicken their assault.

Five miles from where they started, Tantur is the first to arrive at the wall, cupping his hands for his young brother, Wahota.

A lanky teenage boy handles an armful of luggage on the other side of the wall. The boy has light, ebony skin and appears to be in good shape, carrying the bags with ease. There is a soft thud by the wall and the boy turns around, blaming the noise on some critter he saw the night before.

In a dingy corridor filled with portraits and impressions where others once hung, Nathan and his grandmother are talking about family relations—Margaret's eyes filled with regret. "Now I spend my time," said Margaret, "looking at photographs of those I have no memory of. Come," she turned to Nathan, "… I promised we would sit and talk."

Margaret took Nathan to a sizable parlor where a swamp-cooler churns the musty air. A monstrous fireplace stands guard over an ancient pair of armchairs and she offers Nathan a seat. A table-lamp with a shade full of jaundice looking tassels sits between the two chairs. Like a pitched tent, a copy of *Gone with the Wind* adorns the table.

"I see you're into the classics," said Nathan, an opportunity to add some light and conversation to the room.

"Oh, that? I pick it up every now and then."

"May I," asked Nathan, reaching for the book.

"Of course," answered Margaret. She switched on the lamp and Nathan's eyes question her cotton gloves. "I have a skin rash," declared Margaret. "The gloves keep me from scratching."

Returning to the book, Nathan inspects the binding. "They don't make 'em like this anymore. A first edition, is it not?"

Margaret invites him to read the inscription.

"To Margaret Lewis," Nathan read the inscription aloud, glancing at Margaret "… a young and vibrant admirer whose company I enjoy. I am pleased that we share the same name. Sincerely, Margaret Mitchell." Nathan put the delicate treasure back on the table. "You knew Margaret Mitchell?"

"I've spoken with her briefly on a few occasions. A pleasant and articulate soul," said Margaret. Pausing as though she is in deep thought, Margaret then turned to her grandson with a quizzical look on her face. "Nathan," she asked.

"Yes."

"There are a number of things I wish to tell you. And to be honest, I'm quite nervous about it. You're probably wondering why I keep to myself; never calling upon you until now."

Finally, thought Nathan, *she's going to reveal the mystery behind her reclusiveness.*

"I think it best to start with your mother and father's untimely death. I know this is an arduous time for you. A sensitive subject, but we must press on."

"The last two days," said Nathan, "have been exhausting, *painful to say the least*. I'm sure it's been like that for you as well … but go ahead," he encouraged her, "I'm all ears." *And I need answers,* he thought.

"For you, Nathan, it must have been a terrible shock. I, however, feared this might happen. But not to your mother."

Nathan appeared confused.

"It was no accident," said Margaret, "… not with your father at the controls."

The frightening vision of a reoccurring scenario crept into Nathan's jaded thoughts—what it must have been like moments before his mother and father crashed into that mountain. Nathan envisioned the terror on their faces as his father relayed the aircraft's position; his mother questioning their decent. He can hear their screams and the terrible sound that followed.

"Nathan, are you all right?"

"I'm fine," he answered.

Nathan felt as if he were going to weep. Stepping away from Margaret, his eyes are fixed on a section of marble above the fireplace. "I can't stop thinking about what went on up there."

Margaret rose slowly from her chair, placing a hand on Nathan's shoulder.

"I lost those dearest to me," said Nathan, "… and what's so strange … *so intuitive* … I never believed for one second it was an accident. Dad's been a pilot all his life. He knew that plane better than any airline mechanic. This is all happening so fast," blurted Nathan, avertedly stepping away. "It's like I've known you all my life— but I haven't. I'm here for ten minutes and you tell me exactly what I've been wondering myself."

Nathan can feel the surging of his pulse, sitting once more beside Mitchell's classic, rubbing his forehead.

"Nathan, I am truly sorry. No one wants to hear such news about their parents. But it's the truth. They were murdered."

A delay in his response, a rap on the door beckons Nathan's head around. Someone peeked inside the doorway, then full-figure stepping forward. "Gonna be takin' off now, Miss Margaret. The bags is in from outside. Anyth'un else ya wants done 'fore I take off?"

"No, that will be all for today, Shadwell. Come inside for a minute before you leave though. I'd like you to meet someone."

Margaret introduced the seventeen-year-old as her spirited helping hand and Nathan to the teenager as her salvaged grandson.

"Pleased ta' meet ya, Mist'a Lewis." An energetic hand reached out and Nathan shook it.

The boy's fingers were long and he had a strong grip for someone with such a wiry frame. Margaret expressed her gratitude for his help around the house. "I don't know what I'd do without him," she concluded.

The boy, Clarence, offered to bring Nathan's bags upstairs and Nathan thought it considerate of him; accepting only because he's tired. Grabbing one of the bags, Nathan followed Clarence down the hall, as Margaret, a roast needing her attention, told them to go on ahead without her.

The two warriors are laying low in the confines of the withering estate. Tantur is stationed in a coppice of wilted azaleas in the front while his brother, *scratched and bruised from crawling around*, recuperates underneath a backyard gazebo.

Bare skinned like his brother Wahota, strangely Tantur is unscathed. Cursed with an unusual thirst, he takes a drink from a nearby hose.

Wahota has dried meat in the pouch around his neck and takes a small portion for the time being. Tantur, however, a plastic device in his pouch, has nothing to eat; even though Wahota offered to share what little he had before they split up.

Looking at the mansion, neither hungry nor thirsty, the wilting ivy is a disconsolate site to Tantur. Neglect ravaging the roots, destroying its healthy vine, Tantur is desperate to look away, but having a job to do he can't… the once luscious plant souring his watchful eye. He wished he could do something. Salvage a clipping and take it home.

One day, as he's been planning all along, Tantur will take back what rightfully belongs… his people and the ivy thriving together.

Nathan stopped in the middle of the stairs, his mind fabricating visions of that horrible mountain. Eyes yawning to stay awake, he focused on the foyer below. He imagines the mansion in its prime for he did not expect to see it in such ruin. It should be as elegant as depicted by his father. The layout appears as his father said, the only thing missing is the rich glaze of paint and fresh air to the lungs.

The past grandeur of the mansion, deplorable now, Nathan recalls the far-from-ordinary, somewhat prominent life of his family. "In times of innocence and malevolence," his father told him, "… our lives never change. Everything good is tarnished by everything bad."

Regardless of the past, Nathan is quite proud of his heritage. His grandmother, an only child, her father was killed when she was barely five, and now Margaret, as old as she is, most memories of him are vague—or suppressed because of what happened.

Despite her father's untimely death, Margaret did exceptionally well in school; exceeding all others no matter what the subject. At twenty-two she fell in love with Nathan's grandfather, Stuart Morgan, a writer from New Orleans. Two years later, on September 16th, 1928, a week before their wedding, Stuart disappeared during a savage hurricane off the coast of Florida. He could not have survived where two-thousand others perished. Margaret, however, escaped the ordeal, as did Nathan's father, safe in her womb.

Clarence stopped at the top of the stairs, putting one of the bags down.

"Be right there," said Nathan. "I just need to catch my breath."

Returning to his ascent, Nathan counted every step to the top, recalling the tragic death of his great-grandfather, Alexander Lewis.

An inheritance of land from Alexander's great, great-grandfather, Benjamin Lewis, a distant cousin to the explorer Meriwether Lewis, Alexander became a wealthy and influential man early on; his sugarcane and lumber profits making him one of Louisiana's wealthiest land owners.

Unfortunately, Alexander did not live long enough to manage such an abundance of wealth.

Nathan's father, Stewart, spoke of that only recently. Reaching the top of the stairs, Nathan lowered his head envisioning that horrific day. One man hurried to the spot where Nathan stood, throwing a rope over the chandelier, tying it to the banister. Another man grabbed a footstool below as a third fashioned a noose slipping it around Alexander's neck… young Margaret playing in the gloomy room Nathan just came from. She must have heard her father pleading for his life, rushing in as the men balanced Alexander on the stool.

One of the men pushed her away and Margaret fell to the floor, returning to her father in an instant. Margaret tugged at her father's pant-leg and he had a loving smile on his face, one he could not maintain as the man who knocked Margaret down pulled her to the side. Margaret looked up at her father. There was a short period of silence, Alexander's eyes adoring his daughter for the longest time, when suddenly, the footstool spinning across the floor, the last thing Margaret saw was that same loving smile on her father's face.

The awful vision faded and Clarence brought Nathan back to the present, asking if he's okay. Nathan told him how tired he is, elucidating on the need for a shower and full night's sleep.

Clarence took the luggage to a cozy, well lit room. An inviting bed, relative to those in Mitchell's classic, its mattress high above the earthy, Savonnerie carpet, Nathan pays it no mind, eyeing instead the adjoining room with its cast iron tub and snowy curtain.

"How ya like it," asked Clarence.

"Very nice," replied Nathan. "I especially like the table and chair next to the window."

"Thought ya might. Miss Margaret says ya don't take kindly ta' bein' boxed in."

"You arranged this room, Shadwell."

"Clarence," the boy accentuated his name.

"Well, you did a nice job … *Clarence*."

"Thanks. It took near all day cleanin' it up. Ca'webs mostly. Miss Margaret, keepin' t'erself and all, she don't mind an untidy house."

"She's always been so reclusive. Why is that, Clarence?"

"I don't rightly know. My Uncle Will, I reckon he could tell ya."

"That name sounds familiar," said Nathan, sitting on the bed removing his shoes. "William Shadwell from New Orleans, right?"

"Yep, that's 'em. Only I calls 'em Uncle Will. Can't recollect anyone callin' 'em William 'cept Miss Margaret."

"Wasn't he my grandmother's personal bodyguard or something?"

"Uncle Will, *a bodyguard?*" The boy laughed, amused at the thought. "Naw, he was more like a personal s'tent. He u'sta travel everyw'ere with Miss Margaret. Even foreign places, stayin' in fancy hotels an' eatin' rich food. Told me 'bout a swamp in Florida one time, an' how he almost got ett by a gator. 'Da way he was tellin' the story, I don't 'thank he was no bodyguard."

"Florida, huh?"

"Yep. He say Miss Margaret left 'em there and they ain't talked ta' one 'nother since. W'ile later, Miss Margaret heads back 'erself … 'cept she bolts ever' now an' then ta' N'awlins fer a spell."

Another piece of the puzzle in place, Nathan thought about what Clarence said, remembering a conversation between his mother and father about William. "Clarence Shadwell, things are starting to clear up. Not much, but the fog *is* lifting."

"Shadwell's my uncle, Mist'a Lewis. My last name is Brooks."

"But my grandmother calls you Shadwell."

"Miss Margaret been callin' me that ever since Uncle Will talk'd me in ta' cleanin' up roun' here. Bothered me the first day 'er two. I kept tellin' 'er my name was Clarence Brooks but it didn't do a bit a good. She's real nice ta' me so I gots use to it. Sides, makes me feel good t'way she carries on."

"You admire your uncle very much, don't you?"

"Yeah, you could say that. 'Cept, he's been more like a best f'rin than an uncle."

"I'd like to meet him someday."

"We don't live fer, two miles down 'da road, first dirt road ta' yer left."

They talked a little more, Clarence mentioning how nice it is to have Nathan visiting Miss Margaret, then how terribly sorry he is about Nathan's tragic loss. When Clarence bid goodnight, it took Nathan a short time to pry himself from the bed, easing into the shower and cranking but one handle, the refreshing, cold water pelting away his fatigue.

His spirit replenished, two days of strife spinning down the drain, Nathan grabbed a towel. Sitting on the corner of the bed, the thought of his father in the same room, grief worms its way deep into Nathan's battered heart.

Outside, his bike next to the garage, Clarence wonders if his uncle started supper. Margaret had asked him to stay, but the teenager said it was getting late, wanting to make it home before the roads disappear.

Clarence looked at the aging horizon, and Tantur, a dart missing from his armlet, points his blowgun at the boy's dusky silhouette.

With one end of the blowgun between Tantur's lips, a deep breath filling his lungs, Clarence stepped out of the shadows.

Tantur knows right away who it is, and without hesitation, no sudden movement or faint sound, he lowered the blowgun, young Mr. Brooks then speeding away.

Two

THE MOON TOOK siege upon the torturing sun and the afternoon heat surrendered. An intolerable kingdom by day, a score of empty stomachs emerged; unwittingly, the cottontail, rodent, and insect alike—an army of hungry mouths rising at their heels. Countless nocturnal wings rage the blackened sky as the wildcat prowls voraciously the boundaries of its realm. The hunters, chasing the hunted, at one point all are pursued. A multitude of surging appetites, they abstain to catch their breath, moving methodically lest they be dead.

Among the shrubs and bristled weeds, Tantur stalks Margaret's home with incredible vision; the scent of his prey emanating from an open window. Checking the pouch around his neck, Tantur's hand trembles unexpectedly, the plastic device milling in the throes of his powerful grip. Without warning his stout posture buckles and he crashes head first into a rabble of jimsonweed.

The episode lasts a short time and Tantur is rejuvenated, the azaleas and withered brush around him appearing as a ruffled bed. He listens outside the kitchen window and Margaret's conversation with Nathan is no longer private.

Nathan explains to Margaret his regret for having made no

attempt to patch things up with his father. He loved his father dearly, but never having said so as an adult, Nathan is afraid the guilt may plague him for the rest of his life. "Too late to reconcile differences now," he confessed.

Margaret is aware of the falling out, insisting that Nathan explain his point of view. *Better to let it out than have it fester*, she thought.

Nathan fidgets to stay awake, sleeping a burden he's put off before. "He wanted to control every aspect of my life. Grades nine through twelve he chose my courses, my friends … everything. He had my life all mapped out. My senior year in high school he came to me during finals, explaining how easy it would be to take up engineering. He spoke to a friend of his at Pitt and there was no need for a discussion, the enrollment papers were ready to sign. He said I was on my way."

"What did you do," asked Margaret, taking a seat across from him.

"I said I was on my way all right. You should have seen the look on his face when I told him I was going to Princeton instead."

"You didn't do anything wrong, Nathan. Most young men in your position do the same thing. But you mustn't blame Stewart for what he was trying to do." *If anyone,* Margaret told herself, *blame me*. "A good number of skeletons remain locked in our family closet, and detrimental to the wrong people, your father threw away that key a long time ago. Now I'm the only one with any knowledge of our reprehensible past. A past that needs explaining, but not until you've had a good night's sleep."

A puzzled look appeared on Nathan's face. "What do you mean by *reprehensible?* We're not part of the Mafia are we?"

"Heavens no. There, you see, I think I've said too much already. This family has some very old secrets. Unfortunately, there are others determined to preserve what we know and will stop at nothing to keep it from the rest of the world."

Nathan suppressed a yawn, his jaw aware of its new purpose, *to speak when need be*—many questions running through his mind. As fatigued as he is, his back succumb to sitting, both hands clinching his knees, Nathan steadies an anxious ear, intent on learning the truth behind his parent's death.

"The people who did this were afraid," said Margaret, squaring her shoulders, "… afraid of their precious secrets being known. Secrets that could change their way of life forever. Killing two innocent people meant nothing to them. *Nothing at all!* All they care about is keeping what they have to themselves, making examples of those who start snooping around."

"Who, Grandmother?! Who?!" Nathan could not believe his own ears. He was a passive man, literally losing his temper in that college argument with his father. Now here he is raising his voice once more, and his father, regrettably, the cause of it. "Who killed them, Grandmother? Who killed my parents?!"

"Desperate souls, Nathan. Powerful men with one common goal. One man in particular is responsible."

Once again Nathan looked confused and Margaret continued without realizing it. "Stewart was never a danger to them. He didn't know enough. But they felt threatened anyway. And they had no idea your mother was in the plane."

Margaret paused for a moment, a tear swelling then racing down her cheek. "Nathan, your father was never controlling. If anything, he was watchful of you. He chose your friends because he knew their fathers. The university he wanted you to attend was nearby so he could keep an eye on the facility and students."

Scowling as if the blame were seated across from him, Nathan delivers a quiet but harsh statement: "These are people … *you know!*"

"I've not seen nor associated with any of them for over fifty years."

"Who are they," demanded Nathan, his bold voice taking charge of the conversation.

"I think it would be best if you didn't know … although, from what has transpired it doesn't seem to matter. I love you a great de—"

"You don't even know me!" Nathan scornfully cut in.

"I suppose I deserved that. But you must understand I had to stay away from you. Your mother and father as well. It was the only way to keep you all safe."

A lot of good that did, thought Nathan, holding his tongue.

"I have no idea what triggered this. Sending for you was not an option. These people rid themselves of any and all threats. They can make it look like an accident, suicide … you name it."

"What about the police?"

"The police are of no use. It's best that I keep quiet, never revealing what I know to anyone. The consequences, as you are aware, are much too severe."

"I don't care. Please, tell me everything."

"Tomorrow, I promise. I know you won't sleep well, but you must try. We're safe here. Surveillance cameras monitor the grounds and every room has a keypad to the alarm. There are motion detectors along the perimeter of the house, and if that's not enough," Margaret points her finger, "… the pantry has a panic-room. There's a switch under a box of pancake mix on the middle shelf. It activates a latch and the shelves swing out."

After an explanation of operating the alarm, Margaret mentions an early appointment with her doctor she can ill afford to miss. "You can go with me," she said. "I'll explain everything on the way."

Nathan refused. He'd had enough conversation for now. Besides, a morning of undisturbed sleep sounded so much better.

Once a month, Dr. Laurian Webster takes a private plane to Ruston, her appointment with Margaret always at a predetermined hotel. Margaret pays for the flight and all expenses, though Laurian insisted from the beginning she stop by her office in New Orleans—which Margaret did the first time, taking her to lunch and shopping afterward.

Laurian now looks forward to these trips each month. She and Margaret have much in common, reading classics like *Gone with the Wind* and horticultural at the top of the list. But poor Margaret, forced into pretermission of the latter, the flowers Laurian brings each month are intended for something else.

If the thirty-eight-year-old doctor had any complaints about the trip, it would be the weather. It's 6:30 and the morning is already muggy. A restless night behind her and a ninety-minute flight ahead, Laurian considers a power nap. She had too much on her mind, however, so she couldn't possibly fall asleep. Purple, tuberous begonias are on the seat next to her. Moving them aside she takes out a thin, paperback novel from her briefcase.

Laurian's daughter, Amy, the first of two rented movies still in the machine, fell asleep early last night—a quality Amy did not inherit from her mother. Laurian was up until 3:00, reading the *Steinbeck* classic now in her hand. Up before dawn, consorting a fading star in her cozy bathrobe, like every morning she had juice and toast at her windowsill.

Margaret's twin-engine Cessna, a fully loaded 340A, still has that new-plane smell. Margaret paid cash for it and trusts no one but Richard Gregory as her pilot. An employee at Gulf Coast Charters, an air service provider at Lakefront Airport, Richard is one of Laurian's closest friends. She introduced him to Margaret last year and he's been her pilot ever since.

"All set," asked Gregory, securing the hatch.

"Good morning, Richard. Yes, I'm ready."

Gregory sat down reaching for a clipboard, Laurian two seats behind strapping herself in. An attractive woman, Richard considers Laurian to be an Audrey Hepburn lookalike, though not as tall. They've been good friends since the early days of the war in Vietnam; Richard serving for nearly six years. He now leads a harmless civilian life. Battling his wife for the TV remote, he too looks forward to these monthly excursions.

A rare expression, Laurian smiled at Richard who is flipping switches and pressing buttons. A single mother for nine years, Laurian lost her husband, Michael, to Leukemia long after he and Richard returned from Nam. Amy was two at the time and Michael entrusted Richard to keep an eye on both her and Laurian. "Jungles of a different war," Richard told his dying friend, "*I've got your back*."

Margaret Lewis moved rather well for a woman her age. Wearing dark slacks, a long-sleeved blouse and leather gloves, she hurried out the door. At precisely 7:30 her presence is well observed, pulling her BMW out of the garage. While on his stomach, Tantur has but one wayside shot, spewing a low, whizzing dart at Margaret's impregnable sedan.

In a matter of minutes, the BMW's fender pulsating in a perfect, unwanted rhythm, Margaret pulls to the shoulder. The driver's-side tire is flat and while inspecting the sidewall,

Margaret finds what appears to be a dart protruding out.

They're here!

Grabbing her purse in a frenzied rush, some of it spilling onto the seat, Margaret takes a quick look at the road before disappearing into the trees.

A limousine pulls alongside the BMW shortly thereafter, a pair of smooth, cinnamon legs stepping out, embellishing the rich soil. "One set of tracks, Father. She's gone into the woods."

"I expected as much," said the man with the leafy tattoo. "Come back inside, Ariel. It's up to Tantur now."

The slender, twenty-four-year-old Ariel listens to her father. At 306 pounds, a solid six-foot-six to the top of his smooth head, his massive chest a cathedral for his demanding voice, Ariel knows all too well her father is accustomed to having his way.

Aware of her frailty, Ariel does not fear anyone or anything, and her father is no exception. Even at the age of nineteen, watching him strangle a man did she cower. Her father's illicit nurturing, grafting ethos of bane contempt upon Ariel's budding maturity, the killing actually brought out an emulative desire in her. Ominously motivated by that agnatic side, Ariel too is accustomed to having her way. A cunning instinct, she would rather go after Margaret herself, but with nothing to gain arguing with her father, she submits to his onerous voice.

Twisting her short-skirted hips around, her shaded eyes peering into the front seat, Ariel's calculating fingers glide atop the BMW. Joining her father, a drink in his hand, she crossed her legs and spoke impassively while staring out the window. "She left her mobile phone behind."

"Good fortune smiles upon you, my daughter. It will make your job much easier."

Having dozed off around midnight, Nathan slept soundly until a disturbing noise beckoned him to wake. Drifting in and out of an insufficient sleep his eyes remain closed, pleading for the ringing to stop. Tenfold of normality, the phone calls him from across the room. *Wake up. Wake up, Nathan. It's time to wake up!*

His mind switching from standby to alert, the phone twitching on a corner table, Nathan remembers his grandmother's appointment, reluctantly climbing out of bed.

"Hello."

"*Hello*," a female voice replied, somewhat surprised. "I think I may have the wrong number. I hope I didn't wake you."

"No," said Nathan, too tired to say otherwise.

"I thought I dialed my friend Margaret's number."

"You did. I'm her grandson."

"Her grandson? Oh, wait a minute … I remember her mentioning you the other day. Nathan, right?"

"Correct. And you are …?"

"Ariel," answered the voice, "… *an old friend of Margaret's*. Sorry to disturb you. May I speak with her."

"She's away at the moment. A personal matter in Ruston."

"Oh that's right, her doctor's appointment. I forgot about that. Could you be a dear and do me a favor. I think I left my purse in the gazebo the other night. Can you get it for me. That is if Margaret hasn't done so already. I'm afraid if a raccoon discovers it I'll never see it again."

"Expensive?" Nathan sounded sympathetic.

"Not very. More of a sentimental value."

"I could check on it now if you don't mind waiting."

"Umm … I'm calling from a mobile phone. Rather costly you know. I'll be by in a few days and will pick it up then. Tell Margaret I'll call her later."

"I will. It's … Ariel, right."

"Yes, that's right. Thank you, Nathan. It's sweet of you to do this for me. I have to go now. Thanks again."

"You're welcome," Nathan replied, yawning at the end.

Ariel pressed the cancel button, sitting the mobile phone next to her father.

"Nicely done," he said, swirling his thumb over a piece of smooth sandstone.

Three

ARIEL DIALED ANOTHER number and the pouch around Tantur's neck buzzed and quivered; a signal that Margaret had strayed from her car. Tantur then cut the phone line, motioning to his brother to stay alert. The plan now in motion.

Nathan disengaged the alarm and opened a window, the warm air advising him on how to dress. Rubbing his eyes, he considers whether or not to look for Ariel's purse or go back to sleep. Turning toward the bed, Tantur appeared at the front gate—a gate that is now closed. Startled, Nathan took a step back, Tantur then scaling the gate, vanishing behind the wall.

Recalling what Margaret said about the people who killed his father, Nathan fled to the back of the room, believing the person out front to be one of them. Slipping into an old Princeton jersey, he peeked outside… a plausible notion involving explosives and how to trigger them coming to mind.

Grabbing his favorite running shoes, Nathan sat down. *Where would it be? In the house*, he questioned himself. *No, I turned off the alarm like two minutes ago.* A chill then besieged his skin and Nathan sprang from his chair. "The back door! The woman on the phone. I've been setup!"

Nathan thought it best to call the police but his conversation with Margaret told him otherwise. *All these bars and this high-tech alarm in the middle of nowhere. Who are these people?* "I'll call and report a prowler. What's the worst that can happen?"

There was no dial tone and Nathan slammed the receiver down. "That's it, I'm dead."

Lacing his Reebok's, the panic-room in mind, Nathan froze instantly while reaching for the doorknob, a dozen spy novels unraveling in his mind. The possibility of the gate-climber having broken into the house, *in all likelihood planting a bomb*, Nathan examines the trellis outside his bedroom window—the one he opened without being blown to pieces.

Wahota, quiet as a mouse, waits patiently for the deadbolt to snap. He is aroused instead by a disturbance out front. Crunch … crunch … crunch. Crunch … crunch … CRASH!

A resounding thud fills the air and Nathan lay on the grass covered in pieces of trellis and sallow looking ivy. Rising to his feet, unscathed if not for a sore back, Nathan wonders where to go next. Setting his sights on the conquistador, from there he'll scale the gate and look for his grandmother. He'll need a ride for that, however, and there's only one place he can think of to find one.

We don't live far, two miles down the road, thought Nathan, recalling what Clarence told him. "Great," he grumbled, checking the road outside the gate, "… which way is down?"

Crouching at the base of the fountain, the gate relatively close, Nathan took a long look around… no sign of movement anywhere; even the clouds screening the horizon are at a standstill. Judging whether or not he can scale the gate, Nathan glanced up at the conquistador. Weathered cracks below the eyes of the soldier made him look old, and what the birds left behind like he just returned from a snowy march. Nathan then caught sight of a cavity at the base of the fountain where a plaque used to be. He wondered what became of it. If he had more time to examine the rest of the sentry-like figure he would, but its security had been breached and Nathan felt he was in harm's way.

His attempt at the gate did not go as smooth as Tantur's, but Nathan made it over, something moving in an upstairs window as he looked back. Squinting for a closer look, a small animal is pacing the windowsill. *Probably a cat,* thought Nathan, rubbing his brow. *A big, sharp-clawed cat.*

Reluctant to leave his post, Wahota had no choice but to investigate the noise. Avoiding the motion sensors in the shrubs and trees, he discovers the broken trellis and two sets of tracks leading to the gate.

Nathan found a number of bicycle tracks heading north, following them along the shady side of the road. It was the same wooded stretch he came through yesterday and he tried to run fast but his lungs held him back. The last three days were catching up and he tells himself to take it easy. *Short strides, Nathan. No sense in collapsing on the way. Wisdom versus strength. It's the smart thing to do.*

Unearthing a buried memory, Nathan recalls where that expression came from. It was an adage his father used during Nathan's high school and college years. Not only were the last three days catching up, but part of Nathan's past as well.

The characteristics of a bloodhound, and far more stamina than Nathan, Wahota scales the gate with ease. Shifting into high gear, his iron legs churning at Olympic speed, Nathan lagging in the soaring heat, Wahota too is catching up.

Approaching the turn to Shadwell's house, his jersey soaking wet, Nathan stops for a quick breather, unaware of his barefoot tracker abandoning the road, slicing through the trees.

With his aleatory stride determining his fate, Nathan increased his languid pace, the change in velocity rather weak and Wahota having to slow down. Curving to his right, Nathan sees a dirt road of rich, lobster-colored earth ebbing between the trees. *This must be the road Clarence was talking about,* thought Nathan.

Stepping out of the woods, Nathan sees a truck coming down the main road. Shaken by the sight of it, he does an about-face, moving erratically along the edge of the trees.

Unable to get a clear shot, a number of trees separating them, Wahota got down on his stomach, grinning contently as Nathan, his unsuspecting prey, wandered into a small clearing—a stubby oak the only protection in the middle of nothing.

Slithering on his belly, using every muscle in his body to smother the sound of pine needles and foliage, Wahota takes a a dart from his armlet, eager for his prey to step out from behind the stubby oak.

Nathan had stopped for a moment at the tree to catch his breath in the shade. Grabbing a low branch, he moved it to one side as he was leaving. The soft pop of Wahota's blowgun distracts him and the branch snaps back in place. A sharp pain in the web of his thumb and finger, Nathan thought he was stung by a bee. What he felt and saw, however, was a tiny, feathered dart dangling from his skin. Scrutinizing the dart, he is compelled to look around.

Wahota took out another dart, drawing the blowgun to his mouth.

Like a deer caught in the headlights, staring into the glaring eyes of what appeared to be a cannibal or headhunter, Nathan's heart dropped. "And here I am worried about the Mafia," he said to himself, ducking behind the stubby oak.

Once again Wahota is looking to gain a new vantage point, while Nathan, extracting and tossing the dart aside, sprints into the open. A second dart is launched, whizzing through the sleeve under Nathan's arm into the open air.

Breathing heavily while mustering the last of his adrenaline, Nathan made it to another tree. He can see Wahota loading a third dart and he knows he's running out of time.

Wahota is impressed with Nathan's agility. The dirt road, now a stone's throw away, the young warrior can see where Nathan is heading and he positions himself accordingly.

The sultry morning, having absorbed all his energy, Nathan isn't sure if he can make it across the road without getting shot. With the underbrush thicker on the other side, he can see there are more places to hide, but more importantly, he might find something sharp or heavy to fight with.

Nathan took a deep breath. Time to run.

Wahota also took a deep breath, calculating Nathan's probable speed and the distance from one side of the road to the other. He figured on at least three good shots… but that could change if Nathan fell.

Bolting from the trees, Nathan did not weave or dip or shift his feet. He ran a sprinters race and the first dart hit him square in the back. He flexed his shoulders to absorb the pain as Wahota, stepping from the trees, fired his second dart.

The dart threw Nathan off balance and he staggered, veering to the right while struggling to stay on his feet. Wasting no time, Wahota leveled his blowgun and took a third shot, anxious for a forth but Nathan disappeared into the trees.

Nathan hit the ground on all fours. Looking around the deciduous forest, it bore no hope of escape, nor any weapon to puncture the skin or use as a club. The only weapon Nathan can think of, he can't reach around to pull them out. He tried taking his jersey off, but it was pinned to his skin and the more he tugged the more the darts gouged his flesh.

Aargh! Nathan grimaced, one of the darts mercifully

popping out. With his teeth clinched and knees dug in, a numbing sensation taking hold, Nathan pulled the bloody jersey over his head, dislodging the remaining darts as he slid face first to the ground.

Too disoriented to stand, a grim reality is sinking in. Nathan freed himself from the pain but the relief he felt was not right—the numbness was spreading.

Crawling to the edge of the bosky soil, Nathan sees a house at the end of the dirt road, a few hundred feet if not more. Palming a tree for support, he clambers to his feet, and what seems like drowsiness, accepts the fact he may have been poisoned. Not the type of death he expected, and certainly not this soon, unless on the Capitol Beltway in some massive pileup. At forty-one life was just beginning; what about his plans of touring Europe or one day writing that best seller.

This can't be it, thought Nathan, *on some dirt road in the middle of nowhere!*

Dizziness then took over and Nathan's vision became ovate and hazily distorted. A red clay-like substance, he made it to the dirt road, moving sluggishly but in the direction of the house. Between his sixth and seventh step he managed to take a deep breath, once more empowering himself to run.

Straining to keep his eyes open and stay on course, his back and chest cavity suddenly numb, Nathan feels as though he can run forever. The inevitable, however, came to quickly, his limbs faltering like he'd been dipped in Novocain. His arms swing less determined, as his stride, like the rest of his body, he can no longer control. He does not hear nor feel the warm breeze floating through the trees, only the slow cooling of his heart. Unaware of his surroundings, or of life fading fast, Nathan makes it to the house collapsing on the front steps, a gash in his shoulder from the fall and fresh pair of darts lodged in his back.

Four

DETECTIVE SAMUEL Taylor, noting the time on the wall clock at 8:45, pulls a chair from under his desk and settles in. Twenty-seven-years-old, a slender five-foot-ten, Taylor has brown hair feathered with gel and clean shaven cheeks with a pointy, dimpled chin. A breakfast sandwich and Styrofoam cup in front of him, Taylor's work space is the most organized at the Eighth District Station—two other detectives in the room recollecting when they too dressed well and kept a tidy desk.

A seasoned street-cop from Atlanta, now a rookie detective in New Orleans, this being his third week of nothing but paper work, Taylor is longing for a little excitement.

Biting into his sandwich, the Cajun flavor compensating for another bland day, an attractive female, Connie—*something*, strolls across the room over to Taylor's desk. A three-page facsimile in her hand, Taylor fastidiously wipes a droplet of sauce from the corner of his mouth.

"This just came in. Give it to Alcott when he gets here."

"Sure, Connie. So, another Sunday volunteer, huh?"

Connie gave Taylor a polite smile, mostly for remembering her name. "No, I just happen to have quick fingers on the typewriter. I always get the call for these last minute filings."

"Tough break. Sounds like you had something planned."

"Yeah, my day off. Make sure Alcott gets that right away."

Sedulous eyes from the other two men, Connie swaggers back to her desk, an ostentatious display of long legs and masterful hips.

Assistant to Louis Alcott, the District Homicide Captain, one of Taylor's jobs is to sort Alcott's messages, separating work related business from the everyday junk. Glancing over the fax, Taylor is suddenly overshadowed by Detective Cary Monroe, a heavyset Creole with a square, pinkish face and light-blue eyes.

"Wha'd ya got d'are, Samuel?"

"An FAA bulletin. MSY faxed it over this morning," replied Taylor, taking a bite of his sandwich as he continues to read.

"Not d'at," Monroe pointed to Taylor's breakfast, "'da sandwich ya got d'are. A right dressed one by 'da looks of 'et. Wha'd ya get?"

"God, Monroe, is that all you think about?"

"D'at an' sex. So, wha'd up wit' d'at fax?"

"Hold on," said Taylor, sipping from his cup while flipping to the next page. "Apparently, the FAA was investigating a plane crash on Friday … two dead, man and a woman … happened Thursday … Appalachian Mountains … small aircraft out of Pittsburgh. The FAA contacted the airport the plane originated from … blah, blah, blah … here we go … on Wednesday a mechanic at the airport noticed a suspicious looking man leaving one of the tarmacs. He approached the individual and the man said he was just admiring one of the planes. Local authorities went through the security tapes and a positive ID was made."

Taylor then turned the page, gazing intently.

"Well," asked Monroe.

"There's a picture of the guy and a description from the mechanic."

"'Les have a look."

"It's not very clear," said Taylor.

Monroe squinted, reaching into his breast pocket for his glasses. "I'll be damned. So ya finally slip up after all d'ese years, a' Carlo."

"Carlo?"

"We got a 'o filing cabinet on d'ez one," said Monroe.

"So you know this guy."

"Yeah, everyone 'ere know Carlo. 'Da State a Louisiana know 'em as Carlos Ernesto Somoza. A heavy player d'at man."

"What's his story?"

"'E pretty good at what 'e do an' even better a' not getting caught. It's been five years and nobody's seen him. Lucky d'at mechanic showed up when 'e did."

"Five years," Taylor speculates, "… I was cutting my teeth in Atlanta five years ago."

"I was assigned to 'ez case back d'hen. Two months a surveillance, six court appearances and a year a fillin' out paper work, all flushed down 'da shitter cause a 'ez connections. 'Ad 'em fer murder we did. 'E kill a doctor outside 'ez home over in 'da Garden District. 'Da evidence was solid an' when 'ez lawyer asks for bail, 'et was denied 'cause a 'ez priors. 'Da man was in every t'ang from muscling folks to extortion. But 'e escape from jail two nights after 'ez locked up."

"Sounds like he's got a few friends out there."

"Most of us 'ere d'ink 'et was an inside job, but no one knows how 'e got away. 'E slipped right pass 'da surveillance cameras."

The other detective in the room called out to Monroe, asking him to leave Taylor alone and bring him his file. "Be right d'are," Monroe hollered back. "Better give d'at to 'da Captain soon as 'e get 'ere. 'E gonna be t'rilled wit' d'at one."

Waiting for Margaret, Laurian sits alone at the Ruston Airport, Richard having flown to Shreveport to visit his mother; a short hop Margaret insists he take rather than hanging around the airport. Richard spends about an hour with his mother and sister, and at Laurian's request, carries a pager in case of an emergency.

Margaret would have called if she were running late and Laurian's concern, not so much for Margaret's health but for her safety, is growing by the minute.

Laurian knows Margaret's medical history better than those unscrupulous friends of hers. But in regard to her personal life, only one man, William Shadwell, knows more about Margaret than Laurian does. Unbeknownst to William, however, who knows little of Dr. Webster, Laurian knows a great deal about him because of Margaret. In fact, Shadwell has no idea Dr. Webster is a woman, or that her area of expertise is in Microbiology—Research and Development. All Shadwell knows, from what Clarence told him, is that Margaret meets with Dr. Webster once a month. And Margaret, being a notorious eccentric, William wasn't at all surprised she flies Webster in from New Orleans.

A payphone at the terminal, Laurian punched in Margaret's home number, letting it ring for a couple of minutes before trying her mobile.

Ariel's father and Tantur are at the BMW, estimating how long Margaret's been gone when her mobile phone interrupts them.

"You have to move quickly," said Ariel's father. "It won't be long before the doctor realizes something's gone awry." Handing Tantur a bottle of water, he tells him Margaret will be thirsty. "And remember … she is not to be harmed."

Tantur left his blowgun behind, bolting into the woods; Ariel then climbing out of the limousine, making her way over to her father. "Shall I answer it?"

"No," her father replied. "It must be Webster. The grandson would not be calling … unless—"

"He has a mobile phone of his own."

"Yes."

"Wahota must have taken him out by now. Let me answer it, Father."

"If it is the grandson and he recognizes your voice … what then?"

Ariel grinned. "I shall tell him I met up with Margaret at a restaurant and she's in the ladies room. I'll let him know she hasn't seen my purse and if he's not gone out looking for it to do so now."

Her father smiled. "And if it is someone else?"

"I shall tell them—" the phone stopped ringing and Ariel paused.

"You are a clever girl, Ariel, but if it rings again we do not answer. Tantur will arrive with Margaret soon enough and all will be right once more."

Margaret stays alongside the 148, as the next road, Mt. Zion, comes into view. As narrow a road as the one she's been following, Margaret turned left on Mt. Zion, the passageway caressing the pines and the temperature dropping a degree or two. Chafing through the brush, she plucks a thistle from her ankle, cursing the Cariban Warrior responsible for puncturing her tire.

Out of breath, Margaret doesn't have much time. She knows she's being hunted and wonders if traveling in the opposite direction, to the home of William Shadwell, will he help her after what she did to him.

Keeping to the trees along Mt. Zion, Margaret spots a capacious, chalky-white building across the street. A car is parked on its grassy lot and there is a small cemetery surrounded by a low-lying fence next door. *Why the fence,* Margaret asked herself.

Taking a deep breath, the warm air drying her throat, Margaret thinks about crossing over, both spiritually and the narrow road. Fearing her soul would be trapped, she did not like the idea of ending up in a cemetery with a fence around it. Her estate, however, without question her spirit would find a way out of that prison.

Another deep breath, Margaret longs for the refuge the building across the street can offer—a ligneous, white sign posted out front: Mount Zion Baptist Church, est. 1830, Sunday Worship 10:30 am – 11:30 am. She can read everything on the sign from across the street, except for the time of worship in small print. *Surely God is close by*, she thought. *We haven't spoken for a while, I suppose now would be as good a time as any.* Margaret stepped forward and as she did the branches beside her swung back, giving way to a body blocking her path.

Tantur stands before her, flaunting his achievement.

Startled, but unafraid, it's a look Margaret has seen before. Her anger, the last of what she has control over, she dropped her purse, pounding Tantur's chest vigorously. Her face tearfully swelling and arms weakening, Tantur grabbed her by the shoulders calming her down. "If you had anything to do with Stewart's death," said Margaret, backing away, "I swear to you … you'll be the one running for your life. And not from some skinny savage with a blowgun, but a real professional. One who's into smashing bones and pulling teeth!"

Tantur snickered. “You don’t know anyone like that,” he said in his best English.

“I can find someone! The right price and a man will do just about anything. Your boss knows all about that.”

“*Boss?* He’s not the boss of any Cariban, you know that,” blared Tantur. “Your son and his woman,” Tantur then spoke softly, picking up Margaret’s purse, “… I am sorry for your loss. A terrible accident as I was told.”

Margaret shut her eyes, a contorted face and teary cheek. “I thought you were brighter than that,” she spoke harshly. “He had them killed.”

“I do not think so.”

“Why not ask him the next time you see him,” said Margaret. “Tell him you want the truth.”

“Ask him yourself,” Tantur replied, handing Margaret a familiar bottle of water.

Overcome with fear, Margaret took a long swallow, her pungent face confused by the taste.

“What’s the matter,” asked Tantur.

“I don’t know. Something’s different.”

Tantur took a drink. “It tastes fine to me. What do you mean by different?”

“Never mind,” said Margaret. “It’s not important.”

“Then why mention it,” uttered Tantur. Negating his concern, he then nudged Margaret toward her abandoned car.

Raymond took the spare out of the BMW just as Margaret emerged from the woods. She is overwhelmed with fatigue, Tantur stepping aside as Raymond, wiping his greasy hands, escorts Margaret around the BMW to the limousine. A motionless face and wide, bullish-chest, Raymond leaned forward, opening the door for Margaret.

Margaret's stomach curled as she sat facing the man with the ivy tattoo, his attire and shaved head the only thing different when she last saw him. Ariel is sitting beside her father, eyes peering out the window and Margaret having no idea who she is.

"I believe an introduction is in order," said the tattooed man. "Margaret, this is my daughter, Ariel."

Ariel turned, scowling intently at the frail looking woman, returning then to the window and the muscular physique of Tantur outside.

"You look much older than when I last saw you, Margaret," remarked Ariel's father. "Rhytidectomy does not appear to be a part of your vocabulary any longer."

The man reached for Margaret's face and she slapped his hand. "The enormity of your behavior sickens me, Marcus! You killed Stewart, I know you did. I stayed away. We both stayed away and still you murdered him. He had no intentions of going to the island. And his wife, she knew nothing of it … or the cave as a matter of fact. Outside of your little entourage here, I'm the only one who knows its secret now."

"What about your grandson … *Nathan?* You spent a few hours with him last night. How much does he know?"

Margaret had a feeling Marcus knew everything there was to know about Nathan. "Do not do this, Marcus. He doesn't know anything. I swear to you, no one knows. It's been so long I doubt if I could find it myself."

"You're a terrible liar, Margaret. You know where to look," said Marcus revealing his tattoo. "It's behind the ivy. You do remember the night your betrothed Stuart found it. He was going to take you to it. But he never made it back."

"Stop it! Stop it, Marcus!" Margaret could feel his animosity choking her, and though Marcus would never physically harm her, he used the death of her fiancé like the back of his hand. "What do you think, Ariel? Do you believe Margaret is telling the truth?"

Ariel studied Margaret's reflection in the window. "I think she could find her way back. She doesn't appear that stupid to me."

Marcus grinned. "I must apologize for my daughter's harshness. Although, I have to admit, I agree with her assessment."

With an appeased look, Marcus told Ariel to go outside. "Raymond will be finishing up soon. Now leave us."

"You're an intelligent woman, Margaret, undoubtedly you could find your way back if you had to. Perhaps you could take along Dr. Webster, or that half-wit butler friend of yours. That is to say," Marcus lowered his voice, "… if the two of you were to reconcile your differences."

Margaret became fearful, Marcus knowing so much about her personal life. "Don't worry, your friends are safe. All of them busy in their trivial little worlds. I am somewhat concerned with Dr. Webster, however. But the situation will rectify itself. As for Mr. Shadwell," Marcus paused while rubbing his head, "… after that incident on the island, he's inclined to believe that I'm dead. Isn't that right?"

"What you say is true. I have no idea how you found out, but yes, neither they nor Nathan know the whereabouts of the cave."

Marcus then drew close to Margaret's ear. "*What about its contents,*" he whispered.

Margaret froze, expecting the worse, Raymond then getting behind the wheel. Her BMW stirring up a cloud of dust and gravel, Raymond switched on the intercom, telling Marcus that Ariel and Tantur are on their way.

"I believe you were about to have breakfast," said Marcus,

looking intently at Margaret. "I too am hungry. Hungry for a great many things." Flipping a switch, Marcus spoke casually to the air: "Raymond, follow Ariel. We are all going to Margaret's for breakfast."

Wahota's father taught him to hunt when he was only five. An anxious pupil, he listened carefully to his father's experienced tongue, but it was Tantur, the oldest of five brothers, Wahota would later emulate. A long way to the porch, using the woods as a shroud, Wahota surveys the area around Nathan's body. He knows Marcus will be angry with him for letting the grandson escape. *Perhaps*, thought Wahota, *if I bring him back safe and sound that anger will turn to praise*.

A breeze tickles an arch of limbs, and Wahota, stepping from the woods, moved like a cluster of lolling branches. Approaching the wooden porch, the steps likely to creak, Wahota proceeds with caution along the edge, the dusty surface undisturbed while crouching beside Nathan. A sudden crackling on the ground behind him, Wahota turned his head, just as the butt-end of a shotgun comes crashing down.

A tall, black elderly man with polished gray-hair, William Shadwell points the shotgun at Wahota, inspecting his handiwork. A bloody gash in Wahota's forehead, Shadwell lowered the gun, yelling to an open window, "Keep a sharp eye, Clarence. Especially to the woods. There may be more of them out there."

A gun barrel protrudes from the window, a sign that his nephew is paying attention. Nathan, belly down with his left profile up, blood staining the porch from where his shoulder hit, Shadwell pulled the darts from his back, promptly rolling him over pinching a blood vessel in his neck.

"He's got a pulse. A rather weak one, but he's alive. Open the door, Clarence, then go back to the window and cover me."

The old man drug Nathan into the house, breathing heavily as he closed the door. He bandaged the wounds on Nathan's back and the gash in his shoulder, placing a damp towel on his forehead and pillow under his neck. "How is it out there," he asked Clarence, "… are things still quiet?"

"Nothin' out there but the breeze, Uncle Will. Yer eyes 'er workin' p'erty good fer yer age. What made ya 'thank there'd still be somebody hangin' around?"

"The darts in that man's back. Someone had to claim him."

Clarence turned and for the first time saw the body's face. "Tha's Mist'a Lewis. Jesus! He gonna be all right?"

"I'm not sure. We'll know in a few minutes. Do you remember what I told you about that tribe in South America?"

The boy's eyes exploded. "Them cannibals?"

"Yes."

"I think I's near twelve when ya told me that story. D'ay never know if they's usin' poisonous darts, or … what's them other ones d'ay load in them pipes?"

"A tranquilizer dart. And they're called blowguns, not pipes," Shadwell corrected his nephew. "The Cariban, or cannibals as you refer, relish a challenging hunt. Especially if they're stalking a man. If the victim is to be brought back, in most cases tortured and eaten, the hunters receive nothing but tranquilizer darts. They only dip them in poison for a death sentence … and no one knows if they have the fatal darts or not. The condemned were given a chance to clear themselves of any wrong doings if they escaped. But that didn't happen too often. As you can see, a plain dart can be just as lethal."

"What kind 'a darts er those, Uncle Will?"

"Only the man who gave those darts to that Cariban

warrior knows the answer to that question. One thing's for certain, *they're not plain.* These are minor wounds. He collapsed on the porch because they were dipped. We'll soon know which ones they are. Poisonous darts will kill a man in a few minutes. We'll give him ten minutes and if he still has a pulse, he'll remain just as he is for an hour or so."

"But what if ya can't find a pulse by then?"

While picking up his shotgun, his head down low, Shadwell raised his eyebrows at the boy.

Clarence realized it was a foolish question.

At ten o'clock, Laurian finished her second diet soda, pumping three more quarters into the machine. She'd once been instructed to sit tight if Margaret was ever late. And never, no matter what may arise, was she to leave the airport alone. She thought about that for a moment, searching the local directory for a taxi.

Clarence kept an eye on the body outside, edging the curtain open with one hand while balancing his scatter-gun in the other. There are no fences around the property, and with a hundred feet of bare forest in every direction, it's easy to spot unwelcome guests. The two-bedroom house is dimly lit, modest furnishings with Nathan lying unconscious on the floor. Clarence felt he should be on the sofa but his uncle said no. The boy had to keep one eye on Nathan and the other on the perpetrator outside.

The morning breeze, steering a cloud in front of the sun, Clarence starts to worry about Miss Margaret, a shadow then crossing over Wahota's face. Clarence caught the shadow out of the corner of his eye. Excited and perplexed, he hollers to the kitchen, "I 'thank he moved, Uncle Will."

Shadwell came into the room empty handed, stepping over Nathan and joining Clarence at the window. "Let me have a look." Seizing the boy's shotgun, Shadwell took aim at the front steps, Clarence watching as his uncle cocks both barrels.

Wahota grabbed his aching head, moaning and turning toward the window. Their eyes meet and Shadwell squeezed one of the triggers, the jolt knocking him into Clarence, who then stumbles over Nathan.

Shocked by the blast, his uncle actually killing someone, Clarence sprang to his feet rushing to the window. He'd never seen a dead man before and braced for the worst, only to watch as Wahota staggered into the woods.

"Ya missed 'em, Uncle Will."

"You sound disappointed."

"How could ya miss 'em from 'ere?"

"I just wanted him to know what it's like to be afraid."

"But he's gettin' away."

"We won't have to worry about that one anymore."

A groan came from behind them, Nathan grasping his head, struggling to sit up. "Looks like we woke someone up," said Shadwell, kneeling beside Nathan. "Try not to make any sudden moves. It's best if you place your head between your knees for a few minutes."

Nathan did as the voice said, the towel on his forehead dropping to the floor. He inhaled the fresh air, casually exhaling thereafter. "It's cool in here."

"I take it Margaret still enjoys a sultry house?"

"That she does," answered Nathan, not knowing who he's talking to. "Ooh… my head. It feels like it's going to explode."

Shadwell told him to breathe in and out in deep intervals, expressing the importance of regulating his heart. Wincing with pain, Nathan looked up, trying his best to focus on the room. "Where am I?"

"My Uncle Will's house, Mist'a Lewis."

"It's good to hear your voice, Clarence," said Nathan, cupping the back of his head with both hands; resting his elbows on his knees. "I could die right now and I wouldn't feel any better."

"You'll pull through," said Shadwell, rising to his feet.

Nathan turned to the unfamiliar voice. "You must be William Shadwell."

"Yes," replied Shadwell, peeking through the curtains.

"How did I get here?"

Clarence told him what took place on the porch and afterward when his uncle patched him up.

"You saved my life," said Nathan. "Thank you."

"You would have done the same for me," answered Shadwell, his cliché remark somewhat insensitive. He wasn't even looking at Nathan when he said it and Clarence felt his uncle's fifty year shunning of Margaret inclusive to all her relatives. Clarence, however, took a liking to Margaret and Nathan, the two of them befriending him with a caring tone; one that is similar to uncle's tone—the kind that makes him feel wanted. He is slower than most boys his age and treated with little respect. Margaret and his uncle are his only friends, and he sees Nathan as another.

"Is there anyth'un we can get fer ya, Mist'a Lewis. Some water maybe."

"Water sounds good, but what I really need," said Nathan, his head resting between his knees, "... is for someone to explain what's going on around here."

Clarence started talking but Shadwell gave him a stern look, one that said, *you get the water and I'll tell the story.* Clarence bares a disappointing smile, one that he follows into the kitchen.

"Clarence said you arrived yesterday afternoon."

A muffled reply from Nathan, he flashed back to his grandmother, recalling how oddly she looked at him on her front porch.

"I'm sorry that your mother and father are no longer with us. I took care of Stewart when he was younger. He was a good man."

Nathan lifted his head, no words necessary as the expression on his face thanked Shadwell.

"What did Margaret have to say," asked Shadwell. "About what happened?"

"Not much. Only that my mother and father were killed by some people she used to know. She didn't explain the details, not wanting to get into them right away."

"Left you in the dark, did she?"

Nathan placed his head back down to ease the throbbing. "She must have some reasonable explanation for not telling me everything. She warned me my life was in danger and she was right… but she never said why and I wish she had."

Clarence returned with the water and his uncle asked him to keep an eye out back.

"*Awe*, Uncle Will," said Clarence, dragging his feet across the floor, "… ever' time sumpin' interestin' happens I gots ta' leave."

"Is he gonna be safe back there," asked Nathan.

"Yes. The Cariban don't hesitate once they find you. They would have attacked by now if they were going to. And rest assured, the warrior who brought you down won't be coming back anytime soon."

"You seem to know a lot about their customs."

"Experience is our best teacher. Margaret didn't tell you everything she should have. I suppose I can. There are many things about her you deserve to know. Our relationship, however, I'll keep to myself. I believe that to be fair."

"Anything you can tell me is more than fair."

"Good. How are you feeling?"

"Not that great."

"As I've told you, it will pass. Believe me, I know."

Five

BEGRUDGING THE TIME at hand, Clarence patrolling the woods from the kitchen window, *a discommodious but necessary task*, he'd rather be in the next room hearing firsthand what his uncle is saying to Nathan.

Shadwell spoke with an elevated voice, in total command of his pronunciations which are uncommonly precise, working the room as though looking out from a Victorian stage. The account he conveys of his first conversation with Margaret is so explicit, the event taking place sixty years ago, if Nathan were to close his eyes he would see himself there.

A bell from a distant trolley along Canal Street declares its position, eighteen-year-old William, self-described as then fit and assiduous, running as fast as he can. Adventure filling his lungs, he can't help but look back, checking on the distance he traveled—all the faces and landmarks he left behind.

Avoiding a car at Baronne, he heads downriver cavorting across the tracks at Carondelet. The parched air along the Mississippi lingers and he perspires heavily down Bourbon Street. Another long stride and anxious breath, the crowd intent on slowing him down, with the excitement of running, he maneuvers through the swarm of people like a cowboy in a barrel race.

William rarely spoke back then but many people of the Old Square knew him well. They saw and greeted him on his way to Antoine's, an upscale restaurant where he washed dishes and cleaned tables. Speeding around the corner at Bourbon and St. Louis, street vendors and people on verandas wave to him; a bashful smile from William in return.

"Don't worry, chérie," shouted a busty woman from above, "… you'll make it on time."

Catching his breath at the backdoor, William infiltrates the noisy kitchen, a vigilant and true stride heading for his station.

"Shadwell," said a hurried voice, attacking his blindside, "… why you get 'a-here so late?!"

William avoids the question, stepping around the heavy mustache and loud vocals of Anthony La Pérouse, a crabby Italian whose livid finger berates young William. "You get 'a-busy now, uh."

William forced a smile as the crabby Italian, shouting something derogatory to one of the cooks, loaded his tray with French cuisine. He then screamed at the pastry chef while balancing the tray on his lapel. Two doors, one marked IN and the other OUT, his face red with anger, the crabby Italian leaned into the proper door, a pastel smile appearing on his chubby face while vanishing into another world.

Grabbing an apron, William assumes his appointed duty; a sink full of scathing water and endless scrubbing. He only tolerates the crabby Italian so he can clean tables in the main dining room—his favorite part of the night. Once inside the elegant room, every table brimming with knowledge and success, William dreams of living that kind of life. All things considered, however, in his dream he is without reservation, taking a back seat to no one.

William had no father, and his mother died when he was thirteen, he and his sister living with their aunt—a generous woman who had no husband or children of her own.

Growing up, William was never as tough as the mean boys in his neighborhood, but he was smart and very nimble; a fighter not by nature but by the streets that raised him.

Dreaming of that *better life*, more so for his aunt and sister, William works hard, saving his money for college. Living in the poorest district of New Orleans, he often wonders about the upper class… what it would cost to attend one of their universities.

Whenever he's in the main dining room, in addition to the fashionable coats and stylish shoes men are wearing, William longs for the command of their rich vocabulary. Referred to as colored, a word William cannot stand, it strengthens his desire to have those things.

He once saw Louis Armstrong in the main dining room, elbow to elbow with all manner of society. An inspiration to so many different people, a black musician rising to the top in that day and age, William felt it was just a matter of time and he too could dine wherever he pleased.

The crabby Italian returned with an empty tray. "André," he shouted to the cook, "… you not 'a-hear me. I tell 'a-you more béarnaise on the chicken … no? Signorina Margaret, she love 'a-you sauce. But 'a-you listen to your brother Anthony? No."

Apparently, André was not listening, then or to his half-brother now, ranting and raving with an exclamatory hand gesture at the end.

"Now she want 'a-more," the crabby Italian continued. "You know what 'a-this does to my tip?" He slid his finger across his throat whistling in unison, André then slamming a bowl on the counter between them.

"There, go and save your neck my poor brother."

Leaning over the counter, the crabby Italian said something in his native tongue and André quickly fired back in French, the duel going round and round until the crabby Italian shook his finger in his brother's face, forewarning him to knock it off or else!

Enraged, the crabby Italian left the kitchen and everyone congratulated André on how well he handled the situation.

"What an ass my brother has become," said André, his French accent as thick and Americanized as his brother's Italian.

They all laughed.

"William," said André, stirring some egg-yokes in a bowl, "… do not let my brother's edginess upset you. You know how he gets with Mademoiselle Lewis here."

William turned and smiled at the tall Frenchman, tipping his head to let him know he understood.

"I do not see what all the fuss is about," remarked one of the cooks. "She comes here every spring. It is our fameux cooking that brings her back. There is no reason for Anthony to be so nervous."

"It is her wealth that makes him nervous," another cook replied.

"One should not have to worry over money," André's voice rang out.

"My friend," the oldest chef, Jean Claude, spoke up, the kitchen suddenly quiet, "… if not money, it would be something else. Look at me. Do you believe my greatest worry in life is wealth?" André shook his head as did a few other countrymen. "Be more concerned about your well-being and those around you. One day when you are as old as I, you will realize fortunes are unimportant. Good health and reliable friends are all you need. Those are your riches. Remember, the day you call upon others to care for you, those who felt your foot will not lend their hand."

William held back his scrubbing, gazing at Jean Claude as everyone agreed. He too believed in what the old man said, reexamining his need for those fashionable coats and stylish shoes. The kitchen door then flung open and the crabby Italian let loose again.

"Shadwell! Stop 'a-you starin' and 'a-finish those dishes! Some nice 'a-people next to Signorina Margaret just 'a-finish their meal. If 'a-you hurry, you can 'a-give us a hand cleanin' the table."

William got busy right away, soap and water spinning like a small hurricane—a barrage of thunder coming from the sink.

"That's 'a-more like it," said the crabby Italian, picking up another order.

Nathan rose from the floor, Shadwell bringing him a knit polo and pair of loose trousers. The shirt rubbed against his wounds and Nathan cringed, but not as much as when he sat down.

"How are you feeling," asked Shadwell.

"Better," said Nathan, swallowing the last of his water. "I can open my eyes without the room spinning around."

"Good. Would you like some more water?"

"Thank you, no. Please, continue with your story."

"I hope I'm not boring you with all the details."

"No," replied Nathan. "Not at all."

Shadwell stayed on his feet, describing the main dining room and how relaxed he was once inside. Elegantly dressed, the women wore expensive jewels to accentuate their beauty, the men sitting handsomely in their tails and slicked-back hair. His kitchen uniform and white apron against his dark skin, William felt very much at the low end of society. He shrugged off the occasional smug look, making his way through the crowd. His dream to one day sit and eat with all of them, he also made a pact with himself to remember his roots. The way people treat him, not just for the apron he wears but for the color of his skin, when he reaches their status, he will never look down upon anyone. *No one chooses to whom and where we are born*, thought William.

A silver bus tray at his side, William makes his way between the candlelit tables, antique gaslights illuminating softly overhead. No one needed a napkin or their water glass filled, not even the time of day in his passing. They were all too busy talking to interrupt the kitchen help—trivial gossip and the news of Amelia Earhart crossing the Atlantic.

Reaching the table he was sent to clean, a young woman across the way gave him a friendly nod. She sat alone, a delicate thing with sandy-colored hair and short bangs exposing two lusty curls. Her cheek bones were low and when she smiled the crest of her lips brought them up, the glow from the candle at her table bringing out the deep-green in her willful eyes. Diamonds hung from her ears and a shimmering peach creation from her shoulders. No one knew her true age, guessing that she was in her early to mid-twenties. She was a widow and William was sad because he knew her three-year-old son had no father.

Crystal glasses and china pasted with sauces, uneventful to the quiet multitude, William put them on his tray, balancing the load on his shoulder. Retracing his steps, he remembers what the crabby Italian said about the kitchen doors: *You don't 'a-stick yer ass in front 'a-the wrong one!* The two doors opening in different directions, it was an important rule to follow, and for many years the rule stood unchallenged. But rules, as everyone knows, are made to be broken.

William perfected his technique months ago and with his

rear against the door eased his way back, *the door then flinging open the wrong way!*

The jolt knocked William forward, sending his tray across the cavernous floor. Silverware, china, and crystal went everywhere and William stood there in awe—now recognized by all.

The door swung shut and he could hear laughter erupting from the kitchen. The cachinnating grew louder and William knew it wasn't directed at him, fearing the worst by the uninterrupted howling.

He looked back at the broken glass and dishes, the dining room quiet and everyone staring at him. Even the young widow had a surprised look on her face, one that turned into an expression of hope, prompting William to open the door.

Cracking the door, William peaked inside, the crabby Italian sitting on the floor with a clump of vichyssoise dripping from his fat head and mess of creamy oysters swimming in his lap.

André came to his brother's side with a glass of wine. A sudden hush filled the kitchen and with his best Italian accent, André offered his brother the glass. "Would 'a-you like a little vino to go with 'a-you meal, Signore La Pérouse?"

Again there was laughter… crazy, thundering laughter, unabated until William walked in.

The crabby Italian rose to his feet as though he'd been knocked down by a bull, his chest soaked in steaming Café au lait and lumps of cold potatoes running down his face. Fire in his eyes, he reached out taking William by the collar. "Are you 'a-crazy?! Everyone 'a-know you don't 'a-stand in front 'a-the wrong door." The crabby Italian cursed at William, the boy having no part of it and breaking free, his head hanging down and not a word to anyone.

André grabbed his brother. "What's the matter with you,

Tony? You barreled into that door like a horse out of a gate. You tell everyone to slow down when they push it open and now you yell at the boy?! You deserve to be covered in soup."

Some of the men in the kitchen agreed with André, the crabby Italian then screaming at them. "Don't 'a-you all have 'a-work to do?! André, you don't 'a-talk to me like that!"

"Calm down, Tony. Go in the back and clean up. I'll take care of the order. A small inconvenience but the customer will understand."

"Shut up, André! I don't 'a-care about some customer. I been 'a-humiliated here."

The crabby Italian then turned to William, cranking it up a notch so everyone can hear. "Shadwell! You 'a-fired!"

William looked at André and then the Frenchman at his half-brother.

"Now who's the crazy one," said André. "Come on, Tony … don't be an ass! The boy is good worker. He needs this job."

"You don't 'a-call me an ass!" Stepping away from André, the crabby Italian bumped into William. "What 'a-you still doin' here? I said 'a-you fired!"

William's eyes pled with André's for help, but the Frenchman just stood there. "I'm sorry, William, there's nothing I can do. My brother's promotion went straight to his brainless head."

That better life for his aunt and sister slipping away, though William rarely spoke he knew the embarrassment would soon escape him. "I … m-m-made a m-m-mistake. P-p-p-please don't f-f-fire me. I'm s-s-s-sorry."

The crabby Italian had his face in a towel, soaking up the vichyssoise while gesturing toward the back. "You turn 'a-that uniform in now!"

"André," the crabby Italian then commanded, "… you take 'a-this stutterin' idiot and 'a-pay what we owe him."

Flushed with contempt, André turned away. "Come on, William," he whispered, "… I've had enough of this."

The crabby Italian stood silent as they walked off, William suddenly turning around, glaring into the crabby Italian's smoldering eyes and having the last word. "A-a-a-asshole!"

Much to the delight of everyone, even more so to Jean Claude, young William stumbled upon the need of a well-placed foot. An act of defiance certainly, but a salubrious act nonetheless.

André unlocked the storeroom door, rows of expensive wine, caviar, and other canned goods inside. A writing desk in one corner and rack of uniforms in another, William took a seat next to the desk. "I didn't b-b-bring a c-c-change of c-c-c-clothes."

"I wouldn't worry about that," said André, remembering when he first met William, sixteen-years-old selling apples on Rampart Street. He asked how much the apples were and the boy's stuttering triggered the better side of André's vanity. The next day William was off the streets, a steady job washing dishes and bussing tables. *Now he goes back*, thought André. "Keep what you have on, William, but take off the apron." The generous Frenchman grabbed two shirts and the same number of trousers off the rack. "These are for you. Now you have no excuse not to change. And remember, no one has the right to treat you like my brother did. No one."

André poured himself a glass of wine and offered one to William which he refused. "A real horse's ass that man," said André, taking a drink. "It was good what you said to him in there."

William removed the apron and André withdrew a stack of

bills from a cashbox. "Here, this is your week's pay," said André, giving William some of the money. "This is your holiday pay," he reeled off a few more bills, adding bonuses and retirement which left André empty handed.

It was the most money William ever had at one time. He stared at it momentarily, wanting to give it back. "You'll g-g-get in t-t-trouble."

"No, you keep it, William. Let me worry about my brother. What he did to you was wrong. This money doesn't make it right or even things up, but it's yours now. I only wish it could be more."

André told him he would talk to some friends about another job and William gave him a grateful nod. Taking hold of the boy, André gave him a fatherly hug, vowing to get back at his brother for what he said.

William shrugged it off, André going through a set of keys unlocking the outside door. Stepping into the early part of the night, William is mindful of his surrounds, the old carriageway behind Antoine's much too dark to feel at ease.

"Wait," said André, running off and returning with a bottle of wine. "Here, take this with you as well, a 1914 Pinot Noir. Château Lafite-Rothschild, the best vineyard in all of France. Both of you are of the same age. Good luck to you my young friend."

A bottle of France's finest wine under his arm and fifty dollars in his pocket, William felt pretty good about losing his job. It would have taken him forever to save that kind of money. *Besides*, the optimist in him thought, *I'm better off now than I was two years ago*.

Heading lakeside along the old carriageway, William wonders what to do with his newfound money. First, he will buy his aunt and sister something nice. Nothing too expensive, perhaps a colorful scarf or frilly hat—women like those silly things. Next, he will do something for himself, an expenditure bringing him closer to the upper class.

A moonless night, the air is somewhat cool, typical along that part of the river. William stopped beside a garbage can switching his bundle of clothes from one arm to the next, footsteps then pummeling along Bourbon Street bearing his way. Crouching behind a pile of broken crates, the foot noise replaced by voices, an angry little man argues with a lady no more than ten feet away.

"Look missy, hand over that bag or—"

"I am not giving you my bag!"

"Ya either gives it ta' me or I takes it."

"Here," said the lady, removing her earrings, "… take these instead. They're worth a lot of money. I have personal belongings in my bag I dare not part with."

"Ya don't understand, do ya missy. I been told ta' bring back nothin' but that fancy little tote 'a yours. The fella don't want me ta' hurt ya … just give me the bag."

The man stepped closer and the lady backed away. William, looming in the background, the lady stole a look and the angry little man turned his head, William then hitting him as hard as he could, right in the jaw with the bottle of Pinot.

The man hit the cobbled stone head first and William was confident he would be out for a while.

"Thank you. A thousand times, thank you," said the lady. She could not make out the face of her rescuer, nor William hers. "What was I thinking, going for a walk on a night like this?"

William said nothing, following her to a safe location under a nearby streetlight.

"Why, you're the young man from Antoine's," said the lady, pinning her earrings back in place.

"Yes, m-m-ma'am," replied William. He recognized her

from the restaurant, sharing only a gregarious look now and then, her voice unfamiliar because they never spoke.

"I would have lost something very valuable, irreplaceable in fact if not for you."

"Glad I c-c-c-could help," stammered William, dropping his head.

The young lady extended a tender hand lifting his chin. "It's all right. You don't have to lower your head. I should be lowering mine to you. Your name is William, is it not?"

"Yes, m-m-ma'am."

"Glad to meet you, William. My name is Margaret. Margaret Lewis."

Six

RETREATING FROM THE impending storm, the sultry air fled the shores along the Gulf Coast. A hot afternoon in New Orleans, the lethargic pace of the streets quickened, everyone watching the sky for the first sign of trouble.

In one of the office buildings along Poydras Street, two men take to the stairs, ascending to the fourth-floor. The leader is of stocky build and average height, his pale, rather spindly partner carrying an old doctors bag. Dressed conservatively in dark suits, shirt collars loose and jackets open, they are looking for a particular office; door after door until finding the right one.

Each silent in their subverting task, the leader keeps an eye out for his partner who is picking the lock on a huge glass door. Breaking into some kind of medical facility, a waiting-room full of science and chemistry journals, the leader takes a seat, motioning to a door marked PRIVATE, his partner then going inside.

Waltzing through a dark corridor, the partner came to a sudden stop at the last door. Dropping to one knee he jimmies the lock, the tiny room filled with nothing but filing cabinets and storage boxes. Two windows overlook the street and the room has just enough light to do the job. Pilfering through a drawer marked K–L, the partner makes off with one of the files, retracing his steps to a laboratory infested with microscopes, centrifuges and refrigeration units.

The partner set his bag atop one of the workstations—a clay pot with purple begonias to his left. Digging into the doctors bag, he takes out a thin bar covered in waxy cellophane. The bar is half the size of a cigarette carton and he pulls two more out of the bag, grabbing a handful of electrical components at the bottom; sorting it all into three piles. In less than a minute his task is complete and he's on his way out, all the bars connected to a small timer.

The door marked PRIVATE opens and the leader throws down a magazine, his partner handing over the file and not one word between them. They approach the stairs at 10:15 a.m. and the sidewalk two minutes later.

At 10:24 a.m. the leader is on a payphone across the street. "We have it," he told the person on the other end. "...That's been taken care of too. Here," he seized his partner's wrist, looking at his watch, "... you can listen for yourself." The secondhand ticking down, the leader aimed the phone across the street, stretching the cord as far as it will go. At precisely 10:25 a.m., a loud, violent burst rattled the air.

Chunks of concrete and shattered glass pelt the street, an old IBM monitor flying toward them and the leader ducking out of the way, his partner gritting his teeth, raising his arms as if to say, *oops, too much*.

A livid brow, the leader is back on the phone. "Did you hear? ... Yes, the lab and all her files. There's nothing left."

Traffic comes to a halt and the onlookers start to gather.

Hanging up the phone, the leader popped a cigarette in his mouth. "Let's go," he smirked, celebrating their destructive success with a rush of nicotine.

"Terrytown, right?"

"Right," said the leader. "Then we meet up with Raymond at the airport."

An ink pen smothered in his left hand, Captain Alcott, an obstinate, stocky man with a round face, stern eyes and tight lip, slid the paper to one side, taking another and reading what needed to be signed.

"Sit down, Detective," said Alcott, the look on his face telling Samuel he didn't like paperwork. "What have you got there," he asked.

"An APB from MSY," replied Taylor. "A private plane went down outside of Pittsburgh and two people were killed. Someone may have tampered with the plane and the FBI needs our help if we can spare it."

"What do they think we are, a lost-and-find? We've been workin' twenty-four-seven all week. They should be helping us."

"I just spoke to Monroe on this one. He didn't sound too happy about it either. Said the perp was a real hard-ass."

"Now that's something coming from Monroe. Who's the perp?"

"Carlo Somoza."

Alcott's eyes sweltered and he dropped the pen. "Let me see that," he motioned to Taylor, grabbing and scanning the report. "When did this come through?"

"About 90 minutes ago. Connie said to bring it to you when you got here."

"This guy Somoza," said Alcott tapping the paper, "… he's the kind of trouble that looks you in the eye and you know hell is not a place. I doubt anyone will ever find him. And you can bet your ass he did something to that plane."

"I agree, but I don't think he was acting alone. Not after

what Monroe told me."

"Very good, Detective. That's not something Somoza would do out of spite. He's one of those death by torture animals. This has contract written all over it."

Taylor responded with a nod, eager to explain a motive but Alcott shifted gears. "I see you and Monroe have gotten close this past week."

"Pretty much."

"Good," said Alcott. "You deserve a break from all the paperwork I've been shoveling you. I want you and Monroe to partner up on this one right away."

Gratitude etched on Taylor's face, he's compelled to say something but Alcott cut him off. "Before you start thanking me, I want you to know everyone's had their fill of the Somoza case. Especially Monroe. I can't send you out on this alone or I would. Anyone else would hate me till their death if I gave them this case and you as their partner. Cary, however, is easy going compared to most cops. He'll still be pissed… but only for a little while."

"I understand."

"First thing we need to do is give Pittsburgh and the Feds a call. Somoza's on the NCIC and any dope we have on him they can get it there. Next, get a hold of MSY and Lakefront security. Tell 'em we've got a positive ID on the saboteur and he's a local boy."

"Anything else?"

"Not that I can think of. Just be careful out there."

Taylor had something to add but Connie stuck her head in the office. "You better come out here, Captain. Dispatch has been swamped for the past ten minutes and it doesn't look good."

"Now what, I'm up to my neck in paperwork."

"It's the Central Business District. There's been an explosion at the Mobil Building."

Clarence stepped out of the kitchen and Shadwell saw the frustration on his affable face. "Ther' ain't nothin' movin' out there, Uncle Will. How much longer does I have ta' tend watch?"

Finished with his story of saving Margaret in the old carriageway, Shadwell advised Clarence to keep an eye out just a little longer. Clarence frowned, going back to his post, Shadwell then taking a seat beside Nathan.

Rubbing the back of his neck, Nathan wanted to know all about his grandmother. "What was she like back then?"

"She was soft spoken and had an imperative use of grammar. Her eyes captivated me with every word and I knew whatever she said was the truth—it was in those emerald eyes of hers. She always looked so calm and self-assured, her courtly voice leaving no doubt she had everything under control. I always admired people like that, the ones who spoke so eloquently. As I've told you, I had a speech impediment of my own. When I first spoke to your grandmother, I thought how refreshing it would be if she could teach me to speak like that."

"I've seen pictures of her at that age," Nathan interrupted, "… but I never had a personality to go with them."

"The pictures do her no justice what-so-ever. Margaret possessed both inner and physical beauty. Something rare in most women these days. She cared about the people around her and was more concerned about what happened in the kitchen that night than in the carriageway. I told her about the crabby Italian and she put her hand on my shoulder. 'You should have opened the door,' she said, 'everyone would have loved seeing that starchy Italian covered in soup.'

"I didn't realize it at the time but she said that to comfort me—to bring about something we both had in common. A white woman confiding in a black man didn't happen that often back then. It was an act of decency if you ask me. One that I will never forget."

Shadwell then paused for a moment, going to and looking out the window. "I remember showing Margaret the fifty-dollars, asking if she could help with my stuttering. I told her I would pay forty if she did and she was curious about the other ten. I said it was for my aunt and sister and she told me to keep the money—losing my job and all. It was then, Margaret giving me a lift home, I realized we were put on this earth as a comfort to each other, *to not let indifference take that away.*

"I've spent my whole life dealing with all sorts of people, Nathan. It doesn't take me long to study a person or look someone in the eye to know what they're all about. With Margaret it took less than a city block. She offered me a job and I took it. She then told me to pack everything I had because we'd be doing a lot of traveling."

"Can I ask you a question?"

"Of course," answered Shadwell, abandoning the window, "… but make it quick. A car just turned off the main road heading this way."

Nathan got up and peeked outside. He saw a yellow taxi coping with the bumpy road.

"Clarence," Shadwell yelled to the kitchen, the boy sticking his head out. "There's a car coming down the road. Keep your eyes open. *And Clarence …?*"

"Yeah?"

"Go ahead and cock that shotgun."

Clarence disappeared and Shadwell went back to the window. "What was your question," he turned to Nathan.

"It can wait."

"You're wondering what was in Margaret's handbag that night."

"How did you know?"

"I asked her the same thing before I took the job. Margaret said it was a fair question and if I were to be involved in her affairs I should know what I was getting myself into."

"Well ..." asked Nathan, the taxi pulling up to the house. "What was inside?"

"*A waste of time.* Just a ridiculous old map leading nowhere."

Marcus stood at the parlor window looking out at the fountain, punishing the sandstone in his hand with an abrasive thumb. "Why must you keep it so unbearably hot in here?"

"I have no problem with the heat," jeered Margaret, snug in her chair. "It pleases me that you are so uncomfortable."

"My unpleasantness," said Marcus, remaining calm, "stems from the incompetence of others. I can tolerate the heat ... failure I cannot." He then turned and gave Margaret a cold look. "That grandson of yours' will pay dearly for this inconvenience." Mashing his thumb into the sandstone, Marcus paced back and forth, Margaret sinking in her seat.

Ariel descends the staircase joining Raymond at the bottom and together they enter the parlor with Ariel shaking her head. "We checked everywhere, Father. He's not in the house. All we found was Margaret's cat."

"Then we wait for Tantur. In the meantime, we haven't had our breakfast yet. Take Margaret into the kitchen, Raymond. Pancakes would be nice."

"And, Margaret," Marcus stops her. "You know I disapprove of what you are wearing. I'd like to see the real you when you get back."

Margaret left the room in a petulant mood, Marcus back to the window staring at the gate. "What time is it?"

"Close to eleven, Father."

"Good, we are still within our time frame. I wish to be alone now, Ariel. I need time to rethink our departure."

"Yes, Father."

"Wait! Where did you find Margaret's cat?"

"Upstairs."

"Bring the little troublemaker to me," said Marcus, rubbing the sandstone's smooth surface—the best way for him to lull his angry disposition.

Tantur came into the parlor from outside, and Marcus, *a harsh thumb upon the sandstone,* did not look happy.

Full of malice, Tantur fends off an ominous glare from Marcus. Setting his blowgun aside, sweaty from head to toe and catching his breath, Tantur confronts Marcus up close.

"He left through window," said Tantur. "Fell and hit the ground hard. Wahota followed his tracks into the woods and I believe they are still out there."

"Tantur, you serve me well. Your father would have been proud. Your brother, however, angers me. He has brought shame upon your tribe. Need I remind you of your custom?"

"I assure you I will find the grandson and my brother. Wahota is young and there is no need to punish him."

"I need Nathan here within the hour. Alive and unharmed. You know what is at stake. Now go, Toncha!"—*quickly!*

Grabbing his blowgun, Tantur gave Marcus a fierce eye, bumping into Ariel on his way out. She has Margaret's cat and the animal is startled, jumping to the floor and dashing through Tantur's legs.

Giving chase down the hall, Ariel is called back. "Forget about the cat," said Marcus, stepping into the hall. "You can tend to that later. We have a situation to sort out first. Come back inside," he motioned to Ariel, an uneasy eye directed at Tantur.

A cigarette in his mouth, the leader is driving a black Lincoln, his partner navigating a street map and both men listening to the radio; a news broadcast describing their handiwork. "The explosion sent glass and debris as far away as Rampart Street. No injuries have been reported and the cause is under investigation. In other news…."

"Nobody got hurt. Good," said the partner, his nose in the roadmap. "Hang a right at the next intersection."

"You're full of shit, you know that, Vincent? We go through this every time. Why do you even bother with that map?"

"It's off Carrollwood, right?"

"It's off National and that's to the left."

"Are you sure?"

They pass a maintenance van from the city of Gretna parked beside a water main. "There's the shutoff valve," said the leader. "You and your stupid-ass directions. If you keep your trap shut for two seconds I'll remember how to get there."

A few minutes of silence the Lincoln rolls to a stop. "You need to hurry," said the leader, sticking his head out the window, "… I don't want the neighbors coming out asking me a lot of stupid questions."

"Sure, Carlo. It won't take but five minutes."

Laurian grabbed her briefcase, moving quickly to the other side of the cab; instructing the driver to wait.

"Friend of yours," asked Shadwell, he and Nathan stationed at the window.

"I've never seen her before, but I recognize the driver from yesterday. He picked me up at the airport." Nathan shut the curtain, a little woozy while heading for the couch.

A knock on the door, Shadwell told Nathan to sit tight, the old man scooting down the hall into one of the bedrooms.

"Here," he whispered on his return, handing Nathan a shiny, Pug revolver. "I'm going to open the door. You know how to use a gun?"

"Sure," said Nathan, rising from the couch. "Zero in on your target and pull the trigger."

"*And the safety* … is it on or off?"

Nathan tilts the 44-special to have a look, inadvertently pointing the stubby barrel at Shadwell's chest.

A frightful look, even though the safety is in the off position, Shadwell redirects the gun. "You mustn't point that at anyone but her. And don't get trigger happy. It would be a shame if all she wants is to use the phone."

Another knock, louder than the first, they turn to one another. Nathan's face is terribly pale and Shadwell wonders if he's up for the task.

"*Ready,*" asked Shadwell.

"Ready," answered Nathan, taking a deep breath.

Shadwell reached for the knob but Nathan suddenly cut him off. "Wait! Ask who it is first."

"Why? We'll find out soon enough."

Nathan got close to Shadwell's ear. "A woman named Ariel called this morning," he said, scratching an itchy shoulder with the gun, "…*she could be in on it*."

"Tell you what," Shadwell grabbed the revolver, "… I'll take this and you answer the door."

"*Good idea*. Who is it," Nathan spoke up.

"My name is Laurian Webster. I'm looking for a Mr. William Shadwell."

"*What for*," mouthed William.

"And the reason for your visit," asked Nathan.

"I'm Margaret Lewis' doctor," Laurian elevated her voice. "I had an appointment with her in Ruston this morning. She didn't show or call and I got worried. She once told me Mr.

Shadwell lived down this road."

"Sounds good so far," whispered Nathan.

"Tell her you're going to see if I'm awake yet. I'll be right back."

Shadwell went to the kitchen, asking Clarence the name of Margaret's doctor.

"Dr. Webster."

"She never mentioned a first name?"

"No, sir."

"Keep your eyes open, Clarence," said Shadwell, patting the boy's shoulder.

"Go ahead and let her in," Shadwell said to Nathan. "But be careful, it may be the woman that called this morning."

Nathan opened the door and Shadwell made sure no one could see him standing behind it. "He's just getting up and about," said Nathan. "Would you like to come in?"

"Yes. This is very important." Laurian stepped inside and with Nathan closing the door Shadwell startled her. He then turned to Nathan. "Take the lady's briefcase," he said, flaunting the gun in front of Laurian. "See if there's anything inside with her name on it."

Nathan did as instructed. Apologizing while rummaging through the case, he pulled out a pocketbook, reading aloud to Shadwell what he found inside. "Laurian Webster, State Operators License ... her picture's on it ... *nice picture*. Laurian Webster, Medical Staff card ... *another nice picture.* L.W. on the wallet, credit cards in her name... Well, I'm convinced."

"Well I'm not," said Shadwell stepping in front of Nathan, peering into the doctor's eyes. "What are you treating Margaret for?"

"I'm not treating her for anything. Margaret's in good health ... exceptional for her age. I've been taking blood samples that's all. But if you're William Shadwell you wouldn't know that. It's been more than fifty-years and the two of you haven't said a word to each other."

"Fifty-six to be exact," answered Shadwell, shamefully lowering the gun. He then directed Nathan to give Webster back her briefcase. "I must apologize for all this. We're a bit— *tense* this morning. Margaret sent you down the right road. I'm William Shadwell. But you already knew that judging from what you just said."

"Margaret spoke of you from time to time," said Laurian, stepping aside and addressing Nathan. "She talked about you too. Her only grandchild. She said you were— how should I put this? *A man of integrity?* Tell me, *Nathaniel*, what honor is there in snooping through a lady's belongings."

"Now that we're all … *acquainted*," exclaimed Nathan as he sat down, "… honorable or not, I never said I was Margaret's only grandchild."

"She has several photographs of you in her wallet. You've gotten a little gray on top since the last one. Did you know that?"

Unamused, Nathan figured his mother was to blame— photos in the mail and social status over the phone. "Why would my grandmother show you my picture?"

"Grandmothers do that sort of thing."

Nathan fought with a throw-pillow to get comfortable, his weary eyes upon Laurian Webster's enthralling features. Her hair pinned up, black and lustrous, it seemed a perfect color to him. She has a pleasurable face, narrow with round dusky eyes and thick lashes, but most important to Nathan, is the innocence behind those eyes, evident also in the tone of her voice and solemn posture.

Shadwell grew tired of the silence. He wanted to ask Dr. Webster about Margaret. Clarence kept him posted on most everything, but he was curious of her feelings toward him. *I should be a little circuitous about it … ease my way into it,* thought Shadwell. "Tell us what happened, Dr. Webster."

"As I said," Laurian spoke to both men, "I had an appointment with Margaret in Ruston. We meet privately once a month. That's how I know so much about both of you."

Shadwell and Nathan looked at one another with great concern.

"An hour after she didn't show this morning, I called her house and mobile phone and she didn't answer. Something's happened to her, Mr. Shadwell. She would have called the airport and left word if she were running late."

"*The airport,*" Nathan questioned Laurian.

"I live in New Orleans. Margaret has a plane, several in fact, and she insists on flying me out here instead of coming to my office."

"That's Margaret," said Shadwell. "But why come to me? Her estate is only a few minutes away."

"A year ago she told me to stay away from her house in a case like this."

"Why," asked Shadwell.

"To keep me safe from any— *dangerous situations,* I suppose."

Shadwell gazed into Webster's blue eyes. "Dangerous situations?"

"Did she ever mention," clamored Nathan, "… blowguns and half-naked men running around?"

"Nathan, please," Shadwell plangently cut in, "… you can see she's upset. What kind of trouble do you think Margaret was talking about?"

"The kind that involves blowguns and half-naked men running around."

Shadwell was not amused. "Very funny, Doctor."

"It wasn't meant to be funny. I believe the correct term is

Cariban … as in Caribbean headhunters." Laurian then paused, thinking about what she just said. "Oh, my God! They've got Margaret! Haven't they?"

"We don't know that for sure," said Shadwell. "They may just be after Nathan. He was attacked by a young tribal member this morning. Margaret has entrusted you with a great deal. I don't have to tell you how serious this is."

"This is one of those dangerous situations she was talking about, isn't it," asked Laurian.

"Now that we've established the situation is dangerous," said Nathan, "… what are we going to do about it? I vote for calling in the police."

"No!" screamed Shadwell and Webster in unison.

"Margaret said, 'never contact the authorities.'"

"Dr. Webster's right," said Shadwell. "There's nothing the police can do but complicate matters."

"So what do we do," asked Nathan, lumbering to his feet ready for action.

"We'll need all the help we can get," Shadwell answered in return. He then called out to Clarence… bringing the boy up to speed. "We could use another hand," he entreats his nephew, assuring the boy he'll be on the first plane home if things go awry.

An alacritous spirit, Clarence gave a fearless nod, unafraid of what may lie ahead. It reminded Shadwell of himself at that age. André La Pérouse was so proud of young William back then. And now, as Shadwell put the moment into perspective, he is the proud one.

"I believe I've stayed away from Margaret long enough," said Shadwell. "Clarence, go and get a blanket to wrap these shotguns in. We don't want to scare anyone unless we have to."

"Quit wasting time," hissed Raymond, Margaret arranging her kitchen utensils. A skillet next to the burner, everything she needs minus the pancake batter is on the island-counter. The pantry, with its panic-room at her backside, Margaret toils at figuring a way to distance herself from Raymond and his handgun. She imagines pulling the hidden switch, the shelves swinging out and Raymond there to grab her before she can open the secret door.

A plan in the making, Margaret spun around opening the pantry. "What are you doing," barked Raymond—tugging at her leash.

"Pancake batter. Would it be all right if I used an electric mixer? It would speed things up."

"Sure, go ahead."

"Can you get it for me while I grab the batter?"

"Where is it?"

"In the cupboard over there… behind the bowls."

She did it! The mixer wasn't even there and by the time Raymond realizes it she'll have a secure line to the outside world, safe and sound behind twelve inches of concrete.

Moving boxes and cans to the side, Margaret can't find the switch. Trembling where she stands, the manual latch is missing as well!

"I couldn't find the mixer," said Raymond, his voice mauling Margaret from behind. She turned around and Raymond grinned. "I did find this though," he spoke derisively, bouncing the panic-room latch in his hand.

"How did you—"

"Nice try. Now get out of there," exclaimed Raymond pulling Margaret aside, grabbing the batter demanding she get busy.

Mournful over the defeat, Margaret poured the proper amount of water and mix into a bowl. Heating up the skillet, she wonders if she should try something else. “How about some hash browns with these?”

“Just the flapjacks, Margaret. You don’t need to use a knife when making flapjacks.”

“Sausage?”

“Flapjacks! Nothing else,” snapped Raymond.

“Fine,” said Margaret taking out a spatula, Raymond then twisting his gun motioning that she close the drawer.

A very large kitchen, Raymond leans against the refrigerator to get a close look at breakfast. His attention on the skillet, Margaret casually scans the room spotting another opportunity above his head. “Do you object to having orange juice with your—*flapjacks*, Raymond?”

“Juice is all right as long as you’re not planning on cutting any oranges.”

“Don’t worry, there’s a carton in the fridge.” Setting the spatula aside, Margaret strolls peaceably toward Raymond. “May I?”

Raymond stepped out of the way and Margaret flung open the refrigerator door, his gun pointed away and her cat leaping from atop the refrigerator. Landing on Raymond’s shoulder, the cat swiped at his face, and Raymond, so easily startled, dropped the gun. Stooping to pick it up, his eye on the cat darting out of the room, Margaret moved in for the kill, slamming the hot skillet on the back of his head.

“*Thank you, Bourbon*,” Margaret said to herself, picking up the gun and throwing it in the trash—Raymond sprawled out on the floor.

A spare set of keys in the kitchen and her BMW parked out front, Margaret makes her way outside. Slumping in the car she turns the key; no dashboard lights, radio, starter… nothing!

Wasting no time, Margaret is out of the car rushing toward the open gate. Keeping an eye on the parlor window, the curtains closed for the time being, Margaret is only a few feet from the gate. Proceeding alongside the wall, she stopped dead in her tracks, Tantur appearing suddenly from around the corner.

There is a body slung over Tantur's shoulder and Margaret knows she has no chance of escaping now.

Checking the face of the young man Tantur is carrying, Margaret wants to know who he is.

"My brother, Wahota. The last of our great tribe."

"Your brother?"

"Yes."

"What happened to him?"

"Someone hit him in the head."

"Is he …?"

"Dead? No, he's alive. I found him outside your stone wall. Why did you build that? It does not stop a man from climbing over."

"Ironically there was a time I felt safe having it around me. Now it surrounds and traps me."

"What does that mean, 'r run-ic—"

Wahota moaned and Tantur stepped off the driveway, placing his brother on the lawn; his forehead covered in blood.

"How do you feel, my brother?"

His eyes now open, Wahota answered in their native tongue.

"What did he say," asked Margaret.

"He is great pain. If you ever had a cut like that you know how it feels."

"I've never been cut that bad. Despite our differences, Tantur, I do hope it's nothing serious. He's far too young to die."

"When the day comes for you to pass on," said Tantur, looking Margaret in the eye, "I will be sad for a long time."

"I think it will be a good day," Margaret responded in a most peculiar way. "One that I look forward to."

Margaret entered the parlor with Tantur close behind, Wahota resting in the foyer at the foot of the stairs. Ariel stood next to her father who leniently attacks the piece of sandstone—his pacifier as she calls it. Tantur explained his brother's condition and Margaret's attempted escape.

"How did you manage to slip away from Raymond," Marcus questioned her.

"I crowned him on his head with your breakfast," answered Margaret. "Verily he'll awaken and wish he were dead."

"I see," said Marcus, easing off the sandstone. "Tantur," he imperiously redirects his tone, "… you failed to bring back the grandson but I've a change of heart. Tend to your brother… and Raymond as well." Slipping the sandstone in his pocket, Marcus said it was getting late, telling Margaret to head upstairs and pack for at least a week.

Margaret turned, heading toward the door but Marcus stopped her. "Wait! Before you go," he grabbed Margaret with one hand, clawing at her face with the other, "… get rid of this façade!" Digging into her cheek, stretching and distorting the side of her face, Marcus ripped apart what he knows to be a latex mask, a portion clinging to Margaret's fair skin as the rest, Marcus tossing it aside, ends up face down on the parlor floor.

Seven

VINCENT GRABBED a briefcase from the trunk, putting his doctors bag atop a knapsack and two canvas duffels. The house he approached is in Terrytown, verdurous landscaping on a spacious lot with pudgy trees and high shrubbery. To the unsuspecting residents, he looks like a salesman itching to throw his latest pitch. Stopping all of a sudden, the onset of the casuist walkway split between two hedgerows, he turned around looking at Carlo who seems impatient; a threatening glare persuading him to keep moving.

Stooping on the cement porch, Vincent opens a thin pouch filled with everything he needs to pick a lock. Seconds later he's inside the house, his Italian shoes silent over the parquet surface. Narrow windows sandwich the ornate door as a pair of cheap Venetian blinds let the outside light into the foyer.

That's odd, thought Vincent, *they should be closed.*

Passing through a short hallway, Vincent admires the photographs on the wall, his favorite an 11x16 portrait of a father and his two-years-old daughter. Red hair and a cheery smile, the daughter had no idea her father was sick when the photograph was taken. She also had no understanding of death back then… only that it brought pain taking her daddy away.

How unfortunate for the little girl, thought Vincent. *At least she has this portrait, the two of them together.*

Vincent entered a spacious room with two recliners and a long sofa cincturing a glass-encrusted coffee table. An entertainment center along with French doors, which Vincent knew led outside, engrossed the far wall. Vincent noticed a lofty row of flowerpots on the porch he hadn't seen before. The swing-set in the yard he knew about, judging it to be a safe distance away. These were the jobs he hated most, the uncomfortable ones he tried to get out of—the ones Carlo forced him to carry out.

On top of the coffee table, Vincent swept a set of keys to the side, an empty video sleeve and box of Captain Crunch at the edge of the table. Setting the briefcase in the open spot, he removes a squeeze bottle filled with liquid. Saturating the furniture and stereo equipment, he then unplugs the television set, pulling from the briefcase a shiny, tin box the size of a cigarette pack. Double-shielded wire with two bare ends sticking out of the devise, he inserts them into the outlet, wedging the television plug inside—the shiny, tin box receiving 115 volts.

"*Come on, Vincent!*" Carlo said to himself. "*I'm not getting any younger out here.*" He can't see the front door from where the Lincoln is parked and gets out of the car to check on Vincent, who all of a sudden appears between the hedges.

"Finally," said Carlo crushing out a cigarette, he and Vincent getting in the car. "It shouldn't have taken that long. What happened?"

"I made sure no one was home," said Vincent, slouching in his seat.

"I don't care if anybody's home. That's their tough luck. Go ahead, let's get this over with."

"Right now? We can drive across the river and still be in range."

"I wanna make sure."

Vincent reached inside his jacket, taking out a remote transmitter, extending the antenna. Looking away, he held the thing in his right hand, a tiny bulb on top and his thumb over a button switch.

"What are you waiting for," grunted Carlo, a car pulling into the driveway and an elderly woman getting out.

The old woman is followed by a little girl with short red hair—a fifth-grader maybe—strolling merrily along the front walk.

"Jesus! What are they doing here?"

"I don't know, Vincent. And I don't care. Now hurry up and trip that thing."

"*Carlo* … one of 'em is a kid!"

"I can see that, do you think I'm blind. They'll be flying out of that house in no time. It's not like they'll be trapped inside."

Vincent hesitates, having a vision of the little girl setting on the sofa when suddenly she is overcome by fire—thick smoke and toxic fumes suffocating her. He takes his thumb away from the button, fixing his eye on the front walk.

"I can't find them, Amy," said the old woman, rummaging through her purse. "*Where could they be?*"

The little girl cupped her hands against one of the narrow windows peeking inside. "Do you see them," asked the old woman, hovering overhead.

"Vincent, either you trip that damn thing now or give it to me. We're running out of time here."

Vincent looked at Carlo for a moment, then over at the house, turning to Carlo again and the house once more.

"Damn it, Vincent, give me that fuckin' thing!" Carlo

reached across the seat unable to grab the transmitter, Vincent turning to the side with his face against the window. Both men glance at the house, the old woman and little girl appearing in the driveway.

"Maybe Paw-Paw has an extra set," said the old woman, opening the car door for the little girl.

Furious, Carlo snatched the remote from Vincent, thumbing the button and the miniature bulb glowing red. The old woman fastens the child's seatbelt while at the same time an electrical pop goes off inside the house. Likewise, the whooshing sound of an igniting fire and the old woman shutting the car door take place simultaneously.

Backing out of the driveway, focused on the street, the old woman put the car in gear, too busy checking out the Lincoln behind her to notice the array of fiery colors coming from the front door windows.

"You're starting to piss me off, Vincent," said Carlo, tossing the remote in his lap. An ireful glare while starting the engine, Carlo pulled alongside the house, the two men looking at the whitish-yellow crown of a surging inferno. "Oh, look, Vincent … someone's house is on fire."

"Funny, Carlo. Real funny."

"Come on," said Carlo, grinning as he turned the car around. "You should be happy … nobody got hurt." Carlo then took hold of Vincent's wrist checking his watch. "*What do you know?* Despite your lack of efficiency, we have enough time to grab a drink at the airport."

Vincent said nothing, staring at the houses one street after another.

"*All right*, I'm buying," said Carlo—the expressway just ahead.

Vincent turned from the window in due time, indulging Carlo at the thought of a free drink. Carlo smiled, but then suddenly he scoffed, "Hey, where's your map? Was that maintenance van there on our way in?"

"You're a barrel of laughs today, aren't you, Carlo."

Not far from the road, a man observes the oncoming traffic, in particular Carlo behind the wheel of the black Lincoln. A Gretna Water District shirt and sporting a Saints cap, the man draws a 24-inch Crescent from his van, tipping his head at Carlo while shutting off the water main.

At the rim of the airport peninsula, riverside of Lake Pontchartrain, the sun peeks through a patch of dark clouds, eavesdropping upon the lake's rippled surface. Jerry Holiday, the far side of overweight, bites into a ham sandwich at precisely 11:00 a.m. The fifty-six-year-old doesn't care much for work, and his current job, sitting in a golf cart at the base of the South Harbor promontory, is prevalent to that.

Jerry never thought of himself as lazy, he just doesn't like doing much of anything. He hoped airport security would suite him. Two years and twenty pounds later it hasn't. He swapped places with another guard last month, giving up his indoor post to rest his feet. The other guard said he'd rather be inside with central-air and hot globetrotting chicks anyway. It turned out beneficial to both Jerry and the other guard; one playing it cool on his feet inside the terminal and the other lolling in a golf cart, checking out all the racy numbers on the tarmac and tightly rigged vessels at the neighboring marina.

Presently, a few head turners grace the water in front of Jerry. But more so, anchored at the end of the promontory, is an attractive looking seaplane. *A DHC Beaver*, thought Jerry admiring the aircraft. *I'll take a closer look after lunch to see if it's the same one.*

Taking a bite of his sandwich, the stagnant air trudging

heavily above the asphalt, Jerry reached for a cold soda, his quiet meal interrupted by a burst of static on his two-way radio. “Jerry … You there?”

Jerry rolled his eyes at the radio, contemplating whether or not to throw it in the lake. He popped open the soda instead.

“Jerry … Pick up, Jerry … *Jerry?*”

Jerry took a drink and the liquid sugar and gross amount of caffeine jumpstarted him right away. “Yeah, what is it,” he answered.

“I got a Detective Taylor from the Eighth District on the line. Wants to know if we received an FAA bulletin. You know anything about that.”

Jerry keyed the radio. “No, I don’t. I’ve been outside making my rounds.”

“Thought so, just wanted to check.”

“Ten-four.”

The radio stayed silent and Jerry replaced it with his sandwich. Poised for a third bite, the sandwich in front of his mouth, another crackle of static erupts. “Jerry … You still there?”

Jerry glanced at the radio, taking a long gander at the lake. He sighed and put his sandwich on hold. “Riley, where else would I be? I just talked to you ten seconds ago.”

“*Right*,” the voice on the radio agreed. “Thought you’d like to know a couple of detectives are coming out here this afternoon. They wanna go over this bulletin thing with you.”

“Why me?”

“It’s Sunday, Jerry. You’re high man on the totem pole.”

“Where’s Fuller?”

“Didn’t show … Sorry pal.”

“All right. Guess I better get inside and cover for ‘em.”

“Roger that … base clear.”

Jerry threw the radio on the seat, devouring his sandwich and gulping the rest of his soda. *Nothing ever happens out here anyway*, he thought, jumping on the accelerator while spinning the cart around.

For the second time in as many days a limousine appears on Parish Road 8214, Adams paying close attention to the stretch of road ahead. "Whoa! Déjà vu," he declared.

"What is it," said a disgruntled voice in the back seat, Nathan squeezed between Laurian and Clarence.

"Another limo headed my way," answered Adams, turning to Nathan. "What are the odds of that happening out here two days in a row?"

"It could be the same one," said Shadwell, seated next to the driver.

"*Maybe*," replied Adams, the limousine zipping passed in the opposite direction. "A rental out of Shreveport most likely."

Curious, Clarence looked back. "It stopped, Uncle Will."

Everyone with the exception of Adams turned around—four pair of eyes gaping at the brake lights. "You folks don't get out much, do you? It's just a limousine," said Adams.

"I think someone's taken an interest in us," observed Shadwell. "They better not follow us. Not with my revolver on board."

"Revolver!" screamed Adams.

"Relax," Shadwell took the gun out of his boot. "*It's just a limousine*. Keep driving and everything will be fine."

"No one's going to hurt you," said Nathan.

Rattled about the limousine and Shadwell's gun, Adams starts asking a lot of questions, all of which no one is willing to answer.

"It's all right, Nick," said Nathan. "Once we get to my grandmother's we'll all have a good laugh. I'll fix you a nice sandwich for lunch and you'll be on your way."

"What the—" Clarence swung back around, "it's gone!"

"There, you see," continued Nathan, "… you needn't worry."

"You're sure," asked Adams, looking at Nathan in his rearview mirror.

"Absolutely," replied Nathan. "They're not after you."

Stuffing the revolver in his boot, Shadwell dug into the trunk handing the 12-gauge pump to Clarence, keeping the double-barrel for himself. Clearly the one in charge, Shadwell instructs everyone to wait by the taxi, taking a quick look inside Margaret's BMW.

"I don't see any keys," he told everyone on his return.

"Got one right 'ere, Uncle Will," said Clarence dangling a handful—the keys entrusted to him by Margaret.

"Good," said Shadwell. "We can send Mr. Adams on his way."

The dubious party entered the house with caution, Adams screeching his tires in the driveway. "I doubt if she's here. Or anyone else for that matter," said Shadwell, lowering his shotgun.

Still fixated, the thought of a bomb in the house, Nathan forewarns everyone to stay alert; an amusing comment from Laurian that he's overreacting.

"Far too much," scoffed Shadwell, handing Nathan the revolver. "Here, don't be so paranoid. You and Dr. Webster head upstairs and search the bedrooms. Clarence and I will check things out down here."

Nathan went up the left stairwell and Laurian followed. "And, Nathan," Shadwell yelled up at him.

"Yeah?"

"Try not to shoot anyone on our side."

Unpleasantly quite, Nathan lingers shrewdly behind the snub-nosed revolver. Laurian is aware of how fearful he is and breaks the silence outside the first room. "I never did get a chance to say how sorry I am about your parents."

His weary face thanking her, Nathan kept quiet, pressing an index finger against his lips in order for Laurian to do the same. He then pointed off to the side where he thought she should be.

Reluctant to open the door, his face cringing, Laurian is entertained that Nathan anticipates an explosion. Turning the knob slowly and cracking the door, Nathan breaths a resounding sigh of relief, nothing but the smell of dust saturating the air. From outside the darkened threshold, sticking his hand in the room, he feels around the corner flipping the light switch, anxious to get in and out as quick as possible.

"Stay here," he whispered, angling through the doorway.

With Nathan on the other side of the door and Laurian waiting patiently outside, she hears a noise down the hall—*or was it Nathan*, the door closing behind him.

"All clear," reported Nathan, "… let's move on."

Laurian scoots beside him, a peculiar look on her face.

"You okay?"

"I thought I heard something at the end of the hall. Probably just the house settling."

"It's old. Bones creak, houses creak … everything settles in time."

With the exception of a missing trellis outside his window, Nathan's room appeared exactly as he left it. He did a quick sweep, sticking his head out the door gesturing for Laurian to come inside.

Laurian glanced at his personal effects. "I had a feeling Margaret would give you this room."

"You've been here before?"

"Margaret gave me a quick tour of the place my first time out."

"Good, you can give me the layout of the next room."

"I said it was a quick tour, not the grand tour. This room and the one at the end of the hall are the only ones I've seen up here. She said the rest are filled with too many bad memories."

"I wonder if William sent his nephew to help with the cleaning or to watch over her."

"The boy does a few chores and that's it. Margaret wouldn't take advantage of someone like Clarence—only his company."

Every musty room leading to the last was the same. They all had dusty sheets over shapely furnishings dripping with cobwebs. The windows had so much dirt on the outside you could not tell the time of day.

"You look tired," said Laurian, she and Nathan standing at the end of the hall; the last room now in front of them.

Nathan initiated a response but a resounding thud behind the door cut him off.

"What was that," asked Laurian, appearing a little edgy.

"I'm not sure," answered Nathan, his face telling Laurian he expects the worst. "That didn't sound like the house settling to me. Something hit the floor."

"I'll go and get Mr. Shadwell."

Once more Nathan put a finger to his lips, pointing the gun at the door as if to say, *I have everything well in hand*.

Laurian stepped back, debating whether or not Nathan is trying to impress her… or if he really is the courageous type.

Nathan turned the knob. *The foolish type,* thought Laurian, stepping back again. The door creaked and a flash of light entered the hallway, a shadowy gust of life then darting out of the room brushing against Nathan's leg.

Nathan jumped and the gun went off unexpectedly, his eyes tracking a furry, little beast down the hall.

"Are you all right," Nathan cried out, advancing to Laurian's side.

"Just a little startled. What did you shoot?"

"Nothing— *I hope*."

Crossing the threshold, Laurian has a nervous hand upon Nathan's arm. "I'm a bit shaken myself," he admits.

"Afraid of cats, *are we?*"

Nathan didn't answer right away, his shadow casting a trace of umbrage upon the fancy, papered wall. "When I was seven I met my grandmother for the first time. I saw her for no more than an hour. The only thing I remember about that day is that she brought along a black cat. That's how I got this scar. I was afraid to touch it and she said it wouldn't hurt me. I should have trusted my own instincts.

"*That's funny?*"

"What," asked Nathan, sweeping the floor with his eyes— attentive to what's on his mind.

"Margaret never mentioned that. And I never noticed the scar in your photos. It's too close to your brow. When I saw it up close I wondered what happened."

"Well, now you know— Ah! There it is."

"What?"

"The bullet. It's lodged in the floor."

Nathan inspects the damage. "It's not that bad," he exudes a smidgen of relieve, the Pug revolver at his side and Laurian mindful of her actions.

The layout of the room was uniformed, immoderate furnishings in demand of an envious eye. Adversely dwarfed around a king size bed, there stood a towering wardrobe and chiffonier. Huge rectangular rugs protected the floor as heavy drapes guarded the outside balcony. Several antique chairs sit randomly in the cavernous room; a stool with rolling wheels residing in front of a huge curved vanity—complete with a lighted mirror and fancy middle drawer. Topped with perfumes, beauty aids, expensive jewelry… *everything imaginable*, the curvature of the dressing table appears to be a pair of welcoming arms.

"Look at this," said Nathan, letting out a faint whistle tallying the cosmetics. "There's more makeup here than all of Broadway."

"I know. A little bit of Hollywood too."

"That's right, you've already seen this."

"*This*— oh yes … *this I've seen before*."

Loud footsteps fill the corridor and Nathan raised his revolver, Laurian gently touching his wrist coaxing his arm back down. "We're all right," she declared to an empty doorway, Shadwell and Clarence emerging with shotguns pointing everywhere.

"What happened? We heard a shot."

"Nothing," answered Nathan. "A cat startled us, that's all. The gun went off by accident."

"That'd be Miss Margaret's cat, Bourbon. What happen to 'em?"

"It ran down the stairs I suppose."

"Oh no!" Clarence cried out. "Them doors is wide open out front. Miss Margaret don't care too much for 'em ta' be outside." Clarence looked at Shadwell for his approval to go after the animal and the old man motioned his head toward the door.

"Shouldn't one of us go with him," queried Nathan.

"He'll be fine. The place is clean. I never expected anyone to be here anyway."

"Then why all the guns?"

"I know the type of people we're dealing with," said

Shadwell. “They can afford a lot of muscle—money to burn and the audacity to fan it. They must have kidnapped Margaret while she was in her car. I saw a mobile phone on the front seat. This we found downstairs,” he shows them the panic-room latch. “You’re not the only one to visit Margaret this weekend, Nathan.”

Nathan appeared worried but Laurian looked calm. “I know where they’re taking her,” she said.

“Then we need to go there,” said Shadwell.

“Where,” asked Nathan.

“I’ll explain on the way to the airport.”

“The airport!” Nathan suddenly had an anxiety attack. “I’d like to pack a few things. Do I have time?”

“Not much,” replied Laurian. “Once I call Margaret’s pilot he’ll expect us at the airport as soon as possible.”

“You two get busy then. I’ll check on Margaret’s car,” said Shadwell.

Laurian followed Nathan back to his room, sitting atop the bed with his carryon suitcase on one side and Shadwell’s handgun on the other. She listens needlessly while he packs; something about his being cooped up in an airplane. *He’s quite handsome*, thought Laurian, his speech telling her he was well educated. He was nowhere near articulate, but he didn’t have to be because he spoke with such great confidence; she’d give him that.

Nathan didn’t have all that much to say when Laurian asked where he went to college, changing the subject to the conversation he had with Margaret last night; his parent’s death being no accident.

After the part where his father told him to stay in Pittsburgh and attend school, Laurian wanting to hear more, Nathan grew quiet, taking a handful of under-garments from one of the large bags to the carryon.

"Big mystery solved," observed Laurian, sensing the need for Nathan to think about something else.

"What big mystery?"

"Boxers or briefs."

Nathan looked down, closing the outer flap on the carryon, a drawn out grin on Laurian's face too playful to conceal.

"That's enough," said Nathan, somewhat on the serious side.

"You're sure? *I'd pack a sweater if I were you.*"

"You know what I mean," Nathan's voice ripened, his face baring a lighthearted smile.

A pair of thin trousers and loose fitting shirt—one to hide a gun—Nathan slipped into the bathroom. "Be right out," he said, looking at Laurian while closing the door.

Fidgeting upon the bed, Laurian tilts her head back, wanting to talk but no idea what to say. "What if something should happen to me while you're in there," she questioned the ceiling; Nathan oblivious to her affectionate tone.

"You'll be safe," answered Nathan. "I think Will was right," he spoke up. "Whoever they are they're long gone by now. I wouldn't worry if I were you."

"I'm not," replied Laurian. *I've worst things to consider*, she thought.

Shadwell reconnects the battery cable on the BMW, Laurian using Margaret's mobile phone to call Richard. "Clarence! Forget about the cat," screamed Shadwell—the boy still searching for Bourbon. "We need to put our things in the trunk."

Going through the keys, hastily one after another, eventually Clarence found the one for the trunk, Nathan placing his carryon and Laurian's briefcase inside. Shadwell put the bundle of shotguns on top of everything, Nathan handing over his revolver and Shadwell stuffing it back in his boot.

Shadwell then closed the trunk. "Clarence," he said, motioning to the front seat, "… you're driving."

Sliding behind the wheel, a much better mood than standing guard at the kitchen window, Clarence has never been more anxious to drive Miss Margaret's BMW than he is now.

A true gentleman, Nathan opens the rear driver's-side door for Laurian, Shadwell climbing into the front passenger seat. Despondent, Nathan having to sit in the back, he gradually made his way to the other side, sliding in next to Laurian.

Latching her seatbelt, and Nathan doing the same, Laurian flinched all of a sudden.

"What's wrong," asked Nathan.

Laurian points to the floorboard and there lay Bourbon nestled at her feet. "*Oh, no*," exclaimed Nathan, leaning to one side.

"What is it?" Shadwell turned around.

"We found Margaret's cat," said Laurian, "… or rather, it found us."

Stuck behind the wheel, Clarence pushed his body up out of the seat, angling his head around. "Ther' ya are … *ya sneaky cat*."

Laurian picked up the orphaned feline, coddling him in her lap. "Poor thing," she stroked his side, the cat then purring.

"He likes ya, Doc'ta Webster. Can we take 'em with us, Uncle Will?"

"We have no choice. There's no one here to care for him."

Wonderful, thought Nathan. *It's going to be a long trip.*

Eight

CLARENCE BROOKS, like most teenagers, drove the family car whenever he could. And that's what Margaret considered him to be—*family.* His uncle did not own a car and Margaret taught Clarence to drive when he was fourteen. *A fine way of travelin' from one place to another*, the teenager glorified Margaret's German sedan. She constantly told him to slow down and Clarence felt shackled respecting the speed limit with so much power at his feet. The roadside leaves stood still when he passed by and the countryside made him drowsy. The only way to stay alert was to crank up the radio to a lively, vibratory-station out of Shreveport; hip-hopping and rapping between moronic drivel and a steady dose of commercials. Oddly enough, the music never bothered Margaret.

When Clarence first got his license, he drove Margaret into Ruston euphorically… the familiar road now gloomy and his uncle none too happy when he switched on the radio, despotically expressing the need to hear himself think.

"You're driving like an old woman," said Shadwell, glancing at the speedometer. "You know we're in a hurry. Open her up."

Clarence thought this day would never come. Every teenager

dreamed of it. *But to have permission!* So what if he couldn't listen to the radio, he'd manage. *Go ahead… floor it!*

"That's better. Now, Dr. Webster," Shadwell spun his head around, "… where are they taking Margaret?"

"Cape Coral."

"And where's that?" Nathan wanted to know.

"Florida," answered Shadwell. "I know it like the back of my hand. You know where Fort Myers is, right?"

"Of course."

"Cape Coral is across the bay."

"Why take her there?"

Laurian put a hand on William's shoulder. "I can explain the significance of Cape Coral but you may want to tell him yourself. Some things are better left unsaid. *Details* you may want to leave out."

Stunned at how much she knows, Shadwell said he'd rather not, that *such things* were unimportant to him; his light, ebony cheeks abashed with modesty.

Shadwell's dark eyes, as Laurian can see, showed a little discomfort. "Margaret told me what happened out there," she declared, "… the French Quarter … what took place on the steamer… San Juan … *everything*."

"Very well," Shadwell complied, her delicate reasoning changing his mind. "Clarence, most of the particulars you already know. *The questionable truth*, however, you may find hard to believe. Be mindful of the road and remember to slow down around these curves."

Clarence gave an attentive nod.

"I assume she mentioned how we first met," Shadwell queried Margaret's omniscient friend.

"Yes."

"I'll start with the map then."

"It was late June, 1932," said Shadwell, "... after the carriageway incident. On a paddle-steamer bound for Fort Myers we entered Charlotte Harbor at sunrise. Margaret took her three-year-old son, Stewart, and the boy's nanny, Dorothy, along. We also had a cat I found abandoned on the steamer; jet black except for a white, diamond-shaped spot on its chest. The feisty little creature hissed at me so I palmed him off on Margaret."

Shadwell gave the rest of his account as though it were yesterday, he and Margaret standing over a small table, the nanny and three-year-old Stewart sleeping in the adjoining room—Margaret's nameless feline at her feet. Under a gas light, Margaret unfurls the map with young William seeing it for the first time. The markings were barely visible, a disgusting piece of hide appearing as though it had been ripped from someone's body. Sketched in 1521, seven islands inundated the tawny hide with a lengthy portion of land curtailed along the right side. Names did not appear on any of the islands, only a compass-rose in the corner and the faded words *pascua florida* underneath.

"Pine Island," said Margaret, tapping the map. "It's just outside our window... thirty-four miles of sandy beach surrounding a jungle-like interior. The one below," she slid her finger down the map, "... is Sanibel. Not a very accurate drawing I'm afraid. It's much larger in proportion to the others and has a thick, wooded area on the northwest side. I've searched the other islands top to bottom and found no clue as to what I'm looking for. This time I— or rather *we* will find it together."

"F-f-find what? B-b-buried treasure."

"You might say that," said Margaret. "See these dark regions on the rim of our two islands. I believe they were once explored and later colored in. If that's true, we don't need to search the whole island. We'll start here," said Margaret, pointing to the southern tip of Pine Island. "I'll procure a boat tomorrow and make arrangements for our provisions. If you need anything or something particular you would like to eat, I must know by this afternoon." Margaret folded the sordid pelt, placing it in her handbag. "Any questions?"

"W-w-what about yer son?"

"Dorothy will look after him in Cape Coral. I have a summer place there. Not very spacious," said Margaret looking out the cabin window, "… but they'll have plenty of room once we leave. Now," she breathed in the morning air, "… why don't we go out on deck and take a look at our first island."

William answered as always, nodding in silence; Margaret promising herself she'd soon put an end to that.

The surface remained calm as the serried boat made its way through the estuary across the subtle waters east of Pine Island. Margaret pointed to a spot along the beach, the carious smile of the captain—as he liked to be called—expressing his approval, maneuvering his twelve-foot skiff accordingly. An old Mississippi helmsman, the captain timed his landing perfectly. Teetering the engine out of the water, the boat drifted until the bow stabbed the sandy shore.

William jumped from the boat and muscled it further in, extending a hand to Margaret. "Thank you, William."

Margaret received his customary nod.

"What a beautiful day to start. Is it not?"

The lengthy portion of beach lie abandoned, as well as the surrounding waters. Last year, preferring not to draw attention to herself, Margaret told the captain she didn't want anyone bothering her while exploring the islands. Upon her request, the captain started a rumor that she was a rich ornithologist. A local tavern gave her the entitlement of *Lady Bird* when they saw her for the first time. Margaret knew very little on the subject, something she came up with at the last minute. Socializing with the townspeople and area fishermen, Margaret soon discovered she was an expert by comparison.

Supplies were offloaded and Lady Bird Margaret told the captain where to rendezvous next and on what day to arrive. It didn't seem too far up the coast to William, until Margaret proved otherwise, pointing out they'd be scouring every inch of it. "By the end of the day," said Margaret, "... it will seem like a thousand miles away."

The owner of Shreveport Limousine is waiting patiently for the return of his vehicle. Looking out the lobby window, he admires the virescent belly and glossy-white dome of a Learjet lounging on the tarmac. Disembarking minutes ago from the private jet, the snug terminal filling to capacity, the owner checked his watch, adding another hundred to the bill. *And why not*, the customer can afford it. A down payment of a thousand dollars and the hourly rate doubled, the customer's driver handed over the money without bargaining. And to sweeten the deal, *as if the owner needed more*, an extra five-hundred for the inconvenience of having to pick up his limousine; flying from Shreveport to Ruston in a private jet.

Outside the terminal, the seductive Learjet a short distance away, the owner's limousine comes screeching around the corner to a sudden stop. "Finally," the owner said to himself, finishing his coffee as the passenger door opened. "*What the hell*," gaped the owner, those seated in the lobby rising to their feet staring out the window.

Two dark and seemingly tall individuals head for the Learjet with female companions at their side. Both are carrying a lengthy walking-stick and appear naked at that distance. One man moves rather briskly and the other somewhat gingerly, the spryer of the two men grasping the woman next to him. It looks as though she's struggling to free herself, but then she appears reposed, the driver and another man exiting the limousine.

"Hey!" yelled the stocky owner, making his way to the edge of the tarmac. He recognized the driver but the other man, much taller, he'd never seen before.

The driver glanced at the owner, locking the limousine door. Tossing the keys on the roof, the driver ran across the tarmac boarding the Learjet. With the cabin door closing, the owner of the limousine is stretching for his keys. He looks through the front window, spotting a manila envelope on the seat.

The Learjet swaggers to the runway and the owner of the limousine tears into the envelope; an eye-popping bundle of C-notes inside.

Clarence wanted to hear more about the map. The other stuff, Pine Island and Miss Margaret's bird name, he knows all about that. Pulling off the 146 and taking the 148, Ruston just minutes away, Clarence cut into his uncle's narrative. "Miss Margaret didn't tell ya what the map was 'fer."

"She did," replied Shadwell, frowning at the interruption, "… after our first week on the island."

Returning to his chronicle of what happened during that first week, Shadwell describes the wooded inland and open beaches on the island, leaving out what he thought to be minor details in Margaret's behavior.

Pine Island, a drawn-out cluster of several anorexic ones, separated by shallow waterways and calm lagoons, did not appear all that promising to Margaret.

"This island," she confessed after the first day, "may turn out to be a waste of time. None of it looks familiar. There are very few palm trees here and not a single vine of ivy."

By the end of the fifth day, William memorized nine varieties of tropical birds. Margaret brought along a few books to keep up appearances and was excited that the two of them shared something new. William carried the books in his pack as they trekked through the heavy brush, Margaret on occasion taking one out, identifying the species they were unfamiliar with.

That night, Margaret encouraged William to read from the book. An attentive pupil, no distractions except for the mosquitoes, *and no schooling beyond the third grade*, surprisingly William learned quickly. The hindrance of that period's injustice, discouraging blacks to learn, in the quiet of the woods it disappeared. The intolerance, the superficial men… this thicket of solitude proved beneficial to young William. He gathered as much nourishing information from Margaret as he could. Feasting on her knowledge, like oxygen he could not survive without it. He now had a new purpose in life. To not only exist but to actually live.

Margaret told him he progressed admirably—a new word for him. "I still feel t-t-the same," answered William. "I might be able t-t-ta' point out a b-b-bird or two. T-t-tell ya its species… what's so admirab-b-b-le about that."

Margaret said he could soon ask Dorothy for her opinion.

"W-w-we's leavin'?"

"Day after tomorrow we head for the mainland. I miss my son. Besides, there's not much here we haven't explored already. It's time to move on to the next island."

“I have a q-q-question … n-n-needs answerin’.”

Margaret looked at William with much anticipation. Everything revolved around his loved ones back home. She asked what it was and William replied almost perfectly, “I should like to know w-w-what we are searching for?”

Somewhat proud, his tone more confident, Margaret knew the question would come sooner or later. He deserved to know and keeping it from him was just as dangerous as revealing it. She thought for a considerable amount of time about the consequences and whether or not to comply.

“Those close to me have died because of this. I think it is unwise to tell you, but if you feel it is necessary….”

Clarence eased off the accelerator, his uncle about to reveal what he and Miss Margaret were searching for. The car slowed to forty-five and no one questioned the change in speed; for all they knew they were heading for a curve.

“Margaret told me we were searching for a treasure beyond all others,” said Shadwell. “‘One so costly it changes your life forever. Hunger and pestilence are vanquished upon its discovery. Death is cast aside and time becomes no more.’ She said she and her fiancé stumbled upon it four years earlier; on one of those seven islands. With my help we’d find Stuart and bring back his remains. After that she would come back on her own and destroy the thing that caused his death.

“And what might that be,” asked Nathan.

“The fountain of youth,” answered Shadwell. “Margaret said it was out there, and for me to not only trust her, but have faith in what she believed.”

Nine

NATHAN KEPT QUIET, staring at the back of Clarence's seat, wondering what to make of it all. Laurian, having heard the story before, showed little emotion. *Don't look at me*, her eyes tell Nathan, *I believe in this stuff.*

Clarence checked his rearview mirror and Nathan saw how confused the boy was, as though he were in a different ballpark compared to everyone else. "Sorry, Uncle Will, but I ain't never heard a no foun'in a youth."

"You're serious, *aren't you*," blasted Nathan, right in Shadwell's ear. "*The,* fountain of youth."

"Yes."

"The one Ponce de León thought to be real?"

"Yes," answered Shadwell once again.

"Ponce'a *who*," asked Clarence.

"I asked Margaret the same thing. I had no idea myself back then. But she did. She knew everything about the man."

Returning to an earlier time, the island of Sanibel, Shadwell describes what took place when he first learned of the Spanish explorer, Margaret sitting across from him with a congenial campfire between them.

"Juan Ponce de León," Margaret explained to William,

"accompanied Columbus on his second voyage to America when he was thirty-three years old. He soon commanded a ship of his own and in 1510 conquered the island of Boriquen. Spain renamed the island Puerto Rico and in 1512 Ponce de León became Governor. During that year, the Boriquens told him tales of an island north of Cuba called Bimini. It possessed a magical fountain with immortality bestowed upon those drinking its water.

"Ponce de León setout immediately in search of the legendary island and its reputed spring. For whatever reason, he discovered Florida instead. The Biminis were fifty miles to the east, a diminutive group of islands in the western part of the Bahamas. Many believed his quest for the fountain ended upon his return to Puerto Rico, which for some unexplained reason the Spaniards and Boriquens were at each other's throat. Two years later, enmity between the Spaniards and Boriquens manifested into war. Ponce de León and his men fought the natives for six years.

"Vanquishing the rebellion in 1521, Ponce de León led an expedition to colonize Florida. The battle-ridden men, two-hundred of them, landed somewhere on the west coast where they fell under attack by a fierce army of Native Americans. The great explorer was severely wounded during the bitter confrontation, and having been defeated, the expedition retreated to Cuba. Soon after their arrival Ponce de León died."

William leaned over the fire. "How did you get h-h-hold 'a that map?"

"*Of* that map," Margaret corrects him. "I met a man one night in some shoddy little tavern in the Quarter. He smelled of salt water, a stout and very tall man with long dark hair. Much older than I, he enjoyed flirting with me. Unlike the other men, he appeared quite sober, determined at bedding me down for the night. The less attention he received the more he told me about this map of his. 'I have a room down the street' he said, 'come with me and I'll show you.' I asked him what kind of map it was and he said it belonged to Ponce de León. 'A puzzle in itself,' he emphasized, 'rightly interpreted the map will lead you to the fountain of youth. You are knowledgeable with the legend,' he asked. I told him I was and he took my hand caressing my fingers. I have no idea why, but I granted him this one indulgence. Only for a minute mind you, regaining my senses and pulling away. Without warning, he left me there promising to return."

The fire going out, Margaret stokes the weary flame fortifying the darkness. "When the man returned," she went on, "there was another in his place. He too was tall, though much thinner and closer to my age. The man who left took a chair across from me, demanding that the other fellow leave. The young man cursed at him and continued his conversation with me. I was impressed. The younger man wasn't afraid. Looking back, he should have been. The man with long hair rose from his seat. He had a chilling, iniquitous grin, grabbing the other man's head twisting it to one side and back again. I heard something crack and saw the eyes and jaw of the younger man stiffen. His forehead smacked the table in front of me and I remember how quiet it got. Either no one in the room saw what happened or no one cared. The killer then sat next to me … his foul breath spoiling my air and lowly eyes examining mine. Though I don't recall mentioning my name he spoke it rather seductively, telling me he would have me, if not that night then another. Rising to his feet he tossed the map on the table, confessing that it belonged to me. He said it had been stolen from my family's house years ago and if I showed it to anyone he would snuff them out like the boy in front of me."

"You showed it t-t-to me," said William.

"Yes, I know. And against my better judgment. If you wish to leave I will understand."

Young Shadwell sensed Margaret's fear. To keep her from sensing his he got up and sat next to her, drawing courage from her despair. He said she needn't worry because he wasn't going anywhere.

"I was looking over my shoulder for a year," Margaret continued, "… then I met Stuart. We fell in love and I'd forgotten all about the map. Stuart discovered it by mistake two years later. That's when this all started."

"The man in the t-t-tavern found you?"

"No … *I found him*. I should have destroyed the map when he gave it to me. Stuart was intent on finding the fountain and we got lost in a terrible storm. Our boat crashed on one of these islands. I don't know which one but there he was … the man in the tavern. He didn't bother looking for me because he knew I'd come to him. He and his companion, a Cariban warrior, tracked us during the storm. It was then that Stuart stumbled upon the cave leading to the fountain. With the Cariban warrior on our heels we had no time to look inside. Stuart hid me in the brush to save me and it was the last I saw of him."

"Five miles to Ruston," Clarence spoke up.

"Finally," said Shadwell with a yawn. "I think I can finish up by then."

"Would you like to know what I think," asked Nathan.

No one objected, especially Shadwell, the old storyteller had been talking for twenty-minutes and needed a break.

"My grandmother," commenced Nathan, "… one tragic event after another, I can understand her eccentricity. No one can deny she's associated with some undesirables; most likely after her money. They killed my parents and then came after me. Taking into account what I've learned, I think she may be ready for a long rest… someplace with overbearing nurses and pills that keep your imagination from running wild."

"There's nothing wrong with your grandmother," refuted Laurian.

"Do you believe in all this fountain nonsense, Will?"

"No, I do not. But I've always pondered the possibility. The older one gets the more they dream of such things."

"And you, Dr. Webster?"

"What do you think," Laurian asked Nathan in return.

"You're a believer. I can tell. Clarence, how about you?"

"Naw. What ya said 'bout Miss Margaret is p'erty much ta' way I sees it. 'Cept I don't think she belongs in no home. She ain't dangerous or nothin'."

"No, I'd say she's *in danger.* Putting this tall tale aside—" Nathan concludes, "that's what I believe. Sorry to have interrupted you, Will."

Shadwell said he didn't mind, but Clarence knew better. He knew how his uncle felt toward others. The old man outlived his family, and his friends have long since disappeared—irreverence and spitefulness driving them away. He's less objectionable with Nathan, however. And Dr. Webster too. *Maybe it has sumpin' ta' do with Miss Margaret,* thought Clarence. *Carin' about 'er like they do.*

"Nathan," said Shadwell, "your grandmother was obsessed with so many things. She told me three men killed her father because he knew about the fountain. The maid who found Alexander swore it was suicide. Even his wife said he killed himself. As a child other children tormented Margaret because of it. They made up stories as to why her father hung himself. One boy said Alexander had a black daughter in another parish and someone else said her mother was a harlot.

"I told Margaret I didn't believe in the fountain or that her father was killed because of it. She insisted on finding it however, along with the men who murdered her father. Her paranoia soon expanded into wild fabrications about the cave moving from island to island… also the adverse effects the water had that first year of immortality. One of the things she claimed that wasn't far-fetched, was the Cariban tracking and killing people who jeopardized the location of their sacred pool. I believe it was all a hoax to extract money from wealthy families.

"In 1809, long before her father's death, Margaret told me the explorer Meriwether Lewis died at the hand of one such warrior. The first in a long line of innocent men."

"*Meriwether Lewis*," Nathan said to himself. "I don't understand."

"If I may," Laurian addressed Shadwell, "I'd like to explain what actually happened."

"By all means, go ahead," said Shadwell, gazing sternly out the window. *It's all ancient history to me now*, he thought.

"Meriwether Lewis never searched for any such fountain. A distant cousin claimed he knew where to find it and Meriwether believed him because he had Ponce de León's map. On their way to see the President with proof of the fountain, Meriwether either committed suicide or was murdered in Tennessee."

"Hold on a second," Nathan interrupted. "That's ridiculous. I know my history. True, he was found dead on his way to Washington … but traveling with a cousin? That's something you won't find in any historical document. Even if the cousin were real, I doubt if the two ever met."

"You're so stubborn," said Laurian. "The story alone would suggest reason for murder. Murder *made* to look like suicide."

"Okay, let's say he was murdered. But the fountain of youth— *come on*. I'd really like to believe in something like that. The fact of the matter is you have no proof it exists."

"All the proof I need is sitting right here on my lap."

"My grandmother's cat?"

"This is the same cat that gave you that scar when you were seven. The same cat Mr. Shadwell found on that steamer in 1932."

"That's not the same cat. The cat that scratched me had a white spot on its chest."

Webster lifted the cat from her lap, precariously above Nathan's head. "All I see is a black underside. Not a speck of white anywhere," said Nathan.

"I don't understand," Laurian examines the animal. "This is Margaret's cat, Bourbon."

"Bourbon number three or four maybe. You need something more tangible than a cat to validate your story."

"*You know*," said Shadwell, as they pull into the regional airport, "... I never believed it myself. I wanted to at the beginning, but the man from the tavern stalking Margaret turned everything around. He was a psychopathic killer, yet he never harmed her. He couldn't ... he was in love with Margaret. I think she made all that up to forget about him. I put a bullet in that psycho's head when he came after me in 1936. It was the last I saw of Margaret until— now I don't know what to believe." Removing from his shirt the torn prosthetic face he found on the parlor floor, Shadwell hands it to Nathan. "Tell me, it's been over fifty years ... is this or is this not Margaret Lewis?"

Clarence held the door and Laurian Webster is the first to enter the terminal. She believes what she told the others about the fountain to be true. She felt despondent, however, having no evidence to confirm her story. Shadwell, following in her footsteps, reconsiders the matter. *Was Margaret telling the truth all these years? Everything makes sense if she did. But how— how could it be true?*

Nathan, far behind them, doesn't accept the mythical concept, as Clarence, the last to enter the terminal, is indifferent. The fountain is of little importance to him. He wonders instead whether or not he'll be flying for the first time.

Bypassing the service counter, the dissenting group assembles in a modest lobby. Two pilots are talking baseball beside a self-serve coffee pot and Shadwell tossed a dollar into a tumbler full of change. Everyone grabs a cup except for Clarence, heading for the picture window overlooking the tarmac. Seated in the lobby next to Clarence, a handful of passengers await their small commuter flights, still buzzing over the Learjet and what appeared to be a kidnapping.

Laurian joined Clarence at the window, pointing out Margaret's plane to him. "I don't see Richard anywhere," she said. "He must be around here somewhere. Maybe he—"

"Is that 'em," gestured Clarence, a man climbing out of the plane.

"Yes, that's him. Excuse me," said Laurian, rushing to the door.

Richard is making his way to the terminal… embracing Laurian for the longest time.

"Are you all right," asked Richard, looking her over as though she'd been in an accident.

Laurian appreciates Richard's concern—his potent hug and sensitive tone as well. When last they spoke, Margaret's mobile phone died and Richard was cut off before Laurian could explain everything.

"What happened? I tried calling Margaret but there was

no answer."

Laurian gave a brief summery as to what took place at Margaret's. The others made their way over and hasty introductions are exchanged. Shadwell then excused himself, the coffee rousing his bladder.

A man leaves the lavatory, crossing Shadwell's path taking a seat at the far end of the terminal. *I've seen him before*, thought Shadwell, approaching one of the urinals. *Was it in Ruston or somewhere else?*

Pouring a cup of coffee, Richard questioned Laurian as to how she's holding up. "I'm fine," she replied, Nathan and Clarence stepping aside and Laurian's face suddenly grim. "I'm worried about Margaret, that's all."

Richard knows how close they are and is cognitive of Margaret's troubled past. Watching over Laurian, his number one priority, Richard has a strong bond with Margaret as well and will do everything he can to help find her.

"Clarence," Shadwell announced on his return, pouring another cup of coffee, "… I need you to do something right away."

Grimacing at his uncle's tone, without question Clarence agreed.

"I want you to head back home. And take Margaret's cat with you."

"*Aw*, Uncle Will."

"Clarence, I'm sorry. I have a bad feeling about this."

Nathan sided with Shadwell. He couldn't understand why he brought the boy along in the first place.

Richard's discussion with Laurian is at an end and he discloses a plan to fly everyone to New Orleans, then on to Cape Coral.

"We should be all right," he said to Nathan. "I see no danger of flying in that area until tomorrow."

"What do you mean," asked Nathan, his blood pressure rising.

"They don't know," Laurian said to Richard.

"Know what," inquired Shadwell, the same nescient look on his face as Clarence.

"There's a hurricane watch along the southwest coast of Florida … early to mid-morning."

"Hurricane Andrew," said Nathan, recalling last week's news.

"Yes. I wouldn't worry if I were you. We'll be in Cape Coral this evening. We won't have much time to look around, but it's better than doing nothing."

"I need to call my folks and let them know I won't be coming home tonight," said Laurian.

"Wait a minute," blared Richard, "… you're not planning on going with us, are you?"

"Yes, as a matter of fact I am. Once I grab a few things from my office. Is there a problem with that?"

"I just thought it would be best if you sat this one out. These men can assist me if I need help."

"*Assist you*," answered Shadwell rather harshly, unaccustomed to playing second fiddle to anyone.

A chauvinist stance, Richard directs a stern voice at Laurian. "You didn't tell them, did you?"

"No. Not yet," replied Laurian. "I promised Richard we'd go along with whatever plan he comes up with. He's ex-military," Laurian paused for a moment, "… 2nd Brigade, 25th Infantry Mechanized Di—"

"I was a helicopter door-gunner," Richard cut in. "Two tours. Cu Chi in '67 and Long Binh in '71. I was about his age when I enlisted," Richard glanced over at Clarence, giving him a creditable nod.

"Did ya hear that, Uncle Will?" Clarence nearly hit the floor begging to come along. He had a war veteran to back him up now so maybe his uncle will change his mind.

"No sense in leaving him here," advised Richard. "He can keep Laurian company once we get there."

"What?!" Laurian's tone and the look she gave Richard, he knew she wanted him to renounce that idea.

"If you're going with us," said Richard as gracious as possible, "... I'd rather you stay on the beach. We'll take Margaret's seaplane. It will save us a lot of time hopping from one island to the next. And there are a few things we need to take care of beforehand." Richard then turned to Shadwell. "Laurian tells me you have some guns tucked away."

Shadwell is reluctant to answer, replying with a slight nod. "Good," Richard smacked him on the shoulder. "Now I have someone to cover my back. *The boy*, is he coming with us?"

Clarence pled his case once more and Shadwell gave in. "I suppose—" answered Shadwell, "his role having been decided and my position on the battlefield settled."

Richard forced a smile, commandeering Clarence to help him transfer whatever they have in the BMW to the plane; one temperamental cat included.

"Richard's a good man, Mr. Shadwell," said Laurian, realizing how much time has passed since her husband's death.... "Michael would have been forty-two this month," she said to herself, unaware Nathan is standing behind her.

"I just turned forty-one," said Nathan, recalling the day and those deplorable hours that followed.

"Yes ... I know," said Laurian, delivering a wishful birthday, none too happy as she consoles the floor.

Nathan's reply mirrored her congratulations, Laurian aware of what it's like when a loved one is taken from you. But to lose your parents on your birthday—to have them murdered—she can't imagine his pain. *Can he imagine mine*, she thought, Nathan and Michael's birthday occurring on the same day.

One whose mood changes frequently, a familiar sight or spoken word often the catalyst, Laurian felt like crying but held back. The waning days of the wrong month, she buckles down to get through.

A quiet, elegiacal moment surrounds Nathan and Laurian, and Shadwell, having forehand knowledge of Nathan's grief, and now a hefty slice of Laurian's, can't help but share the couplet's harrowing silence. In an attempt to overthrow his own emotions, like any soldier, William fought off the attack by clearing his throat, attracting their attention. He reached over wiping a tear from Laurian's eye. A beholding gaze from Laurian, the old man withdrew a stiff upper lip and a layer of pride fell by his wayside.

Heading for the payphone, Laurian gave Shadwell both a feeble smile and grateful hand to the cheek. Nathan then set his coffee down, his face pale and Shadwell questioning his health.

"I'm all right," answered Nathan. "Just a slight stomach ache."

"It's the darts. You'll be nauseous for a day or two."

"Now there's something new," quipped Nathan.

"How does your back feel?"

"Like a sun-dried sponge."

"You need to walk it off. Why don't we check on our ex-military friend? Clarence is likely to enlist if we stay inside much longer."

They pass Laurian on the way to the parking lot, as she is talking on an old rotary payphone. "Hold on, Dad—" Laurian muffled the phone. "*I'll be right out*," she gave Nathan a subtle smile.

"Still there," Laurian questioned her father. "...When did they leave?"

"You just missed them. Something about a spare set of keys."

"I'll be leaving here shortly. Would you mind watching Amy for a few days? Something's come up, I'm afraid."

"Sure, sweetheart. Is everything all right?"

"Yes, everything's fine. I have a medical emergency to tend to in Florida. I'm flying out late this afternoon."

"*Florida*. Laurian, you do know—"

"I know, Dad. There's a hurricane headed there. Don't worry, I'll be up north. Far from any danger."

The suspicious looking man William saw earlier takes a seat by the window, mindful of those who are boarding Margaret's twin-engine Cessna. Scrambling to the payphone as the plane is taking off, a recording instructs him to stay on the line while locating his party.

"They're on their way," said the suspicious looking man.

Ariel is on the other end of the line. "How many," she asked, stepping out of the hanger office.

Two flatbed Cushman's and a mechanic's rollaway are at the bottom of the stairs, Ariel making her way to the middle of the hanger; a '91 Blazer towing a 16-foot skiff and her father checking it out.

"She's on her way, Father," Ariel said to him.

"I suspected she would be. Who does this belong to?"

"Raymond. He asked if he could park it here for a couple of days. I said it would be all right."

"*Not a bad rig*," said Marcus, his intonation abhorring. "Now get rid of it! Torch everything and dump it somewhere."

"Why?"

"You should have known better, Ariel. The vehicle has a

numbered plate. The boat is also registered. The hanger, I venture to say, is in my name … is it not?"

"I'm sorry, Father. I wasn't thinking."

"*No*, the problem is you think too much."

Ariel was indignant with herself. She hates making mistakes, especially in the presence of her father. This time she put his life in jeopardy.

A limousine, similar to the one in Shreveport, pulls into the hanger and Raymond gets out carrying a manila folder. He can see something is bothering Ariel, having a hateful look on her face.

"Carlo sends his regards," said Raymond approaching Marcus, "… and this."

"Where is he," Marcus grabbed the folder.

"Where else, he reeks of whiskey already."

"Good. He becomes more callous when he drinks. Now that we have the last of her research," Marcus flips through the folder, "… he can extirpate the good doctor. In the meantime, our guest has had plenty of time to freshen up. Raymond, see to it that she's ready for lunch."

"On it, boss."

"What of Webster's friends, Father?"

"Are they on the plane?"

"Yes. The old man, his nephew, Margaret's cat … and believe it or not, the grandson is with them."

"Stay here with Carlo and make sure the doctor's body is disposed of properly. As for the others," Marcus caressed his propitiating stone, "… bring them to me."

"What about the cat?"

"It belongs to Margaret. *It always has*."

Ariel took a few steps in the direction of the terminal, none too happy by the way she lingers off.

"And, Ariel—"

“Yes, Father,” she turned around.

“If Carlo’s taken in, I’ll not be there to free him this time.”

“That was a long time ago.”

“For you perhaps. I do not wish for the connection between the two doctors to be made. Is that clear?”

“Yes, Father. Perfectly clear.”

Ten

TANTUR STEPPED OUT of the hanger office with a young woman, his swarthy fingers cuffing the arm of the fair-skinned beauty. The young woman's eyes bursting with anger, she twists her arm, a defiant protest knowing full well she cannot escape.

Standing between the limousine and Raymond's boat, Marcus revels in the young woman's presence. Captivated by her proud walk, the way her sandy curls flop upon her forehead, he can think of nothing else. "You look like a new woman, my dear."

The complement upset her and the young woman tugged at Tantur's firm grip. "I look and feel as I always have."

"Yes, isn't it wonderful?"

"No, Marcus," the young woman broke free, "… it is not *wonderful*. Nothing has changed in sixty-four years. I did not ask nor ever recall wanting any of this, and I certainly don't expect to spend the rest of my life with someone like you."

The face of Margaret Lewis can be altered from time to time but the tone of her voice and eloquent tongue cannot. Even when angered her speech is unmistakable. "Why do you treat me like this? To experience your impassive will is to know the true meaning of terror. Even during the lull of not thinking about you I grow weary. My aberrant life, scorned forever, the only solace I have is when you are not around. I don't need you showing up on these cloudy days reminding me of how miserable I am. Go away. Just go away and let me live as I please."

"Don't you mean, *die as I please?* Why would you want that, Margaret? Do you think I'm blind, someone such as myself unable to see what you're up to. This treatment of yours," said Marcus, shoving the manila folder in her face, "… endangers not only my existence but others as well."

"I care not about *your* existence, Marcus, only how well I manage my own."

Margaret incites an unpalatable flavor in his mouth but Marcus held his tongue. "We'll discuss this later," he said, the bickering deferred and Marcus opening the limousine door. "I'm hungry, Margaret. Our breakfast ending up on the floor, in all fairness I trust you to join me for lunch."

"I have no stomach for being around you no matter what the circumstance. And I've never known you to be hungry. Eager to satisfy your palate— yes… *but hungry?*"

"Just get in, Margaret," snapped Marcus, proceeding to the other side, Raymond then stepping forward with an angry look on his face, purposely slamming Margaret's door.

Tantur drifts toward the office and Marcus stopped him at the bottom of the stairs. "Wait," he called out, then to Raymond, "What time is it?"

"One o'clock," the chauffeur checked his watch.

Marcus then turned to Tantur. "Have Walter file a 3:30 flight plan nonstop to Cape Coral."

"Are we going home," asked Tantur.

"Yes," replied Marcus, stepping closer. "Your brother, how is he?"

"The same. He's sleeping right now."

"You can do nothing to heal his wound?"

"No," Tantur lowered his head. "We are of the same blood."

"I understand. I know of another empowered with your gift but I have no idea where she is. Wahota treads an uncertain tide, Tantur. Do not let his fate trouble you. By tomorrow's end he will be as right as rain." *Or dead as night,* thought Marcus, *if things do not go as planned*—ascribing Wahota's injury as a casualty of war.

Richard Gregory throttles the Cessna to a cruising speed of 230 knots. The plane is stable over the State of Louisiana and all is quiet except for the whine of the engines. Sitting in the cockpit next to Richard, Clarence takes off his headset, no more questions as the windshield steals his attention, miles of ripe forest glistening below.

Comfortable high-back cushions with plenty of legroom, both facing one another, Nathan and Laurian are asleep in the aft pair of seats. Shadwell, wanting to take a nap as well, is sitting portside with Bourbon sprawled out on the seat next to him. It has been several years, a lifetime actually, since Shadwell's last time in a plane. The view from the cabin looks like it did back then, uneventful for the most part but too enthralling to miss. Gazing at the terrain, it defies consistency, miles and miles of plush forest changing from one shade of green to the next. The land could be mistaken for a number of places if not for the ocherous soil; patches of blushing earth swimming in a mottled ocean of trees. Nowhere else in the country is there such a scarlet hue than in Northern Louisiana. The fiery color, exploding from the ground, imprints a sublime memory in Shadwell's head. His mind, a bountiful assortment of sight and sound, the moment takes the place of another—but not that of the one he so desperately needs to forget.

Midway through the flight, Shadwell is dozing off. He can hear Richard tugging at his eyes, inviting anyone awake to take in the view. Curious as to what the pilot presumes so important, Shadwell turns to the window.

His reflection beside him, the countryside collapsed, wallowing in the Mississippi River. A relative life and steadfast death, the Old Man appears to be in a state of infancy, suckling through the land in a moment of time.

From beginning to end, the falling rain to the open sea, the snake-like river separates the country. The people's traditions and ideals, however, remain inseparable. More than just a body of water it is a way of life, or to one's perspective, life itself.

The river gave Shadwell just what his morning needed, a reposeful end to a rough beginning. Debating whether or not the fountain exists, the engines drowsing his train of thought, Shadwell takes into account the synthetic mask he found in Margaret's parlor.

"There must be some reasonable explanation," he told himself. Everything he said in the car was accurate, and with Dr. Webster's version, Margaret may have been worse off than he thought. Webster supplied the link that coupled Margaret's delusional obsession with reality. *All those years,* thought Shadwell, closing his eyes... *my obsession too*.

Slipping into a dream, the muffled engines of the Cessna surging into a solitary roar, Shadwell envisions the cabin swelling to almost twice its size. A step-up cockpit with a slender teardrop fuselage, the horizon turns from Mississippi mud to Atlantic blue, the single-engine Vega rumbling toward the island. It was William's first time in a plane, a generation where only the privileged flew.

Lady Bird, or Miss Margaret as William calls her, insists he look out the window, adventitiously discovering something he's afraid of. Two years ago in the old carriageway, William was as bold as a medieval knight, but here among the clouds, he cowers like a child afraid of the dark.

"William," said Margaret, his hands clutching the armrest, "...take a look, you're going to miss it."

"I looked at Cuba. It was very nice."

"You looked at Cuba when we got off the plane. This is a different view. Much better than what you saw on the ground."

"I'll look when we land."

The other passengers took notice—all nine of them—Margaret intent on prying William from the armrest.

"William," she said quite firmly, "... it will not kill you to look out the window."

"She's right, young man," said an old, pasty-faced woman across the aisle. "One can only describe it as breathtaking. Not too many of your kind have an opportunity like this. Listen to her. You've nothing to be afraid of."

Afraid! That did not bother William. He knew of many things that would scare that old woman. When she said *your kind* it was like calling him the N-word right to his face. And nothing fueled William's fury more than racial insolence.

"I'm not afraid," declared William, leaning over Margaret.

"Look up ahead there, William," Margaret said to his chest, "... off to the right."

The word William used describing Puerto Rico only Margaret could hear. It was the closest he'd ever been to her and Margaret was quick to clear her throat letting him know just how close. Not that it bothered her, he finally mustered up enough courage to look out the window. It was the way he positioned himself that worried her. A black man pressing up against a white woman, even this far from home was never taken lightly—a dangerous mishap if the wrong people were offended.

"Oh— sorry, Miss Margaret," William withdrew from the window.

"It's quite all right, William," replied Margaret, arching forward while glancing across the aisle. "There are far worse things to worry about on an airplane than taking in the view."

"*Huh,*" puffed the old woman, jutting her head around.

"Well, what do you think," asked Margaret.

"Too many mountains. It would take us years to explore."

"Yes," laughed Margaret, "... it would. It's no Sanibel or Pine Island. But we're not here for that. We came to research the map, remember."

"No exploring?"

"There may be some exploration. A library most likely." Margaret took another look at the island, convincing William to switch places. "Now," she began, "... do you see that large cluster of gray over there."

William scoured the northeast shore. "Yes, I see it."

"That's the city of San Juan. We'll be landing there shortly. Hopefully the man I sent word to hasn't gone anywhere. A historian, he's also a native of the island. If he can't decipher the map he may know of someone who can."

"You said you figured that out already."

"We've scoured every inch of every island and still no cave. If this turns out to be another dead-end, we'll make the best of it by having a nice vacation."

"I don't need a vacation, Miss Margaret."

"Yes ... *you do.* You have certainly earned one."

"I have no choice in the matter, do I?"

"None whatsoever."

"A vacation it is then," said William, sneering at the old woman across the aisle.

Peering down from the cockpit, the pilot informs everyone to secure their belts, as they will be landing in a few minutes.

The aircraft commencing its descent, William fidgets in his seat, begging Margaret to trade places. His face, suddenly flush at the thought of dying, Margaret squeezed his hand and an ounce of courage kindled his spirit. In a daring move, William takes a deep breath peering out the window. The mountains, fading in the background, the grainy faraway colors change dramatically into a forest of kaleidoscopic buildings. The glossy runway, racing toward the plane, a city rises from the spinning earth and everyone is caught off guard by a sudden jolt and screeching tires.

William's heart dropped and he collects himself, relief vested on his face as the plane travels not in the air but on the ground.

"There, you see," Margaret pats his hand, "… nothing to be afraid of."

The city of San Juan overlooks a busy commercial port, miles of white beach gleaming with patches of dark and fair-skinned bodies. Ponce de León named it *rich port,* four-and-a-quarter centuries ago. Ships carrying both goods and passengers thrive off the island's fair weather. If Margaret can decipher the map, undoubtedly it will warm her as vitally as the sun satisfying this tropical paradise.

A 1931 Packard arrives at the airport, the driver putting their bags in the trunk. With reservations at the Hotel EL Convento in Old San Juan, the car is one of the amenities there—one the average guest knows nothing about.

"Fortress de El Morro, por favor," Margaret said to the driver.

"Sí, señora."

Now a world traveler, William sat in the back with Margaret, both reluctant to talk in front of the driver.

El Morro Fortress blankets the northwestern tip of a lengthy island hugging the mainland; an ancient bridge over Condado Lagoon connecting the two. From the center of capitalism preceding the fort, the Packard drove across the ancient bridge into Old San Juan.

The colonial streets of The Old City remind William of the Vieux Carré. The colorful, adobe buildings are a contrast, but similar to the Quarter, and other social districts, are its people. Like one gigantic heart, the people are the city and the streets the arteries that pump life into the suburbs.

Relative to the Old Square, some cities grow too fast, either to lofty heights or obese proportion. Progress in their shadows, the older the district the more weary the streets.

Everything born of this earth will eventually die, yet there are countless avenues that stand the test of time. The outskirts of Old San Juan is full of new structures and William can see a vast ocean of people moving from one point in time to another. If the heart of one's infrastructure exudes originality from those unacceptable to change, William is confident that in two-hundred years the Vieux Carré will be as meaningful and desirable as this old city is to its people.

"Fortaleza de El Morro," said the driver, the fort coming into view.

Entering the vast stronghold, the Packard stopped in an open courtyard, brown and gray ashlar walls surrounding them. Margaret advises William to stay in the car, instructing the driver to wait. "Debo estar detrás pronto. Veinte-minutos, por favor. Wait here… usted espera aquí. Veinte-minutos, debo estar detrás."

"Sí. Sí, señora. You return in twenty minutes. I wait. No pro'lem."

Margaret dug into her handbag, removing something wrapped in a white handkerchief. The driver opened her door and Margaret made her way to the nearest corridor, William sitting timorously in the back seat.

Everything the driver said was in Spanish and William thought he was talking about the fort the way he clocked his hand around the courtyard. Wide archways, placed amorphously underneath their turrets, squaring to a number of steep, decaying walls, the driver pointed out an inconsistent proportion of asymmetrical towers along the perimeter. Various levels connecting the corners at random, he threw his hands in the air shouting at the sea before imitating a number of cannon blasts. Turning to the back seat he rattled off some more cannon fire, startling William who shook his head indicating he understood.

Ten more minutes of fast talking and hand waving, William recognized one of the driver's words. "Señora, ella vuelve," said the driver pointing his finger.

Disappointment on Margaret's face, the driver opened her door. He proceeds to the front and Margaret whispers to William, "Our contact here was of no help. He did, however, give me the name of a cartographer in Caparra, specializing in sixteenth century maps."

The El Convento started out as a convent in the late 1600's and Margaret swears it's the best hotel in Old San Juan. A five level complex spanning several blocks, it offers a plush atmosphere in the center of a worn and tranquil district.

When Margaret and William travel together, she books a second room in advance, not wanting to deny William his privacy. If Dorothy comes along she rooms with Margaret, but neither is the case this time around. Dorothy is caring for little Stewart back in Louisiana and the hotel is unable to comply with Margaret's request for separate quarters.

In the middle of the Grito de Lares Festival, rooms are hard to come by. The manager at The El Convento offered to find William lodging at another hotel but Margaret told him it wasn't necessary. She booked her usual suite and privacy was not an issue.

William examines the suite's lavish interior and agrees. He would have said no if they were back in the States but the people here are more tolerable. And as the manager said, *others ran into the same problem*.

"I'm going downstairs to arrange a vehicle for tomorrow," said Margaret.

"What time are we leaving," asked William, his stuttering a thing of the past.

"Not too early, I'm tired," replied Margaret. "You must be tired as well."

Placing his bag next to a divan, his body somewhat stiff from the flight, William shrugs his shoulders.

"Is that a no or a not very."

"Not very."

"Well," Margaret stepped closer, "… then I too am a *not very*. The hotel has a fine restaurant but I'd rather dine out this evening. The streets will be festive and full of excitement tonight."

Again, a slight shrug from William.

"Was that a, *doesn't matter* or *fine with me?* Tell you what, why don't we dine here and afterward we'll take in some of the festival. As much as we can," said Margaret, stepping into the hall, "… we are after all … not very tired."

Margaret left and William smiled at her playful side, something he's never seen before. A vibrant spirit, he wonders if Margaret takes nourishment from that, starving the bad memories with a structured disposition. *Two years*, he thought, *has it been that long? This is the happiest I've seen her*.

The further she is from her past the more Margaret shines, but she persistently sneaks back, taking the luster with her. *All this searching… for what?* It seems to William she's after the wrong thing. *How does one find happiness in something that doesn't exist? She'll search her whole life burdened with the prospect of false hope.*

Margaret deserved better. William had a good life because of her. His sister attends a private school and his aunt takes care of all the bills with the money he sends home. *How can I repay someone that's given so much?* He thought about that… a difficult task because Margaret has enough money to buy anything. The last gift William gave her was a first edition by Gertrude Stein and it will take more than a book to do what needs to be done.

William then recalls something he heard in Antoine's kitchen. *One should not have to worry about money.* He could not place the voice with a face, only the doctrinal speech and haggard look of the old chef who agreed. *Fortunes are unimportant*, William recalls Jean Claude's testimony. *Good health and reliable friends are all you need. Those are your riches.*

William realized what he must do. To purchase happiness he must put away his wallet. *Think, Will. What can you give Margaret that no one else can? You can do this. It can't be that hard to figure out….*

A multitude of ships in the harbor, the backwash of freighters and speedboats gave William an idea. *Now,* he thought, Margaret returning from the hotel lobby, *how do I drag her away from that road leading nowhere?*

"Good news, William. The same car and driver are available tomorrow."

Paying no mind to what Margaret was saying, William turned from the window.

"Beautiful view … is it not," said Margaret.

"Yes, *very.*"

"You seem distant, William. Is everything all right? Are you displeased with the room? If you feel uncomfortable—"

"No, the room is fine. I could sleep on the floor and it would not bother me. I need to figure something out, that's all."

"Can I be of assistance," asked Margaret.

"I— um … well. Yes. Yes, I believe you can … *maybe.*" William saw this as an opportunity. An opportunity for what, he wasn't sure. In order to take Margaret's mind off the fountain he needed to come up with something quick.

"Come, William. Sit down so we may talk."

Margaret grabbed a chair from across the room—eighteenth century by the look of it. She put the hand-carved relic beside another, her legs skewed courtly to one side, looking up at William. "Are you in some kind of trouble," she asked.

"Trouble, no— that's not it," answered William, stepping aside. *Wait. That could be it! If I have a problem it will take her mind off the fountain.*

"Do you wish to talk about it?"

"Yes, we could do that."

"Good, I'd hate to pry. Are your aunt and sister all right? I know you didn't spend much time with them when we were in New Orleans."

"They're fine." *Why did I say that? A sick relative would have been perfect. No more traveling. Margaret would stick around until they were better. No— wait. One of them would have to lie.*

"What then?" Margaret pats the seat next to her.

"It— you see— the thing is—" William sat down, rubbing the back of his neck. "This is difficult. Much too hard to—"

"—explain. I think I know what's bothering you," said

Margaret. "Does this have anything to do with a girl?"

William hesitates on that one. He doesn't have any female friends. Margaret's the only one he spends any real time with. Six years his elder he likes her very much. If he were to meet someone special, as special as Margaret, he'd certainly make his presence known.

"I thought that may have been it," said Margaret. "Wayfaring with me these past two years you haven't had any free time to yourself. I sometimes forget how important a social life is for others. Please, forgive me. I will see to it you have a room of your own somewhere." Rising from her seat—that luster fading—Margaret walked away.

"Wait," William sprang from his chair, "… you don't have to do that, Miss Margaret." William can tell she's hurt by what he's ineffectively doing—his plan taking a back seat. "That's not what I'm looking for. Why would you even think that?"

"William, a handsome man such as yourself needn't be cooped up all night. You should be out living your life. I have no right to keep you all to myself." Margaret smiled and put a hand to William's cheek then turned away. "Go to the festival," she said. "Meet someone— someone nice. Enjoy yourself, dear William."

"No," cried William.

"*What?*"

"No, Margaret. I will not." Disquieted, his shoulders square with Margaret's, William gazed earnestly into her eyes, his young heart reeling for the first time. "I won't go out there searching for something that doesn't exist."

"What are you saying, William? This isn't about the fountain. *Or is it?*"

William turned and stepped away. "I don't know. It feels wrong. But it can't be, because you seem— so … so—

perfect. Everywhere we've been I could have gone out and—*met someone*. I realize now I could never do that to you."

"William, don't—"

"I think I— I may be … I … I—" *Oh God, what am I doing!* "I need some f-f-f-fresh air."

William backed up, pulling a light jacket from his bag bolting for the door.

"William, wait! William! William…."

"—Shadwell. Mr. Shadwell. Wake up, Mr. Shadwell."

Shadwell woke up with Laurian rocking his shoulder. "We're going to be landing soon," she said. "Time to fasten your belt."

His body ached and Shadwell moved tactfully to sit up straight, focusing on his surroundings.

"You all right," asked Laurian.

"Fine. Just a little sore," replied Shadwell, twisting his neck. "I had a dream about the time Margaret and I were in San Juan. I suppose she mentioned that as well?"

"Yes. And her visit to Caparra about the map."

"That's it. Nothing more?"

"Only that the trip lasted far too long."

"She said that?"

"She said after San Juan her life was never the same."

"Because of the map," asked Shadwell.

"No … something else."

Eleven

DETECTIVE TAYLOR skimmed through the last page of the Somoza file, closing the folder and pushing it aside.

"Finished," asked Monroe.

"I skipped the petty stuff," answered Taylor, leaning back in his chair.

"'Ez a mean one. Come on, it's time we went out ta' Lakefront."

Taylor snapped to his feet grabbing the file. "You want this back?"

"Naw, you keep it. Got it memorized."

Taylor tossed the file on his desk as two more detectives entered the room.

"Looks like we got a couple more volunteers," said Monroe.

"Very funny," clamored the first detective. "I was just getting ready for an afternoon nap."

"So, what's up," asked the other detective.

"Grant's workin' on it right now. 'Da Le Petit shooting. Trial starts on Tuesday an' 'da DA needs everyt'ang by tomorrow afternoon."

"I thought we had enough people on that already."

"Not anymore. Somet'ang else come up d'ez mornin'."

"Now what, it's Sunday for Christ sake," said the first detective.

"I'm wit' you on d'at one," Monroe agreed, "… but our old friend Somoza 'az resurfaced."

The two detectives turn to one another then to Monroe. "We'll take the Le Petit case," they said in unison.

"Relax," said Monroe. "D'ats why you're here. Samuel and I got stuck with Somoza. 'Da Captain," Monroe motions to Taylor, "… 'e want to break 'em in on d'ez one."

"Good luck," said the first detective, patting Taylor on his shoulder, heading for Alcott's office.

"The Captain's not in," Taylor stopped him.

"Where is he?"

"'E out investigatin' an explosion over in 'da Business District."

"Yeah, I heard about that on the way in. You hear about that," the first detective asked his partner.

"Sure. The Mobil Building."

The four detectives discuss the explosion, hoping it to be a gas leak or accident of some kind. Connie then enters the room and they quiet down. "Glad to see the reinforcements are here," she said.

"Afternoon, Connie," grumbled the first detective.

"*Connie*," the second detective acknowledged, flashing a cordial smile.

Connie kept a serious face. "Monroe," she said, squaring up to the Creole. "The boss just called. He wants you and Detective Taylor out at the Mobil Building right away."

"Now what? We were on our way ta' 'da airport."

"Some parking attendant on Lafayette recognized Somoza from this morning's APB. Alcott said another man was with him and they left the garage no more than ten minutes after the explosion."

Carlo is having a drink at the airport with the man who shut off the water-main. Both men are nursing a cigarette and the man is sitting across from Carlo with his back to the wall. Ariel walks into the lounge and the man hurries with his cigarette before crushing it out. Excusing himself from the table, the man shuffles through the crowded room and out the door.

"Who was that," asked Ariel, taking the man's seat.

"A friend of mine," said Carlo. "He's moonlighting for the Gretna Water District right now."

"Why the cold shoulder?"

"He's very shy. Even around Vincent. He did ask about you though. Got scared when I told him what kind of girl you are."

"Really?"

"It's true. You saw how fast he let out of here."

"I noticed that," replied Ariel, taking inventory of the drinks on the table. "Where's the half-wit?"

"He went to the john, why?"

"My father has a job for us."

"Yeah, I know. Raymond told me this morning. You and your jungle friend botched an easy kidnapping."

Ariel doesn't answer, glaring intently across the table.

"You seem a little pissed."

"Listen, Carlo. My father likes you but that doesn't mean I have to put up with your shit. You're being paid for your services not your smart-ass remarks. Lewis got away but that doesn't matter because he's no longer a top priority."

"Calm down, sweet-thing. You wouldn't want that pretty little face of yours to freeze up and stay that way." Carlo took a drink then a puff from his cigarette. "Now, what do you mean— *a job for us?*"

"What do you think? I'm in on this one."

“No thanks, sweet-thing. I don’t work with girls.”

“So, *you prefer men?*”

“Now who’s the smart-ass?”

“You have no choice in the matter. Besides, I’d much rather wrestle an alligator than work with you.”

“I can arrange that,” replied Carlo, leaning back in his chair taking a long drag on his cigarette, blowing the smoke across the table. “Maybe your father wants you to learn a thing or two,” he said with a smile.

“From you? I don’t think so,” said Ariel, looking around to see if anyone is listening. “There are a number of things he wants done and I’m coming along to make sure they’re done right.”

“Like what?”

“First of all,” Ariel lowered her voice, “… we no longer need the doctor.”

Carlo turned from side to side mocking Ariel. He then announced rather causally, “*You want me to kill her … right?*”

Ariel rolled her eyes at Carlo. She then passed along her father’s instructions concerning the others.

“Doesn’t sound too difficult. How long do we babysit?”

“What do you mean *we?* You dispose of the doctor’s body and hide out like always. You know my father will never meet with you in person.”

“I’m sick of hiding out.”

“Would you rather end up in jail? Which, by the way, would be permanent this time. No one’s coming to your rescue if that happens again.”

“If what happens again,” asked Vincent, strolling up from behind.

“Nothing,” replied Ariel.

Vincent sat down and took a sip from his glass.

"You boys need to hurry up," said Ariel. "We need to go over a few more details and I'd rather we discuss it someplace else."

Carlo drank the rest of his whiskey. "Don't be so dramatic, sweet-thing. I'm ready for another one … how 'bout you, Vincent?"

"As long as you're buyin'."

"Let's go," Ariel got up. "There's plenty of booze in the hanger."

A variety of tastes sandwiched together on a hot afternoon, the narrow streets of the French Quarter are seething with weary travelers. The atmosphere changing at every corner, either the architecture or the people—both concealing or parading their suggestive appetites—unlike other popular districts throughout the world, it's hard distinguishing the tourists from the residents.

Once the sultry air along Bourbon Street takes hold, some people find it necessary to drink the afternoon away; a reputation for gaiety and wandering flesh thus clouding the air. Waiting for nightfall and the day to begin, one can listen to these squandered souls who in due time are part of the experience.

At the same time, around various corners along that adverse bankit, a different kind of people gather, the midday sun much too beautiful to drink away. They take delight in the history and ambience instead. The light, exposing the good of the people, its wondering flesh is a body of knowledge having a sober taste for something real, indulging in the cultural surroundings like that of Jackson Square.

Near the corner of Royal and St. Louis, the back entrance to Antoine's, Raymond pays no attention to the people around him… or to Marcus, clutching the manila folder as he steps from the limousine. Margaret, however, Raymond keeps a close eye on. She never shuts out the Quarter, watching the people as they stroll by. More of the subdued, Jackson Square type, on occasion Margaret will expose herself to the stentorian chants of mirth and foolishness. Depending on her Bourbon Street or Jackson Square mood, she has experienced most of what the Old Square and its people have to offer. Taking a deep breath, she feels more at home in the French Quarter than anywhere else—her own little corner of the world.

On this day, however, she wants to escape from both Marcus and that corner she's in. But when either takes hold, you can't escape. You can only choose the mood in which to escape. For Margaret the mood is a sullen one, much like that of death. And where else than in New Orleans can one see death so prominently displayed… its many cemeteries—*cities of the dead*—shoulder to shoulder with the living.

Margaret becomes a symbolic crypt, a stone-cold shell showing no emotion.

"You seem tense, Margaret. Don't be," said Marcus, sticking his arm through the iron bars covering Antoine's back entrance, his giant fist knocking on the door.

The door opened and the iron bars swung out over the crowded bankit, a young waiter in a black coat and dark bowtie stepping out of the wine cellar. He cordially invites them in and Marcus sweeps the manila folder outward, gesturing for Margaret to go first.

"Monsieur Córdoba, de bon après-midi," said the waiter. "Mademoiselle," he turned to Margaret, tipping his head.

"Jón René, de bon après-midi," replied Marcus. Margaret was unaware Marcus spoke French but said nothing, looking back as Raymond closed the door, returning to the limousine.

Following Jón René through a row of vintage wines,

Margaret recalls the wine cellar used to be an old carriageway, Shadwell rescuing her one night with a bottle of pinot.

Jón René led them through several dining rooms. With the exception of a few holidays and the week of Mardi Gras, most afternoons are slow at Antoine's. They turn left at the escargot room, a giant, white caricature of a snail smiling at them. Heading down a corridor that was once an alleyway, they arrive at a private room. Part of an old Spanish garrison, Margaret is familiar with the small enclosure.

Jón René pulled out a chair, and despite her apparent mood, Margaret sat graciously with her hands in her lap. Marcus is seated and Jón René recites the day's wine selection. "Et le mademoiselle voudriez-vous commencer avec un verre de vin."

Marcus asked his fellow bon vivant in English what she would like and Margaret replied in French, "If I must go through with this I would like a Pinot Noir. Château Lafite-Rothschild, si vous l'avez."

"Shall I inquire on the year or would mademoiselle prefer I chose for her," Jón René answered in English.

"Vous choisissez, je ne me sens pas jusqu'à lui cet après-midi."

"Oui, mademoiselle." Jón René complements Margaret on her French, commenting on her familiar voice. "Have we met before?"

A regular at Antoine's, without her makeup Margaret informs Jón René she is the niece of Margaret Lewis.

"Ah, oui," Jón René envisions another Margaret. "Monsieur Córdoba?"

"An excellent choice, Margaret. I will have the same. Jón René, s'il vous plaît, la bouteille et deux verres."

"Oui, Monsieur." Jón René closed the door on his way out, and though the casement window had no bars, it seemed like a prison cell to Margaret.

Taking out his familiar sandstone, Marcus rubbed his thumb over the smooth surface. "I remember visiting some soldiers in this very room, long before the renovation."

"How utterly wonderful for you," said Margaret, her sarcasm having no effect on Marcus.

"Yes, but sad for the ones executed that week. I also recall walking outside the corridor when it was an alleyway. Antoine's was a small establishment back then, only one dining room and now all this."

Margaret was already looking around. Their tiny room lay in the center of the hallway, the alley's old brickwork on the walkway and exterior walls still intact. A roof was constructed years ago to protect the venerable façades. Across the walkway, on the other side of the wall, Margaret knew people were having lunch in the main dining room, the one where young William dropped his service tray.

"I also remember," continued Marcus, "… after I saw you here one night, I sent a man to take the map from you."

"Yes, I know. It did not pan out well for that little hooligan."

"It was the last mistake he ever made. I despise failure."

"Yet you surround yourself with those who are successful at it."

Marcus dug his thumb into the sandstone. "True," he said in a bitter tone, "… I find myself replacing them much too often."

"Replace me in their stead. That would free up some of your time. Speaking of which, what are we doing here?"

"This is somewhat of an anniversary, Margaret."

"Is it the unfortunate day we first met in that tavern?"

"No, that happened in the spring. This occurred three years later in mid-September."

Margaret realizes Stuart found the map early that month and they got lost searching for the fountain; Stuart then sacrificing himself to save her. "I don't understand. Why would you bring me here in August for something that happened in September?"

"It's not the month we are celebrating but the season. You do remember what took place? Shall I give you a hint?"

"I have no patience for these guessing games, Marcus."

"Tomorrow there will be another hurricane, and if the conditions are favorable, as they were back then, the fountain will arise once more."

"And why should I care about that?"

"You will be at my side, Margaret."

"Why?"

"Do not play dumb with me. I know what you're up to."

"What are you talking about?"

"The doctors, Margaret. I know all about the doctors you've been seeing."

"Everyone sees a doctor at one time or another, Marcus."

Slamming the sandstone on the table, Marcus grabbed Margaret by the wrist. "People like us don't need to, Margaret!" A razor appeared and Marcus looked Margaret in the eye. "Or do we," he flicked the blade.

Blood dripping from her arm, Margaret tries to pull away but Marcus won't let go. "Marcus, what are you doing?!"

"The wound will not heal quickly will it?" The expression on Margaret's face gave Marcus the same answer as the blood on her arm. "Why did you do this," asked Marcus. "I gave you eternal life and in return you spit on me by giving it back." He pushed her away and Margaret grabbed the table napkin for the tiny cut.

"It should have healed by now," said Marcus. "I don't understand you, Margaret. Just like Tantur's father. Why would you do this?"

"Tantur's father? He was the one who killed Stuart. Was he not?"

"Yes. The darts were somehow mixed up. He never forgave himself for that mistake. They are a proud people, the Cariban. His guilt got the best of him two years ago. But unlike you he wasted no time in taking his own life."

"*He killed himself?* How is that possible?"

"Come now, Margaret," said Marcus. "We are not completely immortal. There are many ways we can die. *Think.*"

There was no need to think about it, Margaret had a short list in her mind already, blurting out the first one. "Decapitation."

"Yes. That is an appendage we cannot live without. However, he died another way."

"Suffocation?"

"That too would do it. We must be able to breathe. But that was not it. You are getting—"

"Drowning! He drowned himself, didn't he?"

"Yes, Margaret. Nearly five centuries of life, he strapped himself to a boat anchor in the middle of Primo Bay."

"But William shot you in the head— *and you fell into the water.*"

"I did not die because my body healed itself as I sank. When I regained consciousness I swam to the surface."

Margaret was primed for another question but Jón René came into the room with a bottle of Château Lafite-Rothschild. Marcus gave a nod of approval and Jón René poured a small sample to taste. When the ritual is complete, and their glasses filled, Jón René saw the napkin on Margaret's arm.

"Oh mon! You are bleeding."

"It's nothing."

"Shall I bring you a bandage?"

"Yes, but please, let us order first."

He wanted to get a bandage right away but Margaret's eyes

told him she was all right. "Très bien," he conceded, handing out the menus while going over the soups.

"Ils tous bruit merveilleux, Jón René," said Margaret, returning the menu without looking, "… mais je voudrais une Fonds d'artochauts Bayard, avec des Pommes de terre soufflées, et les Pompano à la marinière."

"Monsieur Córdoba," inquired Jón René.

"I have been craving turtle soup—"

"Nous ne pouvons pas servir ce ici, Monsieur Córdoba, ni peut n'importe qui autrement," Jón René informed him.

"Oui, je sais. It was a little before your time… and quite good here I might add."

"How could you know that, Monsieur Córdoba? You are not that old."

"My grandfather told me," Marcus ripostes. "Now, what can I order that is not protected? J'aurai la Avocat à la vinaigrette, un petit bol de Consommé froid en tasse, et les Pompano à la marinière que mademoiselle a commandés. Et s'il vous plaît, apportez deux portions des Huîtres Bienville."

"On servant, Jón René," insisted Margaret.

Jón René turned to Marcus, his eyes asking permission to cancel one order.

"I thought you liked oysters?"

"On occasion, yes," answered Margaret, then to Jón René, "Je voudrais le Chair de crabes ravigote à la place."

Jón René bows, telling them he will return shortly with a bandage.

Each taking a sip of wine, Marcus questions Margaret once more on her motives for reversing her immortality.

"I already told you at the airport. What must I say to make you understand?!"

"What must I say to make you understand the way I feel about you? And why can you not feel the same way for me?

I've met many women over the centuries but none like you. How can *you* not understand that?"

"You had my fiancé killed, Marcus. Whether it was deliberate or not, he died because of you. I also know you had something to do with my son's death; as well as my father's. I despise you. There is nothing left in this world for me but death. I long for its natural course, for without it I am lost. You ask why I saw those doctors. I went to them because I'm afraid of life and too much of a coward to end it myself. But you, Marcus, you fear nothing! And that is this world's problem— *your immortality.* Your lack of fear has destroyed your conscience and you are uncontrollable without it. Nothing can stop you from having or doing whatever you want. I imagine it would be far less distressing if you wanted to do good in this world, but you're motivated by something dangerous to us all. Your true self."

Marcus does not react timely to her convictions, nor does he show any form of anger. He picked up his sandstone, sliding his thumb back and forth. "Yes," he agreed, "I am all that." Grinning, his thumb now in a circular motion, Marcus put his elbow on the stolen file. "I doubt I will ever change. The world has changed many times over, yet I still expect those around me to heed my words. If they protest they shall not be around long. The same can be said of you, Margaret. I see that now. Tomorrow we go to the island and *you will* drink from the pool along with Ariel and Tantur's brother. If you choose not to, your life will change far worse than you can imagine. I will not kill you, *that would be a gift*. Instead I will take from you what matters most in your life. And you know of whom I speak. By tomorrow evening if you fail to do as I ask, your grandson will reunite with his father."

Twelve

JERRY HOLIDAY is scheduled to make his rounds every forty minutes, and with the marina adjacent to the airport, he takes a sightseeing tour of the harbor every time, no one caring or paying much attention until today.

The man who had a drink with Carlo circles the parking lot in front of the terminal. A strip of trees separate the east and west stalls and he parks his maintenance van at the far corner of the west lot.

After five minutes, the man wonders where the security guard is; unaware that Holiday had to cover for someone else inside. The man sat there another five minutes, climbing out of the van expecting the security guard to show up any second. Lowering the bill of his cap, he strolled passed Carlo's black Lincoln, stopping beside a Town & Country minivan. Stepping between the minivan and a midsize car, his vigilant eyes sweeping the area, he drops to one knee. Digging between his sock and ankle, he removes a magnetic object, securing it to the minivan's undercarriage. In an easy, insouciant fashion, rising to his feet and pulling the bill of his cap even lower, he casually makes his way to the terminal.

Midday shadows are cast upon the oval tarmac from a number of private and corporate planes. A fueling truck is stationed alongside a Learjet and Richard stays clear as he taxis the Cessna along a row of hangers. He positions the aircraft in front of Gulf Coast Charters, the fueling truck and Learjet not far away.

"Can we hurry it up," screamed Shadwell, the aircraft idling and his bladder ready to burst.

Richard shut down the lusty engines, swinging around in his seat, peeling back his headgear. "There's a restroom inside the hanger," he announced. "You can all leave your personal belongings in the plane for now … especially your little bundle, Will. We'll load everything on the seaplane after I check in."

Shadwell agreed and Richard dropped the hatch making his way down the folding steps. Clarence then followed and Shadwell gestured to Laurian she was next. Laurian swiveled her seat around, picking up Bourbon then swinging back, the animal taking a swipe at Nathan

"Shame on you," said Laurian, handing the little terror to Shadwell. "Sorry, Nathan."

Nathan rose from his seat and Laurian gave him a quizzical smile. "Still think it's a different cat," she said, eyeballing Nathan's scar.

"Yes, I do … they're all out to get me."

Shadwell was the last to disembark. Taking a deep breath, the sultry air no different than what he's used to back home, he led everyone away from the plane, expeditiously guiding them to the hanger as if marching into battle.

Richard then took over his command, directing their attention to the promontory fortifying the marina. "That's Margaret's seaplane over there," he said, gesturing toward the Canadian aircraft.

"Where," asked Shadwell, squinting to locate the plane.

Laurian pointed the way and Richard continued his orientation. "Two things to remember about the De Havilland, he said, "… it's slow and the ride will be extremely uncomfortable."

"How slow," asked Nathan—he had a good idea what uncomfortable meant.

"It will take us nearly four hours to get there."

"*So if you think you're sore now—*" quipped Shadwell.

"You don't have to do this, Will," elucidated Richard, having a brash tongue. "Things can get a little rough over the ocean in a plane like that."

"Don't worry about me. I've flown in weather that would make your head spin," boasted Shadwell.

"About the weather," Laurian said to Richard, "… a hurricane watch is something we shouldn't ignore. They say Andrew will make landfall sometime tomorrow morning and if—"

"And if it does," Richard ventures to say, "—we'll be miles up the coast."

"It still sounds risky," said Laurian.

"Don't worry. I've been to Cape Coral before. If the hurricane watch upgrades to a warning we'll make it out in time."

"Yeah, if the water's not too choppy," warned Nathan, recalling what his father said about flying in bad weather.

"We'll be fine," Richard reassured them. "Like I said, the first sign of trouble and we're out of there. Now … let's get inside. I'd like to grab a few things before we leave."

Dreading the thought of another claustrophobic flight, Nathan would have called the whole thing off if not for his missing grandmother and those responsible for his parent's death. Dragging his feet across the tarmac, he looked at Clarence, wishing to be young again, thinking how fortuitous it would be if the fountain were real.

Entering the hanger, Richard led everyone to the office, Laurian stopping at the bottom of the steps with an inquisitive expression on her face. "When were you planning on leaving," she asked.

"As soon as I grab a few supplies. Why?"

Laurian insists on going into town and entrusts Richard not to leave without her. "I'll be back in less than an hour. I just need to grab something at the lab."

Stationed at the back of the pack, Shadwell said no. He felt out of the loop with Richard in control and would have said more but Richard preempted him. "We really should stick together," he said to Laurian.

"I know but this is important," answered Laurian, stroking Bourbon's side to calm herself down; the cat purring against her abdomen. "All the research I've been doing for Margaret has finally paid off and the results are in the lab. I need that information if something goes wrong."

"Fine. But hurry. I'd like to leave by 3:30. That should give us enough time to get there before dark."

"I don't like it," conduced Shadwell. "We really should stick together like you said."

"She'll be all right," answered Richard.

"Are you sure about that? You know the old saying … strength in numbers."

"You're right," said Richard. "Nathan would you mind going with her?"

"Not a problem," answered Nathan.

"Good," concluded Shadwell, removing the revolver from his boot. "Here, take this," he gave the gun to Nathan. "And please, be careful this time."

"Where did you park," Richard asked Laurian, "… the marina?"

"No. I'm out front."

"Take one of the carts," he said to her. "Restrooms are in the office everyone." Richard then points the way and Shadwell scurried up the office steps.

"Clarence and I will take care of everything here," Richard said to Nathan, "… we'll have the De Havilland ready to go by the time you get back."

A sleek, red and white Aerostar with one of the propellers missing is parked in the middle of the hanger. There is a roll-away tool box next to the plane and several Cushman utility carts off to the side. A four-foot cargo bed and bench seat, Nathan and Laurian climb into the nearest cart, Nathan compulsively peeling out and their heads jerking back.

"Easy there, Mario," said Laurian, "… they've got the yellow flag out."

"Sorry," Nathan let off the pedal.

"I'm kidding. We are in a hurry— go ahead, *pedal to the metal*."

Nathan punched it and Laurian spoke up again. "Wait! I have to get something out of my briefcase."

Once more Nathan let off the pedal, looking at his wristwatch to remind her they didn't have much time.

"It's okay… keep going. I won't stop you," promised Laurian. "*Unless—*"

"Unless, *what,*" said Nathan, a prophetic eye upon her face.

"You think we should tell Richard first?"

"It's your briefcase," said Nathan with a firm voice.

"Yes. *Yes it is*. Onward then!"

A slender, middle-age receptionist named Phyllis manages the service counter at Gulf Coast Charters. She's rereading a copy of *People Magazine* as Richard and Clarence enter the tiny lobby. Normally, when a pilot brings a client into the office, she'll respond with a quick greeting and return to her magazine. Clarence, however, has Bourbon in his arms and she jumps to her feet.

"Where are the animal carriers," asked Richard.

"Behind the paper towels in the back," replied Phyllis, shuffling to the other side of the counter.

"I'll be right back," Richard said to Clarence.

Phyllis took it upon herself to hold Bourbon, almost prying the cat from Clarence while asking its name. Clarence is reluctant to tell her but doesn't see any harm it doing so, Phyllis then realizing the cat belongs to Margaret. She introduced herself to Bourbon's curious face, questioning Clarence on the animal's breed.

"*He's a cat.*"

"No silly, I know he's a cat."

This prompted Phyllis to educate Clarence on the domesticated varieties and how many different breeds she has at home, rifling off each cat's name, where they came from and how old they were. "How old is this one," she asked.

"Not quite sure ma'am. P'erty old though," answered Clarence.

"He doesn't look that old," said Phyllis, her expert eyes studying Bourbon's face, coinciding with a little pampering and baby talk. "You're practically a new born. *Yes you are, just a fresh little bundle*. You're not that old— are you kitty?"

"No," a voice from behind agreed, "I don't believe so."

Phyllis turned her head and Shadwell is standing there, asking if she knows where Richard is.

"He's in the storeroom getting a kennel for your friend here."

"Would it be all right if we joined him? There are a few things we need to discuss before we leave."

"Sure. Go ahead, mon chéri."

"Thank you. Mind keeping an eye on Bourbon until we get back?"

"No, not at all."

Phyllis points the way to a large storeroom with several rows of high shelving. "Richard, where are you," called Shadwell.

"Over here."

Halfway up a ten-foot ladder, Richard is sorting through a number of boxes on the middle shelf. "What are you looking for," asked Shadwell.

"You name it. Blankets, flashlights, batteries… anything I can think of we might need."

"What about food and water? I'm starving."

"We've got cases of bottled water here. We'll pick up some sandwiches at the— Ah! There they are," exclaimed Richard, pulling out a bundle of airline blankets. "That should do it," he said, handing down the blankets.

Shadwell looked at the stack of supplies on the floor and made a sarcastic remark about Richard's military expertise. "What, no machine gun?"

"I keep that at home with my bazooka and grenades."

"If only that were true," said Shadwell. "We need something like that going up against the Cariban."

Richard made his way down the ladder. "I doubt any of the local gun shops carry anything like that," he joked. He knew Shadwell wasn't happy with him taking charge, but Richard couldn't help it. Therefore, he didn't mind a little sarcasm. "I do have a few connections if you think we need a bazooka or machine gun."

Shadwell smiled, regretful for what he said—not the

sarcasm itself but the disparaging way he said it. "I wouldn't know the first thing about handling either one," he reconciled his tone. "Now plastique, get your hands on a stick of that and I'm good to go."

"What's that, Uncle Will," asked Clarence.

"Plastic explosives. C-4," answered Shadwell, jogging his nephew's memory.

"*Oh yeah.*"

"Clarence and I use it to remove tree stumps," Shadwell said to Richard.

Richard was somewhat impressed with the old man and they talked about the different applications and how easy it is working with C-4, Richard preferring a wireless detonator over the conventional fuse Shadwell uses on tree stumps.

Clarence listened to the men with much enthusiasm. He saw his uncle warming up to Richard, but more importantly, he could relate to what they were talking about. It felt good knowing he could do something dangerous—*something soldiers did.*

The rear stow of the Cessna is a small one, the bundle of shotguns, luggage, and Laurian's briefcase crammed together. Taking the briefcase off the stack, Laurian plops it on a table between the cabin seats. Sitting on the larboard side, facing the cockpit, she opens the case rummaging through the contents: her wallet; a copy of *Tortilla Flat*; a text book on molecular biology; an unused syringe with an empty vial; and a manila envelope. She took out the envelope, stalling for a moment before reaching inside. A single page and nothing more, Laurian checks her work and there are no mistakes. She's now positive Margaret is running out of time.

Nathan, still waiting in the cart, is staring at the rear portal when Laurian's face appears. She holds up an index finger. "*One minute,*" she mouthed.

Looking over in the direction of the marina, a tanker crew fueling the Learjet, Nathan spots two people walking alongside the fuselage. He cannot make out their faces, only that one belongs to a man and the other a woman. They quickly turn their backs to Nathan and he averts his attention to the tanker crew monitoring the fuel hose and its components.

"What do you suppose they're up to," asked Ariel, she and Carlo stepping over the fuel hose.

"How the hell should I know? Maybe the doctor left her stethoscope behind."

Looking like a World War II blitz, Poydras Street scattered with chunks of concrete and broken glass, somehow every media outlet in the city found a place to park in the street or on the sidewalk outside the Mobil Building.

The rubble is part of what used to be nine offices on the fourth floor. Now one gigantic room, a massive hole top and bottom from the epicenter of the blast, Detectives Taylor and Monroe are careful with their footing. They enter what was once the reception room, stepping over staves of charred furnishings and pools of smoldering fabric.

Taylor picks up a puce looking flower shaking off the dust. Monroe called to him and Samuel tossed the flower aside, a petal separating in midair and the outside breeze plucking it from the room.

Captain Alcott and Fire Chief Anthony Thomas are standing at the edge of the chalky mess, looking down at the street. "...definitely some type of explosive device," said Chief Thomas; guessing at the type of material as his men sift through the evidence. "One thing's for sure."

"What's that," replied Alcott, Taylor and Monroe fast approaching.

"Whatever it was, they used a shitload of it."

With Alcott addressing his men, Chief Thomas goes about his business. "You two up to speed," asked Alcott.

"Just got 'da word 'bout some fella puttin' 'da make on Carlo."

"Parking garage around the corner," said Alcott. "I talked to the attendant on duty twenty minutes ago. He said two men in a black Lincoln left the lot shortly after the explosion. The passenger in the car said something to the driver, inadvertently mentioning his name. The driver then used a few choice words telling the other guy to shut up. He was so harsh about it the parking attendant said he couldn't help but notice the driver. He described what sounded like Carlo Somoza to me and when I showed him this morning's APB he confirmed it."

"What about the guy with him," asked Taylor.

"The attendant couldn't see with Somoza in the way."

"What do ya d'ink Carlo's up to now?"

"I don't know, Cary. So far there's no evidence of a body. Could be any number of things. Insurance is at the top of the list but I have a feeling that's not the case. We don't know if Somoza had anything to do with this yet. I'd be willing to bet he did, but for now we better keep an open mind."

Alcott and his men inch their way to the center of the blast, a large part of the floor and ceiling blown away. "Anyway," Alcott continued, "… I wanted the two of you down here so you could look around. We know Somoza's in town— or at least he was. He's too smart to be traveling by plane right now. I've already alerted local and state police so I want you to concentrate your efforts on the surface streets around the Quarter."

"Cancel Lakefront," said Monroe, disconcertingly nudging his partner.

"What's out at Lakefront?"

"Airport security never got 'da FAA bulletin. We were gonna pay 'da officer on duty a call an' fill 'em in."

"Go ahead. It wouldn't hurt to ask a few questions either." Alcott then took a step forward, checking out the ceiling. "Look at this place. What a shame. You know they found a typewriter on Canal Street."

Taylor and Monroe, figuring how far it is to Canal Street, look at one another with a sense of urgency.

"We need to find whoever did this," said Alcott in response to their reactions, "... and fast. Before something like this happens again."

The two detectives take off the way they came, Chief Thomas approaching Alcott, placing a hand on his shoulder. "Just got some news you might be interested in, Captain. Some of my men helping with a two alarm in Terrytown just checked in. The homeowner carries the lease on this office."

"Got a name to go with that information, Tony."

Chief Thomas grabbed a note pad from his breast pocket flipping it open. "Webster. Doctor Laurian Webster."

Thirteen

GRABBING THE FOLDER and her wallet, Laurian made her way out of the plane back to the utility cart. “Let’s go,” she said to Nathan.

People are moving in the shadows of the nearby hanger and Nathan is watching the shapely posterior of the woman he saw by the Learjet. Veering off the tarmac, a thundering 13mph, Nathan avoids the fuel hose and tanker crew as they wrap things up.

“I thought something like this might happen,” said Carlo, the utility cart approaching their hanger.

Ariel said nothing, looking at Carlo as if he were to blame for Webster leaving. Ariel then moved away from Carlo, over to Vincent who is hiding behind Raymond’s Blazer.

Fifty-feet and closing, Carlo stood his ground looking directly at the cart. His cold eyes piercing the sultry afternoon, Laurian felt a bizarre chill traveling down her spine.

Four days ago, unbeknownst to Nathan, Carlo Somoza planted a small device under the right aileron of his father’s plane. Somoza now undermines the impending fate of Dr. Webster and Nathan has no clue who he is, or that he stands less than twenty-feet away, staring at his passenger.

"I need a ride to the terminal," demanded Carlo. "Whose SUV is that?"

"It belongs to Raymond," Ariel affronts him, "… and I have no idea where the keys are."

"What about that golf cart?"

"Keys are in the ignition."

"What a shame. A nice looking woman like that," said Carlo, he and Vincent climbing into the cart. "And don't worry about the grandson," Carlo turned to Ariel. "He'll be all right as long as he stays quiet."

"Wait," said Ariel stepping in front of the cart. "You're leaving without me?"

"That jungle friend of yours may need a hand rounding up the others?"

"Tantur doesn't need my help. Vincent, you stay here and watch over his brother. *I'll go with Carlo*."

Vincent got halfway out of the cart and Carlo pulled him back inside. "No can do, sweet-thing," said Carlo, swinging the cart around. "Tell your father Margaret Lewis needs another doctor. One that isn't dead."

Lakefront Airport, originally named Shushan Airport after Levee Board President Abraham Shushan, was constructed in the mid 1930's on a man-made peninsula. Inside the terminal, Nathan took a few seconds to admire the geometric shapes and bold colors of the Art Deco lobby. "Think we have time to grab a sandwich," he said to Laurian, both standing outside the Walnut Room—the airport's prestigious restaurant. "I haven't eaten a thing since last night."

"Neither have I. But they're pretty busy this time of day."

"How about over there," asked Nathan, pointing to the Fly-Away Lounge.

"We don't have time."

"What about a vending machine. I'd settle for a candy bar right now."

"There's a kiosk here," answered Laurian, marching into an area with magazines and snacks. A radio behind the counter is playing jazz music as the shop merchant, who looks to be Shadwell's age, takes his time bagging a few items—even longer counting the customer's change.

Laurian grabbed a bag of pretzels and diet Snapple, pleading with Nathan to hurry and choose something. She got in line and the merchant rang up the Snapple as Nathan set a candy bar and sports drink on the counter.

Nathan took out his wallet, the merchant ready with the total when a live news feed captures his attention. "Lord all mi'dy," said the merchant, turning up the radio, "… y'all been listenin' ta' this."

The reporter said she was at the corner of Poydras and Loyola. "The explosion blew away part of the fourth-floor at the Mobil Building, a major office complex in downtown New Orleans. The cause has not yet been determined. We do know that the offices involved were part of a privately funded research facility. There is also speculation that one lab contained chemicals strong enough to cause an explosion of this magnitude… giving concern as to why a laboratory…."

"Wow," howled Nathan, "… now that's scary." He looked at Laurian who is staring at the radio with her mouth open.

"We have to leave right now," screamed Laurian, stepping out of the kiosk.

Nathan shrugged his shoulders at the merchant, joining Laurian in the main corridor. "What's the matter?"

"That was my lab," she whispered.

Laurian took off for the exit and Nathan grabbed her. "Slow down. Whatever you're after, it isn't there anymore."

"You don't understand. We're not going to my office. We need to go to my house instead. As quick as we can!"

"*Your house?* What for?"

"I'll tell you on the way."

Vincent watched from inside the terminal as Nathan and Webster scramble across the parking lot. He knows which vehicle they're heading for, checking on Carlo outside the Fly-Away Lounge.

The man who turned off the water-main, having a drink with Carlo afterwards, stepped out of the Fly-Away Lounge, busy with a toothpick as he approached Carlo. "All set," the man whispered without stopping, slipping a note and set of keys in Carlo's jacket.

Laurian sped through the parking lot in her Chrysler minivan, Carlo and Vincent watching from the terminal door. Nathan is with her and once they're out on the road Carlo gave Vincent an elbow nudge, "Come on," he said.

Vincent led the way, rushing through the parking lot heading straight for the Lincoln.

"What are you doing?" screamed Carlo.

"We're going after them, right?"

"Not in that car. *I told you that already!* Our new ride is over there," said Carlo, pointing to the maintenance van.

"What about my bag? We can't leave that stuff here."

Carlo figured he was right, cursing at Vincent all the same as he grabbed his doctors bag. "Can we go now?!"

"Yes," said Vincent cradling the bag.

"I'm driving and you navigate," snapped Carlo. "And you better not screw up this time."

Carlo got in the van, popping the door latch for Vincent. Taking a look at the note, he told Vincent to check under his seat.

Vincent pulled out a heavy aluminum case, placing it on his lap.

"Okay," instructed Carlo, "... open 'er up and turn it on. You do remember how to use it?"

"It's been a while but I remember." The case has a control panel in the belly and a liquid crystal screen embedded in the lid. Vincent flipped one of several switches and the screen lit up.

"Where are they," asked Carlo, staring at the case.

A street map appeared on the display and Vincent toggles another switch to zoom in. "They just left Downman heading uptown on the 10."

Jón René sat the appetizers on the table, a cold dish of crab in a seasoned dressing for Margaret and baked oysters in a white wine sauce for Marcus. Pouring water into Margaret's glass, Jón René looked at her bandaged arm, inquiring if she was okay.

"I'm fine. Thank you for asking."

Jón René smiled, pouring water for Marcus before leaving the room.

Marcus dug into the Huîtres Bienville, the dish named after a French colonial who founded the city back in the eighteenth century. Marcus mentioned that historical fact of the former governor, but his words vanished across the table, Margaret's verdurous eyes frowning as he scooped another oyster from its shell.

"Is something wrong, Margaret? Are you displeased at your choice of appetizer? Shall I call for Jón René?"

"I have never had a bad dish here ... ever. It is the company I cannot stomach."

"I spoke of changing others," Marcus reminded her, "... why

must the task be so difficult with you?"

"I change when I feel there is a need to change," Margaret fiercely replied—unremitting in her desire to stay obstinate.

"Oh, you will feel the need," Marcus assured her. "I suggest you sweeten that tone of yours. I meant what I said about your grandson. If I were you, I would focus on the undertaking of absolution toward your enemies, not their condemnation."

Margaret could not imagine a more sickening reply. The thought of spending an eternity with Marcus was bad enough, but having to be civil, she would rather be dead. "I shall try," she uttered, lifting from her face an odious shroud as the hatred in her heart bore deeper. *It's the only way to save Nathan,* thought Margaret. *Perhaps when he's lived a full life I will be free of this monster.* Then an awful thought occurred. *What will I do if Nathan brings a child into this world?*

Grabbing the sandstone, Marcus sensed what Margaret was thinking. "Good choice," he responded, placing the sandstone in his pocket. "You have salvaged your family's existence for now."

Finishing the last of his oysters, Marcus pushed the plate aside picking up the folder Vincent stole from Webster's lab. "I want to explain something to you," he tapped the folder. "This file contains years of research for cell reconstruction on bone marrow and organ tissue. Five of those years I know to be the sole effort of Dr. Laurian Webster. All privately funded by one individual. *Now who could that be?*"

"Spare me the theatrics, Marcus. I'll spend my money as I please."

"Very well. Now, Margaret— and this is the intriguing part," Marcus opened the folder, pulling out the file. "I would have put an end to this long ago if not for Ariel. She made me realize something. Dr. Webster is working on a serum to reverse the effects caused by the fountain—*taking away our immortality.* In theory, if that serum were modified, it could restore it as well. If Webster succeeds, this research will be the key in formulating the modification. And with the results here in front of me," Marcus spoke of the cut on Margaret's arm, "… I see no reason to believe otherwise."

"I don't understand. Why would you need something like that? You'll always have the fountain."

"No one knows until the last minute whether or not a hurricane will hit the island. If an immortal were injected with an accurate dose of Webster's serum they would be vulnerable just as you are right now. They could easily be killed waiting for another hurricane. If that happened to me, the urgency of returning to the state I'm in now is self-explanatory. That's why I waited for Webster to finish her research." Marcus put the file back in the folder, except for the last page, which he blatantly scans. "And now I have it. I can finally—"

"Yes," Margaret perked up. "You can finally what?"

"*Wait a minute*," exclaimed Marcus. The page did not look right and he pulled out the file once more, searching desperately through the pages. "This can't be right!"

Margaret's face bore a sly grin. She wanted to tell Marcus what a fool he was, but for the sake of Nathan, she held her tongue. "Is something wrong?"

"Yes, there's something wrong," mimicked Marcus.

Jón René stepped into the room spoiling the moment for Margaret—Marcus having to calm down.

On his tray, Jón René had an artichoke salad and bowl of cold, jellied soup. Setting them on the table, Marcus then spoke harshly to him, "Jón René, where is my driver?"

"In the kitchen having a salade."

"Tell him I need to see him right away."

"Oui, monsieur."

Marcus reexamined the file. "There is a page missing. The last part of Webster's research."

"Did you think she would keep that in a place you could easily find?"

Glaring at Margaret, Marcus took the sandstone from his pocket, drubbing his thumb along the edge.

The folder from Laurian's briefcase sat on Nathan's lap; Nathan putting Shadwell's revolver in the glove-box at Laurian's request. Heading toward the river, just passed the Superdome exit, Nathan opened the folder. "*One page*," he questioned Laurian. "What's so important about one page?"

"Margaret said it would be a good idea to keep it separate from the rest of her file. It's the only hard copy I have. The rest is on my office computer. Needless to say that was destroyed along with everything else. That's why I keep a backup disk at home."

Nathan studied the text and numbers, trying to figure out Laurian's calculations. "This is a dosage chart, is it not?"

"The top portion is," Laurian replied. "The bottom consists of the properties used for cutting genetic tissue matter. The monthly results and final analysis show the progress of reversing Margaret's— *condition*."

Nathan rolled his eyes.

"You can remain skeptical if you like. I've been giving her a series of injections, and when I ran some blood tests last week, I had mixed feelings with this month's results. Margaret's treatment for some unexplained reason is ahead of schedule. A complete success, but I'm worried about a possible side effect."

"A side effect to what? *The condition she's in?*"

"Something like that," replied Laurian.

Bumper to bumper traffic, the river coming into view, Laurian changed lanes, unaware they are being followed.

"They're crossing the bridge," said Vincent, his eye on the monitor. "She must be going home instead."

"What home," replied Carlo, a smug look while merging on Interchange 90.

Wiping his mouth, Marcus excused himself from the table. "Finish your salad," he said to Margaret. "This won't take long."

Marcus met Raymond outside the private room. "That new phone of yours'," asked Marcus, "… do you have it with you?"

"Right here," Raymond tapped his breast pocket.

"Call Ariel and tell her the file is incomplete. The doctor pulled a fast one and we have to stop Carlo before it's too late. I need her alive, do you understand?! Now go somewhere private and make the call."

Raymond went outside, around the corner to the limousine pulling out one of those new Motorola flip phones, extending the antenna.

"You're too late!" Ariel exploded. "She left not more than ten minutes ago with Carlo in hot pursuit. He'll disappear once he's got his hands on her."

Raymond then asked Ariel if she knew where Webster went.

"I have no idea. Raymond, I have to go, the rest of the group is on the move."

"Do you need any help?"

"No, Tantur and I can handle it. We need to borrow your rig for a few minutes if you don't mind."

"The keys are under the seat."

"Thanks. If Carlo shows up I'll pass along the news."

Returning to the restaurant, the lavish, wood-grained interior of the Annex Room, Raymond chose a quick path along the wall, the room empty except for a waiter appearing out of nowhere.

"Your order is on its way to the airport."

"Good," replied Raymond.

"Shall we put that on Monsieur Córdoba's bill?"

"Yes, of course," answered Raymond, looking back at the waiter as Jón René came out of the kitchen. "Whoa!" exclaimed Raymond, a tray full of food grazing his scalp. "That was a close one."

"Pardon," Jón René tipped his head.

Given the right of way, Raymond continues to the private room, Jón René right behind him.

"Go ahead and start serving," said Marcus.

Raymond moved out of the way and Jón René put the entrees on the table. "Bon appétit!" he announced on his way out.

"Bad news," Raymond whispered to Marcus.

Marcus rose from his seat. "We'll discuss it outside," he replied, dipping his shinny head through the doorway.

"Webster left the airport ten minutes ago and Carlo went after her. We can't get a hold of him right now."

"Why?"

"He has no mobile phone. Doesn't like carrying it around."

"What about a pager," asked Marcus.

"He hates those too."

"How do you propose we contact him?!"

"He won't kill the doctor in the city. He'll take her to his place for that."

"That's more than an hour away. The doctor may be dead by the time we get there. Listen," Marcus lowered his voice,

"… I need that page. If we don't stop Carlo, that information will die with the doctor. We need more help. Get our friend at the Eighth District Station on the phone."

Raymond stepped away and Marcus stopped him. "Make the call here. You dial and I'll talk."

A desk sergeant answered the phone and Raymond gave the name of the person he wanted. The sergeant told him everyone was in the field and would he like to leave a message.

"Hold on," Raymond replied. "Not there," he said to Marcus, "… wants me to leave a message."

Marcus gave his approval and the sergeant asked for a callback number.

"No number," said Raymond. "Call Sucràm. That's the message. It's important."

Fourteen

CLARENCE BROUGHT out a case of water, sliding it on the back of the utility cart with everything else. "Mist'a Gregory says tha's it. Sure is a lot 'a stuff."

"It's going to be a long flight," answered Shadwell. "Our pilot believes in being prepared."

"You scared, Uncle Will? 'Cause I sure am."

"Of what? You're not afraid of flying are you?"

"That don't scare me none. I's just thinkin' 'bout some of the stuff Dr. Webster's been sayin'."

"I've been wondering about that myself. Most everything she said justifies Margaret's behavior. Even if that were true, why would it bother you?"

"Don't know. We all gots ta' die sometime. Never gave it much thought 'till now."

"Young, Mr. Brooks," said Shadwell, putting his hand on the boy's shoulder. "You needn't worry about that for a long time."

"Worry about what," asked Richard, stepping out of the office with Bourbon in one of the plastic kennels.

"Clarence is concerned about my health," answered Shadwell.

"Are you feeling all right, Will?"

"Yes, I'm fine. He gets a little worried sometimes." Approaching eighty-years-old Shadwell is in good health. He just feels tired from all the rushing around. Though not as spry as he used to be, splitting firewood and his evening stroll more of a chore now, despite those faltering piles of wood and dwindling walks, he figures he'll be able to keep up with everyone. *It's not like they're going to Cape Coral on foot.*

Click-clacking her way out of the office—a noisy set of heels—Phyllis makes her way down the steps. "I almost forgot," she reached into her purse, "… here, take these." She handed Shadwell two cans of cat food. "I keep an ample supply on hand just in case. Lots of folks forget when they travel. It'll save ya from goin' to the market."

"Thank you," said Shadwell. The cat food brought to mind an earlier time when Margaret abandoned those closest to her, befriending animals instead.

"Bourbon just ate so he won't be hungry till this evenin'. Make sure his water dish stays full. Y'all have a safe trip." Phyllis said good-bye to Bourbon… from the top of the steps she waved to Shadwell and Clarence, reminding Richard to lock up on his way out.

Clarence, roosting on the tail end of the cart, his arm resting on the plastic kennel, he looked over at Shadwell who gave him a subtle smile from the front seat. Richard is behind the wheel speeding through the roll-up door, thumbing the remote and the hanger's giant mouth closing shut.

Grabbing the luggage and Laurian's briefcase from the back of the Cessna, Richard took the bags to Clarence who loaded them on the cart. He then went back for Shadwell's bundle and a 9mm Smith & Wesson he keeps under the cockpit seat. A satin finish and ebony grip, the pistol was a gift from Margaret, Richard taking it on whatever plane he happens to be flying.

With everything loaded on the cart, Richard put the 9mm next to him, covering it with his flight jacket. "Now we all have a gun," he said to Shadwell.

Ariel popped the hatch on the Blazer, going around to the driver's-side as Tantur put his blowgun in the back. She carries a gun case which she opens on the center console. Approaching the passenger-side, Tantur is visible from his naked chest down, wary of his loincloth before climbing into the front seat.

Ariel appears preoccupied with the case, Tantur, however, is wise to her crafty deceptions—moving tactfully through the door to keep his loincloth in place. She seems undaunted with Tantur being careful, but he knew better, Ariel removing a tranquilizer pistol from the case. "How's your brother," she asked, stuffing a dart in the pistol's chamber.

"He was sleeping when I left."

"*Still?* That's not a good sign. His injury must be worse than we thought."

Ariel nudged the accelerator and the Blazer crept forward. She followed the cart from Gulf Coast Charters across the tarmac at a slow, clandestine pace.

Richard drove along the edge of the promontory, Margaret's seaplane a thousand feet away starting to take shape. Its pontoons, conterminously close to the propeller, Shadwell compares the length of the fuselage to that of the Cessna. *It's not much bigger*, he thought. *Richard was right. It's going be a long, uncomfortable flight*.

Watching the ground speed away from his dangling feet, Clarence pays no mind to the Blazer; Richard maneuvering the cart parallel to the seaplane, stopping in the middle of the promontory.

"Wonder what that fellow's up to," remarked Shadwell.

"Don't know," said Richard. "Probably missed the turn for the marina. Why don't you stay with the cart in case anybody comes snooping around."

Checking the 9mm pistol, Richard released the safety, stuffing the gun back under his jacket. "If anything happens, don't hesitate to use that."

"Thanks, but I'd rather use the scattergun," said Shadwell. "I'd hate to shoot someone I can't see up close."

A steady breeze circulates a string of sailboats around Lake Pontchartrain, the feeble blow brushing against the boats docked at the marina; soothing, lakefront purls lulling them to sleep. On the corner of the headland protecting the harbor, Margaret's seaplane flutters in the water, a berceuse of ripples caressing the floats. Shadwell opens the blanket-roll on the back of the cart, taking out the double-barrel shotgun. The kennel shields him from the Blazer and he's confident no one can see him loading the gun.

Richard doesn't pay much attention to Shadwell, only that that he's loading one of shotguns. He and Clarence are busy offloading the cart, stacking everything next to the seaplane.

"We'll put the shotguns on the plane when Laurian gets back," Richard said to Clarence. "Better to have them with us in case we run into trouble."

"And Bourbon," asked Clarence.

"I'd hate to leave him here. Even for a little while. We'll take him with us."

Clarence shook his head from atop the pontoon, scaling the support-frame to the main hatch. Extended over the water, Richard holds up the first piece of luggage. "Take it to the back of the plane," he said.

Clarence turned around and was practically there. He lifted the bag over the rear seat placing it on the floor. The next item is the case of water, Clarence looking outside trying to spot his uncle but the open hatch obstructs most of his view. Putting the water with the carryon and Laurian's briefcase, he sees Shadwell through the aft window, sitting on the back of the cart.

The supplies are loaded in less than a minute, and when Richard climbs inside the seaplane, Ariel put the Blazer in gear. Slamming the accelerator, gravel ricocheting off the skiff, Ariel urged Tantur to lean forward.

"Why?"

"You'll see."

Shadwell saw the Blazer heading his way, the trailer bouncing on the rocky surface, chafing the skiff on its oversized frame.

Pausing in front of the aft window, the Blazer nowhere in sight, Richard checks on Shadwell who is now standing at the back of the cart. "Still quiet out there," he said to Clarence. "I'll run the preflight then we'll grab something to eat. Mind giving me a hand?"

The Blazer came to a sudden stop less than ten feet from Shadwell, his knee against the utility bed and the blanket covering the shotguns at arm's length. Ariel, who Shadwell considers an attractive female, lowered the window smiling at him. "Nice plane. I was wondering if something like that can be chartered for a couple of hours?"

"I would assume so," Shadwell glanced at the seaplane, Ariel drawing her pistol and catching him off guard.

Her gun pointed at his chest, Shadwell's first thought turned out to be a mistake. He went for the shotgun and a sudden burst split the air, the quick swoosh and ensuing thump striking the outer part of his shoulder. The impact, swirling him to the side, Shadwell fell to the ground, driving a monstrous dart deep into his flesh. The world in front of him a dizzy blur, he grabbed the cart rising to his knees. His rear-end stationed on his heels and the tranquilizer taking affect, Shadwell is unable to focus on the two figures approaching him. In a feeble attempt he reached for the blanket, his body swaying momentarily and his stout frame collapsing to the ground.

Ariel takes another dart from the case. "Notice how fast that worked," she said to Tantur, showing him the dart. "You need to get rid of your frogs. These are much better."

Tantur put his shoulder into Shadwell's waist, wrapping his arm around the old man's thigh lifting him up. "Show me how to make one and we'll see," said Tantur, his wooden armlet stuffed with darts far smaller than what Ariel has.

"You don't make these," replied Ariel, sliding the dart into the pistol's chamber. "You buy them."

"How do you know they have enough poison? I don't like that. I will stick to making my own."

"*Whatever*," said Ariel cocking the gun, her wanton eyes following Tantur all the way to the skiff. "Hurry up, would you," she demanded. "I'm going to need your help."

"You don't need my help," answered Tantur. "That was a well-placed shot and you know it."

"Yeah, but there are two of them in there."

"They can't attack at the same time. The hatch is too small."

Richard turned the ignition key and the panel shut down. "Not as many gauges as the Cessna, are there?"

"Not nearly," Clarence agreed, he and Richard finished with the interior preflight and Clarence leaving the cockpit.

Reaching for the hand support outside the plane, Clarence

checked his footing before stepping out. His body halfway out of the cabin, he looked toward the cart and saw his uncle on another man's shoulder—a tall, bare-skinned man Clarence had never seen before.

The tall man is at the skiff Clarence saw earlier and Clarence screamed his uncle's name as loud as he could.

One more thing to do, taking the keys from the control panel, Richard looked out the cockpit window instead to see what was going on. "Wait!" he shouted, springing from his seat. Rushing into the cabin, Clarence making his way down the support-frame, Richard yelled to him, "Get back inside!"

His head below the cabin floor, Clarence looked up at Richard, another burst from Ariel's gun and Clarence jerking forward, his left hand clawing at his backside.

"Hang on," cried Richard dropping to the floor. Extending his hand, Richard saw a lengthy dart with a red bushy fletching hanging from the back of Clarence's right shoulder. "Give me your hand," he said, stretching out as far as he can.

His face suddenly flush, Clarence reached up but his body went numb and Richard grabbed a handful of nothing, yelling out in anger as Clarence hit the ground.

Scrambling to his feet, an apparent surge of adrenaline hitting him, Richard hid behind the hatch peeking around the corner. He saw Ariel walking toward an empty cart and he knew he was in trouble.

Where are you, Will, Richard said to himself. Looking to his right, he saw Tantur unhooking the tarp from the skiff, Shadwell propped against the boat trailer.

"Damn it!" screamed Richard, turning quickly to hide himself; his back against the fuselage. Shadwell looked to be unconscious and Richard knew he made a mistake on where to leave his gun.

Tantur peeled back the tarp and a quick observation told him he could lay three bodies side by side in the skiff. With Clarence sprawled out next to the seaplane, Ariel put a finger in the air. *One down or one left,* thought Tantur, *either way she can handle it.*

At the back of the cart, the gun case on top of the kennel, Ariel took out another dart. Her attention shifting to Tantur, bending over the skiff putting Shadwell inside, suddenly from the corner of her eye she sees Richard spilling out of the seaplane. Jolting her head around, Richard crouching on one knee, the dart slipped out of Ariel's hand.

Bearing down on Ariel, in a split second Richard sprang to his feet, sprinting toward her.

Moving Shadwell in the middle of the skiff, Tantur is unaware of what's going on behind him—Ariel's eyes fixed on Richard as she fumbles for another dart. Most of the partitions in the gun case are empty and she frantically works her fingers until she finds one. Pulling the capped end with two fingers, the dart is stuck and everything falls out of the case.

Ariel scours the ground for a single dart, her heart racing as Richard is closing in. Glancing at the back of the cart, next to the kennel, she spots one in the crease of Shadwell's blanket, Richard reaching for something on the front seat but her eyes to busy to notice.

Richard dug underneath his jacket extracting the 9mm pistol. He swung around but his arm is frozen in midflight, the gun stopping short of Ariel's head with its barrel pointing toward the Blazer. Ariel has a shotgun aimed at his chest and in an instant Richard remembers Shadwell loading one of the shotguns. *But which one,* thought Richard. Should he call the woman's bluff, disabling her with a round to the shoulder. *Does she have the nerve to pull the trigger?*

Tantur, still hunched over in the skiff, felt the repercussion of a gunshot. Rushing to Ariel's side, he dropped beside her; blood splattered on her face and top portion of her body.

Staring at the sky with her mouth open, Ariel looked over at Tantur. "What a fool," she said, rising from the ground.

With Ariel okay, Tantur went around to the other side of the cart, Richard lying on the ground face up, his chest a pulpy froth of flesh and cinereous vapors.

Ariel stood beside the fallen soldier, his blood and bone-shards everywhere Scarlet fragments of skin, muscle, and fluids are splotched upon the cart, the seat dripping with blood; forming a pool on the floorboard.

Lieutenant Richard Gregory served in Vietnam for five years and had been shot a number of times. The worst was a bullet piercing the hull of his chopper ending up in his chest. He survived a great many things associated with war. Prolonging the inevitable, however, his ironic fate is unjust. No one deserves such a death when they have walked away so many times before. But Richard took a chance… and like those he took in combat the stakes were no different. With all manner of life there is death, Lieutenant Gregory's brought about by an iniquitous female whose birth came as he lay in a hospital bed, recovering from all things, *a chest wound*.

"You should have dropped it," screamed Ariel. "A couple of days and you would have been set free."

"What happened," asked Tantur, his tone extremely bitter.

"I couldn't get another round in the chamber fast enough. He reached for a gun and I did the same. Luckily mine discharged before his. Look at this mess. We'll have to clean it up somehow."

"We need to get the other two out of here first," said Tantur.

"Whatever you need to do, go ahead and do it. I'll look in the plane for something to wipe off the cart."

"Here," Tantur grabbed Richard's flight jacket. "You've got blood all over your face."

Ariel cleaned her face on the lining, handing the jacket back to Tantur. "Put it on the dead guy," she said. "It may soak up some of the blood."

Tantur took Clarence to the skiff as Ariel climbed into the seaplane, looking for something to wipe down the cart. She soon discovered the blankets in the back. "Perfect," she said to herself, uncovering Laurian's briefcase under one of the blankets. "Well, what do we have here?"

Ariel opened the case sifting through the contents for the missing page but it wasn't there. "Damn it!" she exclaimed, staring at the empty vial. *Must be last month's treatment*, thought Ariel. *If so, where's the one for today? I see a syringe. But that doesn't make any sense. Margaret would have to be—* "Wait a minute," Ariel spoke quietly to herself, looking around the plane. "What's going on here?"

Tantur carried Richard's body to the skiff, Ariel joining him with an armful of blankets. "Hold on," she said, wary of the blood dripping from Richard's jacket.

Ariel spread a thick layer of airline blankets in the skiff. "Put him down there and cover him up. This," she set a roll of duct tape on the fender, "… you can use on the other two."

Ariel went back to the seaplane soaking one of the blankets in the lake, wiping down the cart and plastic kennel. Making good use of the duct tape, Tantur takes care of Shadwell and Clarence while Ariel loads the kennel and Webster's briefcase in the Blazer. With everything ready, Tantur strapping the tarp in place, Ariel parked the utility cart over the spot where Richard fell—his DNA all over the place. *Raymond can clean up the rest*, thought Ariel.

Grabbing the shotguns and Richard's pistol, Ariel met up with Tantur who is washing off Richard's blood in the lake. He stares at the skiff for the longest time, then scornfully at Ariel.

"Don't look at me like I'm some kind of psycho."

"Can we go now," asked Tantur, stepping from the water.

"Yes," replied Ariel, chucking the shotguns and 9mm in the lake. "My father won't like this. He won't like this at all."

"*I don't like this*," said Tantur. "That man did not deserve to die like that."

"I'm not talking about the pilot. That was his own damn fault. Margaret's planning something. I can feel it."

Fifteen

AT THE PEAK OF its sultry abuse, the afternoon air invades the wine cellar, Jón René stepping from the doorway into the miserable heat.

Raymond is sitting in the limousine with the AC at a comfortable level and Jón René walks up, taping on the windshield. Emerging from the limousine, perspiring immediately, Raymond buttoned his jacket, rushing to the vehicle's curbside door.

Fuddled from the Pinot and her bandaged arm, Margaret stepped outside, Marcus following her, thanking Jón René for allowing them to use the rear entrance.

"It is my pleasure, Monsieur Córdoba." Concerned over Margaret's cut, Jón René watched as she made her way through the crowd, the limousine not that far away.

Marcus keeps an eye on her as well, but only for a moment. He's confident Margaret will not use the crowd to escape; not after his threatening to harm Nathan if she didn't behave. He turned to Jón René instead, complementing him on his excellent service.

"Merci," Jón René stodgily replied, heading to the wine cellar as Margaret goes quietly into the limousine.

Anxious to get to the airport, Marcus moved quickly across the crowded walk, Raymond holding the door for him and the phone in his jacket going off.

"Hello. …Hang on," said Raymond, handing the phone to Marcus. "Our friend at the stationhouse."

Marcus stepped back and Raymond shut the door on Margaret. "I have a job for you," Marcus blared into the phone.

The voice on the other end had but one question and Marcus explained the situation. "Find him before it's too late. I need that last bit of information. The page is divided into two sections…."

The churches are thinning out and the traffic along Whitney Boulevard is congested. Laurian turns east on Carol Sue Avenue, the road fairly sparse until she crosses the Behrman Highway where there is an unusual amount of cars in both directions.

There is a strong, sooty odor in the air and traffic slows to a crawl outside her neighborhood. Not far ahead, cars line the avenue as a policeman diverts traffic to the right.

"This doesn't look good," said Laurian.

"I take it your house is on the left," quipped Nathan in return.

Any expectations Laurian had that her home was safe decimated around the corner. Six patrol cars, a paramedic team, a TV crew, a fire truck and two engines encompassed her house. Fortunately, she found a parking spot not far from her house, stuffing the manila envelope under the front seat. The damage to her home is visible over a neighbor's hedge and Nathan is observant of how nervous she is—Laurian quivering while removing the ignition key.

"Are you going to be all right," asked Nathan.

"I think so," answered Laurian. Taking an anxious breath,

she gave her pocketbook to Nathan. “Put that in the glove box, please.”

“Sure.” Nathan set the pocketbook on Shadwell’s revolver, considering whether or not to take the gun with him.

“Don’t you dare,” clamored Laurian. “We couldn’t be in a safer place than this. Every policeman in town is out there. Here,” she dangled the keys, “… mind holding on to these? I’m afraid I might lose them.”

Stepping out of the minivan, a smoky, sullen sky, Laurian takes another breath, inhaling the foul air of her misfortunes. She recalls moving into the house a thousand memories ago. Ten years of sacrifice and hard work to make the payments, not to mention raising a child, she exhaled as though dusting off those treasured thoughts. “Let’s do this,” she said, locking on to Nathan’s arm.

Laurian never explained to Nathan the reason they were there. The research disk, a small part of the big picture, was all he needed to know for now. She wasn’t being hesitant about the rest… she had others things on her mind.

Proceeding forward, white ash everywhere, Laurian stopped in the middle of the street, surveying the charred remains of her once beautiful home. It looked like a smoldering skeleton with pieces of skin hanging from the rafters; except for the outer wall of the garage, saved by the firefighters. Most all of the interior studs burned down or toppled over when the roof collapsed. You can see the backyard through the gaps, but not the patio because the roof extension covers most of it.

“I’m sorry,” said Nathan, “… but I don’t think you’re going to find any computer disk in there.”

“Oh my God! NO!” screamed Laurian, running toward her house—dodging people left and right. The police are busy with crime-scene tape and Laurian scuttles passed an officer stringing it across the driveway.

"Hold on there, Miss," a firefighter grabbed her arm. "You can't go in there."

"My— My mother!" Laurian breathed heavily. "My mother and daughter!"

"Are you the owner, ma'am," asked a stocky firefighter.

"Yes. *Oh my God!* They're not—"

"They're fine, ma'am. Turn around," said the firefighter.

In the middle of the street, running through a maze of fire hoses and television equipment, a little girl called out to Laurian. Skinny legs and short red hair, she scurries up the driveway throwing her arms around Laurian's waist. With the barrier-tape between them, Laurian hugged the life out of her daughter. "Thank God. Are you all right?"

"I'm okay, but Grandam May keeps crying."

Laurian's mother followed the same path as her granddaughter, a smile on her weary face as she too embraced *her* daughter.

Laurian wept, relieved that her mother and daughter are safe.

"I'm so sorry," Laurian's mother also wept; *tears of a different nature filling her eyes*. "I don't know what happened. We went to the store and— I must have locked the keys inside…."

"I know, Dad told me."

"It was horrible. I went home for your father's key, and when we got back the street was blocked off. Smoke was coming from the— I made tea this morning. I can't remember if I turned the stove off. Oh, Laurian, I'm so sorry."

Laurian hugged her mother. "I thought I lost you there for a minute," she said. "Don't blame yourself. It wasn't the stove."

Nathan stepped forward and Laurian let go of her mother.

"Mom, this is Nathan Lewis. He's here to help me— *with a patient*."

"Hello," said May.

"Nathan, this is my mother May and my daughter Amy." Nathan gave May a modest greeting, crouching low as he said hello to Amy. She looked a lot like Laurian, same shapely eyes but brown instead of blue; her hair hanging high above her forehead. Wearing a flowered sundress her knees are scraped, Nathan thinking she may be a tomboy.

Laurian gave them a subtle smile. Turning to her mother, Laurian suddenly remembers why she's there. "I need to check on something out back. It won't take but a minute."

"You can't get anywhere near the house right now, sweetheart."

"I know. I'm going to try and talk my way through."

"If you can't," said May, "I have an idea that might work."

"What is it?"

May explained and everyone agreed they would follow her lead. Ducking under the police tape, Laurian checked out all the faces in the driveway. The firefighter who stopped her is close by. She won't talk to him though, *he's to bossy.* The stocky firefighter is in the crowd with a policeman and she'll talk to him; *the friendly one.*

"Excuse me," Laurian interrupted the firefighter. "I wanted to thank you for your kindness earlier."

"You seemed a little distraught. You look a lot better now."

"Yes, I feel better too," said Laurian turning on the charm—attractive women so persuasive. The stocky firefighter smiled as did the policeman. "I was wondering if you could help me out," Laurian continued. There was hint of distress in her voice and one could swear her cheeks flushed on cue. "I'm a doctor. A research specialist and I need to check on some papers I have in the back. I won't be going anywhere near the house I promise."

The firefighter wasn't sure what Laurian wanted to do exactly, asking that she be more specific.

"I have a container with an important medical record I keep in the backyard and I need to make sure it's still there."

"Sorry ma'am, I can't let you go back there. It's too dangerous."

"Can you escort me? It will only take a minute."

"I can't. I'm not the one in charge. You'll have to talk with Chief Larsen about that."

"Which one is he?"

"Right behind you, ma'am."

"Oh him. Mr. Angry Face. *Thanks*."

Laurian approached the firefighter who grabbed her earlier when she ran toward the house. She waved to her mother as she drew close to the man.

"Catch me," said May, turning away from Nathan.

"*What?*"

"Ooh— Ooh my chest!" cried May, falling into Nathan.

"Help! Someone help me!" yelled Nathan, slumping down from having to catch May at such an awkward angle.

Everyone in the driveway turned to see what all the screaming was about, the stocky firefighter and policeman rushing passed Laurian.

Amy joined in the theatrics as well. "Grandam May!" she cried out.

The driveway now empty, Laurian stepped back, angling toward the side of the house with tiny steps, then at the right moment, sprinting in the direction of the one remaining wall.

When the curious and the lethargic have nothing better to do, tragedy is always there to entertain them. A burning building, a car crash, a pool of blood, death or dismemberment… *ill fortune draws a crowd.* Some gather for a short time and disappear, while others camp out until they're made to leave. Don't they have something better to do? It's relative to NASCAR when the last driver crosses the finish line, the possibility of a crash is over and it's time to go home.

That was the case with this fire. Extinguished some time ago, the crowd dispersed on their own; not a single onlooker made to leave. And they seldom are, as long as they stay out of the way. Moreover, it makes sense not to chase them off. The authorities know the significance of panning the crowd for a guilty face. Nearly all fire-bugs mingle with the innocent, including the occasional arsonist—*or two*.

"Do we have to get this close," said Vincent, lowering his head.

The traffic now thinning, Carlo parked the maintenance van down the street from the house they just torched. "Relax. No one's paying attention. Besides, we look like we belong here."

A fire-engine turns the corner and Carlo read the lettering on the door: TERRYTOWN, FIFTH DIST, VOL FIRE DEPT. "Like I said … it won't be long until they all leave. We'll wait a few minutes and take a peek down her street. In the meantime, you keep an eye on that screen."

A white, Ford Taurus turned off Carol Sue Avenue into Carlo's side mirror. "I smell pork. Check out this car, Vincent." Shielding his profile with his arm out the window, Carlo waited for the car to pass. "Tell me that doesn't have pig written all over it?"

Carlo glanced at the passenger from the corner of his eye. "Holy shit," he said to Vincent. "That's the Creole from the Quarter."

"Did he see us?"

"No. He's too busy jawin' with the driver."

"What are we gonna do?"

"Nothing, as long as they keep moving."

Turning the corner, the Taurus stopped in front of the Webster house; a curious group assembled at the curb. Monroe got out and a uniformed cop greets him by name.

"Wha'd you got goin' on 'ere," Monroe questioned the officer.

"Some woman thought she was havin' a heart attack. She got a little flustered and fainted."

Wasting no time, Taylor makes his way through the crowd flashing his badge. "*All right*, give the lady some room," he demanded.

"'Ooh's in charge 'ere," Monroe called out.

"I am," answered Fire Chief Larsen from the driveway.

Monroe headed over and Taylor lifted the police tape joining him on the other side. The detectives introduce themselves with Monroe taking charge. He tells Larsen about the Mobil Building and the offices leased by the same woman whose house burned down.

"Yes, I know," replied Larsen. "I talked to the woman not more than ten minutes ago."

"Where?"

"Right here," answered Larsen scouring the scene. "That's odd. She doesn't appear to be around anymore. Wait a minute— that's her mother on the curb. The woman who just fainted. You may want to talk with her. She was in the house this morning."

"Thanks," said Monroe, heading toward the road and Taylor quick to follow.

Sitting on a fire blanket, May had her feet in the street and a bottle of water in hand. The last of the curious going about their business, she turned to her granddaughter, flashing a cozy grin. Looking up at Nathan, she thanked him for catching her.

"That was quite a show," whispered Nathan, combing the front yard for Laurian. "Looks like she made it."

Leaving the driveway, Taylor and Monroe approach the curb. "Get ready for some unwanted company," Nathan said to May.

"Afternoon," said Monroe, tipping his head. Nathan and May reciprocating, Amy looked up and Taylor gave her a dutiful nod. Cary then took out his shield addressing May. "I'm Detective Monroe, an' d'ez is Detective Taylor. How are you ma'am, feelin' better?"

"Yes, very much. Thank you."

Monroe put the badge away, replacing it with a notepad. "Yer' 'da mother 'a 'da woman owns d'is house, d'at right? *One Laurian Webster*," asked Monroe, checking his notes.

"She prefers Dr. Webster— but yes, I'm her mother."

Monroe then asked everyone their name, wanting to know where they lived and what they were doing there. Nathan gave a brief summary about himself, telling Monroe he was a friend of Laurian's visiting from back east. After his encounter with Wahota in the woods, Nathan wasn't giving out any personal information to anyone. *If this guy really is a cop*, thought Nathan, *he can check me out on his computer.*

Monroe wrote down their information. "Thank you," he said, flipping the page as Nathan and May nervously await his next question.

"Wouldn't happen ta' know where yer' daughter is right now, would ya?"

"She'll be back directly."

His attention on the fast talking Creole, in an instant Nathan looked over at May, an ambiguous plea on his face not to give her daughter's location away.

"She's gone next door to use the bathroom," said May, glancing up at Nathan.

Nathan breathed a sigh of relief, and no one noticing but May. Unfortunately, Taylor saw a faint smirk from May in return.

Considering his next question, Monroe received a nudge from Taylor, asking Cary if he can handle things on his own.

"Yeah, why?"

"Thought I'd have a look around."

"Go ahead," said Monroe, thumbing through his notepad.

Nathan kept his eye on Taylor who met with Chief Larsen in the driveway, Monroe clearing his throat, reestablishing his questioning. "I have a bit 'a information d'at may interest 'da two 'a you." Monroe pulled out the APB with Carlo's photo, handing it to Nathan. "Ever see d'is man before?"

"Rather cold looking isn't he. Sorry, I think I'd remember a face like that." Nathan gave back the APB and Monroe passed it on to May.

"'Ow 'bout you?"

May took a pair of reading glasses from her purse, examining the page. "It's a bit hard to make out." Gradually she put the blacks and grays in perspective. "I saw that man parked across the street this morning."

"What! Are ya sure?"

"Of course I'm sure. He had a long black car and there was another man with him. Right over there," pointed May.

"D'is man may be responsible for 'da Mobil Building explosion."

"Oh my! Laurian works in that building."

"Not anymore," said Monroe. "'Da blast took out 'er entire lab."

"Who is he," asked Nathan.

"Carlo Somoza. 'E kill a N'awlins doctor five years ago. I was on d'at case an' can tell you 'e a dangerous fellow. 'E's also wanted in another state for 'da deaths of two ud'ers."

"Why would someone take out a research facility then

torch their house?" Nathan already knew the answer wanting Monroe to believe otherwise.

"Dunno. But ya can be sure 'a one t'ang … someone else is behind all d'is and when we catch Carlo we'll find out who."

Laurian hid behind the far end of the garage as a firefighter makes his way through the house, poking furniture and cindered wood with his ax. He tramps through the hallway and Laurian creeps around the corner, careful not to rub against the charred exterior. The clay flowerpot she's after is still intact; two of them surviving the fire at opposite ends of the patio. Each pot has the same variety of flower, and the furthest one, *her day not getting any easier*, is where she hid the disk.

The pergola style roof, once shading the back porch now lies on top of it. From where Laurian is standing there is a way through but she'll have to walk across the kindled beams to get there. She could go around, but someone might see her so she decides not to—a choice that didn't matter one way or the other, not with Detective Taylor closing in.

Stepping onto the porch, glass from a table crackling at her feet, Laurian weaves her way through the debris to the other side. Stumbling on a hard piece of lumber, she grabs hold of a corner post to keep from falling. Once she reaches the pot, her hands full of soot, crouching down she's careful not to dirty her pants as well.

The oversize pot, glazed and yellowish-brown, contains a tuberous begonia sopping with ashes. The pot has a wide mouth and in its belly, surrounded by loose soil and organic fertilizer, is a metal container the size of a *War and Peace* paperback. Laurian takes hold of the plant, pulling it out of the pot. A healthy glob of soil clinging to the roots, the hole it made exposes nothing. Shoveling the soil to one side, the soot on her hands rubbing off, she unearths the small treasure. Somewhat bereaved, her prize begonia willfully slain, Laurian put the plant back in the pot.

She takes the metal container out of a Ziploc bag. It once belonged to Margaret and the top is made out of a old brass plaque with a hinge on one side and a decorative hasp on the other. Laurian opens the top with a sigh of relief. Undamaged is Ponce de León's map and the 3-1/2 inch disk. There is a small vial of Margaret's serum in the box as well, uncut and volatile in its present state. Laurian let go of the brass top and when it slammed shut a voice called from across the patio.

"*Dr. Webster?*"

Still crouching in front of the pot, Laurian spun around like a top, cuffing the box against her thigh. "Yes?"

"My name is Samuel Taylor. Detective Samuel Taylor. I work for the Eighth District Station and have a few questions for you."

Curious as to why he didn't scold her for crossing the police line, Laurian considers whether or not to flee across an opening in front of her. "Do you have a badge or ID of some kind?"

"Yes, I have it right here," said Taylor, inching forward while reaching into his jacket.

It was at this time Monroe appeared around the corner with Laurian crouched on the porch, blocked by a smoldering heap of roof and patio furniture. "Samuel," Monroe shouted, heading toward Taylor. "Good news!"

Removing an empty hand from his jacket, Taylor turned around.

Perfect timing, thought Laurian.

"Webster's mother," said Monroe, drawing closer to Taylor, "saw Carlo parked across 'da street d'is mornin'. We need ta' talk wit' d'is Dr. Webster. I d'ink d'are may be a connection between 'er an' Dr. Wainwright."

"Who," asked Taylor. Though Samuel just read Carlo's file he had no recollection of a Dr. Wainwright.

"'E 'da one Carlo murdered five years ago," said Monroe, now face to face with Taylor. "A research specialist just like Webster. 'Er life could be in danger, Samuel. We gotta find 'er!"

"Calm down, she's right behind us," said Taylor.

"Where," asked Monroe. "I don't see nobody."

"She was right over there. Come on, she must have been looking for something," exclaimed Taylor, rushing around to the other side of the porch.

Searching for clues, Taylor found the Ziploc bag. Tainted with dirt, he gave the bag to Monroe, kneeling beside the flowerpot for a closer look. Taylor can tell the begonia was uprooted and hastily replanted. Grabbing the plant, ash flying from the leaves and flowers, he maliciously throws the plant aside. Sticking his fingers in the flowerpot, the soil having an extra cavity, he knows Laurian dug something up.

"Let's go, Cary," said Taylor, rambling to his feet.

"Begonias," declared Monroe, picking up the flower Taylor tossed aside. "Looks like d'ey ain't doin' so good out 'ere."

"*Or in her laboratory*," Taylor replied. "That's the same purple flower I found in the rubble."

Sixteen

THE SMELL OF foul play crept out of the embers as Laurian made her way through the house. Her eyes tortured by the blistering residue, she knew the fire was no accident. A harsh taste clawing at her throat, she believed it died a horrible death; flames consuming the fleshy walls of gypsum and plaster, attacking its structural underbelly. The house, once filled with joy and laughter, cried out in anguish, whooshing and crackling like the wailing of a madman. *Yes*, thought Laurian, stepping through the scorched remains, *my house choked on its own smoke and ash until it could no longer breathe.*

Nathan saw Laurian peering from the shadows, reluctant to leave the house until those outside planted their eyes elsewhere.

Squeezing between two charred supports, hedgerows on either side of the front walk, Laurian dashed across the lawn, crouching behind the hedge furthest from the crowd.

Emergency vehicles are still on the scene, a number of drivers and passengers wrapping things up. Lifting her head, scanning the neighborhood for Nathan, Laurian also keeps an eye out for Detective Taylor. Spotting Nathan next to the curb, as discreet as can be, Laurian waved to him, letting him know she had the disk by boosting the metal container—or map-box as she calls it—high in the air. She then motioned to the end of the block on her side of the hedge.

Nathan is unsure of what she's trying to say, holding his hands in a bewildered state, mouthing the word, "*What.*"

Laurian rolled her eyes, shoving the map-box under the hedge. With one bold move she rose to her feet, standing high above the leafy palisade rotating her outstretched arms in a fisted half-circle. She then points to her minivan down the street, dropping back to the ground.

Nathan understood. Her keys were in his pocket and he held them up.

Finally, thought Laurian, shaking her head. She grabbed the map-box crawling forward, the sun flickering off something in the hedgerow. Scooting along on her hands and knees, Laurian draws closer and closer to the object. A picture frame of considerable size, one of the corners is smashed and the glass appears to be cracked. Laurian can see it came from inside her house; *a portrait of Michael and Amy.*

The two are smiling at one another and the broken glass runs diagonally across the face of Laurian's departed husband. She wonders how the portrait got there, realizing not only has she lost her husband but now her home.

Woven together, her husband and home were her life and security blanket; the house to protect her when Michael was away and his loving arms around her when he returned. She said good-bye to him not long ago and now bids her house farewell.

The stitching of that security blanket, *the fabric of her life undeservedly singed*, it unravels before her sorrowful eyes. A daughter to care for and no home to shelter them, Laurian picked up the portrait, her eyes beginning to swell.

"I've no time to cry," she said to herself, struggling to keep her eyes dry and her body low.

Nathan saw the top of Laurian's head moving away from

the hedgerow. "We have to be going now," he said to Amy, kneeling beside the little girl. "I'm sorry but your mother doesn't have time to say good-bye."

Nathan could see the disappointment on Amy's face; Taylor and Monroe in the distance with the same look.

"Can you keep those two busy for a while," Nathan turned to May.

She knew which two Nathan meant, taking a look all the same. "*Those guys?* I'll talk their heads off if I have to."

The minivan sped around the corner; Carlo and Vincent parked down the street, knowing it would turn up sooner or later. Carlo was surprised, however, that Nathan was the only one inside. "I don't see the woman. Do you see her, Vincent?"

"No. Maybe she's hiding in the back."

"Now why the hell would she do that," said Carlo, throwing out half a cigarette and cranking the engine.

Heading in the direction of the minivan, Carlo pulled into a random driveway on the opposite side of the street. "I see the woman," he said—Nathan slowing down to pick up Laurian.

"Here they come!"

Both Carlo and Vincent turn away, waiting for the minivan to go by.

"They sure let out of here in a hurry," said Vincent.

Carlo put the maintenance van in reverse, keeping an eye on Taylor and Monroe down the street. "Yeah, like they're running away from something."

"*Or someone*," uttered Vincent.

"Looks like the doctor and I have something in common."

"What's that," asked Vincent.

"*Pigs*. We don't care much for pigs."

"...and the little girl," Taylor questioned May.

"I sent her across the street to get something to drink."

"So," Monroe spoke up, "... ya've no idea where yer daughter is?"

"No, Detective, I honestly don't."

Monroe paused for a moment, checking his notepad. "Wha'd about— *Mr. Lewis*. Where'd 'e disappear to?"

"I'm not sure. He was here a few minutes ago."

"How'd your daughter get 'ere d'is afternoon."

"Excuse me?"

"Did she bring 'er own vehicle or did Mr. Lewis give 'er a lift?"

"I think she came in her minivan."

"What kind of minivan," asked Taylor moving closer.

"Chrysler."

Monroe drills her on the model and year and Taylor nudged him to let him know he's going off on his own again.

"Where ya goin' now," asked Monroe.

"Think I'll talk to the neighbors and see if anyone's seen her."

Crossing the street, Taylor went through an obstacle course of a dozen firefighters rolling up hoses. Scouting the sidewalk, he spots Amy at a nearby house with a bottle of water. "Hello," he said, crouching in front of her, "... your name is Amy, right?"

"Uh-huh."

"Do you remember my name?"

"Nope."

"It's Detective Taylor. I'm trying to locate your mommy and it's very important that I find her. Do you know where she is? I need to ask her a few questions."

The eleven-year-old put her front teeth over her bottom lip shaking her head.

"How about the man she's with, have you seen him?"

Same answer.

"Does your mother own a minivan?"

In an instant Amy boasts a resilient, "Yep."

"It must have a lot of room inside. I'll bet she likes to travel."

"I'll say," raved Amy, eager to explain her mother's position in life. She told Taylor about Laurian treating children with leukemia… her compassion, the long hours, the sleepless nights… here one day and gone the next.

"She doesn't stay around much, does she," asked Taylor.

"Some of the kids come here but she's in her lab most of the time researching stuff."

"What kind of stuff," Taylor more or less demanded.

"*Important stuff*," Amy retorted, as if it were classified.

Taylor then asked what was so top-secret about her mother's research. He told her he wouldn't tell anyone, reminding her he was a cop, "…and cops," as he put it, "…are very trustworthy."

"She's inventin' sumpin' that 'ill kill a lot of blood-cells really fast. Not the good ones… only the bad ones. The ones that shouldn't be there. I don't see very much of her because of it. But when I do, we go places whatnot-in' around the whole day. Sometimes two or three days if she's not too busy."

The little girl's face lit up and Taylor knew he could ask her just about anything. "And where do the two of you go?"

"Last year we went to Disney World. Mother did a bunch of tests on a boy over there. *It was my first time in an airplane!*"

"So you like flying, huh?"

"Yeah. Airplanes are really cool. I liked it more than the rides. Mother took me up in a friend's plane on my birthday … and you know what?"

"What?"

"*He let me fly it!*"

"You're very proud of your mother, aren't you?"

"I'm gonna be a spech'list just like her someday. Helpin' folks all over the country. Maybe even the world."

"It's getting late," said Taylor, rising to his feet. "Let's get you back to your grandmother."

Dropping Amy off with her grandmother, Taylor pulled Monroe off to the side, conveying his conversation with the little girl.

Monroe was befuddled, growing impatient as Taylor kept talking. "*—And?*" he cut Taylor off.

"She's up to more than just research, Cary. There was a Chrysler minivan parked down the street when we first got here. Now it's gone. She obviously came here for something important. *Something in that flower-pot.* If her daughter's telling the truth, Webster does a lot of traveling by plane. She may in fact have access to a private one."

"So wha'd ya suggest we do?"

"Like you said, her life may be in danger. First her lab and now her house … Carlo in the thick of it. We need to find her and fast. I say we check out the airport first."

"Which one?"

"Well, we were going to Lakefront," said Taylor. "There are a lot of private planes out there and she has a friend who's a pilot."

The two detectives climb into the Taurus and Monroe calls the stationhouse first thing.

"Dispatch," Connie answered the radio; the staff shorthanded.

"Patch me through to Alcott."

"He's on another line right now, Cary."

Monroe explains the situation, trusting Connie to pass along the information. "Also, can ya get a plate number on a Chrysler Town and Country registered to one *Laurian Webster*…."

A luxury sedan pulled into the hanger and a young man of twenty-three steps out. He's uncomfortably warm in his dress shirt, black bowtie and vest. Putting on a dinner jacket, he curses the thing, yet is complaisant with its fancy lapel.

The car has a spacious interior and there are three boxes taking up the entire back seat. The young man is careless with the first box and a sterling dish-cover topples to the hanger floor, the aroma of palatable sauces and steamed chicken saturating the air. Grumbling, the young man picks up the cover as a Chevy Blazer and fishing-boat pull into the hanger, stopping alongside his skinny frame.

Tantur emerged from the Blazer, his painted face, loincloth and towering physique exuding a lifetime-of-awe from the young man. His nose guiding the way, Tantur stood toe to toe with the young man.

The young man leaned back, lofting his eyes at Tantur's chin.

"And who might you be," asked Ariel, appearing from out of nowhere.

"Delivery from Antoine's, ma'am," answered the young man, his voice quivering. "There's more in the car."

"How much more," blared Ariel.

"Two boxes. Enough for five people."

"Bring everything inside," said Ariel pointing to the office.

The young man tipped his head, eyeing the splotchy blood on Ariel's blouse.

"Fish bait," said Ariel. "My friend and I just got back."

"Catch anything?"

"Yes," replied Ariel flashing a grin. "As a matter of fact we did."

Rather than backtrack, Nathan took the Behrman Highway; left on DeGaulle a short time later, then uptown to the

Expressway. Laurian was silent most of the way, engaging solely to give directions. Staring at the portrait, the map-box at her side, in due time she broke her silence. "I wish I could have said good-bye to my little girl."

"I told her for you," said Nathan, directing a subtle smile. "*She understood.*"

"I hope so. I'm always letting her down. But that will soon change."

"What do you mean?"

"It's been five years, Nathan … Margaret can now live her life the way God intended."

"*An uncontentious life?*" Nathan looked her in the eye, still doubting her story.

"No. Not until the man responsible is taken care of."

"And you're knee-deep in that endeavor."

"I've spent most of my life saving the lives of others. I took no oath. No ethical resolution. If I believed something to be right, I stood my ground no matter what. When I tried saving my husband, our daughter the perfect donor, I felt I was doing the right thing. Now I'm not so sure. The serum I developed for Margaret can be used in another way. Taking a life instead of saving one. I know it's the wrong thing to do, killing someone regardless of what crime they commit. I think we need to question our morality in cases like that. Abandon what is right to set things right. If I don't do this because I feel it's wrong … will I regret not having done so later?"

"So that's why you've been so quiet. Your conscience is telling you one thing and your gut another."

"I'm haunted by it," said Laurian, grabbing the map-box.

Nathan glanced over, reading the inscription on top: Juan Ponce De León 1460-1521. "Where did you get that," he asked, paying no mind to the road.

"Margaret gave it to me."

"The lid, what is that?"

"A plaque. Margaret took it off the fountain in her front yard."

"*The conquistador.* I thought it looked familiar. It's a perfectly good plaque, why would she take it off?"

"I don't know."

"What about the disk," asked Nathan, his eyes back on the road.

"It's safe. Ponce de León's map as well," replied Laurian. "I've never shown it to anyone … and my father's a collector."

"So there is a map."

Laurian took the map out of the box. "It's not important," she said, setting the map and the disk aside. "This is what we actually came for," she exclaimed, removing the vial with Margaret's serum. Showcasing the glass cylinder in the windshield, the sunlight filtered through the lavender mix. Twisting the tube back and forth, the contents opalescent and her fingertips transparent, Laurian is beside herself with grief.

"What is that?"

"Five years of research. Of trial and error … *of what's become of me*. It's the genetic tissue matter I was telling you about. In its present state it would be lethal to someone like Margaret. Once it's thinned and processed with enzymes and the proper dose of white blood-cells, the right amount of bone marrow introduced, it neutralizes the chemical agents preventing someone like Margaret from aging."

"You keep saying, '*Someone like Margaret.*' You're not suggesting—"

"William shot him in the head but he didn't die. He's alive, Nathan. Marcus is alive. He has the same chemical imbalance as Margaret. I know you don't believe all this, but he more than likely killed your parents…."

Nathan gripped the wheel tighter, the throat he wants to get his hands around. "You believe that potion is the only way to rid the world of this killer, don't you. Your virtue's at stake and you don't know if you're capable of— what … injecting him with that stuff."

"Yes."

"When the time comes," said Nathan, execrating his intent, "… if this man Marcus killed my parents, I'll be the one whose virtue is tested."

Seventeen

THE LIMOUSINE arrived at Lakefront Airport around 3:00 p.m. Raymond circled the terminal parking lot, and afterward, the rest of the airport looking for Webster's minivan. There is no sign of it anywhere. He found the Lincoln, and with Margaret in the back seat, Raymond is mindful of giving away Carlo's name. "Our boy must be around here somewhere," he spoke into the intercom. "His car is here and that can only mean one thing—"

"Forget about it," said Marcus. "He could be anywhere."

Returning to the hanger, Raymond opened the door for Margaret but she won't move. Agitated by her disposition, Marcus gave her a nudge, reminding her to do as she's told. Margaret took her time getting out as Raymond zeroed in on his fishing boat. The overhang of the tarp appeared uneven and the bungee-cords are fastened in a different manner. He had a feeling what was underneath, unappreciative of Ariel for the incriminating act.

Unlike the hanger office at Gulf Coast Charters, this one contains a mixture of modern day and Victorian décor. Seated on a 19th-century chair, a glass of wine at her side, Ariel skims through an aviation magazine. Wahota sleeps on a sofa across from her, his head bandaged and body stricken with fever. Tantur sits next to him while the pilot, Walter, dines on a plate of oysters and stuffed crab by the outside door.

A bookcase sits behind Ariel, a few classic sculptures and climbing perennials on two of the four shelves but no books. A mahogany bar runs perpendicular to the bookcase and recessed in the wall behind the bar are a number of glass shelves. Wine and liqueur glasses line the shelves, a vaulted light embellishing the sparkling crystal. The food from Antoine's is spread out along the bar, except for the middle where a bottle of wine and pitcher of water sit. At the foot of the bar, locked in the kennel, Bourbon is dreaming of a way to escape.

The room is quiet and has been for some time. Tantur checks his brother's forehead, the door next to Walter then popping open and the air bristling with sound again.

Margaret is sandwiched between Raymond and Marcus, trying not to show how tense she is.

Raymond is bearing for the leftover food and Marcus shuts the door; Margaret startled by the noise.

Ariel snickered, grinning at Margaret for being so timid.

"Something amuses you," said Marcus, berating Ariel.

"No," replied Ariel rising to her feet. She knew her father's anger had nothing to do with her, giving him a fearful look nonetheless.

"Take a seat, Margaret," said Marcus heading for the bar.

Paying no attention to the kennel, Marcus poured himself a drink. "I trust you have good news," he questioned Ariel.

"I ran into a small problem, Father. Other than that, everything went as planned."

"What kind of problem?"

"One of them is dead," whispered Ariel.

"Which one?"

"The pilot."

"That is a problem. What of Carlo, have you heard from him?"

"No."

"Walter," Marcus spoke up. "Are we clear for takeoff?"

"Yes. We've been advised not to leave too late. The FAA has strict standards concerning hurricane warnings."

Marcus took a drink. "How do you feel about those standards?"

"We have plenty of time. It's not expected to make landfall until tomorrow."

"Yes, I know," said Marcus.

Walter topped off his meal with a quick glass of Merlot, excusing himself to use the head.

Inhaling the rest of his drink, Marcus left the bar. "Keep an eye on Margaret, Tantur," he brutishly imparted. "Come, Ariel. I wish to speak to you in private."

Ariel is on her way to a tongue lashing and Tantur thought it wise of Marcus to take it outside. Margaret would not react well to the bodies inside Raymond's skiff.

The same can be said of Walter. Tantur knew the story. Walter and Richard both served in Vietnam and the two were somewhat close. Richard was looking for a job at Gulf Coast Charters when they first met. An experienced fighter-pilot, Walter knew the people at the air charter service and said he would put in a good word. Having a drink now and then, Walter would extract information from Richard about Margaret's schedule, passing it on to Marcus.

One day, Walter mentioned to Tantur his love of flying. He had time to reflect on things while in the sky—its vast emptiness and uncertain horizon changing his perspective on life. A postwar reaction to those calling Walter a baby killer, Tantur knew Walter associated with a number of known criminals. He was the one who introduced Carlo to Marcus. What Tantur didn't know was Walter's view on society. Governed by men who chastised him for following orders, most of those nameless faces bore Walter's nonconformity. Principles and laws no longer applied to him; *his allegiance belonged to the clouds*. He snubbed democracy not for his beliefs but for the way he was treated. Walter hated the masses for judging and criticizing his patriotism. Even the ruling-class, empowered to forgive him, denounced his loyal service. The narcissism of high-society, which he thought would side with him, indifferent to his military prose he wanted to ram their silver spoons up their lofty noses.

The war was not over for Walter … *not yet*. A wayward soldier, only one man embraced his animosity, Marcus taking him in when no one else would.

Ariel's impassiveness made Richard's killing easier to explain and Marcus rendered the murder as a mistake, immediately forgiving his daughter's vicious act. "The man worked here," said Marcus, *referring to Richard*. "When he comes up missing an investigation will ensue."

"But we'll be in Europe by then," said Ariel.

"Not forever. Where did this take place?"

"On the promontory."

"Was it thoroughly cleaned?"

"Not all of it," answered Ariel. "Raymond can handle the rest."

"Raymond stays here. I'd rather he keep an eye out for Webster."

"But he's good at taking care of situations like this. What's more important, a serum I can figure out on my own or being discovered?"

"Very well. But he's to leave no evidence whatsoever. Is that understood?"

"Yes, Father."

"I'm disappointed in you, Ariel."

"I know," said Ariel, contriving a way to change the subject. "By the way," she popped the hatch on the Blazer, "… I found something out there that may interest you."

"What is it?"

"Webster's briefcase," said Ariel, taking out the empty vial. "Margaret's treatment is complete. This was her final dose. I'm sorry, Father. I know how much you care for Margaret. Webster must have made one last appointment to verify the results."

"I've seen the results firsthand," said Marcus. "Webster's serum did what it was designed to do. But I'll not lose Margaret. I'm taking her with us."

Ariel threw the empty vial in the briefcase slamming the lid.

"I'll take that," said Marcus. "The papers inside may still be of some value."

Ariel already gave the papers a once over but chose not to say anything, knowing her father will look at them regardless.

Leaving the briefcase with Marcus, Ariel went back to the office to tell Raymond the bad news.

At the edge of the hanger, Marcus stares across Lake Pontchartrain, wondering what life would be like if Margaret were not around. He's been with other women but only to satisfy his lust. Regardless of her cold heart, when Marcus found Margaret he found a woman who bore an uncanny resemblance to his first love; a woman he thought he could never get over. *Margaret will learn to love me*, Marcus said to himself. *By tomorrow's end, she'll have all the time in the world.*

The sun burrows into a field of clouds and with the sky

darkening, Marcus constructs a shining vision in his mind. He imagines the pelting rain from Hurricane Andrew working its way into the cave, replenishing the fountain. Inside the cave, the dark of the earth surrounding Ariel, she thirsts for an everlasting life while Margaret turns her back on the anomalous gift. Marcus reminds her of Nathan's fate and Margaret draws the water into a cup. Her brazen lips, cursing Marcus, she's about to drink when the vision abruptly ends, interrupted by the intrusive sound of footsteps.

"Ready when you are," said Walter, strolling up from behind.

"Here," replied Marcus, handing him the briefcase. "I'll be along shortly. Where's Ariel?"

"Loading the Cushman with Raymond. Whatever they're up to, he's pissed off about it. They may end up killing each other."

Walter made his way to the jet and Marcus headed toward the office. Raymond is next to one of the Cushman carts, and doesn't say anything to Marcus. He changed out of his chauffeur outfit into a loose pair of jeans, flannel shirt, and baseball cap. At the mechanics area along the north wall, he grabbed a bag of oil-absorbent—or kitty-litter as most people tend to say. Similar to the cart parked on the promontory, Ariel waits on the front seat, Raymond throwing the kitty-litter on the cargo bed.

The jolt frightens Ariel and she's ready to scold Raymond, but her father is standing there with an overbearing look and she keeps a tight lip.

"I see you and Margaret have something in common."

"And what might that be, Father?"

"You are both easily startled."

A grin appeared on Raymond's face while tossing another bag on the cart. "That should do it," he said.

Marcus gave a rare complement to Raymond on his plan of attack. A flat shovel and several buckets of rags are on the cart next to the kitty-litter.

"This stuff 'ill soak up anything," boasted Raymond. Grabbing the wheel, he slid in next to Ariel, a nasty look on her face.

"If that butcher shows up and Webster is still in one piece," said Marcus, "don't let anything happen to her until we find that last page. Other than that," he turned to Raymond, "… follow through with the instructions I gave you this morning. If you get there first, give Margaret's pilot a decent burial."

Marcus got rid of the ice melting in his glass. There was a little scotch at the bottom and he could smell the alcohol swirling down the sink. Standing behind the bar, the cherished aroma of scotch weakening, he picked up a familiar scent emanating from the floor. A pair of frigid eyes peering from the kennel, Marcus kneels beside the cage. Bourbon hissed, showing his teeth as a reminder they are no longer friends.

"Quiet," blared Marcus, rising from the floor.

Margaret then turned around with a curious look on her face.

"Come and get your cat," Marcus said to her. "If I had sniffed out the animal sooner I would have taken him outside."

Jumping from her seat, Margaret put the kennel on top of the bar. "What are you doing here, Bourbon? I thought—*Marcus, where's my grandson!*"

"Relax, Margaret. I have no idea where he is. He followed us out here then disappeared into the city."

"*He followed us?* But how—?"

"He caught a ride with your doctor friend."

"Why would he do that?"

"I don't know. Perhaps he intends on rescuing you."

"Don't ridicule the boy, Marcus. I've done what you've asked of me so far. I'll behave as long as you leave him alone, you know that."

"No harm will come to him," said Marcus. Opening a bottle of single-malt scotch, Marcus skipped the ice this time. "One thing is certain," he concluded, "… he's smarter than his father."

Margaret frowned.

Marcus took a healthy drink of scotch to satisfy his palate. As expected there was no intoxicating effect. An army of abnormal cells attacked the alcohol right away. Compared to the average man, a fifth of scotch was no more than a thimble full to Marcus; *a side effect he didn't like*. Getting drunk was why he drank in the first place. He threw down a case of whiskey one night to see what would happen and his bladder took over pissing it all away. His harsh temper, now kindled by the lack of that wonderful stimulant, he drinks for the taste and nothing more.

The fountain has a number of side effects both good and bad. All of which, according to Marcus, will soon return to Margaret. In the meantime, Margaret enjoys the feeling of her afternoon wine. It soothes her mind and she treasures the moment, not knowing how long it will last.

With Bourbon locked in his cage, Margaret feels she's in the same situation. She'd been let out for the first time… *but for how long?* "Come on, Bourbon," Margaret reached for the latch, "… I know how much you hate being in there."

"Not now," said Marcus, grabbing her by the wrist.

"When?"

"When I say so."

Margaret lived in a cage, *no mistaking that*, but unlike poor Bourbon, she suffers every waking moment. Imprisoned in a world of time rather than space, bars that accompany her everywhere, she cannot escape her jailer, Marcus Córdoba. Having swallowed the key to her freedom, he relishes the taste, vowing never to release her.

In that moment, *Marcus grabbing her wrist*, Margaret wished for strong hands to spread the jailer's bars, and if no one else, she be the one to do it—to strangle the life from him in order to be free.

Eighteen

THE DOOR AT Gulf Coast Charters is locked, but that doesn't stop Ariel from entering the hanger. Vincent jimmied the lock last month and Ariel ran across a set of spare keys looking for Webster's flight records. Raising the roll-up door high enough to get the cart inside, Ariel wipes the steering wheel for prints. The rest of the cart she checks for any blood she may have missed while on the promontory.

Locking the door, heading toward her father's jet, Ariel wonders what happened to the security guard; the fat one who magically shows up out of nowhere. She doesn't need him snooping around right now. Crossing her fingers, she walks a little faster. *So far so good*, thought Ariel, relieved that the only people on the tarmac are boarding her father's jet.

With Walter tending the hatch, Marcus hands him the kennel. Tantur has an arm around his near-comatose brother to keep him from falling After Marcus boards the plane, the two of them muscle Wahota through the hatch.

Ariel is the last to board and she struts passed Margaret taking a seat in the back. A host of related activities are going on outside, and with the jet taking off, Ariel can see Raymond at the end of the promontory. Too far for her or anyone on the ground to see what's going on, she knows exactly what he's doing.

A maintenance van entered the parking lot, the jet gaining altitude and Tantur taking a moment to look out the window. Two men are exiting the van, the driver heading for the terminal and the passenger positioning himself between the van and another high profile vehicle. Their faces are hard to make out, and with the wing now obstructing his view, Tantur does not see the driver smoking a cigarette at the terminal door.

The parking lot at the terminal has a median strip scattered with trees and Nathan is trying to find a spot in the shade.

"What are you doing? The marina parking is closer. We should head over there," said Laurian.

"We left the utility cart at the terminal, remember. Come on," cried Nathan, jumping out of the minivan, "... we're running late."

"I know," replied Laurian, setting the portrait of Michael and Amy on the backseat.

Laurian grabbed the map-box, walking alongside Nathan coming to a sudden stop. "Wait! I forgot the dosage chart."

And Shadwell's gun, thought Nathan. "Stay here," he said to Laurian, "... I'll get it."

A man crushed out his cigarette between two cars and Laurian stepped on the pavement for a better look. Reaching the minivan, Nathan glanced back and saw the man emerging from the trees behind Laurian. Light on his feet, the man's face is sketchy but his details are defined with each step.

It's him, thought Nathan, recognizing Carlo from Detective Monroe's APB. As Carlo drew closer, Nathan called out to Laurian, "Run! Run, Laurian! Run!"

Vincent, who was sneaking up on Nathan all this time,

drew a gun from his jacket, a placid burst and a dart penetrating Nathan's backside. A stronger dose than those used by the Cariban, twisting and clawing as he did in the woods, Nathan can't reach the dart. Seconds later he buckles to the ground.

Laurian watched in horror as Nathan lay there on his back, a revolver jammed in her midsection and Carlo ordering her to keep still. "Relax," he said, "… he's just sleeping. You on the other hand have a .32 caliber in your gut. Are we on the same page, Doctor?"

Laurian took her eye off Nathan, glancing at the revolver, her brazen face surrendering to Carlo with a stiff nod.

"We're all going for a little ride," whispered Carlo. "Do you see that van over there?"

"Yes."

"Start walking."

Vincent drug Nathan between two cars as Carlo followed Laurian to the maintenance van. "Open it," he said, shoving her toward the door.

Laurian did as she was told, putting her foot on the threshold ready to climb inside.

"Not yet," exclaimed Carlo, demanding she set the map-box on the floorboard. "Good. Now hands behind your back."

Removing a nylon tie-wrap from his jacket, Carlo looped it over her wrists cinching it tight. "Get in," he growled, hoisting her by the arm.

Having driven to the other side of the lot, Carlo warns Laurian to keep quiet, he and Vincent putting Nathan in the back. Firing up another cigarette, the smoke wisping alongside the van, Carlo took his time making his way to the front. "Get back there with your boyfriend," he said to Webster.

Her hands tied behind her back, Laurian is reluctant to move, Carlo heaving her between the seats, face first on the corrugated floor.

One hand on the wheel and the other pinching his cigarette, Carlo takes a long hit. Exhaling while leaving the parking lot, the smoke lingers over to Vincent and he fakes a cough.

Carlo in turn flashed a hateful grin.

Vincent's valor having been challenged, he cowers by lowering his head. The map-box at his feet, Vincent picks it up. "What's this?"

"Doctor stuff," said Carlo, rather sardonically.

"Can I open it?"

"Knock yourself out."

Vincent cracked the lid, peeking inside.

"*Well*," asked Carlo, lofting a temperamental brow.

"I think we may have hit the jackpot here, Carlo. Remember that map Ariel told us to keep an eye out for?"

"The one Marcus gave to the old woman? Yeah, I remember."

"Well," said Vincent, unfurling the map, "… I think we found it."

"Son of a bitch," exclaimed Carlo, turning to catch Webster's reaction.

"That's not all we got," said Vincent, showing Carlo the vial. He then took out the disk looking back at Webster. "This is probably encrypted but I'd be willin' to bet the information is worth a lot of money."

Nursing his cigarette, Carlo changed lanes for the Interstate. Stopping at the light he said to Webster, "You went back home for all this shit, didn't you?"

Laurian had since rolled over, sitting with her back against the side-panel. Carlo saw her in the rearview mirror waiting for an answer, but there was no need for one as Laurian's face explained everything—her anger and bruised cheek both swelling.

"Marcus was right," said Carlo, turning to Vincent. Examining the vial he spun back around. "He said you might have some of this hidden somewhere. All I had to do was wait and you'd lead me straight to it."

"What is that stuff," asked Vincent.

"Some kind of miracle drug. A disease killer … ain't that right, Doc?"

"One can only hope," Laurian said to herself.

Monroe let off the accelerator, creeping into the parking lot, he and Taylor searching for Webster's minivan. "D'are it is, Samuel. Cross 'da neutral ground. Guess d'at old woman was tellin' 'da truth after all."

"I'll check with Connie," said Taylor, "… she must have the vehicle registration by now."

Apologetic for having the information and not responding sooner, Connie gave Taylor the license-plate number. "Alcott is stressing everyone out over here," she explained.

Taylor is very sympathetic. "*Roger that*," he responded. "Tell him we found Webster's van at Lakefront. That should make him happy."

Monroe sped up, heading for a parking spot on the other side of the lot. All of a sudden he hit the brakes, both he and Taylor jolting forward. "Soc au' lait! I don't believe my eyes."

Taylor saw it too. A black Lincoln protuberant among the other cars.

Monroe had a bad feeling, calling for backup as he parked in an open spot near the Lincoln.. "One of us needs to stay 'ere," he said, handing Taylor the keys "I'm gonna see if

Carlo's inside. If 'e shows up while I'm gone don't be a hero. Help is on 'da way."

"Why don't you let me go, Cary? I can handle it."

"Alcott 'ill ream me a new one if I send ya in d'are alone, ya know d'at."

Taylor checked his pistol, demanding that he go instead.

"What's 'da matter wit' you?"

"Cary," Taylor advised his partner, "... this guy knows you, right?"

"Sure. 'E seen me lots 'a times."

"But not me. Come on, I've been in situations like this before. If Alcott says anything, tell him you didn't want to take a chance on Carlo recognizing you."

"All right, go ahead. But don't do anyt'ang stupid. Keep an eye on 'em 'till 'da cavalry arrives."

"If I spot him I'll back off. I promise."

"An' Webster?"

"I don't know. I'll stand down if I see them together. If not I'm going after her. She won't get away this time."

Taylor inspects the terminal through the outer doors. Wiping the sweat from his brow, he's hopeful there is a bustling crowd inside. He figures Carlo to put the make on him in an empty lobby. The way he studies a room, like some spook in a Robert Ludlum novel, Taylor would suspect himself as an undercover agent if he were the perp.

The lobby at the end of the hall is dotted with people. *So much for blending in*, thought Taylor. Two doors of interest are off the main hallway, one marked SECURITY and the other RESTROOMS. Opting to check in with security later, Taylor shuffled passed the kiosk; no one but an old man behind the counter.

A busy runway outside, Taylor ventures through the lobby where a few new faces are arriving and departing. Taking a peek in the Walnut Room and the Flyaway Lounge, Taylor backtracks but Carlo is nowhere to be found, *or Webster for that matter.* Upset with himself for letting her escape, Taylor would have gone to the bar for a drink if not for Monroe waiting in the car.

On his way to the security office, Taylor made a pit stop at the men's room. Muscling open the door, his trained eye can see there are no feet under the stalls. A large security guard is at one of the urinals and Taylor uses the one next to him.

"How's it goin'," asked Taylor.

"Good," answered the security guard. "And yourself?"

"Not bad."

An ID card above the guard's pocket, Taylor speculates his job to be uneventful and mundane. "So … you're Jerry Holiday?"

Confused that a total stranger knows his name, Jerry is mindful of his ID while going about his business. "Oh yeah, the nametag," he proclaimed. "That's me all right, Jerry Holiday."

"Well, Mr. Holiday. I'm here to spice up your afternoon?"

"*What?!*" Jerry turned his head with a worried look as Taylor unzipped his fly.

"I would have given it to you earlier but my partner and I were busy elsewhere."

Jerry's eyes nearly popped. He thought the guy was coming onto him, *and of all places!* He heard about encounters like this and it scared the hell out of him. Emptying his bladder as quickly as possible, Jerry's mind set on skipping the hand washing and sprinting for the door, Taylor promptly mentions the FAA bulletin.

Relieved in more ways than one, Jerry sighs while buttoning his fly. "Excuse me, but— *do I know you*."

"Detective Taylor, Eighth District Homicide."

"*Taylor?*" Jerry said aloud. "You're the one who called this morning."

"Yes."

"Well it's about time. I've been waiting here all day."

Taylor apologized for arriving late, the two men washing up when the door behind them creaks open. With Carlo lingering in his mind, Taylor is quick to reach inside his jacket.

The old man from the kiosk is struggling with the door and Taylor, promptly removing his hand from his jacket, helps the old man.

An outside agency, the security company occupies a small office at the terminal. A microwave and vending machine in the break room, Jerry downs a soda high in caffeine. He listens earnestly as Taylor explains what happened at the Mobil Building and Webster's house.

"Here," said Taylor, handing Jerry the ABP. "This is the man we're looking for. Carlo Somoza."

"I already have a copy," said Jerry. "We received one about an hour ago."

"And?"

"If he's here I haven't seen him."

"Well his car's outside. I'd like to check today's preflight records. Can we do that?"

"I don't see why not."

"After that we need to question all airport personnel. Someone had to have seen this guy."

"Why not just check the surveillance tapes," asked Jerry.

"It takes too long," answered Taylor. "We'll look at them later if we have to."

The Learjet, miles above the ocean, Ariel is seated in a plush leather seat with her back to the cockpit. Tantur is to the right with a tiny aisle between them. Wahota sleeps soundly in front of him and Tantur leans forward taking his brother's hand. "Ceilu tal ja-ungwie," whispered Tantur in their native tongue. *Hold on my brother.* "Ceilu tal."

All the seats in the Learjet recline except for the cushioned bench where Marcus sits. Hugging the fuselage, the bench rests between the main hatch and protruding wet bar. An onboard phone hangs above the head of Marcus and Margaret is strategically seated opposite the wet bar.

The kennel sits on Margaret's lap and she is incessantly tapping its drum-like top. Eyeing a bottle of Scotch whiskey, Margaret is debating whether or not to ambush the pilot. An orphan of society, she believes if not today, death may never claim her. A full life behind her, Margaret has no reason to oppose or argue the Grim Reaper's plan. She wants only to bargain with him. Take her now and she will deliver Marcus as well—two for the price of one.

It may work, thought Margaret. *Nathan's life depends on it.*

It was a tough decision for Margaret. Could she render the pilot unconscious and wreck the controls uncontested? Even if she did and the plane crashed in the ocean, would Marcus be trapped inside; his lungs filling with water. *I doubt it*, thought Margaret. She abandoned the idea, envisioning Marcus yanking her from the cockpit in the nick of time. Strumming her fingers with disappointment, she contemplates another way out.

A glass of rum in his hand, Marcus gave Margaret a testy look, getting up and sticking his head in the cockpit. "Any change, Walter?"

"Weather's fine. Should stay clear all the way home."

"Good. One less thing to worry about."

Marcus return to his seat with a sour disposition. "Must you continue with that irritable tapping," he snapped at Margaret.

"It keeps Bourbon's mind off his imprisonment."

"If you must let him out then do so. But I warn you," said Marcus, pouring the last of the rum, "… he'll not be out for long if he misbehaves."

Margaret fell asleep with Bourbon in her arms, Marcus stretching his legs into the aisle. Feeling somewhat relaxed, the phone above his head let out a placid, beeping tone. "This better be good," said Marcus answering the phone; Margaret and Ariel sleeping soundly with Tantur listening in.

"The doctor's vehicle was discovered not ten minutes ago," said the caller.

"Where," asked Marcus.

"The airport. Carlo must have ditched his car and taken another."

"I'm aware of that. What I need is their present location."

"Both are unknown at this time."

"Then I suggest you find them," demanded Marcus. "That is part of your job … is it not? Finding people."

"Don't worry, they'll turn up."

"It better be soon," said Marcus. His hand trembling, Marcus paused all of a sudden, Tantur now paying more attention to that than his conversation. "Without that file it will take years to duplicate the serum."

"I understand."

Unable to steady the phone, Marcus tells the caller he must hang up. "Call me when you find them."

Clutching his spastic hand, the phone falling from his grip, Marcus called out to Tantur, "The curse is upon me! Hurry! Hurry, Tantur!"

Tantur jumped from his chair, rushing down the tiny aisle. Tripping on Bourbon's cage he knocked the empty rum bottle off the wet bar and Margaret wakes up. She sees Marcus twitching like mad, knowing right away what's going on. An anniversary gift from the fountain, Margaret suffers the same convulsions every September.

Tantur wastes no time restraining Marcus from behind, wrapping his arms around the big man's torso. In a split second, Marcus is a raging tornado threatening to break free. His white blood cells are splitting in half and the stronger cells are devouring the weaker ones at a critical rate. The blood vessels swelling throughout his body, every organ and muscle expanding, Marcus suffers through it, knowing he will blackout in a very short time.

This is it, thought Margaret. *The opportunity I've been waiting for. Tantur can't let go. Marcus will tear this plane apart if he does.*

His flesh boiling and face contorting into a hideous lump, Marcus cried out in agony, slamming Tantur against the wet bar. Ariel felt the jolt in the back and Walter demands that Marcus keep still.

"He's having one of his attacks," shouted Ariel. "Find someplace to land!"

"Are you kidding? We're in the middle of the gulf."

"Time to buckle up, Margaret," said Ariel, latching her own seatbelt, "… we're in for one hell of a ride."

Marcus took his spastic fit up a notch and Tantur reacted by pushing their bodies off the fuselage, steamrolling Marcus to the cabin floor. His intent to hold Marcus in the best location possible, Tantur is unaware he left the aisle wide open.

Margaret kissed Bourbon's head, placing him on the seat next to her. Pinned against the fuselage, Tantur's head vibrates against the empty bottle. He tightens his grip around Marcus to prevent him from grabbing anything. Margaret, however, is the one intent on grabbing something. In one swift move she crouched beside the two men.

"I'm sorry," she said to Tantur, reaching behind his head.

In an instant Tantur figures out what Margaret's up to—helpless as she scrambles to her feet.

Margaret checked on Ariel and Tantur gathered his wits. The great warrior has only one option and it's a dangerous one. He let go of the left arm of Marcus and immediately Margaret felt a crushing grip around her ankle.

Marcus had her, his jumbled brain issuing another reflex order. He pulled Margaret to the cabin floor, her arm slamming against the wet bar and the bottle flying from her hand.

Walter kept the jet steady as best he could. Suddenly, he felt the yoke jerk and the plane reacting with a crazy jolt of its own. "What the hell," he clamored. It happened again but this time the vibration jerked him from side to side. Turning around, the problem is disturbingly apparent. Marcus had reached his epileptic peak.

Pounding the fuselage like a jackhammer, Marcus twitching violently, the underbelly starts to rattle and everyone is feeling sick.

"Hang on!" screamed Ariel. "A couple of minutes and it will all be over."

Walter struggles to keep the aircraft level but the hunk of flying Jell-O won't pull up. "I don't know how much more of this I can take!"

The transfer of energy—a bombardment from blood cell to skin—traveling from Marcus throughout the bodies of Tantur and Margaret, Margaret can no longer bear it. Her body pulsating, in an agonizing effort she leans forward taking hold of Marcus' death grip. A discolored ankle and the pain worsening, Margaret attempts to break free. Unable to move one finger, she falls back hitting the plush carpet. *My God*, she thought, *is there no way to end this*.

"No-o-o-o-o," screamed Margaret, digging under Marcus' thumb this time. With all her wailing strength she peeled his fingers like an orange, somehow kicking herself free. The cabin is a spinning blur and as Margaret regains control of her senses, she focused on the cockpit; the smooth, glass surface of the empty bottle now at her fingertips.

A pulsating floor and sore ankle, Margaret staggered to the back of Walter's head. Raising her arm she let go a vicious blow. Walter caught sight of the rum label just as the empty bottle struck Ariel's outstretched hand.

"What the hell are you doing," screamed Walter. "Has everyone in here gone mad? Take a seat ladies! This ride hasn't come to a complete stop yet."

Ariel led Margaret back to her seat—away from her father's reach. "Not the brightest thing you've ever done," said Ariel, forcing Margaret to sit down. "You could have killed us all."

Tantur looked at them. He knew that's what Margaret wanted. Descending some fifty-feet over the ocean, it may be the end of everyone regardless of her ill-advised plan. But as Ariel had predicted, the episode subsides and Marcus returned to normal; the rebirth of white blood cells and damaged organs complete.

Walter now has full control of the aircraft, pulling up just in time.

"Finally," said Ariel, sitting back down.

"Something to look forward to," Margaret reminded Ariel, "*… the fountain and its consequences*."

"I'd rather keep my menstrual cycle than suffer through that."

"How could you know that," asked Margaret. "I don't recall mentioning it to anyone."

"You think you're the only woman my father granted immortality? Jesus, Margaret, you're so naive."

Nineteen

EVERY TRACE OF gore and drop of blood was removed; rocks and pebbles with the slightest discoloration thrown into the lake. Raymond put the buckets of bloody rags and coagulated kitty-litter on the utility cart. Checking his watch, it took forty minutes to clean everything up. Now he needs to get back before the old man and his nephew regain consciousness.

According to Ariel, who knows more about the effects of the tranquilizer than he does, that time should never be taken for granted. Each dose, at a hundred dollars a pop, will subdue a man of 155 pounds for two hours. Consequently, a heavier victim has less recovery time.

Upon returning to the hanger, Raymond transferred everything to the skiff, the blood from Richard's body seeping through his wrappings. "Damn it," exclaimed Raymond. "I hate that woman. I really do."

Poking Shadwell and Clarence with his knife to make sure they're still out, Raymond secures the tarp in a cursory fashion as he's anxious to leave. In regard to Webster's wellbeing, the sooner he heads out the better. If Carlo takes Webster to his hideout to finish her off and Raymond shows up too late, things will be difficult for him. Marcus takes his frustration out on those around him and Raymond meets up with him in a couple of days. He doesn't care one way or the other what happens to Webster. All Raymond wants is some peace and quiet.

Ariel's tranquilizer gun is on the console, and with a long ride ahead, Raymond considers giving the hostages another dose before taking off. He knows they need to be awake, otherwise he may end up killing them. *Great,* he thought. *Why do they always dump this shit on me? If I wait to drug them again I'm wasting valuable time. Stop along the highway and I risk getting caught. Either way I'm screwed.*

"The hell with it," yapped Raymond, shoving the tranquilizer gun in the glove box.

Racing across the tarmac, approaching the terminal, Raymond saw two police cars entering the parking lot. A detective he's seen before is stationed near Carlo's Lincoln and Raymond slows down.

Shit, it's the Creole, thought Raymond, shielding his face.

Monroe watched as Raymond drove right passed him, the patrol cars tearing through the parking lot and Monroe's attention now on the flashing lights.

"What the hell's going on," Raymond said to himself, a cautious, law-abiding speed while looking back.

Flagging down one of the patrol cars, Monroe gave the APB to the officer riding shotgun. Pointing a finger at Raymond's Blazer, he tells the driver to hurry up.

Red and blue lights racing toward the street, Raymond can see them in his rearview mirror. "Oh, shit," he cried, pounding the steering wheel. Prudent with the accelerator, Raymond left the parking lot, the thundering patrol car skidding into the street blocking the driveway.

Peering at the back of the skiff, the driver of the patrol car turned to his partner. "Nice looking rig," he said.

"Should we check it out?"

"No. I got a good look at the driver. That's not him."

The skies over South Florida remain calm, Andrew now twelve-hours east of Miami festering into a Category 4 hurricane. Advising everyone in the Learjet to buckle up, Walter begins his decent northwest of Fort Myers.

"Time to put the cat away, Margaret," said Marcus, swallowing the last of his drink.

"Why? Afraid he'll attack you once you're strapped in."

"I'm concerned for the animal's safety. Now please," said Marcus in a stern voice, "... put him away."

Placing Bourbon in the kennel, Margaret can't help but notice a change in Marcus. "So now you like cats? You must have hit your head hard this time."

"The animal is important to you, is it not? If it remains unharmed you remain happy. I wish not to upset you more than I already have. End of discussion."

Important to me? Margaret reflects on what was said earlier. *It's not Bourbon that frightens him but his DNA. If the right person were to break it down they could create their own youth serum. No, that can't be it ... he would have drowned Bourbon years ago. He's so protective of him. Why?*

Crossing over the island of Cayo Costa, Margaret recalling her beloved Stuart, she looked out the cabin window, his memory etched in the beautiful but harsh landscape below. The trim of white beach along the western shore, enticing her for a walk, Margaret vows to return but not for an afternoon stroll. *I'll be bound elsewhere,* she thought. *Prisoner of the Sandcat once more.*

Bestowed to a landmark Margaret is familiar with, the Sandcat lies on the eastern edge of the island just below the northern tip. A cluster of sandy paths and chalky buildings, from the plane the area looks like a sprawling cat. Its tail, in fact, is a lazy dock bathing amid the placid water.

The trees below its belly, the Sandcat's kingdom, a separate string of oak and pine rise like castle walls in the shape of a giant A. At the apex, a short distance from the Sandcat's paw, Margaret can see a clump of trees where sheets of ivy hide a secret cave. The Sandcat's dungeon, the name of the cave given by Margaret, is the home of those unfortunate souls lured by the fountain.

The jet circles between Sanibel Island and the mainland, a smooth landing and Walter taxiing the private runway of Marcus Córdoba. Killing the engines not far from the open hanger, he positioned the aircraft for an early departure. The runway, close to the harbor, Margaret can see the hazy treetops of Cayo Costa through the cabin window.

"Time to go," said Marcus, a firm grip on Margaret's shoulder.

"I can manage," she replied, breaking free before grabbing the kennel.

"Never mind that," said Marcus, yanking it away from her. "Ariel," he set the kennel down, "… take this inside."

"Yes, Father," Ariel replied, a smug look on her face. She is helping Tantur with his brother, the boy appearing dizzy as they bring him to his feet.

"You look absolutely peaked," observed Marcus. "Shall I send for a doctor?"

It had been an exhausting flight for Wahota. He wants to lie in a bed that isn't moving and sleep until there's no tomorrow. “No,” he answered in English. “I’ll be fine.”

“By tomorrow’s end you will feel a thousand times better,” said Marcus.

Disembarking, Marcus led Margaret up a small hill. A narrow road winding to the top, knee-high foliage and mangrove trees all around, Margaret watched as Ariel came out of the hanger driving a Jeep Cherokee. Driving up the hill, Ariel passed Margaret and her father who move to the shoulder. Sitting on the tailgate, his brother lying next to him, Tantur has an odd look on his face.

Is he worried or is that a plea for help, thought Margaret. She figures it to be one or the other, the way Tantur is holding Wahota’s hand.

At the top of the hill, a fantastic view of Charlotte Harbor, Margaret is taken in by a noble looking estate along the beach instead. The horseshoe complex resembles a Chinese pagoda; its pyramid roof, however, without the upward curve. Arriving at that moment, Ariel drove into one of the garages protruding from the structure; Tantur jumping off the tailgate, taking his brother by the shoulder and helping him down.

Grabbing the kennel, Ariel went through a monstrous gateway, a long stretch on a cobblestone surface, passing what appears to be the centerpiece of the estate. Gracing a shaded portion of the courtyard, water spills from the top tier of a rousing stone fountain, cascading over a middle and bottom tier into a large octagon pool.

At the far end of the opulent setting, a recent addition to the ancient building, Ariel opened a sliding glass door, Margaret waiting for Tantur and his brother to reappear, for she is concerned about Wahota, *wondering if he’s all right*.

“Come along, Margaret,” said Marcus, grabbing her arm. “I have something to show you before we go inside. A surprise at the bottom of the hill.”

Great, thought Margaret. *Surprise me by dropping dead.*

A man-made lagoon lies at the bottom of the hill, complete with a private dock and boathouse jutting from the synthetic shore. The stationary dock has a gleaming coat of lacquer and the walk to the boathouse is somewhat slippery; the planks, fortunately, remaining firm and steady. Adjoined to the inlet side of the lagoon, the boathouse looks every bit as fresh as the dock. Marcus opened the door, advising Margaret to watch her step. "It drops rather quickly," he announced.

Skylights accentuate the steps and Margaret descends to the next level where a mahogany Chris Craft and fiberglass speedboat are moored. Two wall canopies are at the far end and the operating switches behind Margaret. Marcus flips one of the switches and the boats receive a fresh coat of light—a crescent dawn traveling stern to bow.

Spacious windows all around, Marcus flips another switch and the Venetian blinds covering the glass rise in unison with the canopy doors. The floating platform, now moving side to side, Marcus took Margaret by the arm, escorting her to the back of the boathouse.

The lagoon, a secluded paradise, palm trees and tropical vegetation garnish the shoreline. "Very nice," said Margaret, looking beyond the lagoon at Charlotte Harbor. "You could have just turned on the lights. I've seen this harbor many times."

"Yes, but when did you last see this," said Marcus, pointing to the mahogany Chris Craft—a 1930 Runabout with *Lady Bird* scripted on the stern. Shadows cast from the boathouse ooze across the gold lettering and a bright memory emerges from Margaret's past. She remembers William shooting Marcus and his bloody head smashing against the boat.

"I see this pleases you," said Marcus.

"Yes. The last time I saw the Lady Bird, William got the better of you."

"And I recall what brought that on. This was a gift, was it not? Yet you sold it upon my questioning William's intentions."

"Where did you find it?"

"Panama City. I would have walked passed it if not for the name. It was in fair condition and the owner had no intentions of parting with it. I wanted it so bad he nearly fainted when I told him how much I was willing to pay. Are you surprised?"

"I'm surprised you offered to buy it. When someone tells you no, they usually end up at the bottom of some lake."

"Shocking, is it not? Five years ago I may have done that. Now it's live and let live for me … *when acceptable of course*."

"What are you doing, Marcus? I got rid of the Lady Bird because of the trouble it caused."

"I thought you might like to have it back."

The reaction on Margaret's face made it clear she didn't. Knowing she would refuse, the answer Marcus gave for the boat's acquisition infuriated Margaret even more.

"Your admirer, *or suitor*," Marcus began, "… though he purchased the boat somewhat suspiciously, I'm sure William's intentions were noble. I never understood how a houseboy could afford such a gift. Not until I finished the restoration. It came to me admiring the lusty engine and smooth exterior one morning. I invested a great deal of time and money, and that boy of yours must have done the same, performing more than just servile labor to accumulate such a vast amount."

"How dare you insinuate that I paid for his affections. William earned those wages honorably."

"Yes, I'm sure he did. And what a thoughtful gift for his employer."

"What I pay my help is my business, Marcus. I do not expect someone like you to understand the meaning of generosity."

"I do understand. I acquired this boat to show you such generosity. I am no longer consumed by trifle jealousy. I want to be with you, Margaret, and I'm willing to accept your past relations in doing so. I will not allow myself to be bothered by them any longer."

"No, I wouldn't think so," Margaret agreed. "They're either dead or too old now." *What drives him to such lengths as this,* thought Margaret. *He honestly believes his indifference will change the way I feel. A killer plain as can be, I will never forgive him for depriving me of my family.*

"I sense your disgust, Margaret. But allow me this. Who else has gone through time as long as I searching for his soul mate, only to be denied that which makes him whole? Must I suffer a lifetime of regret knowing I failed to win you over?"

"Love is not something to be won, Marcus. And it's not something you can take. *Yet you've taken from me those I love the most.* How can you even conceive the notion I would willfully love you?"

"There are ways," answered Marcus, removing the sandstone from his pocket.

Why me, Margaret asked herself. *I don't deserve this.*

There is a moment of silence and Margaret stared at the horizon—Cayo Costa the origin of her misery. She sends a prayer that way. Not to God but pleading with the island to take Marcus. She asks the spirit of the fountain to drag him down where evil resides. *Please, I beg of you. Take him. Take him now!*

Marcus, gently caressing the sandstone, both he and Margaret are looking across the harbor. Marcus concentrates on the faint silhouette of the island, the Sandcat's realm floating toward him, drawing close to his eye. He can see the entrance to the cave as though it were in front of him.

Taking a deep breath, Marcus summons another of his heightened senses. With Hurricane Andrew fast approaching, the air around him reeks of precipitation. A beginning without an end, the essence of the storm penetrates his mind's insight.

"It's getting closer," he alerted Margaret. "I can smell it."

"Smell what?"

"The falling rain."

PART II

Running for Shelter

Twenty

BETWEEN IDLENESS and sleep, wonder and dreams, Nathan woke up in a wooden chair with his arms and legs tied to the framework. Lifting his head, he remembers dreaming about a woman whose face is now obscure. She called his name crying for help and Nathan ran to her, a primitive looking man pulling her away and nothing he can do.

The tranquilizer clouding his memory, bits and pieces of the morning begin to surface. He saw the face of a young man chasing him through the woods, Shadwell sitting across from him telling the story of when he and Margaret first met. Nathan can hear the old man's voice as though he were there in front of him. Concentrating on something important, Nathan trying to remember what it was, a smoldering house crept into his thoughts. The woman with the obscure face was there and he saw again at the airport, a man sneaking up behind her, reaching out and grabbing—

"*Laurian!*"

The last glimpse of her, dispelling fear as he slept, with an unbound awareness Nathan knew Laurian was in trouble. He looked around the room but she's not there.

Across from him, a sport-coat hangs over the back of another chair. Between the chairs a tranquilizer gun and spare dart sit atop a wooden footstool. The shabby room, spinning around him, Nathan saw a number of fishing and gigging poles crowding the far corner. He's alone as far as he can tell. No Carlo or pale looking accomplice… only the sport-coat and tranquilizer gun.

Where is she! Where's Laurian?

Nathan tussled with the rope around his arms and feet. "*Wait a minute*," he said to himself. "*What was that?*"

A toilet flushed and a door opened behind him, followed by light footsteps and a man's fidgety voice.

"Finally woke up, huh."

Taking up the other chair is the man who shot him.

"Where are we," asked Nathan, an aggressive, demanding tone.

"Smack-dab in the middle of nowhere," answered Vincent. "Nothin' but swamp for as far as you can see."

"The woman who was with me, where is she?"

"She's all right. More worried about you than herself. You must have been really tired," said Vincent, picking up the spare dart. "They last for a couple of hours but you've been out for three. My partner couldn't wait another minute. He took your girlfriend and a bottle of whiskey out back."

"*Your partner* … you mean Carlo don't you?"

"That's not his name," Vincent skittishly shot back.

"Sure it is. A cop showed me his picture. You two are in a lot of trouble."

"Is that so?"

"If he harms her in any way—"

"Look, mister," Vincent cut Nathan off, slamming the dart on the footstool, rising to his feet, "… I got no say in any of this. I'm as concerned about her as you are. I don't care too much for all this kidnapping and k—"

"—*killing*?" Nathan kept his eyes on Vincent, the timid

little man disappearing behind him, rubbing his knuckles.

"You had nothing to do with my grandmother's kidnapping," asked Nathan. "*Or the death of my mother and father!?*"

"No!" screamed Vincent, swinging his chalky face around. He paused for a moment, stepping from behind the chair pacing the floor in front of Nathan. "He's crazy you know. They all are! But Carlo— he's a different kind of crazy. The rest of 'em don't care one way or the other about killing people so long as it's done. Carlo on the other hand, takes pleasure in it."

"What are you saying," asked Nathan, glaring up at him.

"I'm sorry. I wish I could help but he'd kill me if I did. Sorry about your parents too," said Vincent as he sat down. "I had nothing to do with it. I swear. I wasn't even around when it happened. I stay away from those jobs."

"He killed my parents, this Carlo Somoza. Didn't he?"

"Yes."

"*My God, Laurian!* You have to untie me," screamed Nathan. Jerking the chair back and forth, Nathan stopped all of a sudden, looking Vincent square in the eye. "Please, I beg of you. You can't just sit there and do nothing."

"You don't understand. He meant what he said about killing me."

"I'll take him out," pledged Nathan. "I swear to God … if I have to, *I'll kill him myself.*"

"Even if you did, it wouldn't matter. They'd just send someone else after me. Besides, you're safe. We're supposed to keep you out here for a couple of days, that's all."

"And my friend, what's going to happen to her?"

"I don't know."

Nathan had no idea Vincent was telling the truth. He thought about Laurian in the hands of a killer, lowering his head in grief.

The windows draped with bed sheets, making the 1,200 square-foot shed dark and gloomy, Carlo lights a cigarette. Caressing the filter between his lips, the soft glow from the match reflects ominously off his face.

Hanging from the rafters, a canvas tarp separates the shed. Between the tarp and door there is an empty gurney with a bottom shelf full of bed sheets and plastic covers. Part of the grim atmosphere, a cleaver and hacksaw dangle frightfully from a support post beside the gurney. A small, paint-blistered table with sharp and serrated cutlery stands next to the post; Carlo's .32 caliber and bottle of Jack Daniels sitting at the edge.

Carlo takes a long drag from his cigarette, grabbing the bottle of whiskey for the umpteenth time. Tipping his head, the rush of nicotine and alcohol corrupting his brain, there is a shoddy-looking pirogue in the rafters. Another long hit from the cigarette and now a lengthy exhale, *Carlo swirling the smoke in the canoe*, his little ritual is complete.

The stench of dust and past sins fouling the air, Carlo takes his gun and the bad influence of Jack Daniels to the other side of the tarp—a dim world behind the dark one.

Her back literally against the wall, no way of escaping that world, Laurian's hands are tied above her head with the rope stretching to the rafters. A blindfold hides her innocent eyes, therefore, her ears capturing the unimaginable horror.

There is a window on that side and the sun is creeping down a stack of boxes full of canned foods; Laurian sensing a poignant end to her unfinished life.

Carlo put the gun on another small table. Staggering forward, he reach out, stroking Laurian's cheek with the back of his hand. The smell of sweat and whiskey in her face, Laurian delivers a wild shot to Carlo's thigh with her knee.

"Calm down, little lady," said Carlo, stepping back.

Unbuttoning the top of his shirt, rolling up his sleeves, Carlo grabbed the leftover rope he used to string Laurian from the rafters.

"What are you doing," Laurian cried out. She can feel her pant leg moving; a pair of clammy hands suddenly around her left ankle. "No. No! Please, stop it!"

The rope now secured to her ankle, Laurian can hear Carlo pounding a nail into the baseboard.

"Please don't do this," begged Laurian, Carlo cinching her left ankle in place. "Don't tie me up like this. I won't fight you. I promise."

Carlo drove another nail into the opposite side. He looped the remaining rope around the nail inserting a slipknot, half hitching it to Laurian's right ankle. Pulling the rope, he forced her legs apart, tying the end to the first nail.

With both legs spread open, Laurian is hanging from her wrists. Tears are dripping from the blindfold and she can feel her heart swelling with fear.

"There," said Carlo. "Now you'll behave."

"Why are you doing this," asked Laurian.

"Nothing personnel," answered Carlo, lighting another cigarette. "An associate of mine doesn't care too much for you. I on the other hand," he inhales her perfume, "… can't understand why. A beautiful woman like you."

Another look around the shanty, Nathan saw no plasterboard or insulation on the walls. There are no pictures hanging from the framework, just an outdated Rockwell calendar. The sun, peeking through the clapboard, Nathan noticed a door to his left and another over his shoulder. He knew a bathroom was directly behind him so there must be another room next to it.

Tattered blankets covered all the windows, two in front of him and two more to the left. To his right, a doctors bag sits in the middle of a kitchen table and there are two chairs tucked underneath. Beyond that, against the wall, there is a sink with an old lift pump. Having no lights or television, there doesn't appear to be any electricity in the room.

A mildewed couch behind Nathan, Vincent picked up a book returning to his chair. There is just enough light from the tattered blankets to read and Vincent settles in.

Nathan wiggles in his bindings and Vincent peered over the top of the book. "I wish you'd stay still," he said. "That tranquilizer gun is loaded and I won't hesitate to use it."

"My bladders' about to burst. I need to use the toilet."

"Not until Carlo gets back. Sorry."

"Look man, I've got to—"

"Shh," Vincent interrupted him. "I heard something outside."

Grabbing the tranquilizer gun, Vincent said he'd be right back.

On a remote bayou island, the shanty is surrounded by cypress trees cloaked in Spanish moss. With two hours of daylight left, Vincent abandoning the porch, he followed the tranquilizer gun down a dusky, tree infested trail. The shed Carlo took Laurian to is on the right, but the sound Vincent heard is in front of him; something hollow bouncing off something hard.

There it is again, thought Vincent, drawing closer.

A clearing at the edge of the island, a slope of tender earth meshing with the murky swamp, Vincent discovers Raymond mooring his skiff to the dock; a total of three as there are two more boats on the opposite side.

All the low spots on the island are sectioned off with wire fence to keep the alligators out; the dock having a lengthy section at each end. Plastic barrels secured to its underside, the 15-foot makeshift dock hugs the water and Vincent teeters precariously across. "You sure make a lot of noise," he said to Raymond.

"This lousy dock is movin' all over the place. I don't know which is worse," blurted Raymond, "… a skiff full of bodies I can't control or this floating piece of shit. I had a hell of a time moving these guys to the side."

"We had the same problem," said Vincent. He looked at the bodies in the skiff, the evening sun casting a shadow across its blood-stained hull. "Is that what I think it is?"

"Yeah, Ariel had a little accident. Shot the pilot point-blank in the chest with a 12-gauge."

"And I thought Carlo was the vicious one."

"Speaking of which, has he taken care of the doctor yet?"

"What do you mean? He took her to the shed fifteen minutes ago. Said he was gonna have a little fun."

Raymond scrambled off the vacillating dock with Vincent close behind. "What about the grandson," asked Raymond.

"Got 'em tied up in the house. Matter of fact he just came to. I shot 'em with a full dose at the airport."

"*Jesus*, Vincent … it's a wonder he's still alive. Tantur's little brother pumped him full of pygmy darts this morning."

"Well how was I supposed to know?"

"How's he feelin'?"

"A lot better than the pilot, that's for sure."

"Very funny. Come on, how's he doin'?"

"He's okay."

"All right, you get back inside," said Raymond. "I need to stop Carlo before it's too late."

"*Too late*. Too late for what?"

Twenty-one

LAURIAN CAN HEAR his shoes crushing the ground, the gulping of whiskey and a startling thump; Carlo slamming the bottle on the table. "You know," he spoke to her on the other side of the tarp, "we don't receive many guests out here. Not that it bothers me. One less pig on the chopping block as far as that goes."

Laurian has no idea what he's talking about. The rope she's hanging from is bruising her wrists and she's trying desperately to stand on her feet. A loose knot fastened to the rafters, thrusting her shoulders she constricts the rope just enough to anchor her left foot in place.

"Where are you," exclaimed Carlo, rummaging through his cutlery, "… we have work to do." A swig of whiskey and his worst foot forward, Carlo stepped around the tarp, Laurian hearing nothing but the beating of her heart. "This," he rattled his tongue, "… is the sharpest of them all. I don't know why— *it just is*."

Laurian felt his unscrupulous breath, the blindfold and her body trembling as a sharp blade gradually chafes her face. Carlo, pressing against her, she feels the revolver tucked in his trousers. She is certain he cut her face but doesn't feel any blood. *Is he scraping it away*, she thought.

Running the blade along Laurian's neck, Carlo can feel the writhing of her heart. "My favorite knife," he whispered in her ear. "A merciless edge, not one pig have I slaughtered in vain."

Laurian swallows the bitter air of those words, the knife now under her blouse and Carlo rubbing her thigh. Eyes blind and cold steel to her breast, Carlo slicing buttons down her blouse, Laurian's heart beats faster and faster. "It will be dark soon," said Carlo, "… and he will come for you. I call him El Cid. An abnormality, he feeds every day."

Breath upon breath, Laurian's fear strengthening his desire, Carlo drew closer. "You're the salt of the earth," he tells her, "… what Aerosmith calls, 'queen of the brine.'" Raising the knife to her neck, Carlo ran his fingers atop her bra. "And what good is a meal without flavor. *A little spice in our pathetic lives*."

Stepping back, Carlo takes another drink, his eyes gorging on Laurian's pounding chest. "It's not easy keeping that animal satisfied. But who do I talk to if he abandons me? Tell me," asked Carlo, grabbing Laurian by the throat. "Who … *who do I talk to then?*"

"You can talk to me. I'll take care of you," said Laurian, tempting him. "For as long as you want."

"I'm not supposed to do that," said Carlo squeezing her throat.

"Why not," replied Laurian, quivering under Carlo's strong grip. "No one will know. Not if you keep it to yourself."

"Sure … sure, whatever you say," said Carlo, letting go of her throat.

Scraping the knife up and down her neck, suddenly Carlo pulls away. Laurian heard the noise too. Trading the knife for the revolver, Carlo warns her to keep quiet as there are footsteps on the other side of the tarp. After a long pause,

Carlo points the gun chest high, flipping back the canvas.

"Whoa!" screamed Raymond, throwing up his arms.

"What the hell are you doing," said Carlo, lowering the gun.

"*What the hell am I doing*," Raymond peeked at Laurian, "… what the hell are *you* doing!"

"Never you mind," said Carlo, escorting Raymond to the door.

"You're sick. You know that?"

"Yeah … so?"

"Look," Raymond shook it off, "… there's been a change of plans. She's not dead, is she?"

"Not yet."

"Well keep it that way. Marcus didn't get what he came for and she's to be kept alive until he does."

"Damn it, Ray! How am I going to feed my gator? You best have a pig with you or I'll—"

"Calm down," said Raymond. "You know I never come out here empty handed."

"No, I guess not," answered Carlo. "So I'm to put away my blade this time, is that it?"

"No harm to any of them. His words, not mine."

"*Them?* What do you mean … *them?*"

"Got two more live ones for you," whispered Raymond. "The old man and his nephew."

"I can still have fun with the doctor, right?"

"As long as you keep her alive."

"You're welcome to join us," said Carlo, taking a drink and wiping his mouth.

"I'm not into that, Carlo. You should know that by now."

"Come on, this one's a real looker."

"So I've heard," answered Raymond. "Thanks, but no thanks. I've got my eye on that little waitress in Samstown."

"Yeah, well … whatever chalks your cue."

The two men left the shed, a precautionary length of fence sloping toward the water at the north-east corner; the side Laurian is hanging from. Carlo, staggering along the way, Raymond saved him from falling off the dock. "When are you gonna fix this thing," clamored Raymond.

"Why should I? The only time you ever come out here is to drop off a pig. You don't even get out of the boat."

"Let's get this over with," said Raymond, taking hold of Richard's jacket, he and Carlo then dragging the body out of the skiff.

Taylor followed Holiday into the security office, slamming the door. "I can't believe no one saw him."

"It's late," said Jerry. "If anyone did they left hours ago."

"Or they don't remember," blurted the dispatcher, buried in a magazine.

"*Riley?*"

"Yeah."

"What are you still doing here?"

"Waiting for my replacement."

"This outfit needs to screen its employees better," said Jerry shaking his head. Heading for the vending machines, he turned to Taylor. "Let me grab a soda before we sit down. Want anything?"

"Yeah," Taylor replied, pulling out some change, "… coffee."

"I got it," said Jerry, feeding the machine—money saved from raiding refrigerators throughout the airport.

Returning to the front desk, Jerry asks Riley if he changed the afternoon tapes.

" ' Bout an hour ago," said Riley, immersed in his Monster Trucks.

The control room is an oversized closet. A horseshoe

work-station stacked with monitors and video equipment, Taylor wastes no time finding a seat. “Nice setup,” he said, taking a quick look around.

“Belongs to the airport,” replied Jerry, plopping next to Taylor. “We monitor everything with the exception of restrooms and private hangers.”

“That’s fine,” said Taylor, placing Carlo’s mug shot between them. “How do you suggest we go about this?”

“I’d focus on the terminal for now,” answered Jerry. “Split the morning and afternoon tapes.”

“There’s a woman I’m looking for as well,” said Taylor. “Extremely attractive. Five-six, five-seven maybe. Blue eyes— *I think*. I couldn’t tell from where I was standing.”

“So which do you prefer, Detective. Morning or afternoon?”

“Excuse me,” said Taylor, Laurian’s mental picture still in his head.

“Which tape would you like to review? Morning or afternoon?”

“I’ll take the morning,” answered Taylor.

Once the old bank of Louisiana, the stationhouse with its neoclassical columns out of place in the French Quarter, Alcott and two patrolmen block the front steps.

“Where was he when you left,” Alcott questioned the patrolmen.

“With a security guard,” answered the first patrolman.

“And Monroe?”

“Watching the suspect’s vehicle.”

“You’re sure he said it was his idea to send Taylor inside.”

“That’s what he told us,” said the second patrolman.

“And they’ve been there all this time,” asked Alcott checking his watch.

"Yes sir. We were the first to arrive."

"All right, thanks," said Alcott, the patrolmen heading up the steps.

Connie poked her head out the door calling to Alcott. "There's a sergeant from Atlanta PD holding for you. Said he was returning your call. What do you want me to do?"

"Tell him I'll be right there," answered Alcott.

Alcott took the call with Taylor's file in front of him. "Sorry it took so long," he greets the sergeant, "… I stepped out for a smoke."

"That's all right, Captain. What can I do for you?"

"I need some information on a former patrolman. He's a detective in my department now."

"What's the name?"

"Taylor, Samuel Taylor."

"Doesn't ring a bell."

"Says here," Alcott scans the file, "… he served five years in your department."

"I've been here for over ten and I don't recall a Samuel Taylor."

"Are you sure? I spoke with the Personnel Director myself. He was highly recommended."

"Believe me, Captain, we've never had anyone here by that name. If we did, I'd certainly remember."

Alcott apologized for wasting the sergeant's time. He hung up switching to a private line, dialing the number himself. "Thomas Moore, please," said Alcott, enunciating the name. "Hello, Thomas. …Fine, and yourself? …Sultry. How are things in New York, you and Rachel still together? …You've been saying that forever. …Those friends you have in Washington, the ones with mainframe access … can you get them to run a trace for me?"

Something jabbed Clarence in the back. His eyes are closed and it took a moment to recall what's going on. The last time he woke up, he saw a man pointing a gun at his chest. His hands were bound behind him and his legs wrapped in duct tape like they are now.

The sun arching above the trees, his uncle lay beside him in the skiff, unconscious as far as Clarence can tell. Worming forward, his posterior portside, Clarence takes hold of what's poking him; a loose toe-guard. Struggling to draw close in order to cut his bindings, he took hold of the jagged toe-guard. Anchored to the hull, the narrow strip won't reach the tape. Undaunted, Clarence thought of something else, bending the metal strip back and forth trying to sever the loose end.

His arms are cramping and he's forced to rest. His time is cut short, however, as there are voices heading toward him. Footsteps pounding the dock, he shut his eyes and continued, the metal now heating up.

"They're still out," said Carlo.

"We'll take the boy first," replied Raymond, climbing into the skiff.

Clarence, a moment of victory, the end of the toe-guard broke off but he dropped it—the metal too hot to handle. Keeping still while feeling around for the metal strip, Clarence can't find it, clawing desperately at his backside with Raymond lifting him up.

"Careful," yelled Carlo, the dock shifting and Raymond dropping Clarence.

His back slamming against the fiberglass hull, Clarence held back a groan, franticly searching for the metal strip.

"Damn it, Carlo! Would you mind staying still for a minute?"

Raymond pulled Clarence out by the shoulders, Carlo then grabbing his legs. The boy's head hanging to the side, they carry him from the dock, unaware that he's eyeing the skiff and its markings.

Once inside the shanty, the two men lay Clarence face up next to Nathan, his body motionless on the dusty floor.

"What have you done to him," exclaimed Nathan.

"Just a little sedative," answered Raymond, "… he should be coming around in no time."

"I thought you were in a hurry," said Carlo, stepping forward.

Nathan eyes, screaming with hatred, he grabs hold of Carlo's undivided attention.

"What are you looking at," blared Carlo.

"It's not what I'm looking at," said Nathan, his voice and posture seething. "It's what I'm sizing up."

Angered by the remark, Carlo smacks Nathan in the mouth, Raymond then pulling Carlo away. "Knock it off, will you."

"*What?*"

"You're so annoying," said Raymond, stepping over Clarence. "Come on. Let's get the other one so I can get out of here."

"We'll finish this later," said Carlo, blood oozing from Nathan's lip.

The two men are out the door and immediately Vincent is heading for the sink. "See what I mean," he said, wetting a towel.

"He's not so tough," replied Nathan.

"He doesn't have to be. He wouldn't have hit you if you weren't tied up."

"That kind of intimidation doesn't scare me."

"Well it scares me," said Vincent, wiping the blood from Nathan's chin.

"I don't need that," Nathan turned away. "Check on the boy."

Clarence lay there with his arms under his back and

Vincent knelt beside him, inspecting his forehead. "He's fine. Nothing to worry about."

"Can you get him a pillow or something?"

"I better not," answered Vincent. "Not without asking."

Nathan and Vincent looked at one another for a short time. Vincent then took an uneasy breath returning to his book, unaware of Clarence stirring at his feet.

The porch creaked and Vincent blanched into a deep shade of fear, obediently opening the door.

"All right, I'm outta here," said Raymond, he and Carlo laying Shadwell between Clarence and the outside door.

"How 'bout you bring us a pig tomorrow," said Carlo.

"That gator has enough to last a while. I won't be back for at least a week."

"It's not for the gator," Carlo appealed to him. "I was just thinkin' 'bout our guests here."

Vincent, caught in the middle, disappeared into the other room returning with a pillow in each hand. "They're going to wake up sore," he said, moving away from Carlo over to Raymond.

"We're not running a bed and breakfast here," snapped Carlo. "Put those back where they belong."

"*Just thinkin' 'bout our guests*, huh, Carlo," said Raymond. "You'll be sleeping in shifts, why don't you give the old man a pillow."

"Fine," said Carlo, a stern eye toward Vincent.

"We need to talk privately," Raymond said to Carlo.

Carlo followed Raymond outside and the two men stopped at the edge of the porch. "Remember what I said," Raymond looked Carlo in the eye, "… no harm to any of them. That goes for Vincent too. You got that? I'll bring some supplies tomorrow if that's what you want."

"We need more fuel and something we can barbecue. This canned shit is getting old."

"I'll bring you a nice, fat pig. I'll even get out of the boat. Which, by the way, I'm leaving you the small skiff and taking the 12-foot with me. I'm going to need it to bring you some extra supplies. Now tell me, did you find anything on the doctor?"

"No, nothing."

Carlo lied of course. He would never tell Raymond about the map-box. He thought if that no-good chauffeur took credit for the disk, he'd lose out on some big money. *I'll look after it until the time is right*, Carlo said to himself.

"What about the grandson," asked Raymond.

"He was clean too."

"They had no papers or folder of any kind?"

"You heard what I said … nothing!"

"You nabbed 'em at the airport, right?"

"Yeah, not far from her crappy looking van."

"Damn! She may have left it inside. I'll check it out tomorrow."

"Is that all," asked Carlo, "… I'd like to get back to what I was doing if that's all right with you."

"Take it easy on her, Carlo. I come back here tomorrow and you've roughed her up, you can count on seeing Marcus face to face."

Twenty-two

NATHAN'S THOUGHTS are fighting a nauseous battle over whether or not Laurian is all right. Tugging frantically at his restraints, a rotten feeling inside, with time running out he conjures a mental image of a white flag smothering him. "You have to let me go," he said to Vincent, looking him in the eye. "You know what he's going to do and with his temper he could end up killing her. Please, untie me. You don't want this on your conscious."

"He's not out there to kill her," Vincent assured him.

"You seem like a decent sort," said Nathan, challenging Vincent, "... but if you don't help me he's going to rape her. Why would you let that happen?"

"Because!" Vincent jumped up. "I don't want anything to happen to my daughter. I never see her but I still love her."

Nathan understood. The injustice men suffer, Vincent is more than an expendable pawn. He wallows in a society he was led to believe is free. Carlo, a pernicious heart laden upon mankind, he is the cowed piece pervading the board keeping Vincent in check.

No, thought Nathan, hating Carlo even more, *I can't give up hope. There's more at stake than what goes on here.*

"What's your name," asked Nathan.

"I'd rather not say," answered Vincent, turning away.

"Please, I'd like to know."

"Why? So you can tell the police once you're free."

"I won't. Even if I did, would you really be worse off in jail?"

"I don't know. But I can't give you my name. Carlo warned me not to."

This poor soul, thought Nathan, Vincent pacing the floor behind him. "Make up a name. I have to call you something."

"No," said Vincent, returning to his seat.

All of a sudden Shadwell let out a groan catching Vincent off guard. "*What was that*," he asked.

"The old man," answered Nathan. "Sounds like he's having a bad dream."

Shadwell, a bad dream indeed, he can't wake up. The tranquilizer is wearing off but he's trapped in a recurring nightmare—his suppressed youth torturing him.

Running through a thicket of brush and pine, twenty-two-year-old William looked back without breaking stride. Firing his revolver into the woods, a dart comes whizzing passed his head in return.

Hiding behind a fat tree, William scours the brush for his assailant.

Whoosh! Another dart misses and William wastes another round, his legs up and running down a narrow path.

The path split in two and William immediately undertakes the route furthest from the shore, snapping a select number of branches along the way. Moving slowly through a thick portion of brush, he's careful with his footing, backtracking a short distance and abandoning the path; hellbent on making it to the shore.

Leaving the woods, William turns south with no one chasing him as far as he can tell. Within a few minutes he caught up with Margaret on her private dock, talking to some man; the Lady Bird moored at their feet.

There she is, thought William, quickening his pace. *But who is that man with her?*

William went back in the trees, venturing forward to get a closer look.

"You have a glow about you, Margaret. Are you in love again," asked the man, taunting her.

"Let go of me," answered Margaret, breaking free.

"Answer me, Margaret," the man takes hold of her again.

"Stop it, you're hurting me."

"Let go of her!" shouted William from the end of the dock.

"Is this the man you're in love with, Margaret?"

William strode forcefully across the dock, disclosing his revolver at the last second. "I said, *let her go!*"

"Very well," replied the man. "I must say, Margaret, this one is in better shape than your last beau. I commend you young man on your performance. It is not every day one eludes a Cariban Warrior."

"Who is this, Margaret," demanded William.

"Your help is rather impertinent," said the man. "Not the proper subservience I would expect from one's hired hand … or any good Negro for that matter."

"You hold your tongue," cried William, pointing the gun in a threatening manner.

"Somewhat brash too, wouldn't you say. My, my, *Lady Bird Margaret*," said the man in reference to her boat, "… expensive gifts … first name basis. It appears you have been up to more than just searching for the cave."

Suddenly William realizes who it is he's pointing the gun at. "This is him. Isn't it? The man who gave you the map.

The one who had Stuart killed."

"Yes," said Margaret. "Marcus Córdoba. Or Sucràm, depending on which country he's in."

"I prefer Marcus in this one," he said to her. "But you," Marcus kept his eye on William, "… you shall address me as Señor Córdoba. Or Master, considering the country we're in."

"That's enough, Marcus!" shouted Margaret stepping in.

Marcus could see the hate in young William's eyes, as did Margaret; a look she thought he was incapable of displaying.

"You made quite a bit of noise out there," said Marcus, gazing at the revolver. "By my count you have but one bullet left, and now is not the time to flex your muscles. I suggest you lower your weapon and stand aside."

"No," said William, cocking the gun.

"Stand aside! I shall not tell you again."

His eyes on Marcus the entire time, for one brief moment William looked at Margaret. "It ends here and now," he proclaimed, squeezing the trigger.

The bullet takes Marcus by surprise. A head shot he went down immediately, bouncing off the stern of Margaret's boat into the shallow water. Moments later there is a dark hue rising to the surface.

"My God! *You shot him*."

"It's over," said William.

Margaret then screamed as William foundered to his knees, a harrowing look on his face by virtue of a dart protruding from his neck.

"Will!" Nathan called out, the old man coming around. "You okay?"

"Not particularly, no. Where are we," asked Shadwell, his eyes now open.

"Some shanty in the middle of nowhere."

"And Clarence?"

"Lying next to you."

"We're not going to hurt you," said Vincent. "Sorry about all this. You'll be back home in no time. How are you feeling? Would you like to sit up?"

"I'm seventy-eight years old and my hands are tied behind my back. *How do you think I feel!?*"

"I don't know … *you look okay,*" said Vincent propping him up.

"Ouch! Take it easy," cried Shadwell. "I'm as stiff as a board right now."

"Sorry," said Vincent, helping Shadwell to his feet; the old man's ankles bound with tape.

As Vincent and Shadwell make their way to the couch, Nathan looked at Clarence who is scanning the room with a sneaky eye. Taking his hand from underneath his back, a piece of duct tape hanging off, Clarence glanced at Nathan with a smirk on his face.

Good boy, mouthed Nathan, checking the whereabouts of Vincent, he and Shadwell directly behind him.

"How's that," asked Vincent.

"What's that smell," replied Shadwell, wriggling in the cushion.

"I'm afraid it's the couch. Not much to look at but it is comfortable."

"If I wasn't tied up I'm sure it would be."

"Try not to think about that. You'll be out of those bindings as soon as my partner gets back."

"You can call him by his name," said Nathan, tweaking his head. "Carlo," he blared. "His name is Carlo, Will. And he's got Laurian out back."

"Where's Richard," asked Shadwell looking around.

"I thought he was with you," replied Nathan.

"He was," said Shadwell, lowering his brow at Vincent. "*Where is he?*"

"I don't know."

Vincent stepped away from the couch, and as Shadwell confronts the lie, a scream disquiets the air.

"Laurian! He's hurting her," shouted Nathan. "Do something!"

The tranquilizer gun in hand, Vincent put it on the footstool, the pale little man mulling over what to do. Nathan screamed again and with the terror on their faces colliding, Vincent took a deep breath. He stepped over Clarence heading to the kitchen and the boy grabbed his ankle toppling him to the floor. Vincent landed on his shoulder, the tranquilizer gun within reach. He stretched out, knocking it off the stool trying to grab it.

Clarence, his legs still bound, wriggles across the floor heading for the gun.

Vincent is crawling toward the gun as well, a little closer than Clarence despite the fact it lay between them. The first to arrive, Vincent goes for the gun but Clarence shoved him away.

Scouring the floor blindly with one hand, keeping Vincent at bay with the other, Clarence felt the gun at his fingertips.

Vincent saw this, and while scrambling to his feet, a loud pop rattles the air. With his back in the wrong position, Vincent realized he made a terrible mistake.

Compressed air injects the tranquilizer upon impact and Vincent can feel the effects right away. Lost in a moment of disbelief, he spun around falling aimlessly to the floor.

"My name," said Vincent, staring up at Nathan, his speech tapering off, "… my name is … *Vince-e-e-e-e-e-nt*."

Establishing his bearings, the sun burrowing into the trees, Nathan followed the trail leading to the dock. From there he can see Carlo outside the shed heading for the door, dressed in what appears to be a butcher's apron.

Flaccid and out of breath, Nathan slumps beside the decrepit looking shed. The window on his side is covered by a bed sheet and he peeks through a knothole to find out what's inside. The canvas tarp, separating the room, the first thing he sees is the whiskey bottle on the small table. At that angle the knives are not visible, nor the hacksaw and butcher's apron hanging from the support post. The gurney, as he can see, now has something on top and there is a bloodstained sheet draped over it. Nathan can only imagine what's underneath.

"*Oh my God, no. That can't be her,*" he said to himself.

His face between his knees and anger festering, Nathan gathered his strength, the tranquilizer gun too humane for what he has in mind.

Nathan looked down at the gun, which Shadwell said was easy to use. The old man wasn't up for this and Nathan told Clarence to keep an eye on him.

Rising to his feet, Nathan thought he heard voices in the shed. Looking through the knothole, nothing had changed. He figures the voices are coming from behind the tarp, rushing around to another knothole.

On the backside of the shed, he witnesses the unthinkable. Laurian is strung-up with her blouse open and handkerchief covering her eyes. Carlo has a cleaver ridden with blood, rubbing it across her bra. Suddenly, he drew back his arm, thrusting the cleaver into the wall while latching onto Laurian's blouse. She screamed but it didn't stop him from ripping her blouse away.

Wasting no time, Nathan burst through the door throwing back the tarp. He stretched out his arms, aiming the gun at

Carlo's back, but with Laurian being too close decides not to take the shot.

Turning around, a surprised look on his face, Carlo saw the type of gun pointed at him. He went for the .32 caliber right away and Nathan fired the gun hitting him in the chest. The revolver within reach, Carlo takes hold of the dart instead, wrenching the spurting hypodermic from his flesh.

"You should have shot me in the back when you had the chance," said Carlo. "They're not as effective without a full dose. And like any wild animal, all you did was piss me off. Now I'm gonna rip you apart."

Once again Carlo is heading for the table, Nathan fast-balling the empty gun at his head.

Dodging the gun, Carlo picked up the revolver, Nathan plunging forward, knocking him over the boxes of canned food. Carlo doesn't have a good grip on the revolver and it settles under a section of missing lapboard. Carlo goes for the gun on his hands and knees, Nathan diving for his legs and hogtying him in place.

Carlo can't move forward, and out of frustration rolls over, crowning Nathan with a two-fisted chop. The blow has a rippling effect, and with Nathan relaxing his grip, Carlo broke free, booting him in the throat.

Nathan clutched his bruised thorax, gasping for air. He can't recover fast enough and he sees Carlo tugging at the cleaver buried in the wall.

Drawing back his arm as he did earlier, Carlo gave Nathan fair warning of his intent. Nathan tumbles to the right and Carlo hurled the cleaver into the dirt floor. Rolling under the tarp, Nathan scrambled to his feet, eyeing the knives atop the small table. Rushing to the table, Carlo picked up the cleaver on the other side, slicing through the tarp and letting it fly.

The cleaver barely missed his shoulder and Nathan leaned

over the gurney stretching for the knives. Whatever it is underneath the sheet, he can't reach far enough, having to settle for the whiskey bottle instead.

Bursting through the severed tarp, Carlo lunged forward taking a vicious swing at Nathan. In a single move, Nathan stepped to the side, swinging the bottle at Carlo's head.

The bottle missed but with Carlo lumbering back it was as good as a hit. Trying to maintain his balance, Nathan coming after him, Carlo bumped into the gurney pulling the sheet off as he fell to the floor.

A shocking, grotesque sight, Nathan nearly lost his stomach. Richard lay face up on the gurney, his chest an open cavity and his right arm missing—along with the sleeve from his flight jacket.

In that brief moment, Nathan distracted by the work of something truly evil, Carlo shot up like a guided missile tackling Nathan at the waist. Tumbling into the tarp, ripping it from the rafters, the two men are stuck underneath kicking and clawing at one another—Nathan more so to get away than anything else. He can feel what little space there is closing in on him.

Ironically, in the terror of her darkness, Laurian wants the same thing—to get away. Listening to the braying of both men, she has no idea it's Nathan under the tarp. Carlo, judging by the ranting, his back against the ruffling canvas, has the upper hand.

Laurian can hear the other man struggling to pull Carlo off and by the sound of it he does. But Carlo lands outside the tarp on his feet, violently kicking his opponent over and over.

An agonizing yowl, the man's identity under the tarp is revealed.

Nathan! He got away, thought Laurian. *But how?*

Nathan is of good size and weight and Laurian knows the

genes Margaret passed on to him will certainly help. But compared to Carlo, a homicidal maniac whose foot is relentless upon the tarp, Nathan doesn't stand a chance.

"Stop it!" Laurian cried out. "Leave him alone!"

Carlo let up and Laurian can feel his eyes penetrating her Chantelle laced bra. "Your boyfriend's quite a scraper," Carlo said to her. "Too tired it seems to put up a real fight. Pity, I'd of made pig meat out of him if he did."

"You're the one who's going to be pitied," said Nathan. His back flat on the ground, Nathan gave Carlo a pump kick to his kneecap, the sound of cracking bone causing Laurian to cringe.

Falling to one knee, Carlo grabbed his fractured patella. Nathan did the same to his battered ribs; applying pressure where Carlo kicked him more than anywhere else. Nathan suffered with every deep breath. Moving gingerly, he's on his feet heading for the knives.

Carlo is still on the floor, taking stock of what's around him. One of the canned food boxes lay open on the floor with its contents scattered about. Carlo recalls knocking it over earlier when Nathan slammed into him. With the whiskey and adrenaline rush he's on, reaching for one of the cans the pain in Carlo's knee doesn't feel all that bad.

Nathan is closing in on the knives and Carlo hurls the can striking him in the upper back. Stumbling forward, Nathan topples over the table and the knives take flight toward the outside door. Both men are crawling for their lives, an 8-inch carver at Nathan's fingertips and Carlo grasping his pant leg pulling him back.

A look of determination on Nathan's face, shuffling and kicking to break free, Carlo realizes the tables have turned and he may be in trouble. And he's right, Nathan kicking him in the head, getting away. Both men then scramble to their feet, Carlo limping to the gurney as Nathan plucks the carving knife from the floor. Searching for his cleaver, Carlo spots the handle under the gurney. Rushing in, Nathan takes a swipe but the blade fans the butcher's apron, giving Carlo enough time to grab the cleaver.

The two men then pause to catch their breath; both staring at one another.

"I'm going to enjoy this," said Carlo, circling the gurney.

Step for step, Nathan bracing his ribs, he knows he can't keep Carlo at bay forever. A second trip around Richard's body, Carlo whispered to Nathan, "I'm going to gut you like that pig. It will be a fitting end. Your girlfriend listening to you squeal."

Upon those words, Nathan squared his back to Laurian, blocking Carlo from advancing any further.

Carlo then stepped back, watching the fear in Nathan's eyes evaporate.

Nathan can see he's concerned; more than he was a few seconds ago. *Wisdom versus strength*, thought Nathan. It was a happier time between he and his father when he first heard that. The troubles that followed seem relevant now. What Margaret had said was true. His father was only protecting him. Sacrificing his time and eventually his life.

And it was a good life, thought Nathan. *I can do this. Wisdom versus strength. I draw mine from those who loved me. The two lives this heinous killer should not have taken!*

A courageous look of anger, one that induces stamina, Carlo considers the change upon Nathan's face as a challenge. His size and expert handling of knives a big advantage, Carlo is confident he will defeat Nathan. *This little piggy*, he thought, *will piss his pants. Wee, wee, wee until he's dead, dead, dead.*

Establishing his dominant offense, Carlo made the first move, a crossing forehand slicing open Nathan's shirt.

A tangible incision from his shoulder to stomach, Nathan counters with a deep cut to the side of Carlo's face.

Both men then step away from one another.

Nathan's heart racing, he reached for Laurian. Her heartbeat, just as fast, she can feel it receding with the touch of his hand. "I'm here," he said.

His hand on her hip, Laurian is unaware Nathan is hunched over, glutted with fatigue.

Carlo now defers to defend himself, his face dripping with blood, waiting for Nathan to make the next move. Nathan obliged by nodding to himself, taking a painful breath while straightening up.

Primed for an offensive attack, Nathan moves forward and Carlo counters with a surprise stiff arm to his rib cage. A crushing blow, Nathan doubled over dropping the knife, grabbing and applying pressure to his side.

Carlo kicked the knife away, grabbing Nathan by the throat, pinning him to the wall beside Laurian. She cannot see Carlo's eyes bearing down on them, nor the sharp edge of death hovering overhead. His foul tongue describing their fate, Carlo is indifferent to the will of Marcus. If the blade strikes the woman what does he care, he has the disk and serum to bargain with.

But Nathan, his revenge close at hand, blocking the oncoming wrist of Carlo, the cleaver missed both of them, sticking in the wall as before. Shoving Carlo's hefty frame aside, Nathan has a clear path to the revolver. He's unsure exactly where under the missing lapboard it went, and with little time to look, as Carlo is closing in, he takes a chance by sticking his hand underneath the wall.

Wailing madly in bitter frustration, Carlo found enough strength in his fractured knee for one last running plunge, pile-driving Nathan through the flimsy wall.

The earth unabating his fall, Nathan lay painfully on his back; his sore ribs demanding he keep still. Carlo, however, having had so much whiskey, can tolerate his injuries a little more. Rising to his knees, the area scattered with broken lapboard, Carlo picked up a nasty piece jutted with nails.

Nathan reacts as quickly as possible. Grimacing, he turns on his side intercepting Carlo's arm, *the nails just above his head*. Wrestling Carlo to the ground, Nathan dislodged the board. Their eyes filled with disdain, each man grabs the other by the throat, neither one having enough strength to do any harm.

Locked in each other's chokehold, they tumble toward the water, to a low spot with a thirty-foot section of alligator fence. Landing between two posts, the weight of both men causing the wire squares to sag, they lay there as if anchored to the ground, the sleeve from Richard's jacket dangling overhead.

Carlo's kneecap buckles while getting up and he stoops over for a moment. Wiping the blood from his face, he swears at Nathan for cutting him. "Get up!" he screamed. "I'm not through with you yet."

Clutching his sore ribs, Nathan remained still.

Carlo then kicked him in the hip. "I said get up!"

Not to obey but to rally, Nathan brought himself wearily to his feet. Vigilant in protecting his ribs, he's reluctant in crossing swords again. His strength nearly spent, he knows he must parry wisely. One wrong move and he'll know the adverse nature of defeat.

Carlo swung first, faking with a left to Nathan's vulnerable side, deceptively landing a right cross to his chin. The blow sent Nathan into the fence and Carlo hammered his stomach with a nasty jab. Nathan clinched his opponent around the shoulders but the move gave him no time to rest, Carlo broke free in no time at all. Nathan then shuffled back protecting his ribs—*his one wrong move*.

Carlo delivered a quick blast to the side of Nathan's head, and as he fell into the fence a number of posts broke in half.

Taking the fence with him, fifteen feet or so resting on the ground, Nathan is stretched out between the rumpled wires and murky swamp. In that first moment of lying there, the air is filled with the sound of rustling trees and birds taking flight, Nathan unaware of the stealthy monster he summoned by knocking down the fence.

His healthy foot in Nathan's throat, Carlo calls to the rippling water, "Dinner time, El Cid. Come and get it!"

Both hands around Carlo's ankle, Nathan is struggling to break free, a shadowy furrow drawing closer. Fifty feet … forty … thirty….

"Hurry, El Cid!" shouted Carlo, applying pressure to Nathan's larynx. "This one's trying to get away."

A pair of eyes surface like a wartime periscope… less than twenty feet and closing. *Closing fast!*

At fifteen feet there are nostrils and a snout in the water. At ten feet the body and tail appear … then five … four … three … suddenly there is a crunching sound!

The sound, however, is coming from behind them, pieces of brittle wood under someone's feet. Carlo spun around, just in time to see Clarence lunging forward, spearing him in the shoulder with one of the gigging poles.

Carlo let loose an agonizing cry, taking a firm hold of the pole while dropping to the ground.

A voracious set of teeth speeding toward them, Clarence grappled Nathan from behind, dragging him across the toppled fence.

Crawling out of the water, the gator snapped at Nathan, his powerful jaws inches from Nathan's backpedaling heels.

"Help me up!" screamed Nathan. "Up, Clarence. Up … Up! Up! UP!"

Kicking up the fence while scooting backward, Nathan inadvertently put the wire squares in front of the alligator's snout.

Clarence pulled Nathan to his feet a safe distance away, Carlo breaking the gigging pole slightly below the pronged end, yanking it from his shoulder. Holding the trident looking fork like a knife, his eyes are now fixed on Nathan. The fence, still at his feet, Carlo limps forward unaware of what's behind him.

Sensing the inevitable, Nathan stood his ground, a wary glance at the deadly gator. "Game over," he said to Carlo.

"For you, you bastard pig," screamed Carlo, taking another step. It was his last as the gator, his giant snout caught in the fence, thrashed his head and tail about. Twisting the wires like a piece of taffy, bellowing and loud rumblings churning the air, the gator creates a shockwave Carlo cannot escape; the rippling fence entangling his fractured kneecap.

Carlo gaped into the ravenous eye of the gator, his menacing jaw in a fury of jolting thrusts busting out of the wire.

"No!" screamed Carlo, clawing at the tangled wires around his knee. "El Cid, No! … No! No! No-o-o-o-o-o—"

"*Ooh!*" grimaced Clarence, averting his eyes, the gator crunching through wire and bone. The sight of human flesh being ripped and gnawed, Carlo watching his insides spill out, Nathan had to avert his eyes as well, the gruesome sound of masticated gristle and cartilage supplanting the screams.

Pity took hold just as Nathan said, but from Clarence not him. Nathan felt only sorrow. Sorrow for his parents because he had no feelings for the man who killed them—the taste of revenge he so looked forward to, having no flavor at all.

"Come on," Nathan put a hand on Clarence's shoulder, "… this is far from over."

"What abou' Miss Webster?"

"She's all right."

"She's in there. Ain't she," asked Clarence, gesturing toward the shed.

"It's best if you don't go in there, Clarence. Why don't you head on back. We'll catch up."

As usual, Clarence hung his head low, doing what he's told to do.

"And, Clarence," Nathan's voice turned the boy around.

"Yeah?"

"Thank you, my friend. You saved my life. You saved all our lives."

Twenty-three

THE DOOR SWUNG open and Laurian can hear the panting footsteps of the victor, his shallow breath taking in the last of Carlo's foul air. "Are you all right," he asked.

"I am now," answered Laurian. She still has the blindfold on and Nathan's voice never sounded so good.

"I take it you're ready to come down from there?"

"Now that you mention it—" japed Laurian. She expected Nathan to untie her right away, but he tells her to hold on a second. By the sound of it, he's busy with the tarp, pulling it across the floor over the top of something.

"I wish I could have gotten here sooner," said Nathan. He can only imagine how painful it must be for Laurian hanging from the rafters. Finished with the tarp, he removed her blindfold, both gratitude and modesty on her face.

When Carlo ripped off her blouse Laurian was frightened, but now, adumbrated in her bra she is most uncomfortable in front of Nathan. Oddly, she didn't think about that when he stood beside her with his hand on her hip risking his life to save her.

"Oh my God," uttered Laurian, her eyes adjusting to the light, "… Nathan, you're bleeding!"

"It's just a scratch," said Nathan. Stretching to untie her, his ribs far worse than he thought, Nathan grimaced. He then turned away to hide the pain.

"Ahem," Laurian cleared her throat. "That may not be the best place to start."

"You're right," Nathan agreed. The angle of her tethered feet, had he continued, she would have landed on her face of sure.

Dropping to one knee, Nathan has trouble loosening the slipknot around Laurian's right ankle. "This is taking forever," he said, grabbing a knife and cutting the rope instead.

A sigh of relief, Laurian brought her legs inward standing on both feet. Taking a look around, she now sees what she heard when her eyes were covered. She is most curious, however, as to what happened outside. "All that horrible screaming," she asked, "… is he dead?"

"Pig meat," answered Nathan, slicing the bindings around Laurian's wrist. She is so fatigued her legs buckle, her arms reaching out snaring Nathan around the neck. Reacting quickly, Nathan dropped the knife latching onto her waist.

"You okay," he asked.

Laurian peered into Nathan's eyes and her learned voice responded quickly. "A good feeling, isn't it … *saving someone's life*."

There is a moment of silence between them, and Laurian, no longer uncomfortable with Nathan so close, with a gentle smile she withdrew from their embrace. "I should tend to that," she said, looking solicitously at Nathan's bloodstained shirt.

"It's nothing, really," Nathan reminded her. He then went over to the tarp; where he just covered the gurney. Digging under the canvas, he pulled out a clean bedsheet, draping it over Laurian's shoulders. She thanked him but Nathan saw her appreciation to be somewhat distant. "What's the matter," he asked.

Distress consuming her, Laurian drew the sheet taut against her chest. "He did something terrible in here. I couldn't see but I heard everything that was going on. He said he had to feed his gator. That's all he talked about … that and his aptitude for violence. You covered the body just now, not wanting me to see. But I know it's there," said Laurian staring at the tarp. "He butchered some poor animal … *didn't he?*"

Nathan put his arm around her. "Try not to think about it," he said.

Richard was Laurian's friend. *A good friend*, gathered Nathan. If she believed an animal was under the tarp he would keep it at that. *She need not know the truth,* thought Nathan. *Today or any other day.*

On the second floor, one of two guest rooms overlooking the beach, Tantur put his brother to bed. He then drew the curtains partway, opening the balcony doors for some fresh air. Wahota's forehead is bandaged and with a rueful heart Tantur tells him not to worry, that he should try and get some sleep.

A thriving breeze flustering the curtains, Wahota closed his eyes. The room is uncommonly cool and the lulling cadence of the surf irritable for some reason. Wahota is having a rough time falling asleep and Tantur cannot bear to watch his little brother in such pain.

Stepping out on the balcony, there is a light from below spilling into the night air and Tantur proceeds with caution along the narrow overhang. Sitting beside the pool are Marcus and Margaret. In silence they look beyond the billowing waves contemplating the outcome of the approaching storm. Waiting for one of them to speak, Tantur is distracted by the sound of his brother's wheezing—his breath as it seems in rhythm with the surging tide.

Tantur grabbed a chair returning to Wahota's bedside. "You sound terrible," he said. "How do you feel?"

"Guen-umadra," gasped Wahota.

Tantur sat down looking into a pair of muddled eyes.

"Everything is so blurry," Wahota continued in their native tongue. "Where are we?"

"I can see the island from here," answered Tantur, he too speaking an ancient dialect. "The storm will soon be upon us and you will suffer no more."

"I'm so sorry," said Wahota lifting his head.

"*Sorry?* Why should you be sorry?"

"I brought shame upon our tribe letting that man get the best of me."

"No, my brother. There is no shame in one's first hunt. Father would have been proud. The grandson is a great adversary. The passing of Margaret's blood, he is no ordinary man."

"Then I am worthy of the sacred pool?"

"I think you are too young," reputed Tantur. "There will always be another storm, but because of your injury I know of no other way to save you."

"I don't understand. Young or old what difference does it make?"

"It is a burden to live forever-young, my brother. No one cares about an old man who looks the same as he did yesterday. But a young man showing no signs of aging … the world takes notice. You cannot stay long in one place and are forced to abandon those who matter most. You may find someone to love, but at so young an age it tears apart more than just one heart. Fate, my brother, *has dealt you a troublesome hand*."

"I do not fear that sort of life. I fear only the thought of taking the journey alone. Will you be with me, Tantur … to guide my way?"

"I do not know. I must first honor the servitude of our father to Marcus."

"*Why must you do this?* You owe him nothing!"

"It is our custom. Our father was beholden to Marcus for saving his life. You know that. You also know when a man takes his own life the eldest son serves in his stead."

"Our people—" replied Wahota, pausing for a sharp pain in his forehead, "have long abandoned such nonsense."

"No, my brother. Our customs are not nonsense. Our people through countless generations have forsaken them because the world tells them to fit in … *that they can no longer be who they are*. I am bound to an age long forgotten. An age they know nothing about. An age I shall not dishonor."

"But you also belong to this age," said Wahota in English, "…*to my time!* We could— *Aargh*," gasped Wahota, rearing his head into the pillow.

"Calm yourself," said Tantur. "You need to rest. We have but a few hours until the storm."

Tantur stayed with Wahota until he fell asleep, going downstairs for a glass of water. On his return he ascended the stairs without a blanket or pillow for his bedside chair. All he needed—this and every night—was the nourishing water to supplement his lack of sleep.

A gallery of Carrara marble at the top of stairs, sculptures and paintings between the doors, Tantur noticed one was slightly ajar; a room where only he is allowed access.

Tantur looked inside the room most curiously. Filled with misters and aquariums with netted tops, aside from all the colorful frogs, the tiny room appeared empty. As he shut the door another door opened across the gallery adjacent from Wahota's room.

It was the second floor bath and Ariel stepped into the gallery, an innocent looking face rubbing lotion on her hands.

"So, who do you think did it," she asked, "… the old man or his nephew?"

"Did what," replied Tantur.

"Crack your brother's skull like that."

"It was the old man, William Shadwell."

"I see. I presume you'll be taking out the cauldron now … chopping up a few vegetables and boiling some water."

"No," replied Tantur, dispelling her sarcasm. "Despite what you and my brother may think, that is one ritual I do not care for."

Unconscious, lying on the couch, Vincent's hands and feet are bound with tape. The doctors bag belonging to him is still on the table and Shadwell opens it. Inside is the map-box, and looking at its contents, Shadwell assumes the rightful owner to be Doctor Webster. *So that's what she went after*, he thought, putting everything back. He then called out to Clarence.

"Yeah, Uncle Will."

"I found something of value. What about you?"

"Nothin' but beans an' vegetables— oh wait … found a couple bags 'a chips in the cu'board."

"*Wonderful.* No refrigerator. No stove. No fuel for the generator. Not exactly the Hilton, is it?"

"Maybe there's a campin' stove in the shed."

"Speaking of which," replied Shadwell, "… I wonder what's keeping them."

"Don't know. Want me ta' go an' have a look?"

"No," said Shadwell, willing to give them a few more minutes, Nathan's voice then rearing his head around.

"We're coming in," exclaimed Nathan.

"Thank God," uttered Shadwell, Nathan and Laurian safe and sound. "We were beginning to worry."

Laurian sat at the table, relieved to be off her feet. She recognized Vincent as Carlo's accomplice, and according to Nathan, he was the one who sabotaged her home and research facility.

"He had no choice in the matter," concluded Nathan, clutching his ribs.

Shadwell can see Nathan is in some pain, asking if he'll be all right. "You look like you were knocked into next week," he added.

"I'm okay. You should see the other guy … or what's left of him."

"Yes, Clarence told me about the alligator," said Shadwell. "And how are *you* holding up," he then turned to Laurian.

"*Physically*, I'm fine. I'll never question Nathan's integrity again. First impressions aren't as important as everyone says. *Are they?*"

"Given the type of day we're having," replied Nathan, "… no, they're not."

"What 'a we do now," asked Clarence.

"I'm all for getting out of here," said Nathan. "There's a boat at the dock but I don't think we'll all fit."

"We're missing someone," it occurred to Laurian. "Where's Richard?"

"We were separated at the airport," said Shadwell, explaining to Nathan and Laurian what happened. "He must have somehow gotten away."

"No, something's not right. I can feel it," said Laurian. "Nathan, do you think he got away?"

"I can't say one way or the other. I've been with you all this time, remember."

Changing the subject, a sympathetic glance toward Nathan, Shadwell urges everyone to get moving while they still have enough light.

Laurian asked if anyone has seen her map-box and Shadwell popped open Vincent's bag. "There's something else of interest in here," he said to Nathan. "Do you know what this is?"

"I have a pretty good idea," said Nathan, peering into the bag.

"It's C-4," said Shadwell. "We may as well take it with us. Now, how do we get out of here? Clarence and I were unconscious on the way over."

"I don't know," answered Nathan. "They drugged me as well."

"*Doctor Webster*," asked Shadwell.

Laurian clutched the sheet around her shoulders a little tighter; the thought of Carlo back at the airport giving her a chill. "I can't tell you much either. After our abduction, they threw us in a van with no windows. An hour or so later we ended up on a dirt road. I know because when we got out they had a boat waiting. They put Nathan inside and I had a blindfold on as we got under way."

"How long did it take to get here?"

"Thirty, maybe forty minutes."

"What direction?"

"West. I had the sun in my face the whole time."

"Then we head east," said Shadwell. "Clarence, fetch some water for Doctor Webster so she can freshen up. There's a closet full of clothes in the other room if either of you are interested in trading up."

Clarence took a bowl of water to the bathroom and Laurian went inside with a clean dress shirt—one belonging to Vincent.

Returning to the kitchen, Clarence filled another bowl with water, wetting a towel for Nathan.

Nathan removed his shirt, wiping clean the blood from his chest.

"That's a nasty cut," observed Shadwell.

"It's not as bad as it looks," replied Nathan, slipping into a faded Pendleton.

"The main thing is you're alive and that Carlo fellow is dead."

"A comeuppance long overdue," said Nathan, imparting to Shadwell the conversation he had with Detective Monroe.

"That's what this is all about, isn't it? Webster's research. But why take Margaret?"

"I don't know. To bargain with, I suppose."

"No," exclaimed Laurian, stepping from the bathroom. "They never bargain with anyone. If you have what they want they just take it."

"We certainly have what they want," said Nathan. "I hope you're right about all this. Especially Cape Coral."

"They should be there by now," said Laurian. "Once we get there, all we need to do is keep an eye on the harbor. With a hurricane or tropical storm warning, there won't be many boats out."

"What about him," asked Shadwell, motioning to Vincent.

"Now that Carlo's dead," said Nathan, "… there's no reason for him to trouble anyone. I say we cut him loose."

"That's up to Doctor Webster, don't you think," replied Shadwell. "After all," he turned to Laurian, "… he's the one who set your house on fire, blowing up your laboratory all in the same day."

"Nathan said the man had no choice in the matter. He's the least of my worries," Laurian replied. "I just want to get out of here."

"Fine," said Shadwell. "Clarence, grab those lanterns. We'll need more than a couple of flashlights out there."

There are two lanterns by the outside door and Clarence does a quick inspection. "This 'un ain't got no kerosene, Uncle Will."

"One lantern and two flashlights," said Shadwell taking stock. "We're cutting it close, but what else is new."

Leading the way to the dock, Shadwell is in charge again. "You're right," he said to Nathan upon reaching the skiff, "… it is too small. One of us most likely will stay behind."

"I saw a canoe in the shed… can we tow it?"

"Good idea," said Shadwell. "That Evinrude should handle the extra weight. Clarence, give Nathan a hand… the Doctor and I will manage things out here."

With Shadwell in the skiff and Laurian balancing herself on the wobbly dock, they commence loading the supplies. "It's a good thing Clarence is here," said Laurian, handing Shadwell the lantern. "If we said good-bye in Ruston, Nathan wouldn't be alive right now."

"It was a tough decision. I promised my sister I'd look after him if anything ever happened to her. She could never bare children and Clarence was her only child."

"Does he know?"

"That he's adopted? Yes, he knows. My sister told him early on."

"I know how he feels," said Laurian, confiding in the old man. "My parents told me early on as well."

"I feel for that boy," said Shadwell, setting Vincent's bag beside the oars. "He's been through some very rough times. His father died when he was seven and I helped out as much as I could. But it's never the same. I know how it is not having a full-time father around. You're fortunate, Doctor Webster, adopted or not that both parents raised you."

"You know, *William*," said Laurian helping him out of the skiff, "… after all we've been through it's time to drop the doctor formality don't you think. I did work hard for the title, but friends don't go around using titles, do they?"

"No, I suppose not," answered Shadwell, a slight grin

while stepping away.

"He smiles!" chuckled Laurian. "*That was a smile*, wasn't it?"

"Yes, I believe it was."

A solemn overtone and curious look, Laurian then asked Shadwell something he wasn't expecting. "What happened to you, William? To the man Margaret said couldn't wait to show off his golden smile."

Shadwell thought for a moment. It was a relevant question given his surly disposition. "Too many misfortunes I suppose. It's as though I slipped and fell and couldn't get up on my own. By the time I realized I could, it was too late. All the water under all the bridges turned into one big river."

"You're talking about Margaret, aren't you," asked Laurian.

"I can't believe I'm talking about it at all. Margaret mentioned our past to you I'm sure. She left me with a number of unanswered questions and for a very long time I thought about each and every one. Now I'm down to the question that haunts me the most. Why?"

"I'm sorry," said Laurian. "Margaret spoke of you quite often but no specifics about your relationship. She loved you, *I know that*. I asked her several times why she left but she wouldn't say. I doubt if she knew the answer herself."

"*She said that to you?* She loved me."

"Does that surprise you?"

"When you get to be my age surprises are something you outgrow. Doubt more or less takes control, and I've had more than my share… never sure of Margaret's true feelings until now."

Twenty-four

TAYLOR KEEPS an eye on his monitor as his loafing counterpart, Jerry Holiday, plops down beside him. Having just returned from the break-room, Holiday set his goodies down. "It's getting dark outside," he said.

"I'm not keeping you from anything, am I," asked Taylor, his inimical glance oblivious to Holiday.

"It's either this or HBO," answered Holiday, thumbing the play button on his video machine. He then popped open a can of Mountain Dew, taking a hefty swig.

Great, Taylor said to himself, *fifteen minutes and he'll be takin' another piss. He'll never get through that tape.*

"Sure you don't want anything," asked Holiday. "Another cup of coffee?"

"No, I'm good," answered Taylor in a bitter tone, his patience running thin. "*Where the hell are you, Carlo!?*"

"If he chartered a flight he more than likely went straight to the hanger avoiding the terminal altogether."

"So we could be watching the wrong tapes?"

"He may not be on any of them if he stayed clear of the cameras."

"Don't say that," said Taylor disputing Holiday's pessimism.

"He's on one of these tapes and we're going to find him if it takes all night."

Jerry ripped open a candy bar taking a big bite. "Hold on a minute," he said, chewing faster as the crowd on his monitor dispersed into a small number of faces. "There he is!"

Taylor swiveled his chair alongside Holiday. "Where?"

"Camera three," said Jerry tapping the screen. "Outside the restaurant."

"That's him all right," cried Taylor scanning the APB.

"Fourteen-hundred-hours," Holiday read the time-stamp to himself. "Hey! Somebody just handed him a note."

"I can't see his face with that stupid baseball cap. What is that he's wearing? It looks like a work shirt."

"City of Gretna," screamed Jerry, all hopped-up on sugar and caffeine.

"He's heading for the exit," said Taylor. "Rewind that, would you. Maybe we'll catch the other guy in a better position."

"How far back do you want me to go?"

"I don't know," said Taylor inching forward, "… *ten minutes?*"

Holiday hit the rewind. "This is exciting," he said, people racing backwards in a flickering display of black and white.

"I told you I'd spice up your— Wait a minute!" shouted Taylor, spotting something on the monitor. "Stop the tape!"

Holiday's reaction time, like everything else, Taylor thought to be too slow. "Go back! You went too far," he screamed. "Now pause it. Pause it right there! That's her," exclaimed Taylor. "That's the woman I'm looking for. Her name is Laurian Webster."

"Sure, I know her," said Holiday. "She flies out of here all the time. You should talk to Richard Gregory. He spends a lot of time with her."

"Richard Gregory. Who's that?"

"He's a pilot at Gulf Coast Charters. The number's in the Rolodex there."

Taylor dials the number but the office is closed; the answering service picking up. "I can page Mr. Gregory and have him call you back."

"Hang on," replied Taylor. "Jerry, what's the number here?"

Taylor gave the number to the answering service. Five minutes later he grew impatient; fifteen more, he turned to Holiday with an insufferable look on his face.

"He's not answering his page," said Holiday. "You'll have to try again in the morning."

"I have no choice, do I," grumbled Taylor. "Not a big deal, I suppose. From what you just told me I'll need to examine a ton of flight records as well."

Holiday shook his head in agreement, the door suddenly opening and Monroe stepping inside. "Any luck?"

"He was here all right. And look who else showed up," said Taylor playing the video. "No doubt she went home from here."

"And d'hen she come back to 'da airport. You were right, Samuel. She went d'are for sumpin'. Whatever she pulled outta d'at rubble, maybe Carlo's looking to take it from her."

"Either that or they're in cahoots."

"D'at could also be true. D'hen d'ey fly out a' here toged'er. D'at would explain why d'are cars are still 'ere."

"*That's right,* you've been out there all this time?"

"Yeah, an' I'd still be d'are if not fer Alcott. 'E sent over our relief. No more overtime on d'is one, Samuel."

"I'd like to stick around in case they return."

"Alcott won't allow it. 'E say we got ta' go home an' get some rest … *you especially.* I don't know what ya did but 'e not too happy wit' you right now."

"What if I stayed at the stationhouse instead? It's closer than my apartment."

"Soc au' lait, are you crazy! Alcott gonna be d'are in 'da mornin'."

"As long as I'm close to the airport I don't care. If I did something wrong we can settle it then."

"Go on d'hen. I'm goin' home. Carlo, 'e got to sleep too an' I ain't about ta' lose no more on account a' 'em."

"Thanks, Cary."

Monroe waved him off, marching out of the room.

Taylor then turned to Holiday. "Don't forget what we talked about, Jerry. And don't bring her back here. Take her somewhere a little more— *secluded.*"

The sun withered on the horizon and the bayou turned bleak. It would have been quiet if not for the outboard motor and wildlife scrambling in all directions. Shadwell and Clarence are in the skiff with all their supplies, the Evinrude motor working hard towing Nathan and Laurian close behind.

"Switch hands if you're tired," said Shadwell, Clarence jutting the lantern over the bow.

"I will," replied Clarence turning to the side, the stingy light baring the faces of Nathan and Laurian. Scrunched together in the tiny pirogue, Laurian's head is on Nathan's chest, his arms tucked inside the hollowed out tree.

Laurian is awfully quiet and Nathan is worried she's dwelling on what happened at the shed. "Tell me more about the fountain," he beguiles her attention, intending to get her mind on something else.

"So you're a believer now," said Laurian, tilting her head.

"I didn't say that. Just tell me about the part I'd like to believe."

"And the awful part … do you want to hear about that too?"

"What do you mean?"

"The good outweighs the bad but living forever has its price."

"I'd rather hear the good news first."

"Once Margaret drank from the fountain she never got sick. Not one sniffle. Your father never took ill either, did you know that?"

"No."

"*And you?* How healthy are you, Nathan?"

"What are you saying … I'm going to live forever? In case you haven't noticed I wasn't lying about my age. Every morning I feel each of those forty-one years."

"No, you won't live forever. But you are second generation to Margaret. I'm curious as to what she passed on to you. When you were a kid did you ever have the measles or chickenpox? What about influenza? I'll bet you never missed a day of school in your life."

"That's ridiculous. I cut class lots of times."

Laurian rolled her eyes and Nathan is glad to see her mind on something else. "No silly, you know what I mean."

"I've never been sick a day in my life. So what. It doesn't prove anything. I have a good immune system that's all."

"And when you cut yourself or break a bone, how quickly do you heal?"

Now she had him thinking. Nathan never broke or fractured anything in his life. Even the pain in his ribs seemed to be tapering off. *Funny*, he thought, he injured himself numerous times and the only scar he had was a memento from Margaret's cat. "I'm not sure if I'm ready to buy into all this immortality stuff."

"*But you might.*"

"Okay … I might. Let's say, hypothetically speaking, I

shoot myself in the foot and five minutes later I'm running in the Boston Marathon. What else can be expected if I were immortal?"

"Most of your senses, if not all of them, would be enhanced. So much so, good men often flirt with improbity, capitalizing on private conversations and things they wittingly set their eyes upon. On the downside, you can forget about alcohol to unwind. The brain regards all drugs and stimulants as a threat and blocks them out. Most interesting, however, is the fact that women never menstruate. No cramps to speak of or pain during childbirth. But that's not to say they are without pain."

"*The bad news*."

"Yes," said Laurian, "... frequent migraines and uncontrollable seizures."

"And my grandmother," said Nathan, his skepticism returning, "... she told you everything? All their strengths and weaknesses?"

"Not at first. It took her some time to confide in me. She told me she saw a few of her traits in your father."

"What about the migraines? Did my grandmother suffer from them?"

"Do you?"

"No. Not migraines," confessed Nathan, the boat changing course.

"The migraines are caused from lack of water. Once someone drinks from the fountain they are constantly replenishing those minerals. It took Margaret over a year to figure that out. Your father often had bad headaches and Margaret told him to drink a glass of water whenever he felt one coming on."

"I don't know anyone who doesn't have headaches," said Nathan. "Mine are pretty mild so I must be normal."

"Like I said, you're second generation. The gene pool is weakening. Your children may or may not have the same healthy chromosomes as you. And their water consumption will be the same as everyone else."

If I ever have children, thought Nathan. "You know, that doesn't sound too bad. We all need water to survive."

"But not to the extent of being burdened with it. Most everyone can hydrate on a number of liquids. An immortal, however, needs the unabated minerals from ground water to suppress the migraines."

Laurian saw a slight change of interest on Nathan's face, as though he believed a portion of what she was saying. "There's also sleep deprivation," she continued. "Can you imagine living forever without any rest? Your body on a constant high. Fortunately, your father never experienced that … or the rabid seizures. Every year on or close to the anniversary of that fateful day, you undergo a violent change. Antibodies reproduce themselves and it feels like a thousand hot needles piercing your flesh. The sensation is so painful the Devil himself would cringe."

Nathan was about to comment but the lantern went out. "That's it, Uncle Will," said Clarence, having run out of kerosene.

"Everything okay back there," asked Shadwell, reaching for his flashlight.

Nathan and Laurian answered with a resounding, "Yes," followed unexpectedly by Clarence screaming out, "Uncle Will! Look!"

The lantern having gone out, a set of headlights flashed through the trees, a glimmer here and there before disappearing completely.

"Good eye, Clarence," said Nathan. "We still have a long way to go but at least we're heading in the right direction."

Pitch-dark, the bayou is a universe of spectral earth and somnolent water. A string of starry headlights rising on the horizon, Clarence gazed upon them with great anticipation, his flashlight inadvertently trolling the night air.

"Keep the light on the starboard side," grumbled Shadwell.

"The what?"

"*To your right*, Clarence. How far is the shore?"

"'Bout five feet, Uncle Will."

"That puts us about center," said Shadwell looking back at Nathan. "Any closer and we'll be rubbing elbows with the gators."

"That's encouraging," said Laurian.

"I'm sorry but things don't seem to be getting any better," replied Shadwell, the Evinrude sputtering for a brief time then dying out. "And now, *they're worse.*"

"What happened," asked Nathan, the pirogue ramming the skiff.

"We ran out of petrol."

"What do we do now," cried Laurian.

"We walk," answered Shadwell.

Once the two vessels run aground, Shadwell jumped out conveying as pleasant as he can a set of instructions to Clarence. "And grab that oar. If we stumble upon a gator it may come in handy."

Clarence took a look at Nathan who had the same degree of urgency on his face. "I think I'd like an oar too," said Nathan, fearfully scanning the trees.

"We only need one," warranted Shadwell, handing Nathan the bag of C-4 instead. "Stay close together and we'll be fine."

"We've been out here for more than an hour," replied Nathan. "How far would you say those headlights were?"

"A bit of a stretch," said Shadwell, "… two, maybe three

miles. It won't take long to get there," he assured everyone. Grabbing his flashlight, he then led the way through a thicket of tall brush and lanky tupelos.

Twenty minutes later they are without incident, Shadwell explaining to the city dwellers—Laurian and Nathan—the odds of running into a snake compared to that of an alligator. Halfway through the conversation they run across the very thing they're talking about. The odds, *as Shadwell pointed out*, not only in their favor but right in front of them.

Laurian screamed, leaping to the side as the portentous reptile slithers in her direction. With an insufficient amount of light, she crashed into Nathan and he too is taken by surprise. The snake disappeared into a patch of groundcover and Clarence wields his oar much too late, plangently chopping the brush and the snake jetting into the open.

Shadwell appeared from the darkness, calmly cincturing the snake in a sluice of addled light. "It's not poisonous," he said, Laurian latching onto Nathan regardless.

The snake skeltering away, Nathan then turned to Shadwell. "And people actually live out here," he stodgily remarked.

"It takes a little getting used to," said Shadwell, bypassing the snake's path before continuing on.

"I could never live in a place like this," uttered Nathan, arcing his flashlight across the trees.

"You can take the boy out of the city—" said Laurian, departing with a grin.

"*Hey!* I enjoy the great outdoors as much as the next guy," declared Nathan, scooting alongside her.

"If the sun's out," said Laurian, teasing Nathan.

"Now that's just plain mean," answered Nathan, relieved to see her spirits up.

"Finally!" cried Shadwell, startling everyone but himself.

"There's a clearing up ahead and another set of headlights. Come on, we're almost there."

Aquiver with anticipation, Laurian hugged Nathan. "I can't believe it," she said, a handful of stars melting her fears between a brief parting of the clouds.

Getting ahead of everyone, Laurian the first to arrive at the clearing, stepping out of the darkness she realized Nathan removed yet another blindfold. She wanted to tell him how close they are; about all the turmoil and what side to be on. *But there's more*, she thought. *Am I caught up in the moment or do I truly feel this way about him? It's silly of me to think of such things.* "Especially now," she said to herself, opening the map-box. *I have to concentrate on Margaret and what I must do if we run into Marcus.*

The headlights run parallel with the levee as do the taillights drifting out of sight.

"We made it," said Nathan, breathing a sigh of relief.

"But to where," asked Laurian, Nathan helping her up the levee.

"We'll flag down a car and find out. Hitch a ride to the nearest phone or town if we can."

Shadwell agreed. "But don't get your hopes up," he warned them. "The chances of someone stopping in the middle of the night are slim."

"What about all that Southern hospitality," asked Nathan.

"It's still around," replied Shadwell. "Folks tend to be more cautious than sociable after dark."

A number of approaching cars, Shadwell was right on the money. Laurian is close to the road, yelling and waving but no one stops.

"You may have to pull a Claudette Colbert, Doctor Webster."

"Who," asked Clarence.

"Claudette Colbert," stressed Laurian, depicting Colbert's famous scene opposite Clark Gable.

"Clark Gable?" Clarence scrunched his face.

"You never heard of Clark Gable? Rhett Butler, *Gone with the Wind?*"

"Sorry, Miss Webster, but I ain't heard 'a no Rhett Butler either. Died in some wind storm, did he?"

Laurian shook her head turning to Shadwell. "He's coming to my house on movie-night when this is all over."

"You may want to re-think that," said Nathan. "The part about your house."

"That's right, I forgot. I'll be staying with my folks for a while. Everything is happening so fast."

"Not fast enough," cried Shadwell, pointing to another car.

"Maybe this one will stop," said Laurian.

"If not," replied Nathan, his flashlight beginning to flicker, "… one of us will be showing a little leg."

"Did you hear that, William," jested Laurian. "You have some competition."

Clarence snickered and Shadwell gave him a serious look—*I've no time for jokes* written on his deprecatory face.

"It's slowing down," shouted Laurian.

A flat-bed truck with high railings stopped in the middle of the road. The side rails are sun beaten and a strong poultry odor emanates from the wood. Shadwell is the first to approach the cab, the name of a local chicken ranch on the door and a massive elbow sticking out the window.

"You folks all right," said the rancher, his deep, Southern accent befriending them.

"Our skiff ran out of petrol," replied Shadwell. "Where are we exactly?"

"Well, yer 'bout fifteen mile from White Castle. That's

where I'm headin' if'n y'all need a ride." The rancher weighed at least three-hundred pounds and when he got out of the cab the undercarriage squeaked. Dressed in a pair of taut overalls and sweaty tee shirt, he pulled a handkerchief from his pocket wiping his forehead, the look in his pearly eyes assuring them he was an honorable man.

Shadwell appeared confused. "White Castle," he asked. "I have no idea where that is. How far are we from New Orleans?"

"N'awlins! How long you folks been in that skiff? White Castle's twenty-mile downriver from Baton Rouge."

"Where's the nearest phone," asked Laurian.

"There's a nice little joint this side 'a Samstown. Got a payphone right outside. I reckon we could be there in five minutes."

"Well what are we waiting for," said Laurian climbing into the back.

"Ma'am, it's a bit more comfortable up front."

"I don't mind," replied Laurian, dangling her legs off the tail end. "My friend William deserves the better seat."

"An' which 'un might he be?"

"That would be me," replied Shadwell extending his hand.

The rancher introduced himself as Abe.

"She'll be fine," said Shadwell. "Between you and me," he lowered his voice, "I'd rather be up front… or downwind so to speak."

"I know what ya mean," said Abe climbing into the cab, a jug of water between them. "So where y'all from," he asked, "… N'awlins?"

"Miss Webster resides there. My nephew Clarence and I live up north this side of Ruston. And Nathan— well, *Nathan's come a long way*. Our Nation's Capital I believe."

"'E ain't one of them politicians come out 'ere to stir things up, is 'e?"

"No," laughed Shadwell. "I have no idea what he does. It never came up."

"Are you thirsty," asked Abe, gesturing to the last of his water.

The cab has no air-conditioning and with a naked firewall the heat from the engine is unbearable. Commiseration, sweltering as it seems from his past, Shadwell has always been empathetic with the hardships and misfortunes of others—embracing now the world that troubles him. He never understood why people with so little were willing to offer so much. This man needed the water more than he did. Abe's face pouring with sweat, he's unable to secrete the obvious.

What mother raised a man like this, thought Shadwell. *And who educates the selfish? All those cars and none of them stopped. Who raised those people? And whose God do they not trust to protect them. This man, undaunted, he stopped. How fortunate we are that his mother was there for us—that he trusts his God.*

"You go ahead," said Shadwell declining the water, "I can wait another five minutes. In fact, I may end up quenching my thirst with a glass of bourbon instead."

"Reach under that there seat then. I keeps a pint down there and you're welcome to it."

Shadwell felt around uncovering the bottle, graciously taking a sip. "Smooth," he augmented the double vowel, offering his host a drink.

"No thanks," said Abe grabbing the water. "This 'ill do me just fine."

"Careful, Abe," Shadwell warned him, the big man aiming to sit the jug on his hat. "You almost crushed your fedora there."

"That old th'ang. Some yat used it to ante up t'other night. Thing's too small fer my fat head."

"Well it's a smart looking one," said Shadwell examining the starchy hat. "I recall having one just like it. Back when Kelly's were atop every man's head."

"Don't remember that," said Abe, pulling in front of a squalid looking tavern. "Here ya are, William. Payphone's underneath that light over there. Y'all got enough for long distance."

"We're good. Thanks, Abe."

"Want me ta' wait a spell? Sometimes folks ain't always home when ya need 'em ta' be."

"If you can spare the time," answered Shadwell, "… we'd appreciate it."

"Hold on a minute, William." Abe held out the old fedora, offering it to Shadwell. "Take this with ya, I got no use fer it."

"No, I couldn't do that," said Shadwell, waving him off.

"Go ahead," insisted Abe. "If it don't sit well with ya, give it to some other fella."

Shadwell furrowed the crown with the edge of his hand, resurrecting the stiff fabric. Looking in the side mirror, he adjusts the hat firmly in place, vaunting a finger along the brim. "Perfect."

"And it looks right smart on ya too," said Abe.

Clarence then jumped off the truck-bed. "Uncle Will," he exclaimed. "See that Blazer over there … t'one with the skiff."

"What about it," answered Shadwell.

"That's the skiff them folks at Miss Margaret's plane put us in."

"What makes you say that?"

"Them numbers on the front. I got a good look when they was cartin' me 'cross the dock."

Taking a moment to sort things out, Shadwell tells Abe he

needn't wait any longer. "There's a fellow inside we all know. He'll give us a ride."

"Glad ta' hear that, William. Won't 'e be surprised when you folks come waltzin' in from out 'a nowhere."

"*Yes, quite surprised.*"

Twenty-five

THERE ARE NO painted or neon displays outside, only a boldface placard on the door: NO ONE UNDER 21 ALLOWED. The tavern has a cinderblock façade and the windows are made from old wagon wheels; bottle-green glass between the spokes and ne'er a glint of light shining through. A covered porch runs from one end of the building to the other and Shadwell made his way alongside the decrepit looking planks. A small dumpster at the end of the porch, he cracked open the top, checking out the inside.

"Nice hat," said Laurian, she and Nathan drawing near. "You're not thinking of throwing it away?"

"No. It will come in handy later," he replied. Closing the dumpster, Shadwell made his way to the Blazer. "Anyone know how to hotwire a car?"

He appeared to be joking but Nathan wasn't sure. "Are you serious? What happened to phoning for a ride?"

"Why should we? Now that we know who this belongs to."

Nathan has that confused look on his face again. He turned to Laurian for help but she appears as perplexed as he does.

"Clarence didn't tell you, did he?"

"Tell us what," asked Nathan.

"The man who kidnapped us did so in this boat," said Shadwell. "It's also the same rig I told you about earlier. The one at the lake."

"The woman who ambushed you. You think the two of them are in there," asked Laurian.

"I don't know about her, but he certainly is."

"There's only one way to find out," said Nathan, heading back to the tavern.

"Hold on," cried Shadwell, stopping Nathan in his tracks. "Do you even know what this guy looks like? Because I sure don't."

"Don't worry," said Nathan, "... I got a good look. Why don't we go in there and reacquaint ourselves."

"And if he's armed, what then? He'll recognize us as soon as we walk in."

"He won't recognize me," said Laurian; her hat now in the ring.

"Why not," asked Shadwell.

"I heard him talking to Carlo in the shed. I'm pretty sure he didn't see me. Even if he did, I was wearing a blindfold."

"*No way*," exclaimed Nathan, "... you're not going in there—"

"Hold on," said Shadwell interrupting him. He then turned to Laurian giving her a chance to explain. "What are you suggesting?"

"I go in and persuade him to come outside. You three can handle it from there."

"No," clamored Nathan remaining firm, "... it's too dangerous."

"That's not a bad idea," said Shadwell, "... three against one. Those are pretty good odds. Especially if he's had too much to drink."

Nathan had nothing to say, his expression revealing it all. The plan made sense but he didn't want Laurian going in there alone.

Laurian put her hand on Nathan's cheek. "I'll be all right," she said.

"I don't like this. What if something goes wrong?"

"Like what? Persuading him to come outside is the easy part."

"And how are you going to do that?"

"It's a bar, Nathan. Men come here for two things. I think I can lure him outside for one of them."

Given a description of the man she's looking for, an earful of advice on what not to do, Laurian entered the tavern somewhat pretentious. Her top button is undone and she is showing a bit of cleavage and fortuitous sweat.

The Acadian honky-tonk is swilling in froth, mirth, and tobacco smoke. A thirty-foot bar is opposite the entrance and the people are two and sometimes three deep waiting for a drink. A kettle of mudbugs and simmering pot of boudin are behind the bar on a hooded stove. In the middle of the tavern there are several tables and everyone is clapping to a Cajun two-step. An accordion and fiddle in the hands of middle-aged men, a young lass reels between them, dipping and fluffing her dress to the reveling crowd.

Two doors marked *ladies* and *gents* are behind her and Laurian circles the room scanning all the likely faces. A number of gentlemen, and those not so gentle, gaze at her from every angle.

"Best thing in the house," one man said to another, his voice too low and the tavern too noisy for the complement to travel.

Two televisions are mounted behind the bar with baseball highlights on one and The Weather Channel on the other. Some old toper at the bar is rambling on about Hurricane Andrew to a man who seems more interested in watching the live report. The man, firm and husky—who Laurian doesn't realize at the moment is Raymond—has the same color cap and plaid shirt Nathan said he might be wearing. There's an empty stool beside Raymond, but Laurian is trembling and she turns around, scrambling for the ladies room.

"*What are you doing,*" asked the mirror, Laurian looking at her dingy reflection. "*You're not ready for this, girl. Get out of here! Get out of here now!*" Staring back at her reflection, a hazy look of confidence, Laurian shut her eyes taking inventory of all the women in the tavern. There wasn't one who fit the description Shadwell gave of Ariel. Not even the busy waitress with her short blonde hair and tempered smile. *But the man at the bar! That's him,* thought Laurian, splashing water on her face.

Wiping clean the droplets from the mirror, her reflective voice said to her, "You can do this. Get back in there and sit next to him. He'll take it from there."

A dubious trek through the smoky room, Laurian is paranoid that everyone is watching her. She wonders if they can see how frightened she is. *Relax*, she thought, her body trembling again. *This is the easy part.*

Laurian took a deep breath, courageously sitting next to Raymond. The same brand of whiskey she smelled on Carlo is in the air and for a moment she is someplace else.

Glancing at her with a passionate eye, Raymond is arguing with the old toper next to him; something about the levees around Lake Pontchartrain. "According to Doppler radar," said Raymond, pointing to the television, "… this one's heading for Florida."

It's him, thought Laurian, placing his voice back at the shed.

"It's just a matter a' time," replied the old toper, a heavy slur from his lush mouth. "Some folks never learn. Do they,

Mr. Ray? What makes 'em wanna live d'at close ta' trouble anyway?"

"Location, Wendell," Raymond replied. "Ever been to Florida? My boss's got himself a nice spread right on the beach. He's got so much money, what does he care if he needs to rebuild."

"Rebuildin' is one t'ang," said the old toper, standing up swallowing the last of his drink, "… gettin' caught up in one is another. I used ta' live in 'da Fat City… but no more. Mark my word," he shook a lazy finger, "… one good 'un is all it takes."

"I'm not worried. As long as there's a radio around I'll get outta Dodge in time."

"Ah, ta' hell with it," screamed the old toper, swinging at the air in frustration. He then grabbed his tattered hat and staggered off.

The barkeep, a hefty Creole no more than forty-years-old, made his way to the end of the bar, a welcoming smile and gleam in his eye. "What can I get for you, Chéri?"

Laurian thought about having a diet Coke but ordered wine instead.

"'Ow 'bout a nice Merlot? No," said the barkeep, Laurian cringing her lips, "… a Cabernet would be better."

"Yes, that sounds good."

"'Ow 'bout you, Raymond. Another JD?"

"I'm not in here lookin' to get sober. And if the lady permits," said Raymond, looking at Laurian, "… put her drink on my tab."

"*The lady permits*," mimicked Laurian, a bead of sweat trickling down her face. *So far so good. Glad I ordered the wine instead. I need a little something to calm my nerves. Nathan was right. Carlo would've had his hands full with this one. Now, what do I say to get him outside?*

Their drinks arrive and Laurian thanked Raymond,

inquiring about the disagreement he had with the old toper. They were talking about hurricanes but she wasn't interested in that. What perked her ears was the part about Raymond's boss having beachfront property in Florida. Laurian knew she could pry into that openly. *Women are always asking men about their jobs. No doubt I can get him to tell me the location of the house. Whether or not it belongs to Marcus, I'll pry into that as well.*

"How's the wine," asked Raymond, taking a sip of his whiskey.

"I like it."

Raymond looked at her more closely, particularly the bruise Carlo gave her in the maintenance van. "What happened to your cheek?"

"It's nothing. I slipped and fell," answered Laurian. She then thought about the ligature marks on her wrists, thankful that Vincent left a long sleeve shirt behind. "So your boss has a house in Florida. That must be nice."

"It's huge. He's got his own landing strip and private dock."

"Sounds dreamy," said Laurian in a silly way. "Where is it exactly, Miami?"

"No. Do you know where Fort Myers is?"

"I've been there a few times."

"It's right across the bay. Cape Coral."

Bingo! Time to get this guy outside, thought Laurian. "And what do you do for him, if you don't mind my asking?"

"A number of things," said Raymond rather stiffly. "You wouldn't know it by looking at me but I sometimes chauffeur him around. He's got a thing for limousines."

"*You don't say*," said Laurian, artfully placing her hand on his knee. "I've never been in a limo before," she whispered in his ear.

Raymond tried to look uninspired but Laurian saw the faint

curl of his brow and swelling of his cheeks. *He'll take the bait,* she thought. *It's now a matter of presentation.*

"Say, I've got an idea."

"I'll bet you do," snickered Raymond.

"Why don't you and I go someplace— a little more private. I gather there's a bar inside this limousine?"

"No can do. This one's over in New Orleans. But we can take a ride out there tonight."

"Sure, why not," answered Laurian. "It might be fun."

Raymond motioned to the barkeep that he's leaving. "Got me a party girl," he whispered. "You workin' tomorrow? I have a few things to tend to out this way."

"Yeah. Five o'clock."

"Good, I'll see you then."

Raymond escorts Laurian outside into the stale air, a tank-of-a-car pulling into the dusty lot—the little waitress he's been waiting for. Late for her shift, slamming the car door, the little waitress ran across the parking lot. Not wanting her to see him with another woman, Raymond takes a detour along the covered porch.

Paying no mind to his rig, Nathan and Clarence hiding behind the Blazer, Raymond noticed a man hunched in front of the dumpster. The brim of his hat blocking the man's face, Raymond thinks he knows who the man is.

Oh no! This is all wrong, thought Laurian. *We're supposed to head across the parking lot, not around it. He'll spot them for sure at this angle.*

"Oh crap," said Nathan, a slip of the tongue. Fortunately it was only loud enough for Clarence to hear. "Come on," he slapped Clarence on the shoulder. "We have to get out of here. *And fast!*"

Raymond and Laurian are at the bottom of the steps and the man at the dumpster distracts them with a revolting dry heave.

In a preempted attack, Nathan and Clarence head for Raymond's blindside, stride for stride with the sound of a crapulent drunk.

"Not something I really wanted to see tonight," said Laurian.

"Hey, Wendell, is that you," asked Raymond stepping closer. "You okay?"

"Oh, I'm fine," uttered the man—his voice unfamiliar. He has something in his hand. A package maybe. He then looked up from underneath the hat and Raymond recognized his face in the dim light… the clamant feet of Nathan and Clarence approaching from behind.

"What the hell!" clamored Raymond, turning just as Nathan and Clarence are upon him. Raymond's instincts took over, shoving Laurian aside with one hand, digging into his pocket with the other.

Laurian's feet are entangled with Raymond's and she falls, hitting her head on the wooden porch. Raymond doesn't see this, brandishing a switchblade and the shiv flinging out as Nathan lunged at him.

The knife went deep into Nathan's chest and he fell back into the unsuspecting arms of Clarence. In a festering stupor, Nathan can see Shadwell stepping out of the shadows, Laurian's precious map-box in his hand. Shadwell swung his arm as hard as he could, bashing the back of Raymond's skull with the map-box.

The sharp corner of the box drawing blood, Raymond staggered for a moment, looking rather dizzy and suddenly plummeting forward.

Falling like a puppet whose strings have been cut, when Raymond hit the dirt, he hit the dirt hard; the wonted little scene reminding Shadwell of the time he saved Margaret in the old carriageway… only this time it doesn't end so well with Laurian stretched out on the ground.

Shadwell is the first to arrive at Laurian's side, the knife in Nathan's pectoral muscle slowing him down. The blade went in nearly all the way, and Nathan, gritting his teeth, pulled it out in one quick motion.

"Ouch," uttered Clarence. "That must'a hurt sumpin' fierce?"

"Don't worry about me," said Nathan, grimacing while tossing the knife in the dumpster. "We need to make sure Laurian's all right. How is she," he asked Shadwell, taking a knee beside him.

The old man's eyes are full of sorrow and he doesn't say anything for the longest time … then sadly, "Nathan, I can't find a pulse. What do I do," he grabbed the other wrist.

"No, this can't be happening," cried Nathan. Close to tears, he put his hand upon her cheek.

"*Wait a minute*," said Shadwell, expelling a sigh of relief. "There it is! A healthy pulse."

"She hit them steps p'erty hard, Uncle Will. I hope there ain't nothing broke inside 'er."

"It's all my fault," said Shadwell. "I should have gone in myself."

"She wanted to go, Will. You can't blame yourself for that. Their legs somehow got crossed and she went down."

"And what about you? My God," exclaimed Shadwell, "… we need to get you to a hospital."

"I'm fine," said Nathan, taking a peek at his wound. "She's the one we need to worry about."

"I'll get the keys," said Shadwell. "Clarence, can you lift Doctor Webster without dropping her?"

Clarence put an arm under Laurian's knees, slipping his other arm under the back of her neck. Nathan asked him to be careful, and when Clarence gave a stern nod she began to stir; somewhat like a child in the middle of the night. She opened her eyes slowly, asking Shadwell what happened.

"You fell and hit your head on the porch," he answered, removing a set of keys from Raymond's pocket.

"How long was I out?"

"Not long," said Nathan. "But it seemed like forever."

"I saw a knife," uttered Laurian, leaning forward grabbing the back of her head. "Nathan, you're bleeding again."

"I'm afraid it's a bit more than a scratch this time. But I'm more concerned about you. You're going to need x-rays and right away."

"I'm okay … just a nasty bump. If anyone needs to go to the hospital it's you."

"Me? If you're not going then neither am I. We'll head out to the airport as soon as you're ready."

"We should stop at my folk's place. It's on the way. I can clean and dress that wound for you. We all need to freshen up anyway."

Everyone looked at one another and they all agree in their own way, thankful that no one argues against it.

"You're sure you're all right," asked Nathan.

"I'll be fine," answered Laurian. She felt a little woozy on her feet but didn't want to alarm anyone. "I'll go in for an x-ray after we find Margaret. That's right, I almost forgot! I know where they've taken her."

"Cape Coral," said Shadwell, reaffirming what they already know.

"Yes, right off the beach. It shouldn't be too hard to find. There's an airstrip next to it. And I'm guessing a waterfront dock as well."

"We need to get out of here then," said Nathan, "… before someone spots us."

"What about him," asked Laurian, looking down at Raymond.

"May as well put the trash where the trash belongs," answered Shadwell. "Come along, Clarence. Let's see if we can't find something to tie him up with."

Twenty-six

THE NIGHT AIR is a temperate beast, conspiring with the wind to bring misery and desolation to the Gulf Coast. *The calm before the storm*, thought Margaret, on a day she's been waiting a lifetime to come true—to not only drink the wine but to experience it as well. And now that she's had a taste, her mirror false for so many years, she can hardly wait for a full night's sleep, unveiling an old face to the inevitable dawn.

Knowing Marcus intrinsically, however, he'll not cradle his cathartic talk allowing her to sleep. And Margaret was right, waiting for the temperate beast to storm the coast, Marcus spoke of his life in Andalusia, the verbose chronicles of Sucràm Córdoba when he was a boy of sixteen.

His mother and father, put to death for heresy during the Spanish Inquisition, Sucràm denounced his faith in God, blaming both church and state. That, and a series of events so tragic on his young mind, his hatred in humanity escalating, for centuries Sucràm thought of nothing else … until he met Margaret—not so much as a child when her father was killed, but that night in the tavern when he gave her the map.

Fleeing the city of Córdoba, taking the name to mask his own, Sucràm traveled with Marcelina, his childhood sweetheart. She was two years younger than Sucràm and he remembers pushing her in a swing when she was but a child. They shared secrets growing up and Sucràm stole a kiss on her tenth birthday. The summer she lost her parents, a sickness that took them both, he vowed never to leave her.

When Marcelina moved in with her grandmother, it was easy for Sucràm to convince her to go with him. So strong the need for romance to survive, each knew if they were apart they would have nothing to sustain them.

After a long but civil debate of where to go, Marcelina gave in to Sucràm's desire to leave Spain. He had an uncle in France, and though his father taught him nothing of the path to manhood, Sucràm was determined to find his way. He knew crossing the border would be risky, but speaking French he felt he could travel there without difficulty, teaching Marcelina the language along the way.

The journey would be a long one, 400 kilometers on foot to Cartagena then up the Mediterranean to the transit port of Marseilles. After that, north on the Rhône River to Lyon where his uncle disappeared in exile.

They arrived in Cartagena in the winter, a cold, driving wind in their face and hunger plotting an attack on their stomachs. Marcelina, determined not to harp on the last time they ate, expatiates how good it will be to live in France. With scores of learned phrases to dish out, the rich culture to feast upon, she looked forward to a comfortable life there. But many a Spanish vessel needed to be fattened, and too cold and hungry to realize they were being deceived, she and Sucràm were duped by a band of slave traders.

Seduced by a giant Arab named Khaliq, convincing them he was of royalty and his servants had run off, he promised them free transport to Marseilles in exchange for their servitude on his royal barge.

That night, given a hot meal and warm bed, the inn rather decent, Khaliq and two of his men overpowered Sucràm. His beloved Marcelina, a knife to her throat, Khaliq warned Sucràm of her fate if he did not do as he was told. The next day, Khaliq and Sucràm were on a galleon bound for the West Indies, Marcelina sold into slavery as their ship sailed away.

Several young boys were onboard the galleon, all subjugated to minor tasks. Sucràm worked in the galley with twelve-year-old Tomás, a frail and innocent child. The boys were all mistreated and often beaten by Khaliq, Sucràm receiving the worst of it because of his defiant nature—his punishment brutal for the smallest of things.

The ship's first mate knew of the abuse, but not a single word did he say to the Captain, fearful Khaliq would come after him as well.

At seventeen, Sucràm was the oldest boy, undiscerned with the immoral behavior a man can inflict on a defenseless child. If he knew what Khaliq was forcing Tomás to do in his cabin, bringing him there every fourth night, Sucràm would show no mercy sparing the Arab's life.

An orphan from the city of Murcia, Tomás took Morisco as his surname, and Sucràm, a Spanish Moor himself, became his big brother. Sucràm took good care of little Tomás, often giving his ration of food and water to the boy, for as the weeks passed Tomás seemed very ill; Khaliq warning him never to speak of what goes on in his cabin.

The end of the voyage drawing near, Khaliq sent for Tomás one last time. He was nowhere to be found and Sucràm was called upon to find him. "You know where he likes to hide," said Khaliq. "Now go. And tell him not to drag his feet!"

It did not take long for Sucràm to locate the boy, sitting behind a water keg in the lower hold. He had a galley knife and Sucràm was beside himself. "How did you get that," he screamed. "Khaliq shall be furious. Is this the reason he demands that I find you."

"I no longer wish to live," said the boy, whimpering.

"But why? Have you forgotten our plan to escape… the presence of land closely upon us?"

Tomás could no longer keep secret the terrible things Khaliq did to him—*his big brother fuming.*

"I shall kill him this instant," said Sucràm, taking the knife from Tomás. "Cut a piece of flesh from his body as a reminder of what he stole from us. Upon his death, I shall proclaim, *love and innocence!* You and I shall be free of him this day, Tomás. So no more talk of death. When we drop sail and flee this bondage, we shall do the same for Marcelina; she too bearing witness to the flesh of our enemy, his name never to be mentioned again. Then we shall all grow old together, little brother. Make our home in France and be slaves no more. We can raise goats and drink wine whenever we please, having our fill and slumbering under the night of a thousand stars. And when we wake, it will not be to the sound of chains, but to the coo of the blessed dove."

Margaret turned an altruistic head toward Marcus… for the first time pity in her eyes. "Why now, Marcus? Why mention this at all. It's obvious you never intended to."

His thumb caressing the sandstone, Marcus turned away, staring at the ocean. "I need you to understand something, Margaret. It was fate that brought us together. I never told you how the map came into my possession, did I?"

"No, but I have a pretty good idea. A tattoo, is it not?"

"Yes. I went to Khaliq's cabin and killed him. He never saw it coming. His body lay face down and I proceeded as promised, ripping open his shirt for a portion of his hide. To my surprise, etched in floral colors below his neck, there they were … a string of seven islands off the coast of Florida. Paring his warm carcass, the piece of flesh more than I desired, I left the cabin fleeing to the lower hold."

"So the map belonged to Khaliq?"

"In a manner of speaking, yes."

"Then why did you tell me it belonged to Ponce de León?"

"*That night in the tavern*," inferred Marcus. "Would you have listened if I said it was Khaliq's Fountain of Youth? Ponce de León himself was pleased when I told him whose body the map came from. I was with him in Puerto Rico at the time, eighteen years young and thinking it to be a treasure map. He told me the fountain was no treasure and the legend nothing but a hoax—that I wasted my time tanning Khaliq's hide. For years he searched those islands in vain, urging me not to waste my life on something that wasn't there.

"Preparing for a new voyage to colonize Florida, I employed to him my service as a cabin boy. It was his last journey and I there to witness the event. Tomás was reluctant to leave San Juan and stayed behind."

"The expedition of 1521," said Margaret.

"Yes. And the attack on our landing party," asked Marcus, briskly rubbing the sandstone, "… you are aware of what happened?"

"Everyone fled to Cuba where Ponce de León died shortly thereafter. You must have been relieved to have escaped with him."

"That is where he spent his final hour, yes. But I played no part in that bit of history. I never made it back to the ship. The natives took me for dead and when I came to, the beach was empty. Vowing to make my way back to Puerto Rico, to find Tomás and return to Spain, I saw seven islands nesting on the horizon and couldn't help but stay in what is now Cape Coral. Fortunately, I kept the map. It took ten years, however, to figure out its secret."

"*The compass rose*," said Margaret.

"Yes. Unique, is it not? And you too figured it out."

"No," groaned Margaret, "... I did not. Year upon year of searching, I had nothing to show for my effort. Finally I took the map to a cartographic expert for help. 'The compass rose,' he said, 'look at it. It is different than others of its kind. Specifically the middle.' Much like any other map, I'd seen it a hundred times, a circle with eight spikes and corresponding letters at the base for each cardinal point. But there in the center of the circle, from the north point to the southeast and southwest points, I saw the outline of the letter A. It was then I noticed a faint marking at the right corner.

"The cartographer used a magnifying lens and told me the marking looked like a leaf. One that was added years later. The ink was a different substance and if someone wanted to find the leaf they needed to know what the A stood for. *I knew right away what it was!* Having explored every island on the ground and a dozen times in the air, the shape was unmistakable. I call it the Sandcat's castle, a patch of trees resembling a fortress. I knew the Sandcat was on Cayo Costa. A stretch of beach and tail-like dock, it looks like a cat from the air. The castle is a cluster of trees in the shape of a giant A below the cat's belly. The leaf comes from a rare strain of ivy and I saw sheets of it at the southeast corner of the Sandcat's castle. The exact location on the map."

"I did not have the advantage of air travel back then," Marcus continued his story, "... but scouring for food and hiding from the natives, I knew which grove of trees the symbol referred to. Eleven years and there it was ... behind the ivy.

"That night at the tavern when I went back to my room, I figured it would be impossible to decipher the map with no knowledge of the grove. Therefore, I was not concerned when I drew the leaf to make it easier for you."

"And when did you drink from the fountain? You must have been near forty when that happened."

"Yes. I was 29 when I found the cave, but there was no fountain to speak of... only a temperamental cat wandering in the dark. I sometimes used the cave for shelter, but other than that, I spent my days on the beach... the legend no more a myth to me than a hoax to Ponce de León. But the following year a strange native came to the island. A cannibal by the look of him, he must have been a thousand miles from home. I found out later he was a Cariban tribesman and his name was Takara ... *Tantur's father.*

"I spied on him as he brought animal carvings and human skulls to the cave, never going inside but placing them in front of the ivy. He worshiped the site for weeks on end, always returning the following year... his dugout full of carvings and trophy skulls. This went on for 10 years during the summer months, new offerings and weeks of chanting to the clouds.

"You were right about my age, Margaret. I turned forty the year Takara darkened the sky with his outstretched hands. There was a terrible storm brewing, and by the expression on his face, that's why he kept coming back. He danced in circles in front of the ivy, stirring up more than a rainstorm as an alligator emerged from the brush latching onto his leg. I'd been curious of this man for so many years, coming to the grove each summer, something suddenly came over me that day. I abandoned my seclusion, tearing into the alligator's throat with my knife. But I was too late. Takara had a deep gash in his leg and a river of blood flowing out. It hurt me to see him like that. I shall never forget the look on his face nor the great pain he was in. I fastened a tourniquet above his wound and at first he appeared grateful, then perplexed upon examining the color of my skin.

"The storm turned out to be a hurricane and Takara motioned to the carvings. I imagine he thought I knew nothing of the cave because he spread the ivy apart, the entrance so small you had to crawl around to find it. I managed to drag him down the narrow passage into the main chamber. The rest is rather mundane since you know how the fountain works. Grateful that I saved his life, when the hurricane's inherent water filled the pool, Takara shared its secret with me… gesturing that I should drink first. From the glowing pool, he immediately drank his fill. My eyes were stunned to see how quickly the gash in his leg healed. The blood disappeared and the deep furrow in his leg closed in a matter of seconds. Then my heart beat strange and my body shook. I renounced a lifetime of doubt as I too became immortal."

"And Tantur," Margaret interrupts, "… serves in place of his father because Takara owed you a life."

"Their culture demands it and I cannot argue otherwise. I was present when Takara took Tantur to the fountain. The early nineteenth century, I believe. Tantur was Takara's only child back then. Now he and Wahota are the only surviving members of that bloodline. I do not feel he is worthy, but Wahota may be the last to drink its waters."

"What do you mean, the last?"

"There are but a few Cariban tribesmen left. Forgetting my oath to Marcelina and Tomás, I made such a terrible mistake back then.

"Desperate for money, I sold the map to a man named Benjamin Lewis—the bad-seed of your bloodline, Margaret. Long before I gave the map to you, he figured out the compass rose, showing it to his cousin … the great explorer, Meriwether Lewis. I thought Meriwether was off to Washington to appropriate funds for an expedition. I killed him at the start of his journey but he didn't have the map, nor did Benjamin, searching for the fountain without it. When another tribesman came to worship, Benjamin wanted to know where the fountain was. The tribesman kept his mouth shut, but Benjamin, the stronger of the two, subdued and tortured him. Still the tribesman would not talk, and out of frustration Benjamin killed him. The following year a hunting party came and discovered their kinsman's remains.

"Benjamin started a war, Margaret. But not just between the Cariban and your family. Anyone looking for the fountain was a threat to them. You share Merewether's name but I put no blame on his family. It is the bloodline of Benjamin Lewis that threatens the Cariban, and I vowed to protect them… the fountain's secret as well."

"Protect them!?" Margaret jumped up. "*You kill for them!* Now I understand what this is all about. It's a feud between families and you're a tribal mercenary— paid-in-full with your immortality."

"No! It's not like that at all," replied Marcus rising to his feet.

"Yes, *it is!*" snapped Margaret, the luminous pool at her back and moonlit ocean upon her face. "Tell me Marcus, if not Meriwether, who did Benjamin give the map to?"

"His son, Nathaniel."

"*My great-great-grandfather?* You killed him and took the map, didn't you?"

"No," said Marcus, spinning the sandstone in his hand, "… he was killed by a Cariban Warrior. The map was passed on to Nathaniel's son before he died. And the same was true of his death, passing it on to your grandfather, Bartholomew—long before the Cariban discovered his whereabouts."

"And was he the last to have the map."

"No, Margaret. His death close at hand, Bartholomew gave the map to his son. He was only seven at the time and no threat to the Cariban."

"But they killed him later, didn't they? They killed my father and returned the map to you. You had it with you that night in the tavern waiting to fulfill your promise. *You gave to me the flesh of your enemy.* This is more than just a war, Marcus. For you it's an amoristic quest!"

Marcus turned his back toward the ocean, away from Margaret's blustering voice. He then threw his parallactic stone into the pool, aiming to drown his indignation.

"Marcus, look at me," cried Margaret, grabbing but unable to wheel him around. "Look at me! Why will you not turn and face the truth," she screamed, a fistful of contempt attacking his shoulder. "Look at me! *I am not your Marcelina!*"

"I know who you are," said Marcus, turning to and facing both Margaret and the approaching storm. "Who was it that murdered your father, you ask? It was not the Cariban. Inept to measure my own time, *of when youth ends and manhood begins*, I know nothing of right from wrong—apologizing to no one because of it. But now, I somehow feel responsible for your father's death. I am filled with sorrow for what took place that afternoon. Truly I am."

Margaret stormed into the house, Marcus returning to his seat, full of regret and reflective sin. *For love and innocence,* he remembers shouting, plunging the knife into Khaliq. *I too lost my innocence to him, Tomás. His blood was the first spilled by my hand. And now, little brother, that vengeful act haunts me. Was that the origin of my murderous self? Or do I blame those responsible for the death of my parents? Verily I cannot be held accountable for the whole of my sins ... shunned that I kept watch, never expecting you to kill Margaret's father.*

The incident appeared to Marcus vividly; that afternoon he came for the map. There were no retaining walls around the mansion or iron bars covering the windows back then. The exterior had a fresh coat of paint and all the flowers were dripping fall colors to the ground. The ivy was newly planted and not yet climbing the pillars and walls. A dirt surface ran from the front lawn to the main road and there was no conquistador to guard against intruders.

Out back, a gazebo is under construction and a small child is on a swing with no one to push her. She resembles Marcelina when she was that age and Marcus recalls the promise he made. More than four-hundred years his journey is coming to an end.

Three men join him in the trees and Marcus delivers a set of perspicuous instructions, explaining the importance of their mission. "Remember to watch that temper of yours, little brother. All I want is Khaliq's map. I shall stay and cover your back. Now go before Alexander shows up."

Tomás Morisco shook his head, the other two men, siblings, following him to the front of the mansion. When they turn the corner, a large, spirited housekeeper saunters down the back steps with a basket of laundry. The little girl asks for a push but the housekeeper tells her to leave the swing alone, to play inside so as not to dirty her dress.

Marcus keeps an eye on the housekeeper, pinning shirts and trousers to a braded line. The clothes and linen are all hung, sheets flapping in the breeze and Marcus growing impatient. Suddenly, Tomás and the middle-aged brothers appear at the edge of the trees, the housekeeper lumbering back inside for another load, screaming at the top of her lungs shortly thereafter.

One of the brothers gave Marcus the map, commenting on how ghastly it is. "Did everything go as planned," asked Marcus, Tomás and the two brothers awfully quiet. "Tell me, little brother, what cause was there for the servant to scream?"

Tomás remained silent and Marcus questioned the two brothers.

"It was all his doing," one of them said, pointing to Tomás. "Alexander came in from out of nowhere and he panicked."

"It's true," said his brother, explaining how unstable Tomás was, wanting to get rid of Alexander right there in front of his little girl… clutching onto her father as he dangled from a hangman's noose.

A vision of Marcelina takes Marcus by surprise, of how sad she was when *her father* died. He then recalls how he reacted when his parents were tortured and killed. "You fool! You took his life with the little girl there!?"

Overcome with rage, Marcus grabbed Tomás by the throat, knowing how to strangle the life out of someone such as himself.

The brothers' watch in horror as Tomás falls to the ground. "You have your money," Marcus exonerates them, "… *now take your father and go.*"

Trudging back to the house, nothing can hide in the dim light from Marcus. He can see Tantur on the balcony, knowing he was listening in. But it doesn't matter. Everything Marcus said tonight, Tantur's heard it all before.

The French doors which lead inside are open and Marcus stoops to enter. The room is half den and half kitchen, similar in size to the gallery above. A staircase hugs the wall on the right and a tropical breakfast bar on the left. There are two cane sofas in the middle of the room facing one another; comfortable white cushions on both.

Ariel sits at the bar, watching hurricane updates on a wall mounted screen, paying no mind to Margaret who is parked on one of the sofas with Bourbon curled up beside her.

Margaret quickly lays a hand atop the cat to keep him from jumping on Marcus.

The courtyard fountain is visible through another pair of French doors and every time Marcus sees it he is remorseful. Tomás did the mason work, one by one his little brother removing the stones from the cave, carting them off the island. He and Marcus built that section of house two-hundred years ago. Marcus constructed a master suite on the north wing and Tomás on the south… the latter converted into a storeroom in 1910.

"I know how you must feel," said Marcus, taking a seat across from Margaret—a satellite image of Hurricane Andrew over her shoulder.

"What about my son, Marcus. And his wife? Did you kill them? Or was that an order from your unscrupulous mouth?"

"I am to blame for much of this, Margaret, but there are others as well. Tomás, a long story in itself, I strangled for killing your father. He had two sons at the time and Takara killed the youngest a few years ago. The older brother, an immortal for two centuries, would love nothing better than to get his hands around my neck. I did not ask for this life, Margaret, but unlike you I wish to keep it. All that I live for has but one purpose. To maintain the fountain's secret. To survive this war the Cariban need the advantage of immortality. Wahota is too young, but due to his injury his right of passage takes place tomorrow, joining us sooner than expected."

"*Joining you?* Marcus, there is no one left but Nathan. Do you actually believe he would kill the last of a dying people?"

"Are you that naïve, Margaret? Relevant to circumstances, most everyone is capable of killing. And to live forever … what is that worth? The fountain is tailor made for such a thing."

"No, you're wrong. Nathan would never do that."

"He may not have to. Tomás' son will stop at nothing to have his children drink from the fountain. The Cariban are all that stand in his way. Regardless of Nathan's position, he still has a part in this. I said I would not harm him, but should he involve himself further, others may be less merciful than I."

"I'm tired, Marcus. This is too much to take in all at once. I care not of some silly war. I wish only to fall asleep and dream that I am someplace else."

"Sleep then, Margaret, for I have business to tend to with Tantur. I cannot undo the past and bring back those I took from you. And though I wish I could, it does not change who I am. Tomorrow we go to the island. My life without you, I fear would be unbearable."

Heading for the stairs by way of Ariel, Marcus takes a peek at the television. "Any change?"

"Still on course, Father. A Category 4 with winds of 125 knots. Expected to make landfall in South Florida around sunrise."

"Good. Stay here and keep our guest company while I talk to Tantur."

The lamp on the nightstand is softly lit and Tantur neither reads nor watches television, the light too weak for one and the room absent of the other. A deep basin of ice water is stationed next to the lamp with a washcloth clumped at the bottom. Wrenching the cloth, Tantur applies it to Wahota's forehead, wishing he had gone after Nathan instead. But he had no idea Wahota's genetic cells are insufficient, consequently, rather than helping, they are endangering his life. His blood is coagulating too fast and with the serous fluid rushing into his cerebral ventricles, swelling his brain, there's nothing any mortal man can do to save him.

Marcus tapped lightly on the doorjamb, a quick look inside before entering the room. "*How is he,* " he asked Tantur in his native tongue.

Tantur put a finger to his lips, he and Marcus stepping into the gallery. "Not good. He has a fever and his breath is fading."

"Let me call a doctor," said Marcus, reverting to English. "I can have one here within the hour."

"No. A doctor cannot mend what is broken. Only the sacred water can save him now."

"I agree, Tantur. But Andrew's not expected to pass this way until tomorrow afternoon. Please, let me bring in a physician. He may not last that long."

Tantur showed no sign of changing his mind and Marcus admits it was wrong for him to blame Wahota for Nathan's escape. "I should have sent him after Margaret instead. But you are the elder tribesman now. The decision was yours … as is this one."

"If he were a few years older the decision would not be so hard… but we have no choice."

"So be it. Tomorrow he will drink from the fountain, but we must be careful. The son of Tomás Morisco may be waiting for us. His children are the appropriate age now. Daniel, the oldest, I know to be quite strong. The other one, a daughter who was hidden at birth, I know nothing about. And I've upset Margaret again… she may also cause trouble. How long will it take to prepare a full batch of darts? Nothing too strong. I'd rather not kill anyone this time. Remember, Margaret is now vulnerable to those kinds of drugs."

"It will not take long, now that Wahota is asleep."

"Excellent," replied Marcus. "I shall stay at your brother's side until you are finished."

Tantur went to his private room, arranging everything necessary on a narrow countertop, an aquarium teeming with frogs ready to go.

A large, fat candle, sunken at the top, upon lighting the wick Tantur spreads open a pair of sticks attached to a netted pouch. Next, he opens a box of darts where a small quantity have been pilfered. He thinks nothing of it, however, not with Wahota practicing in the nearby trees.

Placing his wooden armlet next to an empty bowl, Tantur reached into the aquarium for one of the colorful frogs, securing the toxic creature in the netting with its tiny underside over the bowl. Moving the candle close to the frog, it secretes a small amount of venom. Diluting the poison with a saltwater base, Tantur dipped one of the darts into the mixture, smelling it to ensure the appropriate toxicity. Sticking the dart into a wooden armlet, he takes another frog from the aquarium, repeating the process… another frog, another dart … another frog….

PART III

Storms of the Island

Twenty-seven

A FLORID STREAK across the sky, daybreak is upon the Crescent City, Nathan sitting alone with Khaliq's map sprawled out on the breakfast table. Too busy to make coffee or grab a bite to eat, he takes a moment to stretch in his chair, the sun lurking outside and a favorite poem coming to mind.

Monday morning, clouding the air,
birds are chirping and dogs are yapping,
squirrels chattering and motorcars dashing.

"A tainted sibling," the poet doth breathe,
"the enactment of dread
of all seven perceived.

"But why speak harsh of a day not spent;
this morn and those yet to come—
of its divine birthing, so painfully numb."

Guilty too of despising Mondays, Nathan wonders why; especially after what he's been through. *It doesn't make sense*, he thought, *the best Monday of my life. I'm lucky to be alive.*

Laurian is in the next room, a huge, vaulted study paneled in mahogany. Her thoughts of life and death are similar to Nathan's. A number of extant sunrises in her life, she cannot recall one more inspiring than the present. As a child, she used to sit and wait for that first ray of light, her stepfather, *an insomniac himself*, sharing many a sunrise with her. They would nestle at the edge of Laurian's poster-bed, orange juice and coffee on the windowsill and cinnamon toast between them.

Not far from Lafayette Cemetery, the Garden District alive with prosperity, Ionic white mansions line the streets. The Webster house, however, with its olivaceous exterior and decorative iron, appears completely out of place.

Laurian presently sits on the drawn-out sofa she slept on, gazing at her daughter, Amy, curled up on a comfortable settee. The eleven-year-old fancies her mother's old poster-bed upstairs, but with all the commotion, *Nathan who she met earlier and two others in the house*, she slept downstairs not wanting to miss anything.

A tapestry map of the world covers an entire wall and Laurian feels very much alone. The study also has a large globe and lectern for referencing atlases and other books. Medical journals and encyclopedias are the most common in the study; the second being an ample supply of fairytales as Grandam May and Paw-Paw Webster are never without a bedtime story for their granddaughter.

Rising from the sofa, pink sweats and an oversized shirt, Laurian feels well rested, her tender feet navigating the aging, wool carpet. A subtle, Karabagh design, the Axminster carpet came from England at a time when you couldn't buy it anywhere else. Kissing Amy on the forehead, Laurian is drawn away from the simple pleasures of motherhood to her current situation, gazing in earnest at the tapestry map from across the room.

A by-product of old age, fading in spots where the sun

comes in, remarkably, most everything on the map is legible; and though Cape Coral and Fort Myers were deprived of ink, Laurian knows exactly where they are. Stepping closer, she can see the string of islands protecting them—a natural levee if the sea is provoked and the wind succumb to rage.

Freshening up before changing into a pair of black corduroys and sleeveless top, Laurian found herself alone with Nathan in the kitchen. "Good morning," she said with a doting smile, opening a cabinet where the coffee is stored.

"Morning," replied Nathan, engrossed in Khaliq's map.

Wearing a shirt Laurian found in her brother's old room, nothing is said of how Nathan looks or that the map is sitting on a surface where people eat. "How was the couch," is all Laurian asks, turning on the coffee maker.

"I wouldn't know. I've been up all night looking at this map. Your mother came down and we chatted for a while. I put the map away of course, before she could see it."

"Good," said Laurian, opening the blinds and the sun drifting in. "It's best if she and my father don't know about this."

Nathan shook his head agreeing with her, Laurian sitting next to him reaching for her purse across the table. "*There you are*," she said to herself, opening the leather flap.

"Did you get enough sleep," asked Nathan, peering up from the map. "I see the swelling on your cheek has gone down … or did you put something on it?"

"Make-up," replied Laurian, pulling out a compact.

Nathan figures she powdered her ligature marks as well. With the coffee now brewing, he mentions how fortunate they are that her parents' put everyone up for the night. He then thanked Laurian for the shirt… inquiring what her stepbrother does for a living—his name having come up.

"*Jonathan Webster,*" Nathan said to himself. "He wouldn't happen to be a journalist for The Washington Post, would he?"

"On and off for about ten years now," answered Laurian.

"It certainly is a small world. I have a college buddy who knows him. As a matter of fact, Jonathan interviewed his wife for an article last year. A detailed report on the pharmaceutical company she works for. The progress they're having in coronary and pulmonary medication is astounding."

"I remember that," said Laurian. "Maurus Pharmaceutical. Jonathan's rather partial to research and development."

"He must write about you quite often."

"He wants to but I won't let him."

"Why not?"

"Too painful. Most of my early research I did because of my husband. I mentioned that, remember … *our daughter the perfect donor.* Ironically, if not for that decision, she would not be here today."

"It's tough losing a—"

"Let's not talk about that," Laurian cut Nathan off. "I've had too many sleepless nights already and here you are going through the same thing. It's hard to concentrate on anything else, but we need to focus on Margaret."

"You're right," said Nathan. "I just wish I could have spent more time with them. Take back some of the things I said to my father."

"I used to wish that too … but of things not said. There's no reason for that kind of regret though. Not if you believe in heaven. There'll be plenty of time to reconcile later."

"Never thought of it like that," said Nathan, focusing on the map.

"So what do you think," asked Laurian, drawing closer for a better look.

Nathan shook his head. "William was right … it's just a ridicules old map."

"Then why bother with it. We know Margaret's in Cape

Coral."

"And if she's not, what then? What if everything you told me were true? If my grandmother is as young as you say, and this Marcus character still alive, why did he kidnap her? What's changed in the last fifty years?"

"Margaret. I'm certain of it," attested Laurian.

"She's no longer immortal and Marcus scoops her up. Why?"

Laurian thought for a moment. "To take her back to the fountain!"

"Exactly. I think he's planning another trip to the island. *But which one*," muttered Nathan, reluctantly turning to Laurian. "I can't help but think we're running out of time here. She never mentioned the fountain's location, *or how to read the map?*"

"No," replied Laurian, getting up for coffee. "All she said was to hide it someplace safe."

Laurian offers Nathan a cup of coffee but he refuses. He then tells her how awful it would be if they find the right island but arrive too late. "The fountain," he added, "… I care nothing about."

"You know, Nathan, you're starting to sound like a believer."

"It's no myth, I can tell you that."

"So you do believe. What made you change your mind?"

"The talk we had on the bayou," said Nathan, lowering his voice "… about chromosomes and progenies. There can be no other explanation."

Nathan opened his shirt and Laurian is awestruck at the cuts and contusions he suffered. She can barely make out the laceration down his chest and the bruises where he had been kicked are no longer there. But most astounding, there is a scab developing where Raymond stabbed him and his shoulder where he fell. “I always thought I was so lucky,” said Nathan buttoning the shirt, “… never having been sick or injured. Now I feel— *like an outcast*. We have to find her, Laurian. She wants to be normal like everyone else.”

Margaret’s telegram is on the table and Nathan gave it to Laurian. “I’ve gone over this all night as well. Thinking it may contain a clue on how to read the map.”

Laurian crept through the message: “Come as quickly as possible… I have urgent news… pay attention to my address if you do not have it.” Laurian gave the telegram back to Nathan. “I don’t see anything unusual,” she said.

“Then why send it?”

“What do you mean?”

“Why Western Union? Telegrams are obsolete. It would have been easier to call me.”

“Margaret has a thing about phones. Whether or not someone is listening in.”

“That’s what I’ve been telling myself over and over again,” said Nathan. “But it won’t sink in.”

Frustrated, Nathan crumpled the telegram into a little ball casting it aside. “We’ll never figure this out in time,” he groaned, returning to the map. “There should be an X like on a pirate map. Some kind of coordinates or something.”

“You mean latitude and longitude? I doubt if they were in use at that time. The first prime meridian appeared on a map at the start of the 16th century. A Portuguese cartographer, Pedro Reinel, drew the first latitude scale in 1504, hardly enough time for Ponce de León to acquire a decent map.”

“Are you sure?”

“Positive. My father and I spent many a morning talking about the ancient mariners. The early compass made its way from China to Europe in the 13th century; highly inaccurate until the 1500’s. Octants and sextants didn’t exist until the middle of the 18th century. Explorers like Magellan had charts that were misleading so the stars were their main source of navigation. If Ponce de León crafted that map, it would have been difficult returning to the same spot. In fact," Laurian rambles on, "… Magellan knew nothing of the world beyond the Americas. In a dispute over a westward route to the Spice Islands, he renounced his Portuguese citizenship, offering his services to the king of Spain." Pausing for a moment, Laurian quietly said to herself, "*Wait a minute … that's odd.*"

"What?"

"In 1521, Ponce de León fell under attack somewhere around Charlotte Harbor. He later died in Havana from his wound. A poison arrow to the thigh. That same year on the other side of the world Magellan was also killed. The Battle of Mactan in the Philippines. A poison arrow in his foot and spear through his heart. Magellan was the first explorer to circumnavigate the globe and he never made it back home."

"*Home*," wondered Nathan, staring at the crumpled telegram. "*He circumnavigates the globe but never made it back home.* That's it!"

"What," uttered Laurian, questioning the excitement in Nathan's eyes.

Grabbing the wadded telegram, the number 26 atop the crinkled surface, Nathan unfurls the paper. "2641, Parish Road 8214. She picked out the road she wanted and brought it to her neck of the woods. That must have cost her a pretty penny."

"What are you talking about?"

"My grandmother's address. The cab driver got lost looking for it. He said Road 8214 belonged in a different Parish. Look here," said Nathan, showing Laurian the address on the telegram. "These are grid coordinates. 26 degrees, 41 minutes north latitude. 82 degrees, 14 minutes west longitude."

"Clever."

"She did leave a clue, Laurian, in case something happened to her. All we need now is a map to confirm the coordinates?"

Nathan and Laurian charge into the den; Amy still sound asleep. His ribs no longer bothering him, Nathan made his way to the tapestry map, Antarctica at his knees and his head lazily scrolling upward. His eyes are swimming through the South Atlantic crossing the Sudan until his head is level with the Mediterranean. He looked up at Europe, climbing the Alps then trudging over Scandinavia. Finally, out of breath, he's at the top of the world. "That is one…big…map," he strung out the last three words, eyes crossing the North Atlantic over to Laurian.

"My father's a bit of an enthusiast."

Vertical and horizontal lines showing their perspective degrees, the tapestry stiff and somewhat gritty, Nathan slid his finger down the coast of Florida. "I hope I'm right about this," he said. "Cape Coral … Cape Coral— *no Cape Coral.*"

"To small a city. There," said Laurian, pointing to Charlotte Harbor, "… those are the islands we're looking for."

"If those *are* map coordinates," Nathan stepped away from the wall, "… they're in the right place. You wouldn't happen to have a more detailed map of that area, would you?"

"Behind you," answered Laurian, directing him to the lectern.

"Perfect," exclaimed Nathan, flipping through an atlas of the United States and its territories—topographic squares with their parallels fifteen minutes apart and meridians thirty. Florida has five squares at 1:1000000 scale and Nathan troubles Laurian for a pencil and paper.

"What do you need that for?"

"To figure out these coordinates."

"Here," said Laurian, handing Nathan a straightedge scored with two different sized lines. "Minutes and seconds," she tells him. "It's best to determine latitude first."

Nathan put the straightedge alongside the meridian marked 82°, covering the mainland and counting four minutes down from the 26° 45' parallel. "That narrows it down to La Costa or Pine Island," he said, referencing an imaginary line. "Have you got something I can hold this measurement with?"

Laurian gave him a yellow, sticky post-it and Nathan attached it squarely in place, moving the straightedge fourteen minutes west of the 82° mark. "That's it," he announced. "We found our island. La Costa!"

"*Cayo Costa*," said Shadwell correcting Nathan, his haggard body crossing the room.

"We know where the fountain is, Will."

"*On Cayo Costa*," Shadwell questioned Nathan, as though it were the last island he'd ever suspect.

"Somewhere in this general area," exclaimed Nathan, pointing to the northeastern part of the island. He told Shadwell about the telegram and the possibility of Margaret drinking from the fountain again.

"You said you didn't believe in such nonsense?"

Nathan looked at Laurian, his eyes pleading with her to remain quiet. "It's just a theory," he said to Shadwell, "… if we can't find her in Cape Coral, what harm is there in searching the island."

Shadwell moved in for a closer look, sticking his nose in the atlas. "I know this area," he said. "Margaret nicknamed it the Sandcat's castle. Believe me … there's nothing there. If your mind is set on going, I wish you the best of luck. I won't be traveling any further."

"*Why not?*" clamored Nathan, unaware of how weary the old man is. But Laurian knows. Her stepfather, so frail and peaked, like Shadwell he never admits how tired he is.

"If we make it there before the hurricane," continued Nathan, "… it would be nice to have you along. You know that island like the back of your hand. *We're not going there to search for some fountain,*" he lowered his voice. "I just want to find my grandmother and bring her home."

"I can't help you," said Shadwell, the disappointment in his voice matching, *if not exceeding* the look on Nathan's face. "It took a great deal out of me to make it this far. Clarence can help you the rest of the way."

Amy begins to stir and Laurian goes to her, a smile of gratitude aimed at Shadwell. Old age hindering him from the intense pace, Laurian appears rather sad knowing the condition he's in.

It is somewhat of a shock to Clarence, his uncle going home without him. He and Nathan are upstairs in Jonathan's old room, Clarence sitting on the edge of the bed with a dreary look on his face. Likewise, directly below them, Shadwell and Laurian are seated at the kitchen table. Amy, no one else in a better mood, she too sits at the table; an inquisitive, headstrong youngster, neglecting her bowl of cereal on this particular day.

Upon entering the kitchen, Clarence takes a seat next to Amy, filling his bowl with the same frosted squares and not a word to his uncle—he doesn't know what to say.

"I'd fix us a fancy breakfast but we don't have time," said Laurian, transferring the vial from the map-box to her purse.

"What was that," asked Amy, Nathan taking a seat across the table and the serum's lavender glow catching her eye.

"The drug I've been working on, sweetie. Hopefully," Laurian glanced at Nathan, "… one that Mr. Lewis will administer. I need to leave you with Paw-Paw and Grandam May while we tend to this. I won't be gone long. I promise."

Amy looked at her and said nothing. She knew the routine. Her mother's going to some faraway hospital and she'll make it up to her in due time.

"So, what's our plan," asked Laurian, turning to Nathan.

"We'll take the Blazer to the airport. Things get a little tricky once we're there. Without a pilot and our destination questionable, I doubt if we'll find anyone willing to help."

Laurian insists that Richard will show up. Nathan, however, advises otherwise.

"If you must hire another pilot," Shadwell interrupts them, "… do so with a different service. If Richard's not there they'll ask a lot of questions and you don't have time for that. I've been listening to the news all morning. Andrew's on its way to Fort Myers so you've got less than seven hours. Don't waste too much time looking for a pilot to handle Margaret's old seaplane. Charter a jet if you have to."

"Hard to get our bag full of goodies aboard if we do," said Nathan, the right choice of words with Amy in the room.

"We'll figure something out," replied Laurian. "I'm going to leave this with my father," she said, putting the map back in its box—the computer disk still inside. "I'll be back in a minute."

At the end of the hall, bottom of the stairs, Laurian turned the corner running into her mother.

"Good morning," May greeted her daughter. "How are all your friends? Well rested I hope."

"Everyone had a good night's sleep. Except for Nathan, I'm afraid. They're in the kitchen grabbing a quick bite. I want to say good-bye to Dad before we leave. Is he awake yet?"

"Of course he's awake. The two of you are always up at this hour."

"How's he feeling?"

"A little better. He perks up whenever you drop by."

Laurian gave her mother a kiss. "Mind keeping the others company for a couple of minutes?"

"Now what kind of question is that? You always bring such nice people home. I had a long talk with Nathan while you were asleep. He really came through for you this afternoon, the way he handled himself at your house. He's pretty good in a pinch. And quite handsome, wouldn't you say?"

"*Mother!*" exclaimed Laurian, the tone meant to keep her quiet. Heading up the stairs, Laurian leaned over the banister, catching her mother off-guard. "He is rather good looking, isn't he?"

May grinned at her daughter's festive smile, appeased that she may have finally taken an interest in someone.

Laurian's stepfather is sitting in bed staring out the window; a patchwork quilt over his lap and extra pillow behind his back. Looking at his posture one would think him to be much older than sixty-seven. His face is terribly pale and his hands rest upon a hollow stomach. What little hair he has, thin and very gray, looms in a half-circle around his ears and neck. His eyes are dull under a pair of dark-rimmed glasses, glistening suddenly at the sight of his little girl.

Laurian sat on the edge of the bed, the map-box in one hand while checking her father's forehead with the other.

"None of that now," he pulled her hand away. "I'm fine. It's nothing more than a summer cold."

"Dad, we're both doctors here. Stay home and get some rest today."

"Since when have either of us practiced what we've preached. If anyone needs to stay home it's you. Smarty-pants would like to spend more time with her mother. Why don't you take a vacation this year? And when I say vacation, I mean a week or two. Not some spur of the moment trip to Orlando."

"When I get back, I promise."

"Now don't make promises you can't keep."

"You know I wouldn't do that."

"I know, Precious," he said, patting her leg. "So, are you going to tell me what's in the box or do I have to guess?"

"Can you find a safe haven for it," answered Laurian. "There's a research disk inside I can ill afford to lose. I'd take care of it myself but I don't have time."

"Nor the place," said her stepfather, his eyes turning serious. "Your mother told me about your house and I saw what happened to your lab on the news. What's going on, Laurian? I have a feeling you're in some kind of trouble."

"Don't worry, I'll be all right. I have a patient in Florida who needs my help. I'd tell you more but right now isn't a good time."

"I understand you missed your flight yesterday. This hurricane is something you shouldn't take lightly. I wish I could convince you to wait it out but it's your decision not mine. If this is an emergency … go. I trust your good judgment."

"Thanks, Dad." Laurian gave him a lengthy kiss on the cheek, revealing more than just affection.

"You're not going to the northern part of the state, are you?"

"No. We're headed straight for the hurricane."

"You won't think ill of me if I ask you to be careful?"

"I'd be disappointed if you didn't."

Another sunrise flooding the room, Laurian tears up, her eyes drowning with the knowledge of her stepfather's impending death. Her arms, smothering the frailness of fatherhood, she draws from him the courage necessary to confront what lies ahead. She thought for a moment on the possibility of saving him, knowing full well she's rushing off to destroy the very thing that can—a difficult choice over whether or not death survives.

Twenty-eight

IT FELT LIKE a dream to Margaret, running through the trees with sheets of rain cascading from the sky. She cannot remember how she escaped or where she's running to, only that Marcus and his entourage are close behind. *The Lady Bird,* she wonders, *which way do I go?*

All of a sudden Margaret stopped dead in her tracks, thick clumps of brush at her feet and the rain pelting her face like before. It was her worst mistake ever, telling Stuart about the fountain—her world upside-down ever since. *I can blame no one but myself,* she thought.

A slave to the hurricane's will, Margaret can only move wherever the wind takes her. At the moment, she's running from an unknown shadow. It can't be Marcus or Tantur, the spindly form traversing from one swaying palm to the next; Margaret catching a glimpse now and then between bursts of lightening. She can sense herself losing ground, her sluggish pace no match for the shadow's rousing stride.

For the longest time nothing looks familiar. There is no thicket of ivy or pile of rocks Takara used as an altar. Closing her eyes, trying to recall how everything looked in the first hurricane, the shipwreck where she and Stuart stumbled upon the fountain, all Margaret can think about is Stuart dying and Marcus demanding she submit to him.

Margaret did not benefit from the fountain's perceptional gifts that day. While others came away with incredible vision, a keen sense of smell or hearing, or sometimes all three, she received none of that; only the headaches and the curse of immortality. *The fountain takes… it always takes*, thought Margaret.

The first to be taken of those she loved was Stuart. The beginning of no end, William was next; alienated but taken nonetheless. Now her only child is dead. Would Nathan, *innocent Nathan*, an implausible grandson nearly twice her age, be the next victim of this Pandora's Box.

I should have walked away, thought Margaret. *I am no better than Marcus because of it.* "*I'm so sorry, Stuart,*" she whispered to the pouring rain, her tears lost upon the wet ground. *I should have been stronger. Things may have turned out better had I listened to you … and to William as well.*

With the hurricane strengthening, a cold wind swooping through the trees, Margaret can feel herself shivering. She's unsure, however, as to whether or not the wind or the shadow's presence chills the air. Running once more, she stumbles over a fallen branch into a meager patch of ivy. Covered in mud, she follows an abandoned trail where the ivy grows thick on one side. The soft footed area, emerald waterfalls glistening among the pines, in no time she is surrounded by nothing but ivy.

"*This is it,*" Margaret said to herself, the rain falling so hard she can barely hear herself think. *This is where it all began. No wonder it took so long to find. The island takes on a different appearance after each hurricane. The ebb and flow of one storm creating another storm's realm.*

One thing she can see that hasn't changed is the way the ivy kindles to a strong hurricane. From a shimmering green it turned into a placid olive… violet, milky fluid oozing from the leaves. The rain, cleansing this new found spectrum, *the fountain rising again*, a puce looking stream popples at Margaret's feet, dividing into a multitude of stretchy tentacles disappearing into the earth.

Margaret drew close to a twenty-foot wall of clean, hydrated leaves dripping with satisfaction. She doesn't recall the ivy being so high or stretching out so far. Like a child it grew while she was away. Now it's an unfamiliar face and Margaret tramples through the puddled woods looking for the stone altar that goes with it. *It has to be around here somewhere*, she thought, the hurricane tapering off and— "What was that!"

Margaret thought she heard footsteps. *The shadow! Who can it be? I need to get out of here. And fast.*

Margaret took off running again, tripping shortly thereafter over Takara's altar; the ancient pile of rocks sheathed in ivy.

Picking herself up, a bruised knee and scratched elbow, Margaret can't help but stare at the wall of ivy, the entrance to the cave not far from where she stands. *This may be a bad idea*, she thought, spreading apart the ivy.

It's not in there, said a voice in the back of her head. *Whatever you're after has long since passed.*

"No! You're wrong," cried Margaret, arguing with herself. "Love is behind the ivy. I know it is. I have to see for myself. I'm so close. This time I'll find him."

Go ahead then. What are you waiting for?

Curiously, the sun poked through the whirling sky. Residing in the umbrage of her clouded thoughts, Margaret scours the ivy only to discover how tangible it is—that she's not awake.

After all these years, Margaret fell asleep long enough to

dream again. As if on cue, the ivy changed into a colorless gray with shades of blackish white. Spreading the vines farther apart, a bygone horizon at her fingertips, Margaret sees her young-self coming into focus. Vibrant with color and wearing a new dress, she sits on her swing, gripping what appears to be a virescent rope. It's a vine, however, the same ivy in her adult hand.

It begins to sprinkle and the air upon her back turns cold and damp. This was the day she waited for her father to push her in the swing. The sky darkening around her, suddenly the rain becomes a downpour. Rippling thunder travels into both worlds and her father is calling to come in from the storm. With no warning, the vision fades and the portal turns black, Margaret spreading the ivy as far as she can, calling out to her father. Soon after, there is an answer, but the voice belongs to someone else and Margaret is forced to resolve her haunted thoughts.

"Stuart? Is that you," she queried the darkness.

Help me, whispered the voice. *Help me, Margaret.*

It is the shadow in the back of her mind that speaks to her—love's spirit calling from behind the ivy. Guilt nudging her forward, Margaret peered into a vast chasm, a decomposed hand reaching out grabbing her by the wrist. Metamorphosing, the hand turns into an ivy tendril binding Margaret's limbs, pulling her deep into the chasm. Everything is dark for the longest time and her heart is the only sound she hears. Suddenly, a vapor of light looms before her, and in the middle of the darkness the rotting face of her beloved fiancé materializes… his fleeting voice pleading for help.

"Stuart!" screamed Margaret, waking up on the sofa.

"Bad dream?"

"Yes," said Margaret, Ariel sitting across from her. Laurian's briefcase between the two women, Margaret can see

Bourbon has been put away; locked in the kennel on the floor.

"People like you and my father don't have dreams, Margaret. He was right, wasn't he? The cut on your forearm and now this. Webster succeeded in bringing you back, didn't she? Personally I find it to be a blessing. You never appreciated what my father gave you."

"No. You have it all wrong. I was vulnerable back then and he took advantage of that."

"Still, you were never grateful. And you never deserved it. I've been waiting all my life for this day. Ever since he told me I could live forever."

"Good. I hope you and your father have a wonderful life together. Mine will soon be miserable again."

"I'd enjoy nothing more than taking it from you," said Ariel, summoning a hateful glare. "Fortunately for you, I'm not willing to take the chance that my father may find out. Perhaps," Ariel averted her attention to the briefcase, "I should mention to him the full extent of Webster's research. How lethal the uncut serum would be if injected into his bloodstream. I know all about her findings," Ariel looked Margaret in the eye, "… and I have a feeling you know just as much. Did you say anything to my father about it? Though he spared your life many times, you plot to take his away. Isn't that true? Isn't it, Margaret!?"

Margaret did not answer.

"That's what I thought," said Ariel leaning forward. "He read most of Webster's research. Not too keen on microbiology though. But I am. Sooner or later I'll tell him everything he needs to know."

"If you know so much why do you need someone else's research?" Margaret already knew the answer. Marcus told her at the restaurant—*to alter the serum in case he lost his immortality*. Margaret wanted to know if Ariel had something else in mind.

"I intend to reverse the serum creating a new fountain of youth. One can only imagine the value of that. Without the final results, I'll be forced to complete Webster's research on my own. And that takes time. Something you and I will soon have plenty of. My father, however, has a different opinion. He believes we're running out of time. If the right people get their hands on that information," spouted Ariel, staring at the briefcase, "… they could create their own formula. And as I said, this stuff is lethal in its present state to someone like my father."

Marcus mentioned all that, thought Margaret … *except for the part about it being so lethal. Why didn't Ariel tell him? The girl's a lot smarter than I thought. She's protecting her future and herself from Marcus. It all adds up now. Drinking from the fountain isn't going to be enough for Ariel. She doesn't want anyone taking that away. And now that death is part of the equation she'll trust no one. Not even her own father.*

"You don't seem all that surprised, Margaret."

"*Oh I'm surprised.* Surprised at how candid you are."

"You have the right to know," said Ariel. "Being part of the family and all."

Ariel went to the breakfast bar, the morning news broadcasting the latest on Hurricane Andrew.

"I wouldn't drink from the fountain if I were you," said Margaret, counseling Ariel from the sofa. "More than just its side effects you should take into account the moral aspects of what you're doing."

"Do I seem to you, *Margaret*, the type of person who's

concerned about their own morality? I'm going to drink from the fountain this afternoon and there's nothing you can say that will change my mind."

"Don't get caught up in all the solicitous foresight, Ariel … as I once did. You look forward to this because it reverses what everyone believes to be true. No matter what happens in life we eventually end up the same, whether it's underground or atop someone's mantel. For some, that's all there is … end of story. But it doesn't have to end there. The majority believe it to be the beginning. A life hereafter free of pain and suffering. No fear of thirst or hunger … *or of one's own frailty.* No persecution exists in that afterlife. No war, pestilence or crimes against one another. It's something you cannot hide from in this world. The fountain will not give you eternal life, Ariel. Not the way it is intended to be. Its only purpose is to take it from you. Let nature run its course, otherwise you'll suffer for all eternity."

"You're preaching up the wrong tree, Margaret. You lack the insight to understand my reasoning behind all this pious sophistry. You think you're some messenger from God, don't you? Ask the wife of Richard Gregory if there's a God after you tell her her husband is dead."

"What? Richard's dead! How— what happened, Ariel?!"

"It was an accident, I assure you," replied Ariel, turning an impassive eye to the television. "Right on course," she said, a satellite graphic depicting Andrew's current location.

Margaret looked up at the hurricane's colorful graphic on the screen. The outer rim having less velocity is projected in green, rufescent swirls. The next circlet is a whitish-pink then a strong light-gray mass hugging a fiery, destructive wall. The stagnant eye has no color and Margaret thought it to be a looking glass. *But to whose realm.*

"You have no idea," cried Margaret, rising to her feet, "…what you will soon turn into. I see there's no convincing someone like you otherwise … so go ahead. Go ahead and drink from the fountain. You have no conscience during the light of day anyway. Starting tonight you'll never have a single nightmare to induce your guilt."

Grieving for Richard, Margaret had nothing more to say, intent on leaving the room and Ariel's wicked self.

"Where do you think you're going," clamored Ariel.

"Upstairs. I need to freshen up."

"You can do that down here."

"I prefer to be as far away from you as possible."

"Suit yourself," said Ariel, unmoved by Margaret's insult.

Margaret closed the bathroom door, and while splashing water on her face, wonders what happened to Richard. *Did Marcus give another fatal order and Ariel covering for him, or did she take it upon herself committing murder? It's either one or the other. There are no accidents in this foolish game.*

Ariel was the last to use the bathroom and Margaret can see she left the window open. A big window. Big enough to crawl through.

A strong wind blowing from the south, Margaret knows she can easily make it to the ground. But Tantur, always listening, he would certainly give chase and Margaret was tired of running. *A way out may present itself this afternoon*, she thought.

Reaching for a towel to dry her face, her elbow scraping a glob of what appears to be *candle wax* near the sink, Margaret looked around to see if there was one nearby, but more importantly, she can't understand why someone would be using a candle without a holder in the first place.

Twenty-nine

THE PARKING LOT is swelling to capacity and Nathan parks the Blazer in the first available stall. A contemptuous knot in his stomach, never again will he let his guard down. Yesterday he and Laurian were at the threshold of safety; the confines of the terminal no more than a hundred feet away. Today, that sanctuary is no more; not when you're on the run. *Will there be a gang of thugs waiting inside*, wondered Nathan, *or an army of plainclothes watching our every move?*

Doors are slamming left and right on the Blazer and Nathan is without fear—like Marcus, he has an entourage of his own. Lifting the rear hatch, the doctors bag directly in front of him, a look of concern taints his composure.

"What are you waiting for," asked Shadwell. "This is a regional airport, there are no metal detectors here. If you're worried about random searches, I'll carry it. What will they do to an old man with a bag of explosives, *send him to prison for the rest of his life?*"

"I thought you were leaving us," said Laurian.

"Not until you're in the air."

"If we stick to the plan," Nathan said to Shadwell, "… you'll be home in no time. Clarence and I will go in first and police the area. Wait here until we give you the all-clear. If you don't hear from us in ten minutes, you know what to do."

Nathan then said to Shadwell, "I wish you'd change your mind about coming along. But I understand. And thanks, Will. We wouldn't have gone this far without you."

Shadwell felt bad about leaving them. He wanted to see it through for Margaret's sake, but didn't have the strength to continue. "We never talked about this," he imparted to Nathan, "… but what if you can't book a flight this morning. Or find someone crazy enough to pilot Margaret's plane, what then?"

"I'll fly it myself," exclaimed Nathan, closing the hatch. "If I can get her out of the water we should be all right. My dad had a gutsy little Cessna and he taught me a few things about inclement weather. I was in high school at the time but I'm sure it will all come back once I'm in the cockpit."

"*High School!*" Overcome with apprehension—as though Nathan were brandishing a gun—Shadwell shook his head. "It's not like riding a bike! And if you've never landed on water you're in for a big surprise. The ocean can get nasty with or without a hurricane."

"I'll head back if Andrew turns on us. I promise."

"It's still early," inferred Shadwell, "… it may not even come to that."

Walking to the terminal, Laurian and Clarence out in front, Shadwell continued his conversation with Nathan. "If you do end up taking the seaplane, remember what Richard said, 'it'll take four hours to get there.' Hurricanes deviate from their course all the time so stay in contact with the ATC. If it turns south, the brunt of it may not show up at all. Just remember, if you decide to turn back don't hesitate. *Do it right then and there!* And don't attempt to land if the winds exceed 20 knots. You'll hit nose first and the plane will capsize for sure."

Stopping just shy of Laurian's minivan, Nathan made it clear to Shadwell he understood. "Well, this is it," announced Nathan, he and Clarence detracting from the group.

"Be careful," cried Laurian, unable to think of anything better to say; wanting to but her mind jumbled with a multitude of worries.

Nathan then flashed an uneasy smile before going inside, Laurian wondering what became of Richard. *If he doesn't show, can we find another pilot in time? Or will it land on Nathan's shoulders again?*

Despite what Shadwell thought, Laurian felt Nathan proved his worth in a very short time. He saved her life for one thing, therefore, without question, she would put it back in his hands again. *No one can tarnish his radiant armor now,* she thought. If he said he could slay a dragon she would trust him to do so—soaring full gallop into a hurricane no great feat for this crusader. *If he could only handle a gun better*, she chuckled, the mishap in Margaret's bedroom a solaced thought. Laurian then realized she had one more thing to do before leaving.

"I'll be right back, William. I need to grab something out of my van. It won't take but a minute."

"We have time," said Shadwell, a clock in his head counting down.

Laurian popped open the glove box, looking out at Shadwell panning the parking lot with an indiscreet eye. The Pug revolver is what she came for, everything else she gathers on impulse; dark glasses and a powder-blue scarf among the last-minute items.

"I believe this belongs to you," said Laurian, handing over the revolver.

"I forgot all about it," remarked Shadwell, stuffing the gun in his boot. "What else have you got there?"

"A portrait of Michael and Amy," answered Laurian, careful while handling the busted frame. "I found it in the hedgerow along my front walk. Everything else was toast."

Well, almost everything, thought Laurian.

Clarence waved an enthusiastic hand outside the terminal, his eyes full of delight for the entire world to see. Shadwell tells Laurian it's time to go. Stooping for the doctors bag, he let out a muffled groan.

"You okay," asked Laurian.

"I'm fine," he answered, shrugging it off. "*Shall we?*"

Taking a deep breath, Laurian looped her arm around Shadwell's right forearm. Though her intentions are tactful, she looks rather suspicious. A calm morning whose sky is overcast, the scarf and dark glasses are a dead giveaway—she doesn't want anyone to see her face.

Her escort looks to be incognito as well. Not some doctor evident by the bag he carries but an old man portraying one. The fedora Shadwell's wearing would appear normal elsewhere, but coupled with Laurian, the wide brim sloped over his forehead and her scarf shielding her face, even the untrained eye can see they're up to something.

Not to say that Jerry Holiday has a trained eye, but with the right-place right-time scenario playing out, he could not have planned his arrival any better. Hopped up on his morning Big Gulp, he noticed something familiar about the couple in front of him… not so much in the elderly looking gentleman, but in the woman whose distinct walk is unmistakable.

The last time Shadwell set foot in the terminal, FDR was campaigning for his second term as President. The Art Deco construction was only a few years old back then and it still looks the same. Judging the area to be safe, most of the crowd congregating in the lobby, Shadwell took a detour along the back corridor. "I need to use the facilities. Why don't you head on over to the lobby. I'll catch up with you there."

"No, that's all right," replied Laurian, her mind pre-occupied. "I'm going to check in with the Operations Manager first. He and Richard are good friends and if Richard's around he'll point us in the right direction."

"That's fine," said Shadwell, abating his directorial tendency. "I won't be but a minute."

The doctors bag straddling his feet, Shadwell took a quick look at the adjoining stall. A pair of trousers clumped on the floor, the owner pulls them up, sucking in his gut while latching his belt. Shadwell then hears the toilet flush and the clatter of heavy footsteps exiting the stall; unaware that the trousers bare a uniformed stripe on the side.

The office of the Operations Manager is locked and Shadwell knocks several times but there is no answer. Glancing down the hall he sees the old man from the kiosk heading for the restroom. "Them folks ain't 'ere yet," the old man called out. "Not 'till eight o'clock. If yer lookin' fer that woman ya came with, I seen 'er headin' toward 'da lobby just now."

Nathan stepped out of a glass cubicle and Clarence followed. Shadwell is heading toward them and they all gather in the middle of a compass rose embedded in the lobby floor, pointing them in different directions.

"Have you seen Dr. Webster," asked Shadwell.

"I thought you came in together," replied Nathan, panning the lobby and second floor balcony.

"We did," answered Shadwell, explaining what happened.

"She must have gone back to her van," said Nathan.

"No, I don't think so. She grabbed what she needed beforehand."

"Did she have a manila envelope with her?"

"No. Just a couple of small things and a portrait she found on her front walk."

"Come on," said Nathan heading for the exit. "You too, Clarence."

Rushing through the lobby, Nathan turned to Shadwell, a discouraging tone explaining their situation. "No one's willing to fly Margaret's plane across the gulf. I did find a pilot who'll take us there in his plane. He's got a five passenger Piper and is going through the preflight right now. Our window of opportunity is twenty-minutes so we need to find Laurian. *And fast*."

"If she's not at the van," asked Shadwell, "… what then?"

"I don't know. *Where else can she be?*"

A shift change in progress, uniform and plainclothesman are scattered throughout the building. The dispatcher weaves her way down the hall to the homicide division. "Detective," she hollered from the doorway.

His head on the monthly blotter, tweed jacket on the back of his chair and 9mm strapped to his chest, Taylor does not respond.

A stern look on the dispatcher's face, thick heels braying the wooden floor, she clomps into the dark room. "Detective Taylor!" she screamed.

"Yes," answered Taylor, lifting his groggy head. "What is it?"

"You said to wake you if you had any calls. Crescent Security, line four."

"Thank you," said Taylor, rubbing the sleep from his eyes.

The caller spoke for a long time divulging very little. "Get to the point," said Taylor, jumping to his feet shortly thereafter. "I'm on my way," he exclaimed. "Did you take her somewhere private?"

More irrelevant jabbering by the caller, Taylor cut in the moment his question was answered. "Yes, yes, I understand," he grumbled, "… observation deck … right hand side … three doors down."

Taylor put on his jacket, a custom fit right down to the loose stitching over his holster. All he needs now are the keys to one of the unmarked cars and some coffee—*a whole lot of coffee*.

Coming in early to finalize the Le Petit case, Detective Grant turned all the lights on. Taylor bumped into him on his way out and Grant spilled coffee on the floor.

"Sorry about that," said Taylor. "I'm in a hurry to get to the airport."

"The Somoza case?"

"Yeah."

"Where's Cary?"

"He's not in yet."

"That's not a very smart thing to do, Taylor. Leaving here without your partner. Alcott has a policy about rookies going out on their own."

"*I know*," replied Taylor, rebuking the notion. "How 'bout I give Cary a call and have him meet me there."

Grant takes a sip of coffee before sitting down, sliding an old rotary phone over to Taylor. "I'm tired of this already," said Grant, flipping through the Le Petit file. Focusing where he left off, Grant is unaware Taylor is dialing the phone with his thumb on the cradle.

Pausing here and there, Taylor's fake conversation is a work of art. "He'll be there in twenty minutes," he said to

Grant, hanging up the phone.

"Hey," Grant called to Taylor on his way out, "… it's not that I'm being a hard-ass. You know how Alcott is. If I don't say something, I'm the one who gets chewed out."

"Like I said," Taylor stopped at the door, "… *I know*."

Everyone in dispatch is busy, paying no mind to Taylor lingering around a pegboard full of keys wondering which car to take. Grabbing a set, he then poured himself a cup of coffee, heading down the front steps putting on his trendy Wayfarers; the pair of dark glasses shielding him from a nonexistent sun.

Void of early morning tourists, garbage trucks and street sweepers, only a handful of locals roam the streets. Arriving at the Taurus he had yesterday, Taylor saw someone lurking across the street.

"You're up early, Detective Taylor?"

Taylor cannot believe his luck. Captain Alcott ambled into the street crushing out a cigarette. "I didn't recognize you over there, Captain," said Taylor lowering his shades.

"Thought I'd have a smoke before going inside," remarked Alcott. "And you?"

"I'm on my way to the airport," replied Taylor—no other choice but to fess up. "I just got word Doctor Webster's out there."

"*The research specialist!?* Where's Monroe?"

"He's going to meet me there."

"I'll go with you," said Alcott, gesturing that Taylor lead the way.

The look on Taylor's face showed nothing but disappointment. Alcott's inscrutable mug, however, bares a hint of satisfaction. He's been waiting outside the stationhouse all morning, ever since Thomas Moore, his cohort in Washington, returned his call. With Taylor's little secret out, Alcott will keep a close eye on him from now on.

"We're not going to make it in time," said Nathan, their twenty-minute window cut in half.

Shadwell set the doctors bag atop Webster's minivan, taking one last look around. "There's no telling where she's run off to."

"I hope nothing bad happened," exclaimed Nathan, blaming himself for the mess they're in.

Clarence then delivers an encouraging thought—a troubled brow aloft a tinge of optimism. "Maybe Miss Laurian went on over ta' the seaplane."

"You know," Nathan's face lit up, "… he may be right."

"Not the wisest thing to do," said Shadwell, "… running off like that."

"Somehow our paths got crossed and she couldn't find us," surmised Nathan. "And with no one willing to charter anything across the gulf—"

"—she'd expect you to take the seaplane," concluded Shadwell.

"Exactly," affirmed Nathan.

Shadwell gave his nephew a pat on the back. "Good job, Clarence. Why don't you head out there just in case."

"Sure, Uncle Will."

"We'll be out there directly, so stay put. I want to check out the terminal one more time."

"Here," said Nathan, handing Clarence the keys to the Blazer.

Clarence headed for the Blazer but it was short lived as Shadwell called him back. "Take this with you," he gave him the doctors bag. "Stay clear of the buildings and don't talk to anyone."

Clarence smiled. "Don't worry 'bout me, Uncle Will. I'll be like one a them cannibals hidin' in the trees. Nobody's gonna pay me no mind a'tall."

"Good."

Clarence drove away and Nathan suddenly felt uneasy sending him out on his own. "Think he'll be all right? If Laurian's not there he'll be by himself for a while."

"He'll be fine. So tell me about this pilot," asked Shadwell. "I imagine he's a lot like you."

"*Courageous?*"

"I was thinking more along the lines of reckless."

"He seemed okay," replied Nathan, attuned to William's humor. "But now," Nathan looked at his watch, "... we'll never know."

Shadwell suddenly stopped outside the terminal doors. "What about Richard," he asked. "Has anyone seen him?"

"There was no need to ask," answered Nathan.

"He didn't make it, did he?"

Nathan shook his head. "I didn't want to say anything in front of Laurian."

"I didn't want to say anything either. When Clarence and I were tied up I felt something next to me in the skiff. I thought it might have been Richard but I wasn't sure."

"*Wait a minute*," Nathan said to himself. "I saw that rig in a private hanger yesterday. *Carlo!* Why couldn't I have made the connection sooner?"

"You had one to many poison-dart cocktails, remember. You're lucky to be alive."

Luck had nothing to do with it, thought Nathan. "We need to take a look inside that hanger, Will."

"Which one?"

"I don't know for sure. Three, maybe four down from Richard's."

"That's a bit far for these old legs," said Shadwell rubbing his thigh.

"Awe jeez," replied Nathan, patting his pocket and no

keys. "You won't be able to make it on foot, will you?"

"Don't worry about me, I'll catch up."

"Our plan backfired," grumbled Nathan, "… didn't it, Will?"

"I wouldn't say that," answered Shadwell. "You still have time to save Margaret … if you're as good a pilot as you think you are."

"Guess I'll find out soon enough."

Thirty

JERRY HOLIDAY took Webster to a makeshift classroom near the observation deck… no windows and only one way in or out. A small table and pull-down screen are at the front of the room and an 8mm film projector in the back. Holiday is relaxing in a wooden chair with his feet propped up, Laurian front and center in a patch of student desks; the portrait of Michael and Amy next to Jerry's feet. "How much longer must you keep me here," asked Laurian. "It's been thirty minutes… I'm tired of waiting."

"Maybe they're stuck in traffic. And you don't have to be so cross. They're the ones calling the shots. Not me," admonished Holiday.

Just then the door flew open, inciting Holiday to his feet and Laurian to cower at the sight of Detective Taylor. Another man unfurls his badge. "Captain Alcott," he said, "New Orleans Homicide. *And you are—*" he questioned Holiday.

"Jerry Holiday, Crescent Security."

Alcott then turned to Laurian who got up from her seat. "You must be Doctor Webster," he declared, appraising her demeanor from top to bottom.

Laurian stood there neither confirming nor denying the fact and Holiday took it upon himself to answer, explaining to Alcott, among other things, her involvement with children's leukemia. Richard Gregory, which he failed to mention, was the one who told him about Webster. Holiday saw her at the airport quite often but they never spoke.

"Would you mind waiting outside," said Alcott, escorting Holiday to the door. "This won't take long."

"Have a seat," said Alcott sitting on the table, one foot on the floor looking down at Laurian. "I'd like to ask you a few questions, Doctor … if you don't mind."

"As a matter of fact," Laurian responded harshly, "… I do mind." Actually she didn't, but with Taylor in the room she's not in the best of moods.

"I can understand that," replied Alcott, pausing for a moment. "You've been through a lot in the last twenty-four hours, haven't you? I know about your house and I saw what happened to your research facility. But I'm in the middle of a homicide investigation and would appreciate a little cooperation."

Laurian softens up. "I'm sorry," she apologized, "… I have been through a lot." *And you've only scratched the surface,* she thought.

"Detective Taylor, whom you've already met, tells me you crossed a police line yesterday. He identified himself and you ran off. I'm not charging you with anything, but I am a little curious as to what you were doing."

"I've nothing to hide, Captain," Laurian replied, glancing over at Taylor—both fervent with one another. "I just explained to the security guard I'm trying to get to Fort Myers. I have a plane waiting and a patient needing my attention right away. I was scheduled to leave yesterday but ran into some trouble."

"Yes, your house and laboratory."

"That's right," Laurian agreed; though she meant something else. "I went home yesterday to see if I could salvage anything."

"Like what," grunted Taylor, picking up the portrait.

"Be careful with that! It's damaged enough as it is," cried Laurian, stretching across her desk. "The only thing I could find worth saving."

"Husband, ma'am," asked Alcott, gazing at the portrait.

"Yes … and my daughter. He died shortly after the photo was taken."

"I'm sorry," said Alcott.

"What did you remove from that planter yesterday? Certainly not this," snapped Taylor, a curious look at Laurian's reaction as he lowered the portrait, plopping it on the table.

Fuming at Taylor's manhandling of the portrait, his imputed line of questioning as well, Laurian said she had money hidden in the planter. "Here," she cracked open her purse, tossing her wallet on the table. "You want to examine that too!"

"That won't be necessary," said Alcott, dropping the wallet in her purse. He then scolds Taylor for his irrational behavior, apologizing to Laurian on his behalf. "Tell me, Doctor," blared Alcott, eye to eye with Laurian, "… you've spent a little time at Tulane. Ever bump into Doctor Wainwright out there?"

Having worked with Wainwright up until his death, Laurian divulges nothing, maintaining a tight lip given the amount of time already wasted. "I've heard of him. Why?"

Reaching in his jacket, Alcott removed the APB on Carlo. "Have you ever seen this man before?"

Laurian lies to him wholeheartedly for the first time, his stony face bearing no sign of whether or not he believes her.

"This may be the man who torched your house and sabotaged your lab. Five years ago he murdered Doctor Wainwright … *a leukemia specialist.* You can call it coincidence if you like, but with everything that's happened, I'd say your life is in danger. This man is a killer," stressed Alcott, shoving the photo in Laurian's face, "… you're sure you don't know anything?"

"I'm sorry," exclaimed Laurian, turning from the haunting image. "I wish I could help you but I can't. If that's all," she cast a spiteful eye, "… I'd like to go now. I need to see my patient before it's too late."

"Is that what the vile in your purse is for," asked Alcott, searching Laurian's eyes for the truth.

"Yes," replied Laurian; patient or not, she's telling the truth for the most part.

Alcott turned around, staring at the 8mm projector. "Where did you spend the night? Do you have family in town?"

"Yes. But I stayed with some friends."

Looking back at Laurian, Alcott then asked how her mother was doing. Taylor told him about May fainting in the street.

Laurian lied to him again, saying she didn't know.

Apologizing for detaining her, Alcott said she was free to go and would personally see to her departure right away.

Summoning Holiday back inside, Alcott asked if they could borrow a golf cart and Taylor didn't like that, telling Alcott what a big mistake it would be letting Webster go.

"You said her life may be in danger," Taylor pled his case, "… and I agree. Let me take her back to the station until we get a better handle on this."

"You heard what she said about a patient needing her attention," Alcott replied. "She's committed no crime as far as I'm concerned and we're going to extend to her every courtesy possible."

"But sir—"

"That's enough, Taylor," snapped Alcott. "Come along, Doctor. If you're serious about Fort Myers you don't have much time."

Margaret is in deep thought, leaning against the parapet on her private balcony. Hurricane Andrew draws near and the ocean is restless, the morning having no sun as the land is overwhelmed by clouds. Glancing to her left, Wahota's room next to hers, Margaret wonders if the young warrior survived the night. She thought about Nathan too, where he might be and what she must do to keep him alive. *Am I to lose everyone I love,* she questioned the sky.

Waiting for an answer, some kind of sign, there is a sudden knock on the bedroom door. "Come, Margaret," said Tantur invading her privacy, a gentle hand on her shoulder.

"What happened to Richard," asked Margaret, her eyes fixed on the ocean clouting the shore. "Were you not there to stop an innocent man's death?"

"Ariel did not mean to kill him. Of that I am certain. Try not to think about it. I tire from all this madness as much as you. I don't know if my brother can hold on any longer and here we are waiting for a hurricane everyone else is running from."

Margaret senses the need for Tantur's urgency. Wahota is alive but his condition must be worse than ever. "I'm sorry, Tantur. I sometimes forget the role you play in all of this. The fate of our kinship cast from the same mold."

"Yes," replied Tantur. "We share a life of relentless sorrow. *Guen umadra.*"

Ariel sat at the breakfast bar, focused on CNN as Margaret and Tantur head outside. Water is spewing from atop the courtyard fountain, the door to the master suite open and Tantur escorting Margaret inside. A 16th century Mudéar look, filled with Spanish décor, the entire room is made from brick. A cedar trunk sits at the foot of a giant poster-bed while across the room, next to a cavernous door, a roll top-desk hugs the wall with an earthy Islamic pattern on its nearby chair. A wide, cherry wardrobe stands tall between two towering windows and Margaret can see the boathouse at the edge of the lagoon.

The thick, intaglio door next to the desk is ajar. Embedded in the door are the busts of six helmeted Conquistadors, each one confronting Margaret head on. She can see Marcus through the crack, shaving his head with a razor. He is shirtless, donning a pair of snug trousers and a multitude of flogging scars upon his back.

"Tantur," Marcus said to the mirror, "I see Margaret has come without a thunderous tongue. Good, I wish to speak to her alone. You are dismissed."

"There is something you should know before I go."

"What is it," replied Marcus, running the razor over a steamy faucet. Suddenly he stops shaving, a concerned look opening the door. "*Your brother, is he—*"

"He's alive. But his fever never broke. When do we leave for the island?"

"I don't know. Andrew, though bitterly destructive, is taking its time getting here. There may be others on the island, and burdened with the task of lugging your brother around, it would be inauspicious for us to depart now. The cover of a good storm will favor us. You know that better than I. Was it not a storm of this nature separating you from Margaret's servant?"

"Yes. But I found him once the storm broke."

"*After he put a bullet in my head!* Stay with your brother," said

Marcus. “We will leave when the hurricane is close.”

Though angry, Tantur held his tongue, paying no mind to Margaret on his way out.

Wiping his scalp with a warm towel, a clean shaven head, Marcus turned to Margaret asking if she slept well. “*What was it like*,” he added rather sarcastically.

“I dreamt of a horrible encounter.”

“By chance, was it I you encountered?”

“If it were, I would have left you for dead. Not with some morbid scar to remind you of my torment.”

“And I thought you to be civil this morning,” reciprocated Marcus. Reaching for his shirt, Margaret caught a glimpse of the tattoo on his arm—the ivy choking his biceps. “No matter,” he said, looking upon his scars in the mirror. “One of these … that one, there between my ribs,” he pointed, “… given to me by a woman of similar passion.”

“And the lashings on your back? Did you force yourself upon the daughter of some ancient king?”

“No,” said Marcus quietly. “Those are from Khaliq. The others are from the spears and arrows of the early Americans. A reminder of my frailty before the fountain.”

Margaret is filled with remorse, though she cannot understand why. “You remember my son … Stewart,” she asked, glaring contemptuously at Marcus. “When he first cut himself, falling on something sharp as I recall, he bled rather profusely. Despite my better judgment of rushing him to a physician, I stood there waiting for something miraculous to happen.”

“How could you know, Margaret? I too had no knowledge of such things with Ariel. Tell me, what of his wound?”

“I kept him home… a towel over his arm to stop the bleeding.”

“And did he heal in a timely manner?”

“Not as you or I would have, *but in contrast to the rest of the world …* yes, within a few hours."

"With Ariel it was different," said Marcus, having an empathetic tongue. "She inherited instead, as one might say … *a hidden gene*. Her capacity for learning is much greater than mine."

"What of her mother, Marcus?"

"A fancy I once had. I believed her to be unworthy of the fountain and she later died birthing our child. Ariel is a gift I cannot comprehend."

"And she's your only child?"

"I am aware of no other. I've not known you to be so inquisitive of my affairs, Margaret. Do you ask this out of curiosity?"

"I don't know," answered Margaret, sincere but fishing for answers. "I never gave it much thought until now. But that's not why I'm here. Is it?"

"No," exclaimed Marcus. "We have a matter of considerable worth to discuss."

"*Trouble in paradise*," queried Margaret, taking a seat. "You said something about others on the island. Who are they?"

"I spoke of one last night. Tomás Morisco's son. He could be there right now, waiting for us. We must be wary of him, and of his wife, *Rachel*. They'll stop at nothing to get to the fountain now that their children have reached the proper age. That is to say, certainly their son Daniel. I don't know about the daughter."

"Now I remember," said Margaret, complaisant with Marcus. "Tomás was the boy you befriended. The one Khaliq abused. His grandchildren are the ones you're talking about. Should we be fearful of them as well?"

"Of Daniel, most definitely. His sister, however," Marcus stepped aside, "I have no idea where she is. If I had to guess, I'd say she's in a convent somewhere. Put there by her mother for safekeeping."

"—or given up for adoption," said Margaret inadvertently. Her eyes revealing a secret Marcus knows nothing about.

"I thought about that too. Can you imagine? The truth out in the open if the adoptive parents question the girl's abnormalities. Then again, they could be none the wiser depending on Morisco's mutated genes."

"How much do you know about him?"

"*Tomás junior?* Only that he lives to avenge his father's death. He will not breathe lightly until I'm dead. He's taken on many names over the years and akin to any immortal he's a constant traveler. He doesn't realize it, but he's easy to track. One day his bloodline will be the death of him."

"What do you mean?"

"It's obvious, is it not? Pride, Margaret. He will not wander far from his heritage. Tomás junior is of Spanish Moor descent."

All the hangers along the tarmac are filled with people, Nathan having checked all but one. Backtracking, he discovers a husky mechanic in the previous hanger—a pair of white coveralls and not a spec of dirt on him. "Excuse me," queried Nathan, the mechanic stationed at a rollaway tool chest.

"Yeah," answered the mechanic, face down in a drawer full of wrenches.

"Can you tell me whose hanger that is next door?"

"I don't know," he looked at Nathan. "Them folks are in an' out a here so fast we never met. The guy leasing it has one helluva of a jet, I can tell you that."

Grabbing a giant, open-end wrench, the mechanic remembered something. "Wait a minute," he said, waving the wrench around, "… you may want ta' check with Richard at Gulf Coast Charters. He's friendly with the pilot. I see them every now and then havin' a drink at the Fly-Away."

"I know Richard." *He was a good man*, thought Nathan.

"Yeah, everybody knows Richard. But with Hurricane Andrew heading up the gulf he may not be so easy to find."

Nathan wasn't sure if he should say anything more. Though the mechanic was a friendly sort, he may pass on the wrong information if the police show up. But Nathan had no choice in the matter. He had to find another pilot and fast, making up a story about Richard canceling at the last minute.

"You wouldn't happen to know of another pilot as good as Richard?"

"Most of 'em are pretty busy. Folks don't want their planes anywhere near a hurricane. Matter a fact, I gotta get back ta' work. My boss wants that Pawnee out of here this afternoon."

His head in the prop housing, loosening a string of bolts, the mechanic can hear Nathan on his way out; a pair of rubber soles on a slick surface. By way of the tool chest, the footsteps pause for a moment and the mechanic is unaware of Nathan rummaging through the top drawer.

The golf cart has a short, spongy bench, Taylor behind the wheel with Alcott on the passenger-side and Laurian squashed in the middle. Heading around the row of hangers in front of the marina, Margaret's seaplane coming into view, Taylor spots Nathan three hangers down, crouching at the entrance door. "That's the guy from yesterday. The one at your house," Taylor said to Laurian. "What's he doing over there?"

"Why don't we take a little detour and find out," said Alcott—Nathan slipping inside the hanger.

Taylor pulls alongside the hanger door. Pry marks on the doorjamb and strike-plate, he made a move for his weapon.

"Keep it holstered, Samuel," said Alcott. Peeking through the doorway, the hanger void of activity, Alcott turned to Laurian. "Was that the man you were with yesterday?"

"I don't know," answered Laurian, grabbing her purse and beloved portrait. "I didn't get a good look."

"Come on," said Alcott, leading her and Taylor inside.

The hanger is familiar to Laurian, recalling what it looked like when she and Nathan drove by. *That limousine wasn't there but something else was. Wait a minute— the Blazer towing the fishing boat!*

Laurian takes a step back, chills swarming her torrid body.

"What's the matter," asked Alcott. "I thought the two of you were friends." He then snapped his finger pointing to the back. "Samuel, check out that door behind the office. I'll secure the limo."

Advancing slowly, Taylor can see a sliver of light under the door. "I think he went outside," he hollered. "What do you want me to do?"

"Keep an eye on her while I check the office," Alcott replied.

With Alcott out of the way, Taylor immediately confronts Laurian, his eyes projecting a feverish glow. "Hand it over," he said.

"What," answered Laurian, her tongue quivering.

"Don't play dumb with me. The portrait. I know that's where you've hidden it. Now hand it over," exclaimed Taylor.

Laurian staggered back, Taylor drawing his 9mm, pointing it at her head. Her legs limp, eyes fixed on the barrel, she feels her heart pumping like there's no tomorrow—like it did with Carlo dredging her face with that awful knife. But this terror she can see. Taylor's stolid jaw incapable of mercy and his eyes full of contempt.

He abnegates control, however, and there is a gleam in Laurian's eye due to the threatening tone behind his back.

"Don't move!"

"Oh, thank God," cried Laurian, putting her mind at ease when bang!—a shot explodes from Alcott's .38 caliber.

Taylor's jaw shattered in front of Laurian and she jumps from her skin, pieces of flesh and bone splattered across her face. Taylor stumbles forward, knocking the portrait from Laurian's hand, his blood spewing upon the broken glass and busted frame.

Laurian screamed and Alcott snatched her purse right out of her hand. Kneeling over Taylor, he grabbed the broken portrait shaking off the glass, the last page of Wainwright and Webster's research poking out the back.

"Why would the NSA be snooping around here," scoffed Alcott, taking the vial from Laurian's purse. He then extracts the research page from the portrait's loose backing. "Unless it has something to do with this," he said, examining the vial.

Laurian's fear, manifesting into confusion, Alcott peered deep into her eyes, knowing what's on her mind. "I've got two separate clients interested in this wonder drug. Both are at odds with one another and I can't decide which is more deserving. The one with a fat wallet or the one who'll put it to good use. Unfortunately," Alcott turned his gun on Laurian, "… neither one is very charitable. So it really doesn't matter who gets the stuff. Either way, I win," he said, cocking the gun, "… and you lose."

Fear consumes Laurian again and in that brief moment, her eyes pleading for her life, Alcott hesitates. Suddenly, the gun is reeling from his hand, discharging into the back wall. A screwdriver piercing his forearm, Alcott turned around and there stood Nathan. On impulsive, Alcott plants a fist squarely on Nathan's chin, sending him to the floor. Picking up the revolver, Alcott swung around facing Nathan, another shot then ringing out and both men looking at each other, wondering which direction it came from.

Alcott turned, and Shadwell, having missed at a mere 30 meters, appeared utterly perplexed. Wasting no time, Alcott fired his weapon, the bullet jetting out of the barrel just as Shadwell pulled the trigger on his gun.

Each bullet lay waste its mark, Shadwell's .44 caliber a shot to the chest and Alcott's .38 to the shoulder. Alcott went down first, landing on the floor next to Taylor as the hit Shadwell took forced him against the front wall. The old man appeared all right but his legs suddenly gave out, his frail body sliding down the wall until his bottom reached the hanger floor.

"Oh, my God! William!" screamed Laurian, rushing to his side. "Don't move," she said. "You've been shot."

The voice of an angel, thought Shadwell, the outside light casting a blazing silhouette upon Laurian's face.

Pulling the scarf from her head to stop the bleeding, Nathan kneeling beside them, Laurian put pressure on the wound.

"Will, can you hear me," asked Nathan.

"How bad is it," answered Shadwell, sitting there with a calm look on his face.

"You're not losing that much blood," said Laurian. "How's your head? Are you feeling faint or dizzy?"

"No. I don't think so," replied Shadwell. Coughing, he then added, "It's more of an empty feeling."

"Would it hurt if we moved you," asked Nathan.

"It hurts now."

"I realize that, but we've got to get you out of here."

"I'm not going anywhere. All that racket, someone's bound to show up so you need to get moving. Clarence will give you a ride, he's parked outside. Hurry, before it's too late."

"I'm not leaving you here, Will. Not like this."

Clutching his shoulder, Shadwell took an uncomfortable breath. "You don't understand, it's not the pain it's the suffering. Go and save Margaret, Nathan. If anyone can, I trust you to be the one. Tell her that I— *that I was wrong*," Shadwell stammered, his voice now faltering. "I should have believed in her."

"No, my friend," cried Nathan, hoisting Shadwell to his feet, "… I can't imagine you not telling her yourself. Whatever took place fifty years ago, don't let it stand in your way now. The William Shadwell I know would never allow that to happen."

Thirty-one

A PENSIVE SPIRIT, Clarence made a slight adjustment on the rearview mirror, taking a peek at his uncle in the backseat. He can see Laurian in the mirror as well, incessant on tending to his uncle's wound. "Hold still," she said, "… you're only making matters worse."

Writhing in pain, Shadwell shooed her hand away. "I'm going to die one way or the other. Let it be."

"Stop saying that, William. You're just like my father," said Laurian, making another move for his wound.

"Where's my gun," exclaimed Shadwell, tapping Nathan on the shoulder. "I may have to shoot someone back here."

"It's on my lap," answered Nathan.

"And the safety? You didn't forget to— *will you stop that, Miss Webster!*"

Laurian is at it again and Shadwell sidles her meddling attack.

"You'll have to wait until he's asleep," said Nathan, checking the safety on the gun. "Once we're in the air you'll be able to perform open heart surgery on him. *That is, if he has one*."

Shadwell gave Nathan that bravado look of his, the Blazer

coming to a stop and Nathan thankful for the way things turned out. Not that Shadwell took a bullet. With the old man's disposition intact, stern as ever, Nathan is thankful he's okay; moreover, that he changed his mind about coming along.

Clarence, so much more to be thankful for, popped out of the Blazer scurrying to his uncle's door. "Need somebody ta' lean on, Uncle Will."

"Thank you," said Shadwell, shifting gingerly in his seat, "… but no. The bullet encumbers my shoulder not my leg. You can help me board the plane."

Approaching the stocky aircraft, a wing span of forty-eight feet, Clarence and Shadwell climb atop the larboard pontoon. A wobbly first step, they manage not to fall, Clarence having one hand on the framework and the other boosting his uncle to the top rung.

"What's it feel like," asked Clarence, "… gettin' shot like that?"

"Between you and I," Shadwell checked his backside, Nathan and Laurian drawing close, "… *it hurts like hell*."

"I was wrong about him," Laurian said to Nathan, Clarence and Shadwell boarding the plane.

"About who?"

"William. I thought he was leaving us because he couldn't keep up. Turns out he's fearful of confronting Margaret."

"He's a tough old man, that's for sure."

"I should have figured it out. Not everyone his age is as frail as my father."

Nathan tended the plane's tether, detaching it from the rocky shore. "What really happened between those two," he asked.

"Only what Margaret told me. And it wasn't much," answered Laurian, handing her belongings to Clarence before climbing aboard.

Pushing the seaplane from the shore, Nathan jumped on the pontoon… securing the hatch taking his seat beside Shadwell. "Wouldn't you be more comfortable in the back," he asked; Shadwell applying pressure to his wound.

"Someone needs to keep an eye on you. At least until we're in the air."

"*Copilot duties, Will?* I thought you were afraid of flying."

"No more than you are. I don't mind the cramped quarters, it's looking out the window that scares me. Besides, I've learned a few things about adverse conditions myself. Once Margaret procured her pilot's license, she had the option of going up whenever she pleased … ill regardless of the weather."

"Oh, no!" Laurian suddenly cried out, sifting through the cargo. "No! No! No!"

"What's the matter," Nathan spun around, his ribs pressed against the yoke.

"My briefcase," she exclaimed, "… it's not here."

"I put it with the rest 'a the stuff," said Clarence. "Then that woman and her cannibal friend kidnaps' me and Uncle Will."

"You've got the last of your research," declared Nathan. "And the vial's in your purse, is it not?"

"Yes."

"Then why do you need your briefcase?"

"The syringe, Nathan. The only one I have is in that case."

"Don't worry," said Nathan twisting forward, "…we'll figure something out." *I've got problems of my own*, he thought, acquainting himself with the controls. "Mind checking the flaps, Will? I need more time on the preflight with all these instruments."

"Me an' Mist'a Gregory did that yesterday," said Clarence, sticking his head in the isle.

"Doesn't matter," said Nathan looking back. "You have to do the inspection before takeoff. It's a safety issue … right, Will?"

"We don't have time for that," answered Shadwell. Glancing over Nathan's shoulder, he points to a golf cart speeding across the promontory.

"Who is that," asked Nathan.

Clarence grabbed the binoculars they brought along. "Whoever it is, somebody beat his face up p'erty bad."

Laurian took the seat across from Clarence directly behind Nathan. "Let me have a look," she said.

Clarence handed her the binoculars and Laurian is plangently shocked. "I don't believe it," she said to herself. "What's with this guy?"

"Let me see those," said Nathan, taking the binoculars. "You made a quick recovery … *Detective Taylor.* What are you after, anyway?"

"The same thing as the other guy," replied Laurian. "But he's no detective. He's from Washington if you really want to know."

Nathan lowered the binoculars. "The FBI," he asked.

"NSA," answered Laurian. "Same ego, different acronym."

"I suggest you skip the preflight," Shadwell cut in.

"I think you're right," exclaimed Nathan, taking another look.

Taylor is steering with one hand while holding his jaw with the other, his favorite suit covered in blood.

"The water's calm this morning," Shadwell said to Nathan. "You should have no trouble taking her up. Taxi out in a northeasterly direction. And remember, the undercarriage is heavy and the floats have a lot of drag."

Nathan already took that into consideration. The keys still in the ignition, he cranked the engine only to have it sputter and stall.

"You let the choke out too soon," said Shadwell, stating the obvious. "Try it again."

The propeller is hesitant to engage and jerks intermittently. Taylor, now halfway up the promontory, a plume of black smoke billows from under the seaplane's nose.

"Now you've gone and flooded the poor thing," said Shadwell.

"I hate to interrupt," cried Laurian, adjusting the binoculars, "… but I think he intends to shoot first and ask questions later."

Nathan, execrating Taylor, reached under the seat for Shadwell's revolver. "We've got a gun too," he said to Laurian, sticking the barrel out the window.

Shadwell advised him not to discharge a firearm in the cockpit, of the close proximity to its delicate instruments.

"Don't worry," muttered Nathan, "… I'll just fire a warning shot."

Picking up his 9mm, judging the seaplane to be within range, Taylor brought the cart to a complete stop. Calculating distance and projectile drop to the cockpit, he aimed his gun the best he could. Nathan, ready to fire as well, the wind picked up and the aircraft bobbled in the water. Shadwell takes control of the rudder, and as Taylor shoots, the seaplane rotating to the right, the bullet hit the wing support.

Nathan didn't expect the sudden shift and he dropped the gun—watching it land on the cockpit floor. "Nice maneuver," he proclaimed; Shadwell with a subtle nod in return.

Laden with discomfort, Shadwell reached over turning the ignition key, working the choke trying not to flood it. The prop, cranking for far too long a time, the aircraft tweaking proportionately, the 450hp engine suddenly kicked in.

Taylor now reeling with pain, he clinched his shattered jaw as tight as possible. Pausing a few seconds to correct his posture, Shadwell induced a sharp rudder at the same time, causing the aircraft to jet away from the shore.

"Take her up," screamed Shadwell, not having the strength to pull back the column. "Take her up now!"

Nathan pounced on the stick and the plane vaulted from the water—stringy droplets from the pontoons returning to the lake. The tail is in a vulnerable position and Taylor takes aim, firing again and again. Several rounds pierce the sky, Nathan then banking to the left. The last bullet in the chamber and the plane quickly gaining altitude, Taylor squeezed the trigger hoping for the best, unaware he hit the plane's delicate rudder with a miraculous, wild shot.

Margaret stepped in from the courtyard. Closing the glass door, she made her way over to Ariel. "Marcus said there would be no going out to eat. He left you in charge of feeding us."

"Indeed," replied Ariel, taking her eye off the television—of its wearisome hurricane coverage. "There's fruit on the counter and cereal in the cupboard. Help yourself."

Slicing a handful of strawberries and an aging banana with a very sharp knife, Margaret thought about stabbing Ariel, but with Nathan's life at stake she put the knife away, glancing mercifully at Ariel while opening the refrigerator.

"Do you mind," said Ariel, moving her head to the side, "… you're blocking the television."

"Oh yes, the hurricane. *Forgive me*," jeered Margaret, nothing but bottled water and a carton of milk in the fridge. "You're out of cream," she said.

"We're out of a lot of things," answered Ariel. "As long as Tantur and my father have enough water we'll be all right."

Margaret poured some milk over the fruit and a small amount in a saucer for Bourbon. "You'll soon find out what it's like to be on a strict diet of water yourself," she said to Ariel. "And you'll suffer dearly if you run out."

Ariel rolled her eyes. "I know. My father speaks of it often. The headaches and how weak he is without it. But I see no cause for alarm. I'll keep myself well supplied and everything will be fine. A few inconveniences won't matter when I become immortal."

"Immortality is not worth the price of—"

"Keep it to yourself, Margaret," Ariel sprang to her feet. "I don't need another lecture."

"Tell me," asked Margaret, Bourbon jumping on her lap, "...did he divulge to you the pit and windfalls of the fountain."

"Yes, of course. My father tells me everything."

"Who told you about the absence of a woman's curse? Certainly not Marcus, *how could he know?*"

Ariel does not respond, glaring brutishly at Margaret.

"Does he know what you're up to," Margaret concludes, "... *consorting with the enemy?*"

"I suggest you keep your mouth shut about that, Margaret. Lest I do it for you." Without warning, Ariel leaned forward, Bourbon striking at her with a thorny paw and menacing hiss.

"Bourbon! That's not nice," said Margaret, pulling the cat to her chest.

Ariel stepped back. "*Bourbon* ... what kind of name is that for a cat," she scoffed.

"He was yet to be named when I accidentally spilled some on the floor. Stewart had a tooth ache at the time and Bourbon meticulously lapped it up."

"*How touching*," said Ariel, taking a seat at the breakfast bar. "I must remember that whenever the floors need cleaning."

Ariel ended her conversation with Margaret, paying close attention to the television instead, disturbing news by her reaction to a live update. "Why couldn't you have mentioned that earlier," she yelled at the TV, catapulting from her stool and dashing into the courtyard.

The broadcast of Andrew's current position is of little importance to Margaret. She put Bourbon back where he was, enjoying her alone time and what she made for breakfast.

Ariel returned in less than a minute with Marcus leading the way. "Are you sure," he asked, skeptical of Andrew's projected path.

"Yes, Father. It now travels near 80 mph."

"And its location?"

"The last graphic showed it south of Naples. 210 mph gusts in Perrine early this morning."

"And now," asked Marcus, regretful he tossed his sandstone away.

"It's weakening over Indian Hill. 120 mph winds and dropping."

"It's nearly 12:00, Ariel. Why wasn't I told of this sooner?"

"There were no reports of the ground speed until now."

Everyone looked at the satellite image, Margaret a renewed interest in the hurricane. Traveling in a north-northwesterly direction, Andrew doesn't seem as fierce as it did going through the Bahamas and South Florida.

"We have less than an hour. Naples is no more than fifty miles away," said Marcus. "For the sake of Tantur's brother, and yours, my daughter, Andrew must regain its strength."

Wahota appears dead but he's unconscious, cradled in Tantur's arms. Ariel is catching up at the bottom of the stairs, a blowgun in one hand and Webster's briefcase in the other.

"I forgot my armlet," said Tantur.

"I know," replied Ariel, maneuvering around him. "You have a lot on your mind. It's inside the case. Along with the darts you prepared last night. I'll take them to the jeep. Father and that baggage of his are waiting for us."

"Why do you speak of Margaret like that," asked Tantur.

Ariel stopped for a moment in the courtyard—the day cooler than usual. "I just don't like her," she replied, slipping quietly into the garage.

"What kept you," asked Marcus, discontented in the backseat.

"It was Tantur, Father," answered Ariel, climbing behind the wheel. "He insisted on painting his face again."

"That is their way," replied Marcus.

Sitting beside Marcus, Bourbon's kennel on her lap, Margaret wants to tell him it's the way of Tantur's ancestors, *not the way of Tantur.* She kept quiet though, Tantur ducking through the doorway shuffling to the jeep. Despondent, Tantur propped his brother's limp body on the tailgate, their legs dangling off the back as before. This time, however, Ariel's in a hurry to get to the island, driving too fast along the hilly, boathouse road.

On one of the sharp curves, Margaret turned around to make sure Tantur and Wahota are still with them. Moments later, she thought about Nathan and the risk she took sending for him. *He looked lost the other night,* thought Margaret. *Now he's all alone.* She wonders if anyone is lurking on the island, recalling the men who murdered her father—Tomás and his two sons. It was Tomás who strung the rope around her father's neck, kicking away the support beneath his feet. *But his first born ... little Tomás,* thought Margaret, *which one was he? The one who fastened the rope to the railing ... or the one knocking me to the floor?*

Ariel pulled up to the boathouse, a strident brake and Margaret losing her train of thought. Tantur slid off the tailgate, scooping up his brother and carrying him to the dock.

A faint sigh from Wahota, his weary eyes unfurling, he spoke his first words of the day. "Where are we? I feel so cold."

Burdened by the sound of his waning voice, Tantur gave

an elusive reply. “You must not speak, my brother,” he said. “Save your strength for we are nearly there. Look,” he acknowledged the approaching storm, “… see how the clouds gather. They come for you, my brother. To save you this day.”

Margaret put a hand on Tantur’s shoulder. “Don’t worry,” she said, the sky darkening and the sea beginning to swell. “I’ve been out there in weather worse than this. The Lady Bird will not falter.”

Tantur is grateful, dipping his head before moving on.

Margaret recalls what a wonderful gift the Lady Bird was. William saved and invested his money as she suggested. A year later they were jetting from the mainland to the islands in half the time. *The fastest boat in the harbor for many years*, thought Margaret. *I wish that were not the case today. Yet, for Wahota’s sake*, *the Lady Bird must prevail.*

Margaret continues forward, Tantur now in the boathouse and Marcus walking up beside her, escorting her the rest of the way.

“Come along, Ariel,” Marcus called to his daughter.

Ariel is behind the jeep, tossing a hand full of darts into the brush.

“Coming, Father,” she cried, grabbing the briefcase and Tantur’s blowgun.

“Is that not the doctor’s case,” asked Marcus, Margaret on his left side and Ariel passing them on his right.

“Yes. I did not wish to leave her research behind,” answered Ariel, stopping just outside the boathouse. “And I have Tantur’s armlet with the darts he set aside.”

“The special ones I asked for,” queried Marcus.

“Yes, Father,” replied Ariel, her eyes wandering over to Margaret. “*The special ones.*”

Thirty-two

THEY FLY AT AN altitude 3,000 feet below the aircraft's ceiling, 125 mph in a smooth pocket of air. The sky above the gulf is clear and the water relatively calm. Nathan's eye to the southeast, the direction of Andrew's wrath, he expects the horizon to growl and snap at them within the hour.

Clarence sat next to Nathan in the cockpit, as Shadwell, having switched places a few minutes ago, is seated in the cabin with Laurian. A rough field dressing is taped slovenly over his wound, one he kept fussing about as Laurian put it on.

Tucking the first aid kit under her seat, the shrill of the aircraft deafening without a headset, Laurian shouts into Shadwell's ear, "I stopped the bleeding but the bullet is still in there. Try and get some rest if you can."

"Thank you. I'm going up front," said Shadwell. "It's too bumpy back here."

Nathan and Clarence are crowned with radio gear and Shadwell tapped Clarence on the shoulder, motioning to give up his seat.

Clarence inauspiciously turned to Nathan for help.

Anticipating the need for his flight experience, Nathan sides with William, sending Clarence back to the cabin. "Go on now. I'm going to need your uncle's help pretty soon. You can fly the plane on the way back, I promise."

They switch places, Shadwell removing his hat and putting on the headset. "How much further," he asked.

"At least an hour," answered Nathan, his tone indicating how apprehensive he is.

"Is something wrong?"

Nathan looked in the cabin to see if anyone is wearing a headset; neither Laurian nor Clarence listening in. "The rudder's been acting up," he said to Shadwell, a hint of urgency in his voice. "I think we took a stray bullet."

"How bad is it?"

"Not to bad but it's getting worse."

"What about that mess we left behind? Any chatter on the radio?"

"No, nothing. They were upset we took off without clearance. Other than that we should be fine if the rudder holds up."

"Good," said Shadwell, grinding his teeth as a sharp pain roused his shoulder. "I'm going to try and get some rest now. Give me a *land ho!* when we get there."

Impossible to get comfortable, younger days clawing at him, eventually Shadwell falls asleep. Floating toward a previous dream, the EL Convento Hotel in Old San Juan, he picks up where he left off—Margaret pleading with him not to leave.

The hallway void of guests, his body young again, *no ailments or bullet holes plaguing him*, William saw himself circling aimlessly toward Margaret.

"Do not leave here angry," cried Margaret, "… not as you are now. We have much to sort out and things will only get worse if we don't talk about it. I cannot bear the thought of you wandering the streets alone, searching for something that is right in front of you. Come inside, William. Please."

Shadwell takes a deep breath, in both the cockpit and his dream. Returning to Margaret, who checks the hall to see if anyone is watching, she followed William into the hotel room, shutting and locking the door.

William stood before her, neither slouching nor fidgeting, his chest flaring in and out as though he came from a rousing walk. Margaret made her way toward him, an irresolute foot shuffling across the opulent carpet. Gazing at him, their bodies separated by each other's nervous breath, Margaret speaks to him earnestly, her stomach aching with troubling knots and twisted doubt.

"You are a good soul, dear William," said Margaret caressing his cheek—only for a moment, but a stirring one nonetheless. "What pains your heart so? *That I am not within your grasp?* The world we perceive, the one known to us beyond that door, to some it is a bitter dream. I see it as a lonely place where ego and lost virtue gather. A place to bring about fulfillment … *be it something or someone*. On occasion you discover an extended hand or kind word, all the while vast numbers seeking to unearth your faults. They don't know the meaning of acceptance or tolerance, judging you because they believe society judges them. Unwilling to find solace in themselves, they contrive to ruin the lives of others—*those pernicious meddlers!* But here, you and I all alone, that cursed throng is no more. The great evil that rules them, gnawing with a deceptive tone, it cannot dispatch them here. There is no one to judge or take from us our passion. No one to condemn the love we have for one another. When we go out the door, we are spat upon once more by a callous world. Let not society rule your mind, William, nor cloud your thoughts, regardless of which side of the door you find yourself. The great evil expects us to do as society does, and it will darken our hearts and swallow us whole if we do."

It is hard for William to breathe, his chest moving passionately, combatting the issue of his own morality and what others judge to be wrong. He reached out, embracing Margaret by the shoulders. "We live in an insensitively-bred world," he said, one pair of wanting eyes searching for sufferance and the other simmering with tacit consent. "It will be difficult. Pleasing society's eye."

"No, William. It will be permissible maintaining our distance. To every prejudice soul and hateful glare, the color of our skin offends no one this side of the door. A sort of retribution," said Margaret, nestling in William's arms. "Or poetic justice if you please … *your body next to mine*."

It was the moment of a desired vision for William. He held Margaret knowing her thoughts to be absent from the fountain and the men that haunt her. *She has given me so much*, he thought, relishing the experience of their travels and her daily teachings. He stutters no more and is grateful of that fateful night in the carriageway; of the promise Margaret kept and so many other things he takes for granted. *She gave to me my dream and in return what have I to give to her?*

The warmth of her body, *a sweet surrender*, William can no longer disregard his aching heart. Gazing into Margaret's vibrant eyes, his lips defiantly close, if ever a kiss were befitting, this may very well be that kind of kiss.

Margaret's love renewed, and William his first, they kiss for themselves and all the poor souls inequitably left out. They kiss for those who think it wrong, and those who know it to be right… those of beauty and those lacking… the wealthy and deprived… every broken spirit and desirous rein drawn tight, they leave no one out.

A long and passionate kiss, free from the great evil outside the door, William swept Margaret into his arms, gazing at the bedroom then to her trusting eyes.

A window overlooks San Juan Bay, and as they lay together, the cool of a gentle breeze enchants the room. There is no talk of today or tomorrow. There is only the thirst and quench of love, and in a seemingly bitter act of haste, shadows from the outside world cross the room, changing the day into night and the night into day.

Shadwell woke to a blustering thump, the sky outside the cockpit dark and cloudy. "Sorry about that, Will," said Nathan. "I've never flown in anything like this. We're at the edge of the hurricane and there's a little turbulence."

"How's the rudder?"

"Not good. It looks like somebody drove a golf ball through it and it's getting bigger by the minute."

"And Cayo Costa? How far are we?"

"Half an hour at the most."

Suddenly, a hard downdraft hit the back of the plane, slamming down on the elevators and jerking Nathan forward.

Laurian quickly put on a headset. "Are we going to make it," she asked.

"We're almost there," answered Nathan.

Shadwell inspects the altocumulus formations ahead. "Increase your speed to 115 knots," he advised Nathan, "… then drop her down and bank to the left during your descent. That should keep any sudden downbursts off the tail."

Nathan did as instructed, leveling the plane at 13,000 feet.

"That feels better," said Shadwell.

Nathan took that as a compliment, brushing a wisp of sweat from his brow. "I'm glad you're with us, Will. I wouldn't have handled that very well on my own."

"Last time I flew in a storm like this I was looking for Margaret," replied Shadwell. He then turned to Laurian. "I suppose she mentioned what brought that on."

"The argument? Yes … she told me," answered Laurian. "The EL Convento Hotel when the two of you—"

"When the two of you what," asked Nathan. "Is that when you split up?"

"We parted ways twice in a very short time. The first, the one Miss Webster refers to was in Puerto Rico." Somewhat embarrassed, Shadwell contends to regain his composure. *Why should I care what the good doctor thinks*, he questioned himself. *Margaret has always been discreet. We gave ourselves to one another, that's all she said,* Shadwell assures himself. "Do you recall what I said," he addressed Nathan, "… about your grandmother wanting to meet with a cartographer in Caparra?"

"Vaguely," answered Nathan, volleying for an explanation.

"It was our second day in Puerto Rico," Shadwell replied. Promptly turning to Laurian, he told her not to ask about the sleeping arrangements. "Caparra," he then said to Nathan, "… is not far from Old San Juan, and though I begged Margaret to give up that ridiculous quest, she wouldn't listen. Her contact at Fortresses El Morro told her about the cartographer. There was a good chance he could decipher Ponce de León's map. Margaret wanted me to go with her but by then I'd had enough. Things changed the night before, which I thought was for the better. I told her she was wasting her time and to let it go. That the two of us—"

"What?" gasped Nathan, Shadwell gathering his thoughts.

"—that the two of us should take a break from all that. She didn't want to and I stayed behind as she set out for Caparra.

"Later that day she returned with exciting news. She had a

hat box with her. A brand new fedora she purchased down the street. 'Try it on' she said, 'all the men are wearing them.'

"I put the plush Kelly on my head and Margaret's face was all aglow. She then complimented me on how smart I looked."

"And the exciting news," asked Nathan.

"She said the cartographer studied the map and in no time explained where to find the cave. He asked your grandmother if she knew what was inside but Margaret wouldn't say. At some point he told her about the Cariban people on Dominica, an island in the Lesser Antilles whose ancestors inhabited the area surrounding the cave. Anxious to tell me where it was, I tried one last time to convince her how irrational she'd become. She refused to listen and ill words were exchanged. I then realized my value to her. The map meant more to her than anything else, so I decided it was time for me to leave.

"I went back to the islands two years later because I missed her. Hurricane season was underway and I knew she'd be there. What I didn't know, Marcus was also there and that's when I shot him."

"You knew the fountain was on Cayo Costa all this time," wailed Nathan, "... didn't you?"

"No. I left her before she could tell me. Why would I have you believe otherwise? There were no storm warnings back then, and when I went looking for her in a plane I borrowed, a nasty one with high winds and heavy rain appeared from out of nowhere. Disoriented, I saw the Lady Bird but had no idea which island it was on. Ditching the plane, I ran into a little trouble on the island with Marcus. You know the rest... when I came to, somewhere on the mainland, there was a note pinned to my chest. Margaret said I should not have come back and to stay away from her. She never wanted to see me again.

"I loved her and those words stole from me all hope of

holding her again. I should never have walked out that day. It would have been easier believing her." Wrenching tightly the old fedora, Shadwell concedes to the fountain's validity. *Time and time again*, he thought, *I am the beast of my own discontent.*

A strong burst of air rattled the plane and Shadwell is wary of the fierce horizon. "This is it, Nathan. Keep a close eye on your airspeed."

Everywhere they look the sky is saturated with ominous clouds—no blue holes or promising crevices to poke through.

"Take her up to 18,000 feet," said Shadwell, a grave look on his face. "The second you feel a downburst, throttle all the way up and drop back down. Slow your rate of descent and we'll make it through. You can do that, right?"

"As long as the rudder stays intact," answered Nathan.

"You'll scarcely make use of it," replied Shadwell. "Look, those are the white sands of Sarasota. We're almost there."

Thirty-three

360 MILLION SQUARE kilometers of ocean, the sun and moon tug at it, moving and displacing every drop, as the wind, the great wind Tai Fung and Mayan god Hunraken command it, birthing sons and daughters from its latitudes low and warm. Coddling the water's edge, every hamlet and metropolis exists in dire straits. In the advent of jeopardy, strong winds forcing the people inland, multitudes lose everything—those who worship uncertainty, conjuring their own demise. *All hail King Andrew, son of Hunraken, ruler of the mighty sea!*

A cloak of white darkness spinning round his neck, Andrew yields a staggering path of destruction. A radius of 240 kilometers, rot through the miry soil of Florida, his savage breath topples all that stand in his way. At one point, neither concrete nor steel beam is left standing. Peak winds over 200 miles an hour flatten landscape and buildings alike; the instruments used to calculate his force no longer there.

A vicious family circle, Andrew's turn is far from over. Warm water, the sustenance of his throne, he invades the Gulf of Mexico; nothing to stop him for a thousand kilometers.

His reign is destined to fall upon the land, and when it does, there will be another to take his place. Every littoral soul no matter their worth succumbs to ruin, and be it typhoon or hurricane, the antipodal location of their birth, the true fate of man is left not to the wind but in the hands of each other.

Fearful of the rousing blow, the outskirts of Andrew's advance, the Lady Bird plows through Charlotte Harbor, a billowing surge of claw-like water goading her hull. Wave after wave pelting her christened stern, her belly vaulting up and crashing down, those safe in her tender taste the salted air, aspirating promptly on its dank, prickly smell.

Marcus wiped away the blurriness, surefooted while tending the wheel.

"How much further," cried Margaret, nothing but the rough sea ahead.

The boat slamming down, heeling to the side, another salty flagon slapping Marcus, he glanced at Margaret "I can see the dock from here," he said.

"How far is that to the rest of us," asked Margaret.

"We are but a few minutes away."

"And the boat, Marcus? How does my Lady Bird fair… I can feel the jolt of every wave shaking my bones."

"You refuse it as my gift and now it becomes *your boat?* How fitting, the two of you are so much alike. There is not yet twenty knots upon her and you both complain. And for no reason," scoffed Marcus. "This is nothing compared to what's out there. Be grateful it is not yet raining."

In a secluded cove, jutting from the windswept shore, a private dock sways precariously above the water. Andrew's menacing breath rocking the boat, Tantur secures the Lady Bird to a timbered pile, extending his hand down to Margaret. "Everything will be okay," shouted Tantur, his loincloth, along with everyone's loose clothing, swirling in the wind.

"Go on, Margaret," Marcus impels her to leave the boat.

"Yes, do hurry," screamed Ariel, the wind blistering her face.

Margaret is reluctant to move, a foothold on the Lady Bird's railing and Tantur grabbing her hand. Extending her leg out over the water, aiming for the top of the dock, a strong wave rocked the boat and Margaret lost her balance… both feet dangling in the air.

The sea nipping at Margaret's ankles, Tantur holds on tight, one arm around the splintered pile and the other pulling her up.

Crashing into Tantur's chest, Margaret held on for the longest time before letting go. "Thank you," she said.

Tantur grinned. "I told you it would be okay."

"Yes," replied Margaret. "For now."

Marcus followed Margaret out of the boat, Ariel lofting their provisions up to him; tending first to the briefcase and Tantur's blowgun.

A duffel bag and Bourbon's kennel are the last to go, Tantur then stooping beside the timbered pile. "Wake my brother," he said to Ariel.

"Wait," shouted Marcus, scanning the beach for Tomás' son. "Let me give you a hand."

Wahota, sprawled across the rear seat, Ariel nudged him from atop the railing—the young warrior motionless. "Come on, Wahota. We're here. Wake up why don't you," she nudged him again.

With nothing to hear but the wind stirring the trees, Tantur jumped into the boat, putting an ear to his brother's chest. Dead space in a cold shell, he knew there was nothing he could do. Climbing out of the boat, looking bitterly at Marcus, Tantur stepped aside maintaining a safe distance, otherwise he may end up strangling both Marcus and Ariel.

Margaret can sense what Tantur is feeling, relinquishing

his contempt with a lenitive tone. She said but a few words, and in those words spoke his name; Tantur wanting to hear nothing from anyone but her. The sympathy from Marcus, and Ariel's pitiful attempt, which sickened his ears, he listened only to Margaret's mournful discourse, surrendering all thought to bind with her his anguish.

"*Tantur*, are you listening," asked Marcus.

I've listened to you long enough, thought Tantur, the look on his face explaining it all.

"We must be on our way," exclaimed Marcus. "The wind is getting worse and in due time the rain will fall."

Tantur climbed back down, cradling his brother once more as Marcus reached out to steady him. "We can bury him here if you like," said Marcus.

"No. Not here," replied Tantur. "Not where our forsaken father lies. And not in Dominica! I will bury him with our ancestors."

"Then deep into the Orinoco Basin it shall be," said Marcus. "But we must first do what we came for."

Everyone gathered as Tantur nestled Wahota's body in a bed of clotted leaves.

"The ground is high and the trees thick," said Marcus, "… your brother will be safe here." Handing Tantur his blowgun, Marcus opened the briefcase. "What's this," he questioned Tantur, pulling out his wooden armlet. "I asked for a full batch of darts. There are only six here."

"I was the one who loaded the case," answered Ariel. "I grabbed the armlet thinking that was it."

"And if we run into trouble? If we don't have enough? What then?"

"I brought along a gun, Father. There, in the upper partition."

"You know how I hate these things," said Marcus, heaving

the pistol into the trees. "Here," he handed Ariel the briefcase. "Not that I need to say it, but keep it away from Margaret. She's had her eye on it for some time now."

A hearty drizzle is upon them, Tantur leading the way through the swaggering branches and plicated palms. Reaching a narrow clearing, Andrew's squally temperament flogging the open lane, every step they take toward the fountain, the hem of Andrew's cloak darkens.

Suddenly, time stands still for Margaret, and like the shadow in her mind, egging her on, the traverse reflection of the trees do the same. *This way, they wail. This way, Margaret. It has always been this way.*

The drizzle then turned into a downpour, and with the exception of Tantur and his bare skin, everyone scrambled for cover. "Hold on," said Marcus, pulling a raincoat from the bag.

Ariel reached out, a strong gust ruffling the raincoat and Marcus handing it to Margaret instead. Furious with her father's obsequious behavior, Ariel grabbed a raincoat from the bag, stomping off in a puerile tiff.

Everyone putting on a raincoat but Tantur, he ambles off scouting the trail ahead—a looming presence closing in on Ariel now that he's gone. Red hair and a face she recognizes, the figure concealed in the trees, Ariel holds up the briefcase, followed by three fingers in the air. She then points the way to the cave.

The figure understood, a quick nod before fading back into the trees.

Tantur spun around, grabbing a dart from his armlet. An ever-present ear, with everyone on the trail he wonders who it is tracing through the woods behind them.

"What is it," asked Marcus, Tantur returning to the group.

“I heard something,” answered Tantur, motioning toward the source.

“Yes, I hear it too. Difficult to make out in this weather. Probably an animal. Tomás’ son has such an overbearing step.”

“It doesn’t smell like an animal,” said Tantur, sniffing the air.

“A woman,” Marcus surmised, capturing the scent. “We must be careful from here on out. Ariel, stay close to Margaret.”

Aside from a touch of thunder, a frondescent wall of oak and thorny brush trembling along the path, the rest of the way is uneventful; nothing to smell or listen to but the advancing hurricane. The ivy, cordoned round the cave, oddly enough welcomes the incursion with open arms—*tears from Apollo*, the rain will reap the murrey leaf like the blood of Hyacinthus drawn from the quoit. Only then will the water have what is needed, mixing with the bedrock’s vital minerals for everlasting life. A life neither time nor space, but lack of both can claim.

“There! Right there,” exclaimed Marcus pointing the way.

Tantur poked the ivy with his blowgun, punching through and dropping to the ground.

“Excellent,” said Marcus. “Be cautious of Tomás’ son. He could be inside for all we know.”

“Only one way to found out,” said Tantur, spreading the ivy apart.

“Take the lantern,” advised Marcus, flipping it on.

A steep crawl space with little headroom, Tantur made his way inside. Water flowing between his knees, he is careful with the lantern, pushing it in turn with his blowgun.

Quickly, while there is still light in the tunnel, Margaret takes Bourbon from the kennel, kneeling beside the entrance.

"What are you doing?!" shouted Marcus. "Wait until it's safe."

"I'm not staying out here in this storm," Margaret fired back—an escape plan in the making. "I'll take my chances in the cave. I've no quarrel with Tomás' son, and I'm confident he has none in return. I'm coming with you," screamed Margaret, her head inside the tunnel.

Bourbon close to her bosom, the waning light tailing away, Margaret knows once inside the rabbit hole how quickly it turns… catching up with Tantur twelve meters down.

Deep into the earth they reach a massive chamber, its cloven, milky-gray walls spread out as big as a baseball diamond; Tantur and Margaret emerging between first and home. In the center, not far from where the pitcher's mound would be, a bench-like slab of rock sits two feet above the blistered floor. A lofty ceiling, filled with craggy nooks, it slopes to one side and in the middle there is a nodular crevice snaking its way down to a rocky cistern along the second-base wall.

Margaret peeked inside the cistern, its chest-high bowl no more than a foot deep. *Empty,* she thought. *But for how long?*

Tantur held the lamp up high shining the light across the cave, Margaret then sidling up beside him with reasonable complacency. "There's no one here," she said.

Two hollows, one on each side, the right has a tapered recess leading nowhere fast. Holding the lamp out in front, Tantur can see the hollow is empty. The other one, however, *rounding third*, extends deep into the earth with a sizeable pocket at the end.

"I'm going to check it out," said Tantur. "It will be dark for a time, Margaret."

"We'll be here when you get back," answered Margaret, perched on the slab of rock with Bourbon in her arms.

A frosty glow from the lantern surrounds Tantur and he melts into the hollow, Margaret counting his footsteps until they are no longer there. The quietness of the cave and her heart making too much noise, a dozen worrisome things rush through Margaret's mind. Someone like Tantur, *Tomás' son*, she thought, *if he mistakes me for Marcus in the dark, what then?*

Outside the cave, the rain a steady pour, Marcus kneels beside the tunnel.

Ariel is standing beside a wall of ivy, watching her father when a flash of lightning riddles the sky. She thought she saw something and she turns to investigate. A second flash occurs from the dark sky and she is startled by the redhead peering out of the ivy.

A blanket of leaves and sheet of rain obstructing her view, strangely the redhead can see everything. The briefcase entrusted to Ariel, now an offering on Takara's altar, with Marcus so close the redhead stays where she is, afraid of being strangled if caught in the open.

Ariel can sense the woman's fear, signaling for her to stay put. Having fleeced her father's trust, innocence clouding the deceit in her eyes, Ariel stands next to him, making sure he can't see where the redhead is hiding.

Ariel, a liar and thief, Marcus knows his daughter all too well. *But daddy's little girl a traitor?* He could never imagine what she's capable of, her small frame shuddering in the harsh wind.

"Still no word," asked Ariel.

"No," answered Marcus watching the tunnel. "And it's been too long. Tantur should have secured every inch by now."

Ariel is about to reply when a shrill bursts from the tunnel stopping her. "What was that, Father?"

"An all-clear from Tantur's blowgun. Come, Ariel. Soon you will join a select few. And one day," said Marcus, affectionately into his daughter's eyes, "… I hope to see a grandchild or two standing here. Take the flashlight and lead the way. I'll cover us from behind."

"Yes, Father," answered Ariel, kneeling beside him.

"Go on now. And mind your—"

"Mind my what, Father?"

"Where's the briefcase," asked Marcus rising to his feet.

The rain pelting the slick leather, Marcus spots the briefcase… his little girl gazing up at him, giving nothing away.

"Sorry, Father. I'm so anxious, I forgot all about it."

"I'll not be cross with you," said Marcus, "… not on this day. But that was a foolish place to put Webster's research. You need to be more careful in weather like this."

Once inside the cave, Marcus put the duffel bag next to Margaret. Opening the briefcase, paying no attention to its contents, he looked to see if it was wet inside. With Margaret watching, he pulled a silver chalice out of the bag, setting it atop the cistern's ledge—Tomás the one responsible for its flat, chiseled surface.

"Now we wait," said Marcus, sitting next to Margaret.

Lying in Margaret's lap, Bourbon hissed at Marcus, quick as lightning clawing at his cheek then running off into the deep hollow.

"Marcus, you know how Bourbon dislikes being around you," said Margaret, heading for the hallow. "Now he's gone and run off."

"And where do you think you're going," cried Marcus, the claw marks on his cheek vanishing.

"Where do you think?"

"I'd rather have Tantur go after the little terror," said Marcus, handing Tantur the flashlight.

Margaret made her way back to where she was, hovering over Marcus.

"Sit down," said Marcus, taking a deep breath.

A few feet from the tunnel, Ariel crossed her arms, bearing down on Margaret.

"No, I will not sit down," said Margaret sternly, the lantern casting her defiant shadow for all to see. "I've had enough of your demands, Marcus, and I grow tired of the way your wretched child looks at me."

Marcus jumped to his feet. "Have you forgotten our discussion over lunch," he exclaimed. "The fate of your grandson is in your hands."

"I've not forgotten. And frankly, I can no longer be civil to you."

Ariel stepped forward, inches from Margaret. "Do as you're told," she said.

Grabbing the lantern, a move she planned while sitting in the dark, Margaret smacked Ariel across the face knocking her down. Tossing the lantern aside, the cave pitch black, Margaret dropped to her knees so as not to fall on the rough surface. She knew exactly how much time she had until Tantur returned, and by then she'd be out of the rabbit hole into the storm. And no one, not even Tantur, can track her in that.

Tantur's flashlight, abating the darkness, he can see that Margaret is gone and Ariel scrambling to her feet—bruised face and ego heading for the tunnel.

"Now is not a good time for you to go wandering around outside," advised Marcus, pointing to the water seeping from the crevice. "Not with the hurricane at full strength."

Checking the lantern, Marcus found it had been switched off, the lens cracked but the light still working. Grabbing the blowgun, he picked up a small stone next to it, working his thumb back and forth. “Find her,” he said, shoving the blowgun in Tantur’s face.

The rain beat soundly on the windshield, the hurricane closing in and Nathan glued to the yoke.

“You’re drifting too much,” Shadwell grumbled into the headset.

“She doesn’t turn all that well,” replied Nathan, the hole in the rudder spread out like a jester’s crown. “I’ve lost maybe forty to fifty percent of the yaw.”

The bullet from Alcott’s gun is scraping Shadwell’s scapula and he tells Nathan he lost the same amount of movement in his arm. “Keep your eyes forward and your wits about you,” he urged him. “And remember what I told you about the wind.”

“I won’t forget.”

“Good,” said Shadwell. Grabbing his left arm, suppressing a sharp pain, he looked curiously at Nathan, unexpectedly crying out in agony.

Clarence lurched forward sticking his face in the aisle. “Uncle Will!”

Shadwell turned pale and Nathan screams into the headset, “I think he’s having a heart attack! What do I do?!”

Laurian went for her seatbelt but a downburst rattled the plane and her hand caracoles from her chest.

Nathan jumped on the throttle, a steep dive and everyone jerking forward, drooping in their seat. Following Shadwell’s instructions to the T, telling the old man to hang on, Nathan decreased their rate of decent, leveling off at 50 meters.

Suddenly, there is too much wind shear and a hunk of metal from the bullet hole, now the size of a grapefruit, snapped off, wedging between the tail-wing and elevator flap.

In a desperate attempt to elevate the nose, inches from the treetops over Boca Grande, Nathan shakes the column. For some reason he envisions his father beside him instead of Shadwell, Nathan talking about a bully at school.

"Every dilemma you face there are but two things to remember," his father explained, "… what choices do I have and which one keeps me out of trouble. Be mindful what I said about wisdom versus strength. If left with one of those two choices, you more than likely backed yourself into a corner. The good news is you have a 50/50 chance of making the right decision."

Back from the vision, barely missing a cluster of trees, Nathan banks the plane toward Cayo Costa. *You were right,* he thought, remembering what his father said. *Right about a lot of things.* "Wisdom versus strength." *Right now I need a little of both. I've got to find someplace to set down without tearing the fuselage apart. But where? There isn't enough beach or stretch of calm water in sight. Figure it out, Nathan! Pitch, roll, and yaw.*

Nathan tugged on the column in frustration, the piece of metal in the elevator shifting and the nose dropping another degree.

"What's going on up there," screamed Laurian.

"Nothing," replied Nathan, still messing with the column. "We're losing a little altitude, that's all."

"How's William. Is he all right?"

"He's still breathing," answered Nathan, keeping an eye on both Shadwell and the controls. *Wind speed 35 knots,* he thought. *Anything over 20 and we'll end up nose first in the water for sure. I can't park it in the harbor or make it to the mainland descending like this. What do I do?*

"Are we going to be all right," asked Laurian.

"If I can figure a way to land this thing without killing

everyone … yeah, we'll be all right."

"More trees up ahead, Mist'a Lewis," said Clarence. "We come awful close ta' them other ones. They'd a slowed us down fer sure if ya hadn't a turned."

Wait a minute, thought Nathan. "That's it! That's our runaway truck ramp."

Nathan checked his heading, calculating a new course. A hard rudder, he grabs a good tailwind and they gain a little altitude.

"What are you doing," screamed Laurian, looking out over the ocean. "You're heading the wrong way. Isn't that Cayo Costa over there?"

"Yes, but we need to take advantage of the wind. Look at the trees. See the way they're sloped right now. If I come up from behind we may have a chance."

"What are you talking about?"

"Wisdom versus strength … I choose both."

Thirty-four

AS IT WAS BEFORE, in her dream and long ago, Margaret is whisked from tree to tree; the thrashing that arch their backs and undress their limbs the only sound she can hear. But something isn't right. Everything kicked up by the wind is slowing down. The pouring rain turns into a shower and Margaret knows the hurricane is receding.

Standing on a paltry bit of earth, a bare spot at the Sandcat's castle, Tantur is nowhere in sight and Margaret believes the worst is over… or perhaps not, as she is dismayed by the strain of a whiny engine somewhere in the sky.

"We're dropping too fast," said Nathan, muscling the yoke. "I'm not sure we'll make it to the trees William talked about."

"What trees," replied Laurian.

"The ones shaped like a giant A, just below that small clearing. That's where we need to go, remember. I'll use them to slow us down then ditch the plane in the clearing."

"Are you mad?!" screamed Laurian, disputing her courageous knight's plan.

"I have no other choice," said Nathan, a downburst then cudgeling the plane's heavy nose. "Oh no!"

"What's the matter?"

"We're too low and there's no way of pulling up!"

Rolling the aircraft to the left, water spewing from the windshield, Nathan checks the attitude indicator. The wings nearly perpendicular, he works the column back and forth dislodging the piece of metal. A small tear at the stabilizer and elevator, he levels the plane but it's too late. "Brace yourselves," he shouted. "We're going down!"

A fierce burst of speed, the sound unmistakable, Margaret spots her seaplane racing toward her. Forty knot winds rock the aircraft and as the Grim Reaper jockeys for position, *the rudder useless and pontoons scraping the trees*, Nathan kills the engine.

There is a horrible screech overpowering the storm and Margaret finds herself running from the noise. Branches are cracking and from the corner of her eye she sees the cargo door flying out of the sky, the heavy chunk of metal crashing in front of her. Coming to a stop, she hears the sound of metal scraping through the trees, a moment later the earth rumbling and the wind taking over again.

The rain, spawning pools and quick flowing streams, Margaret has no clear path to follow, relying solely on her sense of direction. In the middle of the Sandcat's kingdom, the plane's severed empennage comes into view. Moving passed the tail assembly into the heart of the wreckage, the fuselage jammed between a battery of trees, the nose is planted in the earth and the propeller nowhere in sight. The left wing, Margaret cringing at the damage, one end rests firmly atop the fuselage and the other on the ground. There is a dry patch of earth underneath it and up in the trees a plummeting stabilizer slams into the ground taking Margaret by surprise. She thought it was Tantur and takes a deep breath.

The main hatch, crushed inward, a number of branches

block the opening and Margaret scrambles to clear the way.

Crawling out of his seat, Clarence sees Margaret on the ground, having no idea who she is—a young face and her voice distorted by the wind.

"Are you injured," Margaret called to him, the hatch high above her head.

"Got me a cut on my arm is all," replied Clarence.

Laurian then stirs in her seat, groaning and massaging her neck.

"Who's in there with you," asked Margaret.

Laurian crawled next to Clarence, recognizing Margaret on the ground. "It's me," she answered. Nathan and William are in the cockpit. I don't know if—"

"I'm all right," cried Nathan, a hole in the windshield and the rain coming in. "Will's unconscious and he's bleeding again. We need to get him out of here."

Climbing down what's left of framework, Clarence gave Margaret a curious look. She smiles knowing what's running through his mind but says nothing.

Laurian crawled out of the hatch and they gather outside the cockpit.

Shadwell is pinned to his seat by the column and Nathan is having a difficult time moving it out of the way. "What happened," asked Shadwell, rousing sluggishly. "And why is it raining inside the plane?"

"A slight miscalculation on my approach," said Nathan. "How are you feeling?"

Shadwell grabbed his chest. "I think I may have suffered a heart attack," he answered. Clarence and Doctor Webster … are they—"

"We're okay, Uncle Will," screamed Clarence, beaming with relief.

"Will," said Nathan, provoking him to help, "… I need to

move your seat but I can't reach the handle."

"Here," said Shadwell, handing Nathan the old fedora. He then worked the handle and Nathan moved the seat back.

"That should do it," said Nathan.

Clarence took his uncle by the feet as Nathan grabbed him by the shoulders, gently placing him on a dry spot under the wing. The fuselage is blocking the wind and Shadwell put his back against an evergreen tree.

Laurian then kneels beside him, checking his pulse.

Having gone through so much in a short period of time, Shadwell on the brink of having both feet in the grave, Margaret grabbed a blanket placing it behind his head.

Nathan asked Laurian, not so much in confidence, but openly, who her friend is. He can see most of Margaret's face under the hood of her raincoat, but she's a young woman and his brain is too rattled to put two and two together.

Shadwell looked up, inhaling the freshness of the evergreen tree. "Don't you know," he asked.

"No … I don't," answered Nathan. "Do I," he questioned Margaret.

"I would hope so," Margaret replied, peeling back the hood. "We are related to one another."

A look of doubt crossed Nathan's face and Margaret could see he didn't trust his own eyes. She then dropped beside Shadwell, his eyes revealing something altogether different.

"I don't know what to say," said Nathan. Rationalizing the situation, he estimates Margaret to be in her mid-twenties. "I thought I was prepared if it were true. But it can't be true. It's just so … so—"

"—*so weird*," proclaimed Margaret. "How do you think I feel… *my dear grandson.*"

Margaret took Shadwell's hand and he recalls her delicate touch, his skin now wrinkled and hers unchanged.

"William," said Margaret, digging through the first-aid kit, "… there's something you should know. Marcus didn't die that day. He has a daughter and they're at the fountain so we don't have much time."

"It seems we never do."

"It pains me to see you like this, you know."

"What, that I'm a crusty old man."

"No," Margaret put her hand on his cheek, "… you're as handsome as ever. I was talking about your wound. And you suffered a heart attack as well. You could have stayed home but you came to my rescue instead. You're a hard man to figure out, William Shadwell."

"I should never have doubted you, Margaret."

"It's all right," she said, a subtle smile and the moment touching everyone.

Clarence, completely in awe with Miss Margaret's appearance, sat quietly as she took out a packet of gauze from the first-aid kit.

Working on Shadwell's wound, Margaret congratulated Laurian on the success of her serum. "And the whereabouts of your research," she asked, "… is it safe?"

"Long story," Laurian replied, "… I brought it with me. That and what's left of the serum."

"Good," said Margaret. "We're still in control."

Laurian then informs Margaret about Alcott; Marcus and another party hiring him to steal her research. She then concludes the morning's events with Taylor shooting at the plane. Convinced he's an NSA agent, posing as a homicide detective, Laurian advised Margaret to watch her back from now on.

"This is the closest they've ever been," answered Margaret, securing William's dressing. "I know Louis Alcott and the fact he's working for Marcus doesn't surprise me. I have a feeling who the other party is … *but Taylor?* I know a lot of agents at the NSA and he's not one of them. What does he look like?"

"Well, before he took a bullet in the jaw," said Laurian gloating, "… he was quite handsome."

Laurian then gave Margaret a prior description.

"He doesn't sound familiar."

"Why the NSA," asked Nathan.

"How much does he know," Margaret questioned Laurian.

"Everything you told me."

"When Meriwether Lewis was killed," Margaret spoke to everyone, "… Thomas Jefferson believed he was on his way to Washington with news of the fountain. At the end of his second term, Jefferson put together a team to investigate the circumstances surrounding Meriwether's death. If the rumors of the fountain were true, the United States possessing a treasure like that, the pressure put upon our national security would have been overwhelming. The NSA wasn't the first agency in charge of that task, but they have been for a long time now."

Laurian turned around, expecting a brigade of agents to pop out of the woods. "What can we do to stop them?"

"There's nothing we can do. I'm sorry for dragging everyone into this mess. I'll never learn," she confessed to Shadwell, "… will I? A rumor is one thing but if someone were to prove the fountain exists, there would be no way of controlling the onslaught."

"We have explosives," said Nathan, a destructive look on his face. "We can take care of that problem right now."

"I know what you have in mind and couldn't agree more … but not now," replied Margaret, "…we need to get as far away from Marcus as possible."

"If that means gettin' off this island ya don't have ta' twist my arm," said Clarence, eager to fetch their belongings.

"All I need is my purse," said Laurian. "We'll get rid of that last page once and for all."

"And the map," declared Margaret, "… it too must be destroyed."

"It's in a safe place with a copy of my research."

"Good. We'll tend to that later."

Climbing back in the plane, in order to reach their supplies Clarence must crawl through the crushed interior, the tail section now sagging and Nathan telling him to be careful.

Not wanting to be overheard, Margaret pulled Laurian to the side. "I know who your biological parents are," she said. "Your father is Tomás Morisco, Jr. and your mother's name is Rachel. And you have an older brother, Daniel. My guess is they hired Louis once they found out what Marcus was up too. And like Marcus, they'll stop at nothing to get their hands on your research."

"My biological parents hired someone to kill me?"

"They have no idea who you are. And neither does Nathan. You need to tell him."

"After what he's been through, how can I?"

"Laurian, it was Marcus and the Cariban who did this. You and Nathan are caught in the middle."

Clarence found two bottles of water on his way out, giving one to his uncle and taking a drink from the other. No one else is thirsty so he put the bottle in the doctors bag with all the explosives. He gave Laurian her purse and she tore her research paper into small pieces, stomping them in the mud. The weight now off her shoulders, she tells Margaret there's no syringe for the serum. "I had one in my briefcase but it was stolen."

"Forget about it," said Margaret. "I know where it is and you'll never get it back."

"Be patient," said Marcus, Ariel standing over the cistern with a measly bit of water inside. "You know as well as I how everything works. It takes the water a while to seep through."

"At this rate," said Ariel, another drop falling, "… we'll be here all day."

"You don't need much. One drink and you're forever young."

"I know, Father. You've told me a thousand times. Immortality is guaranteed to all who drink the water. But every hurricane and body chemistry is different. Depending on the levels of tritium in the rainwater, minerals in the ground and residue from the ivy, an inherent quality will develop in each person."

"So, you have been paying attention."

"You once told me Tantur can sense things better than you but you're the stronger one. His father drank the same water as you. The worst hurricane ever and when he killed himself you became the predominate one."

"And that you must learn to accept."

"Why can't I just drink a second time to increase my abilities?"

"I would advise against it. Takara's son did such a foolish thing. Unsatisfied with his regeneration and keen senses he became greedy, wanting more than what his father and brother had. He drank from the fountain a second time and it killed him."

"I can duplicate what's in there… I know I can. One drop is all I need."

"I already told you," refuted Marcus, abrading his newfound stone, "everything dissipates within a few hours."

"At least let me try," said Ariel pleading her case. "We can freeze it once we get home. I have a friend with access to a pharmaceutical lab and we can—"

"You worry too much, Ariel. Take what the fountain gives you and be satisfied."

Tantur ran across the propeller, mangled and blocking his path. Advancing forward there are voices ahead, the wind and rain just enough to make them inaudible—even for his preternatural ears.

"We'll make our escape in the Lady Bird," said Margaret.

"How far is it," asked Nathan.

Tantur's ears perked. *The grandson*, he thought, recalling his voice from the other night. Moving to a new vantage point, Tantur can see and hear everyone clearly, Margaret telling Nathan where the Lady Bird is moored.

"I don't think we should move him that far," said Nathan.

"I agree," answered Laurian.

"What if we bring the Lady Bird closer?"

"How close," asked Nathan.

"No more than a five minute walk," said Margaret. "But we need to hurry. Tantur can't be that far behind."

"Who?" Nathan doesn't recall the name.

"He's a Cariban warrior," Margaret replied. "And he won't be too happy with us. His brother dying and all."

"The boy died," asked Shadwell, his voice teeming with regret.

"Yes."

"I'm sorry to hear that. I meant only to render him unconscious."

Tantur, grief-stricken, lowered his head wondering where it all went wrong.

Nathan parted from the group, unknowingly from Tantur's vindictive view over to the cockpit, tucking Shadwell's pistol under the back of his shirt. "We best get going," he said upon his return.

Clarence handled the bag of C-4, as Laurian, slipping into a windbreaker, stuffed the vial inside her pocket.

"We'll be back as soon as we can," said Nathan kneeling beside Shadwell.

Gripping the old fedora, Shadwell glanced into the woods. "Watch your back, Nathan. Daring to outrun the inevitable is par for the course out here."

Thirty-five

HIS CHEST ACHING, every breath a torturous one, William Shadwell's life is slipping away. He always knew flying would be the death of him. *But I can't blame Margaret*, he thought. *Not for wanting to be with her.*

A fool to reminisce, Margaret's beatific smile coddling his spirit, Shadwell knows there's no going back if he survives. *She's the same as before*, he thought, *and I'm an old man now.*

Losing his grip on life, on the old fedora as well, gazing obscurely into the woods, Shadwell is fearful of letting go. The rain, dripping aptly from the trees, falling to the ground is calls to him, *"Let go, William. Let go!"*

Plop, plop, plop goes the rain. *"Let go of the old fedora,"* plop, plop. *"Let it go, William," plop. "Let it go!"*

His fate stepping from the trees, gliding as it seems, at first Shadwell believes it's the angel of death, but then, the figure drawing closer, he sees it as no angel or messenger thereof. It is death plain and simple, come to take him away.

"How do you feel, old man," asked death, the painted face of Tantur staring down at him.

Shadwell moved his head as far as the pain will allow,

looking up at Tantur. "I remember you," he said, the jarring of his words hanging viscidly in the air. "You chased me through the woods a long time ago but I got away."

"Yes," said Tantur, helping himself to Shadwell's water, his saliva altering the water's chemistry. Taking a knee, Tantur put the bottle close to Shadwell's mouth, instructing him to drink.

The old man hesitated, mustering a swallow to take away the dryness.

"More," said Tantur. "*You have to drink more*."

"I'm too tired," answered Shadwell, his head drooping.

Drawing a weary breath, his last by the sound of it, Tantur forced the water down Shadwell's throat. Heartbeat upon heartbeat, a slow, steady decline, suddenly the old man's grip on life takes a turn for the better, his pulse inauspiciously rising to a more stable rate. His cheeks budding with color and a steady breath, Shadwell raised his head. "What did you just do," he asked.

"You feel better, don't you," replied Tantur.

"Yes," said Shadwell, the pain in his chest subsiding.

"I can do this but one time and at your age it will not last long."

"You're not going to kill me?"

"I see no need to avenge my brother's death by killing a dying man."

"I'm sorry," said Shadwell, his voice full of remorse, "… I meant only to render him unconscious."

"I sense what kind of man you are," said Tantur. "Unlike Marcus and his hateful daughter, your words come from the heart."

Shadwell had no idea how to react. He could see the hatred in Tantur's eyes yet the minacious warrior spoke kindly to him.

"Many good people live too short a life," said Tantur.

"You should be next in line for the fountain, not someone whose purpose in life is to ruin the lives of others."

Shadwell agreed, the pain in chest returning just as Tantur said it would. A small gesture on the part of Tantur, proud warrior that he is, Shadwell can't be sure but it looked as though he bowed his head.

"I must go now," said Tantur, stepping away. "I have the others to deal with."

"Wait!" cried Shadwell, attempting to stand but his legs giving out. "Please don't hurt them. My nephew— he … he's only a boy."

"No harm will come to them," said Tantur, stuffing a dart in his blowgun.

"*No harm?* What do you call that?"

"Don't worry," said Tantur, extolling his work, "… they're not poisonous."

Tracking Margaret through the wind and rain, Tantur must sort through a multitude of sounds. There was a time, *a side effect of the fountain*, when it felt like a thousand hammers attacking his head. If not for Marcus and Takara, it would have taken Tantur years to focus on one particular sound. His sense of touch, however, distinguishing one airborne particle from another, is something he's still trying to master. A spoonful from an enormous collecting pot, Tantur figured out a few of the particles and the benefits are immeasurable. Airborne particles reveal everything from a change in weather to the nearest source of water. The only problem is sorting them all out. Fortunately, with eternity on his side, he'll go through every one, taking into account the particles worth remembering.

The hurricane won't let up, and though Tantur is having a difficult time sorting through the particles, he knows Margaret isn't too far away, and he must stay focused or he'll lose her like he lost Shadwell in the last storm. If not for the ruckus at the dock, Margaret arguing with Marcus, Shadwell would have gotten away for sure.

The rain explodes into one final downpour, Tantur stepping into a thicket of ferns. The wind dithers left then quickly to the right, parting the foliage and Tantur spotting his prey not six meters away. He can hear Nathan through the wind, impatient with their progress and Margaret trying to calm him down. "Don't worry," she said, "… we're almost there."

With Nathan out in front and Margaret close behind, Tantur has a clear shot. Taking a deep breath, pointing the blowgun at Nathan, the wind changed directions and Tantur captures a familiar scent.

Moving purposely along the swaying branches, a sudden blast of air from Tantur and the dart rifling through the blowgun, Bourbon timed his jump perfectly. Grazing the end of the blowgun, followed by a flawless landing and quick getaway, Bourbon altered the shot and the dart missed its mark.

"Not again!" screamed Nathan, the dart buried in a palm tree.

"Run!" shouted Margaret, fleeing opposite the cove without realizing it. "If anyone gets hit," she exclaimed, "… pull the dart out right away."

"Easier said than done," Nathan replied, lifting a branch and everyone scampering underneath.

Processing every sound, a thousand leaves fluttering overhead, Tantur can hear their feet changing course. Judging from the particles passing through the trees, there is a way to overtake them but Tantur must hurry.

With Nathan protecting their backside, Margaret and Laurian squeeze through a handful of squally pines into a small clearing.

Tantur is fumbling with the next dart, his wet hands trying

to load the blowgun, searching the trees for Margaret's cat at the same time. The dart now in line with the blowgun, he's ready to load it, once again Bourbon initiating a bold plan, *a surprise attack coming from below.*

Jumping up, latching his claws in Tantur's chest, an angry, drawn-out hiss, Bourbon takes a swipe at Tantur's face.

Defending himself, Tantur dropped the blowgun. Clenching Bourbon by the throat, he tells the wily cat to let go.

Bourbon dug his claws deep into Tantur's chest. Feeling no pain, only an urgency to track his prey, with the dart still in his hand, Tantur stabbed Bourbon in the belly.

A nonthreatening puncture wound, Bourbon fell to the ground landing in a puddle of water. Motionless at Tantur's feet, the pelting rain is soaking Bourbon's melanistic coat. Tantur, surprised that Bourbon is not moving, he can see the water rinsing some sort of black dye from the the animal's chest, revealing a white-lozenge mark underneath.

Bourbon is lying flaccidly in the puddle and Tantur extracts a third dart from his armlet. Concentrating on nothing else, regretful and rightfully so, he takes a good whiff. An angry brow and gnashed teeth, tossing the dart Tantur can smell a lethal dose of betrayal hanging the air.

Expunging all the darts into the harsh wind, thunder and lightning assaulting the sky, Tantur resumed his pursuit, contemplating on who would do such a thing. *Not Marcus*, he thought, listening to and turning an ear toward Margaret.

Moving briskly through a formation of silver birch, a small clearing ahead, Tantur thought about the vivarium door ajar and the missing darts. "*Ariel!*" he exclaimed to himself.

Passing judgment on her, to kill Margaret and use him as the fall guy, Tantur put that at the top of Ariel's list of shameful attributes. *Poor Bourbon*, he thought, *Margaret will not take the news well.*

Nathan is concerned they will not make it to the Lady Bird in time and he breaks away from the group, scouting the land ahead. Searching for the shore, all he can see are patches of stubby brush and skinny trees. There is a noise behind him and he fearfully turns his head around.

"See anything," asked Margaret, putting a hand on Nathan's shoulder.

"Nothing," answered Nathan, disappointment in his tone.

"I think we lost him back there," said Margaret, a crackle of thunder and burst of lightning marking the spot.

"Lost who?"

"Tantur. I saw him as we left the glade. We better get moving. He's not likely to slow down anytime soon."

Nathan understood. He approached Laurian who is hunched over clutching her side. "You okay," he asked.

"I'm fine," she answered, catching her breath. "I'm not accustomed to all this running."

"How much further—" Nathan turned to Margaret, unsure of how to address her. She was much too young and it would be awkward calling her grandmother. And if she's not his grandmother, which seems less likely at this point, he said what he thought was appropriate, "*—Margaret*."

"The cove is this way," answered Margaret, who can't help but grin at Nathan. "We're on a roundabout path, that's all. Twenty minutes and we'll be there."

"*Laurian,*" asked Nathan, in regard to her stamina.

"I'm good," she answered, straightening her body.

Clarence said he was also good and Nathan spoke openly that the boy keep an eye on Laurian. There is a rustling in the trees and before Clarence can reply he moved closer to Laurian.

At the western leg of the Sandcat's castle, *the foliaged A*, the trees are thinning and Tantur can hear the rustling as well. Footsteps and the scent of the woman from before are not far from everyone. Now a light drizzle, dogwood bracts and magnolia petals scattered about, the footsteps are stride for stride keeping up with Margaret.

What is she doing, thought Tantur, ... *tracking Margaret?* Plotting a new course, Margaret guiding everyone to the cove, Tantur can't believe his luck. With plenty of dark places and sheets of ivy for cover, everyone is heading in the direction of the cave.

Suddenly, Laurian stopped, crouching to catch her breath. The woman doesn't see her, and as she passes by, Laurian saw her among the trees, the wind ruffling her red hair. A short distance ahead, believing that Laurian is right behind, Clarence stopped alongside Margaret and Nathan who are also at a standstill.

"This is not good," said Margaret, she and Nathan at the path leading to the cave. "I thought we were further south. We'll have to—"

"—where's Laurian?" exclaimed Nathan.

Clarence spun around. "She was right behind me, Mist'a Lewis."

Nathan stood in the middle of the path, calling out to Laurian. For a moment everything is quiet. Suddenly, to their backside, the ivy thick and lofty, a gust of wind shows a bit of color other than green.

"What was that," said Margaret, the bedimmed, russet bark of trees and sopping brush exposing something underneath.

"What was what," asked Nathan reaching for his gun.

"I saw something move over there," said Margaret, drawn toward the ivy in a rigid trance.

"Wait!" called Nathan, unable to stop Margaret as he's leaning more toward the direction Laurian disappeared.

Margaret kept going, a lighting flash exposing the dark path. The wind swept through the ivy and Margaret saw something shiny underneath. Nathan is shouting for her to stop but Margaret reached for the wispy vines, the sound of thunder and another brilliant flash showcasing what lies beneath. Margaret stumbled back, in awe at what she discovers canting out of the wet leaves. A human skeleton stood before her, held in place by a ruck of fleshy tendrils and nesting bugs.

Nathan too is startled, aiming Shadwell's .44 at the pasty looking bones. Stepping closer, an empty sheath hanging from the skeleton's torso, Nathan put the revolver away—hiding it once again under the back of his shirt.

"It's Stuart. I knew I'd find you," said Margaret.

Reaching for the skeleton's cheekbone, from out of nowhere a hand grabbed Margaret around the throat.

Nathan reached for the gun but he's too late, Tantur oozing from the ivy thrusting a rusty knife against his jugular.

Letting go of Margaret, Tantur forced Nathan to step back. "What happen to the doctor," he asked, gyrating the knife on Nathan's neck. "Where is she?"

"I don't—"

"—we were separated," said Margaret cutting Nathan off.

Tantur pulled the knife from Nathan's throat, wielding him around while directing Clarence to fall in line. "Go on now, Margaret," said Tantur, pointing toward the cave.

"Tantur, please," begged Margaret, "… let them go. You have what you came for."

"Marcus would not like that."

"He doesn't even know about them."

"Let the boy go, if anything," said Nathan.

"No," replied Tantur, prodding Nathan with the knife. "*If anything* … the two of you are lucky to be alive."

Thirty-six

EVERY HURRICANE alters the island in one form or another—Andrew leaving Cayo Costa ostensibly in one piece. A few uprooted trees and scattered earth is the only damage. But hurricane after hurricane, it all adds up. Who can say what the island will look like in a thousand years. Or, given its size, if there will be an island at all.

Fuming over his brother's death, *the island itself*, Tantur is spiteful with Nathan, pricking his back with the knife; every jab from the rusty blade dangerously close to Shadwell's gun. The cave is just ahead and Tantur ideates what needs to be done to ameliorate his grief. He thought about his last conversation with Wahota, and his little brother certainly hit the nail on the head. *What point is there in honoring their father's debt?*

"An old custom," Wahota told him, "… our people are abandoning such ways." *Times change,* thought Tantur, *why can't I. This will be the last thing I do for Marcus*, he vowed.

Tantur knows Marcus will stop at nothing to preserve Margaret's immortality and that's fine with him. Just as Marcus can't bear to live without Margaret, Tantur cannot bear the thought she will cease to exist. *Who will I confide in if that happens,* he thought.

Takara's altar is within Tantur's patulous line of sight and he reputes his past as they draw near. *Why must everything change,* he thought. *No longer do we worship or give thanks to the wind and rain for the sacred pool. When did this happen?* Tantur gave Nathan a nudge, Benjamin Lewis and the likes of the Spanish, Portuguese and British Navy coming to mind.

When Tantur was a boy, his father told him the history of his people—the Cariban flourishing along the Río Orinoco deep in the Venezuelan jungle. Expanding their nation to the Lesser Antilles, they defeated the Arawak, Ciboney, and Taíno tribes. Two centuries of heinous warfare and ritual mutilation, the Cariban set their sights on the Greater Antilles.

Tantur can hear them on the eve of battle, their faces painted as his, drumming on hollowed out logs, chanting fiercely to the sky. He envisioned hundreds of dugouts storming the sea, attacking the next island. Conquering one tribe after another, all subject to their cannibalistic ways, mercy did not happen that often; given only to the women and children they kept as slaves.

For more than three hundred years, every man, woman and child in the West Indies fearing for their life, the Cariban ruled Venezuela and the Lesser Antilles. Then the great ships from the east came and everything changed.

Hunting on the island of Saint Thomas, Tantur's grandfather spotted the first of many tall ships. It did not take long for the Cariban to confront the invaders from the East. Overwhelmed by their military prowess and superior weaponry, the Greater Antilles, *Puerto Rico* in particular, were no match for the foreign invaders.

Tantur's father, Takara, turned fifteen when his mother and father fled to Morne Trois Piton, a mountainous region on the island of Dominica. Takara and two friends, brothers of seventeen and eighteen, ran into a patrol of battle-hungry Spaniards near Havana while out hunting. The patrol gave chase and the boys escaped in one of the Spaniard's longboats. With no food or water, adrift for nearly three days, they ended up in the Florida Keys.

Continuing north, they explored the islands off Charlotte Harbor. Takara was the first to spot Cayo Costa. Searching the island for shelter, a hurricane fast approaching, one of the brothers lost his footing, ending up headfirst in the fountain's tunnel.

Tantur can't imagine what his father and the two brothers went through back then—the dangers of living in that day and age.

Margaret and Clarence are nearing Takara's altar and Tantur prods Nathan in the back, grazing the revolver with the obtundent knife. Nathan turned his head expecting the worst, but Tantur's mind appears to be on something else, prodding Nathan again for turning his head around.

The flashlight is stationed outside the tunnel and Tantur told Margaret to go first, envisioning what it must have been like for his father and the two brothers, having to crawl down with a smoky torch in their face. *Was it luck or fate the way they happened upon this tunnel*, thought Tantur, squeezing through the dank, opening.

Not far down the tunnel, Tantur caught the scent of a woman— *no … two women*, he thought, tracing through the woods.

Further down the tunnel, no great concern for the women outside, Tantur wondered about his father… descending the same intestinal burrow deep into the bowels of the earth.

They must have been the first to witness it, thought Tantur, *… waiting out the storm and a strange fluid seeping from the rocks.*

All the boys were thirsty, Tantur knew that much, the two brothers cupping their hands and drinking their fill. Takara, however, leery of the putrid color refused to drink. The older brother, as Tantur was told, *an unwieldy, spiteful boy*, spewed a mouthful of water up and down Takara's back.

Margaret and Clarence reached the first turn, and Nathan, his anxiety in the tunnel mounting, obstructs what little light there is from Tantur—his father's intrinsic jealousy coming to mind as he plunged into the dark.

When Takara returned to the Greater Antilles, he noticed something different about the two brothers; something that took a long time to figure out.

A few years later, on the island of Dominica with their families nowhere to be found, they discovered a great number of French and British colonies on the island. Joining forces with a handful of runaway slaves and the last of the Taíno tribe, a gruesome scrimmage took place at the edge of a perilous cliff. Outnumbered ten to one, Takara a man of twenty with the two ageless brothers, whom he thought were invincible, did not fare well until the beheading of the older brother. Overcome with rage, pushing Takara aside, the young brother killed the remaining soldiers on his own.

Halfway down the tunnel, Nathan grumbling about something, Tantur remembers the day he drank from the fountain, his father explaining his regret never returning to their people… missing his chance to be a great warrior.

Tantur ponders from time to time what became of the younger brother. His father never told him and it was a secret Takara took to his watery grave.

Having seen how to kill an immortal, believing as the Cariban do that eating the flesh of your enemy you will inherit their strength, Takara betrayed his kinsman with a Spanish sword. Displacing the young brother's soul and devouring his spirit, to his surprise nothing changed. Takara was the same and the great ships kept coming; driving his people back to the Río Orinoco.

Longing for his emptiness to cower, Takara ventured to the sacred pool offering gifts for the atonement of his peccant deed. Worshiping to the great wind of his people, year after year aspiring to be the next immortal, the one to reclaim the land of his ancestors, Takara prayed for another hurricane.

The light in the cave took away the darkness at the end of tunnel and no one is more grateful than Nathan to be out of that claustrophobic nightmare. Sensing they are not alone, trying to calm himself—a sporadic, agonal breath—Nathan is doing the best he can to focus in the dim light.

Tantur then crawled out behind him, adjusting to the light as well. The setting coming into view, he saw Nathan in front of the cistern, pointing a gun at Marcus and Ariel.

Clarence and Margaret are standing behind Nathan, who glanced at Tantur telling him to move away from the tunnel, otherwise, he'll shoot Marcus.

Six inches taller than Nathan, Tantur stood his ground blocking the way out.

"You don't know who I am, do you," asked Marcus stepping forward, a titan himself and Nathan warning him to stay back.

"A five chamber Pug," said Marcus, scrutinizing the gun. "I believe a— *Mr. Shadwell* owns that particular revolver. Did you know he once tried to kill me with that same gun? And if he could not manage," said Marcus, glancing at Margaret while inching forward, "… what makes you think you can?"

"Don't come any closer," Nathan warned him, checking quickly that Margaret and Clarence are still in the same spot.

"Or what … you'll shoot me? *I'm quivering in my boots.*"

"I'm serious."

"*No*— you're foolish," said Marcus, fifteen feet from Nathan and again stepping forward. Marcus then cut the gap in half and it's more than Nathan cared to offer. He pulled the trigger and the blast echoed throughout the cave.

The bullet went straight through Marcus and he flinched while continuing forward, blood surfacing through his shirt and Nathan firing again. Marcus toppled to the ground on impact and Nathan swung the gun at Tantur, commanding him to step back. Tantur stayed put, however, as Ariel, a curious snicker, watched her father ascending to his feet. Marcus ripped open his shirt and everyone can see the blood flowing from his chest. Suddenly, as strange as it may seem, the bleeding stopped and the bullet holes disappeared… *no trace whatsoever.*

Nathan is paralyzed where he stands, his guard obviously down and Ariel dislodging the gun from his flaccid-looking grip.

Marcus, a maniacal grin, now stands toe to toe with Nathan. His newfound stone in hand, a calm but vigorous rub, Marcus did not say a word. He didn't have to and Nathan knew it. *It's over.* Neither he nor Margaret, *nor Clarence*, can do anything to stop Marcus.

Laurian left the safe refuge of the trees with caution, heading for Takara's altar. Margaret, having described the entrance to the cave in such tractable detail—the scant opening of the tunnel—she should have no problem finding it. The smell of wet earth and moist vegetation all around, enervated and her heart racing, Laurian found the opening, having second thoughts about going in without a flashlight.

No worse than being blindfolded and a knife to your throat ... or crash landing in a bunch of trees. No, thought Laurian, convincing herself to navigate the tunnel in the dark, *by comparison this should be a piece of cake.*

Closing her jacket, Laurian crawled into the tunnel, wary of the silty stream between her knees and the glass vial in her pocket. She cannot see that far ahead as something is blocking the entrance. With barely enough room to turn her head around, she wonders if someone is behind her. Looking back, nothing is there, only the sun dousing the crest of the wayside trees.

Not far into the tunnel the light fades, and Dr. Laurian Webster, brindled with mud, wriggles precariously down the black hole. Drawing close to the end, she can hear faint voices… closer still and Margaret arguing with a man whose speech is unfamiliar. Nathan joins the conversation and his tone is rather submissive. *But that can't be*, thought Laurian, *not Nathan— courageous Nathan. What man, if any,* she manages a waning turn, *could he possibly fear?*

At the end of the tunnel, Tantur standing guard, Laurian discovered the uneasiness in Nathan's voice.

One hand around Nathan's throat, Marcus has him pinned against the wall.

Without warning, as though he heard something, Tantur turned an uneasy eye toward the tunnel. For some reason he shrugs it off, heading over to the slab. A string of supplies are stacked along the edge of the slab, and to Laurian's surprise, wedged in the middle of everything is her briefcase.

With everyone gathered around Marcus, Margaret stood beside Nathan pleading for his life. At the edge of the tunnel, easing forward in the shadows, Laurian takes a closer look.

Tantur sensed her movement and suddenly their eyes meet, but he turned away as before, unconcerned while moving to the far end of the slab.

He had me, thought Laurian. *Why did he back off?*

"You should not have come here," said Marcus chidingly, squeezing Nathan's throat.

"Stop it, Marcus," screamed Margaret. "You're hurting him!"

His face pale and neck squirming, an intractable breath, Nathan can't pry away the fingers around his throat from Marcus' implacable grip.

Swirling the stone in his free hand, Marcus turned to Margaret. "He forfeits his life coming here, Margaret. Had he stayed where he was I would have spared him. You know that."

"He came here for me, Marcus! Nothing else. Don't do this!"

Nathan felt the callous chokehold of Marcus crushing inward, one last hopeful breath while twisting his head in an attempt to break free.

Grabbing Marcus by the arm, Margaret can do nothing to pull him away.

His friend grimacing with pain, Clarence stepped in to help but Tantur pulled him to the side.

Believing this to be her only chance, her briefcase not far and everyone engaged with what's going on between Marcus and Nathan, Laurian prepares herself mentally. "*I can do this. I know I can,*" she whispered to herself.

But it's too late. With the expectation of Nathan dying, Ariel takes her eye off the cistern reeling her head around.

Laurian now has no choice but to stay put as Ariel placed herself between her father and the cistern—water trickling from the crevice into the incipient fountain.

Nathan, his lips turning blue, Margaret begged for his life once again. Marcus, however, incrementing his grip, will not let go. "If not by my hand," he turned to Margaret, "… sooner or later by the hand of Tomás Morisco's son. His family— *and your family,*" exclaimed Marcus, shattering the stone, "… have desecrated the fountain! You and everyone else demanding eternal life from it. Neither family is worthy of such glory."

"Please, Marcus," sighed Margaret yanking his sleeve. "Don't kill him. Please. Please don't kill him."

"Quiet, Margaret! There is nothing you can do to stop me."

Desperate, Margaret is on her knees groveling and Marcus bitter because of it. "You don't understand, Marcus … you're killing your own flesh and blood!"

Rising to her feet, Margaret speaks quickly, divulging everything before it's too late. "It's true, Marcus. I said I was pregnant but you forced yourself upon me regardless. There, on that slab," she gestured, "… what kind of man does that? Well, I lied that day," ranted Margaret, looking Marcus in the eye. "Stuart and I were never intimate with one another. The son everyone believed to be his, belonged to you … and you had him killed. You may as well have sabotaged the plane yourself. Now, I beg of you … *let go of our grandson*."

Marcus surrendered his grip, Nathan grabbing his throat gasping for air, plummeting to the rocky ground.

Margaret dropped beside him, his face horribly confused. "I'm sorry, Nathan, but it's all true," said Margaret. "He led me down here and I drank from the fountain of my own free will. I don't have to tell you how much I've regretted every second of my life. Stuart and I were separated like I said, but only because I followed Marcus down here. I had to. Thoughtless of the consequences, whether or not Stuart was alive, I just wanted to see if the legend was true. Marcus may have forced himself upon me, but he didn't force me to drink from the fountain. He wouldn't go anywhere near it. I think," said Margaret, springing to her feet, "… he's afraid of it. Like it's kryptonite or something."

Seeping from the crevice, the water notably loud to Marcus, every interstice drop falls further and further apart until the last disheartening splash. Approaching the cistern with an uneasy step, Marcus is taken by surprise. The water level is not what he expected.

"It's not that I fear the fountain," said Marcus, dipping a cup into the water. "Like a child heeding his father's words, I must obey the rules." Taking the chalice, a Eucharistic vessel, he poured the water inside. The hue from the amaranth liquid and silver crux interior of the chalice, as Margaret can see, flickers malevolently upon Ariel, Nathan, and Clarence. She too is basking in the radiant water, as Tantur, vulnerable to its prodigious glow, confines himself to the shadows.

"No, Margaret. I am not afraid," said Marcus, swirling the water in the chalice. "Tantur and I know all too well the punishment for those who seek its ill desires."

Margaret had no idea what he was talking about, but Ariel did. She knew her father and Tantur were mindful of the water crossing their lips.

"Come, Margaret," said Marcus presenting the chalice. "It is time."

With the help of Clarence, Nathan scrambled to his feet. "Leave her alone," he said, confronting Marcus. "She doesn't want that and you know it."

"But I do," answered Marcus, inching forward.

"It's all right, Nathan," said Margaret, grabbing his arm. "There's nothing you can do. This time, however, it will be different. Every year I had my seizure I felt I was being punished for Stuart's death. I tried, but I couldn't forgive myself for that. But now, Marcus forcing me to drink from the fountain, I know I can."

"No, I won't let you," exclaimed Nathan, squeezing between her and Marcus.

"Listen to her," said Marcus, Tantur stepping aside the two men as Marcus put the chalice on the cistern. "This is most unnerving," Marcus continued, his tone resentful. "I have not lost the desire to kill you, Nathan. A deplorable situation … is it not? You and I."

Thirty-seven

GILDED IN FLORID rubies, sapphires and emeralds, *a scribed base with gold inlay*, the chalice remains atop the cistern. The water, as Marcus knows, neutralizes in a short time. But there is no urgency as far as he's concerned to rush Margaret.

Nathan held his position, shielding Margaret, as Marcus combats him with an intolerable tongue. "Stand down," clamored Marcus, Nathan spurned to react but Tantur forcing him out of the way.

"Your life," proclaimed Marcus speaking to Nathan, "… once ordinary now belongs to me. And you brought that upon yourself by coming here. I, nor Tantur, will not tolerant the Lewis family straying from their mundane lives… people like Benjamin wanting to claim what is rightfully ours."

"*And Margaret*," disputed Nathan, "… isn't she part of that group? How hypocritical is that?"

Marcus paid Nathan no mind. "This feud," he continued, "…will end when there is but one family left. And Morisco will not rest easy until we are all dead."

"And you think I'm just going to sit around and wait for that to happen," responded Nathan, an air of confidence about him.

"I have no cause to doubt you now, Margaret. He is our grandson … dauntless and obstinate traits common to us both. And," Marcus turned to Nathan, "… it will be your undoing. You have no idea how vulnerable you are against Morisco. Someday, if you live long enough, you may want to rid yourself of him. But no one, myself included, sneaks up on the man with ill intent. He can hear your heart pounding a mile away. Unless of course," Marcus gave an emphatic gesture toward the chalice, "… you have some of that with you."

"*Kryptonite*," Nathan reiterates what Margaret said.

"For the lack of a better term, yes. But it will not compromise his strength. Collectively, Tantur and I have the advantage over Morisco. He would never dream of confronting us together. You, however, once he learns of your Córdoba blood, will more than likely disappear."

Ariel, impatient, inadvertently took stock of their supplies. *Something's not right,* she thought, proceeding to the slab. *What happened to the briefcase?*

Marcus and Tantur, their senses crippled for the time being, Ariel takes it upon herself to investigate. *No one here has moved... so who took it?* Her eyes hateful, surging through the darkness, Ariel found the culprit hiding in the back of the cave.

In front of the deep hollow, beyond the glow of the lantern, Ariel can make out a woman's face—Laurian perched on the rocky floor with the briefcase in front of her. Removing something from her jacket, too far to make out, her hands are busy in the briefcase.

Ariel moved closer because the lid is obstructing her view. Covered in darkness, she found a good spot but Laurian shut the case, leaving it behind as she made her way to the cistern as clandestinely as possibly.

Marcus, his patulous voice treading the length and breadth of the cave, choosing another life for Margaret to consider, he grabbed Clarence by the throat.

"Let him go, Marcus. I'll do as you say," pledged Margaret.

Marcus took the chalice from atop the cistern, Margaret then spotting Laurian speeding toward them over his shoulder.

Holding the syringe like an ice pick high above her head, *Marcus handing the chalice to Margaret,* Laurian's arm swept down upon his neck. Marcus, his eyes fearful, Ariel delivered a crushing blow to Laurian's midsection… a body block causing her to tumble across the slab knocking over the lantern—the syringe falling from her hand.

Positioned alongside her father, Ariel gazed into the cistern, a discouraging look on her once appetent face.

"Well done," declared Marcus, a hasty pat on Ariel's back. "Nice of you to join us, *Doctor Webster*," said Marcus, looking around for the syringe. "It seems as though you've misplaced your miracle drug. Don't worry, there's more where that came from. With all the research involved, undoubtedly you have more than one record. Tell me, Doctor, what happened to the—"

"—*Father?*" inquired Ariel, a rare interruption. "There's not enough water for the two of us!"

"Yes, I know," replied Marcus. "Andrew changed course on us out there. There will be other hurricanes. You know that."

"But you promised," piqued Ariel. "And who knows how long that will take. I'm not spending all eternity with love handles and a fat ass! Let Margaret catch the next one. She's already had a turn."

"No, Ariel. I dare not take the chance of her running away in such a vulnerable state. I suspect this hurricane to supply her with nothing more than eternal life. That should be reason enough for you to wait."

"I don't care!" screamed Ariel. "I've been waiting long enough. That water belongs to me ... *not her!*"

"ENOUGH," exclaimed Marcus. "You will stop this foolish behavior at once. Keep an eye on the doctor and—"

Ariel cut her father off with an ominous look, folding her arms in disgust.

"—GO!" blared Marcus "This instant ... *and stay quiet!*"

Disappointed at the choice he made, over his fallible lust for Margaret, Ariel lingered toward the slab, a hateful eye upon Laurian who is sitting at the edge. Suddenly, without warning, she turned around, sprinting back to the cistern.

"No-o-o-o!" screamed Ariel, grabbing her father's arm.

Marcus forced her back immediately and Ariel stumbled, falling indignantly to where Laurian knocked over the lantern.

Picking up where he left off, a presaged eye on Clarence, Marcus gave the chalice to Margaret once more, demanding that she drink.

Submissive to his bidding, Margaret drew the chalice to her lips, Ariel then appearing from out of nowhere with the syringe in her hand, leaping upon her father's back. Taken by surprise, Marcus spun around. He jostled the chalice from Margaret, the water returning to the fountain and Ariel screaming hysterically into the air, injecting the serum deep into her father's gullet.

Outside the cave, now that the storm has moved on, wildlife shuffles unabated and the island returns to normal. Deep into the earth, however, like a crowd drawn to a burning house, or racetrack anticipating a crash, it is far from normal.

The onlookers are quiet, yet there is much to be heard as

the clamorous sigh of relief is mounting, dinning outward in their deep and foremost memories of that ill-fated soul standing before them.

"What have you done," said Marcus, terror on his face while pulling out the needle. His impregnable shell defeated, death is gaining control. Tantur released Nathan and Laurian lumbers to her feet as everyone surrounds Marcus. Their faces tell all, emotions that pierce and apostatize the cold heart of Marcus.

Of everyone standing there, it is Margaret who affects him the most, her eyes inflicting a worse pain than what devours him from within.

His liver and bladder, intestines, lungs, kidneys, heart… everything is infected—white corpuscles mutating in his bloodstream. A child of the fountain, *of the earth, ocean, and sky,* fearful of the serum, Marcus' protective cells are accelerating.

The perfect host, every last consecrated cell is abandoning Marcus' body. Ariel moved closer and his face changed from a warm russet to a pasty, ghostlike haze. Wavering soberly upon his feet, his mind still active, Marcus grabbed Ariel by the throat.

500 years ago he drank from the fountain, and today, another drink so to speak, the demise of Marcus Córdoba unfolds. The water in his body, ironically the same percentage as the earth, along with the menacing serum and corpuscle extending his life, they're all hell-bent on finding a way out.

His skin bubbling and cells oozing out in liquid form, like the Wicked Witch of the West, *Margaret his kindled broom*, it appears as though he's melting.

His fingers, wrapped around his daughter's throat crushing her esophagus, not like water but of gooey, plasmatic syrup, the harder he squeezed the more flesh he saw seeping from his hands.

Ariel can feel his gelatin-like grip faltering and she broke free, feculent remains of her father's curdled fingers dripping from her neck. His body, the figurative burning house, everyone is reluctant to move. Marcus shuddered and in his waning moments collapsed; the crash everyone's been waiting for as the sound of broken bones and gurgling flesh fill the air.

No one turns away from the grisly sight; his face a waxy pulp and body violently shaking. Globs of him burst into water-shrapnel and the cave of eternal life now becomes a tomb of death. Margaret and those behind her step back anticipating he may explode. His convulsions, though not as bad when his cells reproduce, are so fierce that in a short time bone and muscle blot his face.

Both curious and horrified, Marcus gazed empirically upon his gangrenous fingers. Of his cheek and jawbone—a fleshy, decomposed liquid—most of it splashes sonorously to the ground. His chest, where he ripped open his shirt, shards of cartilage and ribs are showing. Screaming in agony, the brutal sound along with his deliquescent flesh, Laurian can no longer bear it, covering her ears and looking away. Clarence quivers and they are all transiently sickened, except for Ariel who appears innocuous; the goriness of her father's face and squeamish cries having no affect.

All at once, Marcus stopped shaking, the worst of his death canalized in a thundering outcry, his vaporous organs seen through his chest starting to putrefy. A rotting, urinary smell and puce glow seep out of his kidneys and intestinal wall. Drawing a gaping last breath his face is petrified. Margaret, the only one with pity, everything around Marcus turns black and the last thing on his mind is a blithe vision of him pushing Marcelina in a swing when they were young. Suddenly, slipping into desolation, he departs as the falling reign. What is left of him, posh clothing and chalky bones, with no worms to finish his puddled flesh, Marcus Córdoba succumbs to the porous, rocky floor—back to that infernal womb from whence he came.

Thirty-eight

ARIEL BACKED AWAY from her father's skeleton, the inchoate fossil in front of the small hollow and everyone except Laurian inclined to have a closer look. Shuffling passed Nathan, the first to reach the rancid bones, Ariel escaped his exasperate glare. Margaret, a scornful farewell, what little there is of Marcus she kneels beside him.

Tantur's life of servitude ends without quarrel and he drops the knife—no pretext on his behalf or justification declared.

Keeping an eye on Ariel, Clarence doesn't make it as far as the others. Inching her way to the cistern, Ariel lingers in Laurian's direction; the astute doctor blocking the surface tunnel. Concerned that Ariel might try something, her being such an entrancing female, Clarence maintains a contiguous position. He has forgotten, however, as they all have, the gun Ariel dislodged from Nathan lies somewhere between the cistern and Laurian's backside.

Dissolving like ice on a warm platter, all that remains of Marcus are his milky bones. His shirt now covering his ribs, undulating from a drafty fissure, the temptation is too much and Margaret poked the rancid fibers with her finger. To her surprise, everything settles in an instant, the entire length and breadth of Marcus crumbling into a vestige contour.

Margaret now has peace of mind but her repose is laden with anxiety. Tantur is there to help her up and once on her feet he draws her away from the fetid clothes of Marcus.

“You okay,” Nathan questioned her, a teary cheek and muddled look on Margaret’s face.

“I thought this day would never come,” she replied, glancing toward the small hollow with nothing more to say. Margaret felt relieved but it was not how she imagined it. With Marcus gone at last, why did she feel so empty inside? Why were there no trumpets, jubilate in her mind that her heart would be dancing. She felt like a diffident wallflower teeming with desire. Desperate to bloom, yet fearful of the waltzing, *the shuffle in which one’s fortitude transcends*, Margaret can’t muster what it takes to break free of the spell she’s under.

Clarence is taken in by Margaret’s wistful gaze and Ariel regards it as an opportune moment to refill the chalice.

“What do you think you’re doing,” exclaimed Laurian, scrambling to stop her.

Anticipating what Laurian will do, the chalice full again, in one sweeping move Ariel set the chalice at the edge of the cistern, shoving Laurian to the ground.

“Mist’a Lewis!” shouted Clarence, taking hold of Ariel from behind.

Nathan spun around reacting quickly, his heart and feet racing as Ariel wrestled Clarence to the ground; both of them eyeing the rusty knife Tantur dropped. In the same emphatic moment, the knife within their reach, they turn and look at one another.

Clarence hogtied Ariel around the legs, like he did with Vincent going for the tranquilizer gun. Ariel, however, as Clarence sorely discovers, is stronger and far more agile than Vincent.

First generation to Marcus, inheriting among other things a portion of her father's strength, Ariel kicked Clarence in the face; a solid shot to the nose while stretching for the knife.

With all his might, Clarence pulled her back, but in a scurrilous eruption of madness and profanity, Ariel straddled him across the chest, pinning him to the ground.

Lifting her head, Ariel saw Nathan speeding toward her, fending him off in mid-stride. "That's close enough— *Nephew*," she warned him, one hand taking Clarence by the throat and the other brandishing the knife.

The tip is rather blunt but Nathan knows it can pierce a man's juggler in the right hands. Having no alternative he stands fast. Tantur, however, takes a step forward.

"You too, jungle boy! I'm taking what belongs to me so everyone stay put. *You*, Margaret," Ariel motioned to the cistern, "… bring me the chalice, or I swear I'll Frankenstein this kid's neck!"

Margaret did as instructed, stepping around the slab when a voice from behind called out, "Drop the knife!"

Laurian strode into the light between Margaret and the cistern, pointing Shadwell's revolver at Ariel's head. "I said, drop it! *Or, I swear* … you flinch and I air-out your brain."

Her eye on the gun, Ariel clamors to Margaret, "*I'm waiting!* Bring me the chalice and I'll give you the boy."

"Don't do it, Margaret," exclaimed Laurian, asperity rumbling off her tongue.

A bloody nose and obtrusive looking face, Clarence is shocked that Miss Webster is bargaining with his life.

"What does it matter," contested Margaret. "Her only concern is staying young. She'll not victimize us like Marcus."

"She's out of control," Laurian replied, her eye still on Ariel. "There's no telling what she might do."

"Laurian's right," said Nathan, provoking Ariel with his undertone. "If I were you I wouldn't hesitate. Take the shot."

Clarence can feel his skin shudder. "That may not be a good idea right now, Mist'a Lewis."

"You shut up," snapped Ariel, digging her thumb in Clarence's throat.

Nathan is mindful of how close Tantur is to Ariel, his brow swelling outward, giving Laurian the *all-clear.* "Drop the knife," said Laurian, peering over the stubby barrel. "I'm not going to tell you again."

"You're bluffing," refuted Ariel. "Margaret— *the chalice*. Bring it to me now," demanded Ariel, raising the knife.

Fearing she may stab Clarence, Laurian squeezed the trigger. There is a despairing click and Laurian is in disbelief. She pulled the trigger again and again and the outcome is the same. The gun is empty.

Believing she has the upper hand, Ariel flashed a prevailing smile.

"Enough!" said Tantur, grabbing Ariel by her tiny wrist, forcing her to drop the knife. Tantur then hoists Ariel off Clarence, shoving her toward the exit. "Now would be a good time for you to go," he said.

Laurian cleared a path, as Ariel, a bruised carpus and sore ego, swaggered passed her, glancing at the briefcase and then the chalice—the body she assumed would never age, declining with every step. Chagrined at the outcome, her father now dead, moving away from the light and the shadows embracing her, Ariel ascends the tunnel plotting her revenge.

"Why did you do that," asked Margaret, upset with Tantur for letting Ariel go. She then lowered her voice, not wanting Clarence to hear the rest. "She'll take the Lady Bird, you know. We need that boat to save William."

Tantur looked as though he didn't care, dismissing everything Margaret said by walking away. Stooping at the site where Marcus collapsed, Tantur dug into the dead man's trousers. "She can't leave without these," he said to Margaret, showing her a set of keys.

"We should have tied her up and called the police," said Nathan. "She's too dangerous to have let go."

Tantur disagrees. "Margaret was right," he surmised. "Ariel cares for one thing and one thing only."

"Well I for one don't trust her. Whose side are you on anyway? What if I wanted to be an immortal? Would you stop me," asked Nathan, heading for the chalice.

"Nathan, No!" screamed Margaret, urging him to stay back.

"Are you serious," asked Laurian, putting her body in front of the cistern, blocking the chalice.

Nathan spun around, searching Tantur's eyes for an answer. He then turned back to Margaret, her face opposite of what the Cariban warrior tells him. "Go ahead. No one will stop you," said Tantur, glancing at the others. "But you take it from one who is most deserving," he exclaimed, promptly looking at Margaret.

"No, Tantur," cried Margaret, a polite yet harsh tone. "You know I loathe that way of life. And it's wrong to subject Nathan to it."

"You heard what Marcus said," clamored Nathan, defending his intentions. "Morisco will be looking for me— *perhaps all of us*. I need to level the playing field, that's all."

"You don't understand," contested Margaret. It won't stop there. The fountain has a way of changing a man … and not for the betterment of those around him."

"The only thing I wish to change is my advantage," said

Nathan. "I won't allow the fountain to harden my heart like it did Marcus. I think he was too imperious and greedy to begin with."

"It's not greed but power that worries me. If you don't get a hold of yourself, Nathan, you will discover power is the worst desire of all. And the fountain will consume you as it did Marcus. *As it does everyone*."

"But it didn't change you."

"Only because I felt guilty. I suffered with the knowledge that because of my actions Stuart died. Without guilt there can be no absolution. Take advantage of the fountain, Nathan, and it will take advantage of you."

"I just want protection. And not just for myself."

"Nathan," said Laurian, drawing close to him. "Listen to her. You're better than this. You talk as though you're contemplating murder and you've never met the man."

Laurian then looked into Nathan's eyes, a deep plea for him to reconsider the animosity toward her biological father. Harboring the need to protect both men, Laurian wants to tell Nathan who Morisco is, but she's unsure how Nathan will react. "You're only making matters worse," she said, avoiding the issue altogether. "Think about what Margaret is saying. It *will* change you."

"I'm not going to let that happen," argued Nathan, sidestepping Laurian and picking up the chalice. "You can bring me back like you did Margaret when this is all over. I won't let Morisco do to us what Marcus did to my mother and father."

A vague look quelled Laurian stern face. "*Us*," she asked.

"Yes," Nathan replied, raising the chalice. "It's now my responsibility to keep everyone safe."

"Then for me," Laurian placed her hand atop the chalice, "… don't do this."

Out of breath yet moving vigorously, Ariel made it to the dock, climbing onto the bow of the Lady Bird. Swaying in the temperate water, the boat is unscathed and Ariel disregards the lanyard, for as she feared there is no ignition key. She has no idea how to hot-wire an engine and is cursing herself for not learning. Opening the port and starboard engine hatches, now in a crouched position, she wonders which wires to cross… her train of thought disrupted by the sound of footsteps storming the dock.

In a reckless frenzy, Ariel ransacks the life preservers and boating provisions in the engine compartment. "There you are," she said, lifting up an old blanket.

Rising to her feet, the footsteps closing in, Ariel points a massive hunting rifle, *bolt-action with a parallax scope*, at someone wearing a hooded parka.

"That's far enough," cried Ariel.

A pair of gentle hands draw back the hood, a woman in her mid-forties, elegantly attractive with auburn hair and rosy complexion, smiling at Ariel.

"Trouble with your boat," she asked. The woman's voice is subtle, her lips firm and silky. The sun flares through a furrowed cloud and her dark eyes glisten below a thin, rubiginous brow.

"Rachel," exclaimed Ariel, lowering the rifle, "… I didn't realize you were still out there. You can't imagine what I've been through."

"Here," said Rachel, extending a hand to help Ariel out of the boat. "I'll give you a lift to the mainland. My plane should be here any minute now."

Ariel hands her the rifle and a box of shells.

"What's this for," asked Rachel, placing the rifle and shells on the dock.

"Alligators. They don't post signs for the mere pleasure of it."

Rachel disregards Ariel's sarcasm, once more offering to help her from the boat.

Ariel pays no mind to Rachel's outstretched hand, gazing into the woods while ascending the dock. "Where is he," asked Ariel. "Where's Thomas?"

"Thomas would never get this close to Marcus, you know that."

"So he sends his wife into the lion's den instead," said Ariel, a deriding tone followed by a stern eye. "You're lucky my father is no longer with us. If he saw you here he'd tear you in half."

"*No longer with us?*"

"He's dead," exclaimed Ariel, picking up the rifle and box of trundling shells.

"*Dead?!* What about the fountain? What about my son?"

Gazing at the sky, Ariel ignores the question. "Where's the plane," she asked.

Rachel seized Ariel by the arm. "Ariel," she demanded, an edgy voice and harsh deportment. "*Did you bring some for Daniel!?*"

Ariel lowered her head, casting a hapless eye on Rachel. "There was only enough for one."

"*And?*"

"And I wasn't the one," growled Ariel.

"Then who?"

"I don't know. They may not even use it … *the scant-minded fools.* The water sat there ready for the taking when I last saw it. Webster's serum worked and when my father chose Margaret over me … I don't know why or what came over me … but I killed him. And that's not all. Nathan I've just been told is my blood nephew."

"What!"

"My father's grandson. He and Margaret, can you believe it?"

"I suppose he'll be the one."

"Nathan may be next in line for the job but I doubt it. Tantur won't allow it. The Great Protector of the sacred pool stepping down? Not a chance."

"What about the rest of Webster's research?"

"She has it."

"Then we take it from her! With your father out of the—"

"Forget about it, Rachel. It's over. Tantur's gone all Judas on me."

"But—"

"I said it's over! I'll finish what we started without it."

"And how long will that take?"

"I'm not sure. I've narrowed the etiology of her research considerably. But I can't start the reverse diagnostics until I've duplicated what she's already done."

"But that could take a lifetime. What about my son?"

"*Your son?* What about me?!"

"You'll both have to wait for another hurricane, I suppose."

"And when do you think that will happen, *Rachel?* It won't work if it's not a direct hit and it's been seventeen years since the last one."

"It may be sooner," said Rachel. "And we don't need to sneak around now that Marcus—"

"Did you hear what I said," Ariel lashed out. "Tantur has turned against me. He's not rolling out the welcome mat to anyone but Margaret. He always had a soft spot for her and if Nathan joins them it won't be that easy."

"But you said the water just sat there. If no one drinks it," inferred Rachel, "... what then?"

"*Then,*" said Ariel, "... we may have a chance. You and Thomas against Tantur? I like those odds."

Heading south into an airy thicket of Australian pines, the

two women reach a lengthy stretch of beach. The clouds break and the white shore is splotched with sunlight, both Ariel and Rachel searching the sky for their ride home.

Moments later Rachel's seaplane shows up and she waves it in. "I saw a woman at the cave," she said to Ariel, the plane circling back. "Who was that?"

"Dr. Webster."

"*That was Laurian Webster?*"

"You sound surprised."

"I pictured her as an older woman."

"She's thirty-something."

"She looks pretty good for her age."

"Good genes, I suppose," said Ariel.

"For a moment, right before she went into the tunnel, I thought she might be my daughter."

"*Isolde?*"

"Yes, I had this funny feeling. Thomas doesn't know about her. You're aware of that, right?"

"Yeah. You told me a long time ago. A touching story," scoffed Ariel, "… giving her up for adoption."

"You would have done the same if it were your child." *I wonder*, thought Rachel, … *if Webster is a true brunette.*

Nathan withdrew from the cistern, the chalice sitting atop the basin and no one saying a word about the choice he made. Tantur is the first to move and he too is quiet. *Nathan Lewis made his decision*, thought Tantur, *and must live with it for the rest of his life.*

Now the center of all their attention, Tantur opened the doctors bag they took from Vincent. "So many dangerous things," said Tantur, "… for such a timid little man."

Tantur removed everything from the bag except for the

bottle of water Clarence stuck inside. A cigar box, transmitter and receivers, and sticks of C-4 are jumbled together on the slab. "Be careful," Tantur said to Margaret, a firm hold on the doctors bag while heading for the tunnel.

"Where are you going," asked Margaret.

Tantur held up for a moment. "You are fond of the boat? The one called the *Lady Bird?*"

"Yes, very much."

"I'm going to take my brother home now. The boat will be waiting for you in Cape Coral. Farewell, Margaret."

"Can you help us before you go," asked Margaret. "We left William in the woods. He had a heart attack and needs medical attention right away. The Lady Bird has more than enough room. Please, take him with you?"

Tantur pulled Margaret to the side, explaining Shadwell's condition at the crash site. "It's too late for him, Margaret."

Arranging the explosives on the slab, his nose in a bloodstained handkerchief, Clarence turned an unexpected eye toward Margaret.

Margaret's face, sorrowful to begin with, now swells with disappointment.

"I suppose," said Tantur, wiping a tear from Margaret's cheek, "… we can all go together."

"Are you sure? You have such a long journey ahead."

"What are a few hours to an immortal compared to your precious time?"

"And the fountain? You know what we're planning. Are you okay with that?"

"It doesn't matter. I have a plan of my own."

"I'll be coming back for the ivy as well," said Margaret, " … every last vine."

"If that is your wish, there will be no one to stop you. Go to William Shadwell, Margaret. I will meet you there."

Not far from the slab, a shadow sprawls from the lantern, Tantur stepping away and Clarence joining Margaret at her side. “Sumpin’s not right, Miss Margaret. I can tells by the way yer’ lookin’ at me. Is it my Uncle Will … is he all right?”

Margaret didn’t have the heart to tell him, saying nothing and Clarence fearing the worse. Wanting an answer, whether or not his uncle died, Clarence cut Tantur off at the tunnel. “You knows sumpin’ … *don’t ya?*”

Belaying for a moment his aberrant nature, Clarence practically in tears, Tantur opened the doctors bag, the stern warrior kneeling beside the boy speaking softly into his ear.

Clarence is neither sad nor displaced, showcasing complaisant nods, as though listening to a set of instructions.

Thirty-nine

TENDING TO THE matter of the explosives, twenty bars of C-4 wrapped in army-green cellophane, Nathan is apprehensive, having never done what he and Clarence are planning to do.

Two inch wide by one inch thick, a texture similar to modeling clay, the bars of C-4 are stacked together in four separate piles. An aerial transmitter, AA batteries and nine receivers are on the slab next to the C-4. At a safe distance, Nathan opened a felt-lined cigar box loaded with an array of blasting caps and matches. "You're sure this is what you want," he asked Margaret, trusting her to do the right thing.

"All my life I've wanted nothing more. And we'll not have a better opportunity than this," she said, reinforcing her intent. "I only hope it will work?"

"This stuff'll blow up anything," said Clarence, still holding the handkerchief to his nose. "Me an' Uncle Will use it back home takin' out tree stumps. But I don't recall usin' blasters like this," he turned to Nathan, picking one up.

"It's easy," said Nathan. "Attach it to the receiver and a signal from the transmitter sets it off. As many as you want, all at the same time."

"Listen to you," said Margaret, impressed with Nathan's expertise. "You talk as though you've done this before."

"Basic electronics I understand," replied Nathan. "Plastic explosives I've only read about."

"I'll leave it up to you then," said Margaret, grabbing the flashlight. "We need to get going," she nudged Laurian. Margaret then spoke to Nathan again. "You can find your way back to the plane, right?"

Nathan gave Margaret a nod and she promptly turned to Clarence. "Why don't you come with us," she said. "Nathan can handle it from here."

"This is sumpin' I knows how ta' do, Miss Margaret. If Uncle Will were here," Clarence secured a stiff upper lip, "… he'd want me ta' stay an' help."

"All right. Just be careful. Both of you."

Though she looked like a college freshman, more of a snooty know-it-all than a wise old owl, Margaret spoke with an infallible degree of experience. Everyone knew no matter how young her appearance, she possessed a lifetime of empirical knowledge.

As a close friend, Laurian often sought Margaret's sound advice. On this day, no different from any other, excluding the hurricane and formidable events, Laurian gave Nathan an endearing look on her way out, knowing full well she will bring yet another matter to Margaret's attention.

"I'm not sure how to go about this," Nathan grabbed the lantern, he and Clarence scouting the perimeter. "I'd feel better if I knew how much yield a bar of C-4 had. I suppose the best thing to do," he lifted the lantern, "… is to stuff as much as we can in that crevice. The rest we can use to seal up the tunnel and that opening back there. What do you think? Will we have enough?"

"Takes a piece no bigger than a mouth full of chaw to blow

up them stumps. I'd say we have more than enough," said Clarence, looking down at the C-4 then up at the ceiling. "'Cept— how ya figure on gettin' up there?"

It was a good question. The crevice ran the length of the cave and as they both can see the only reachable spot is above the cistern. "We can do it," said Nathan, "… if you stand on my shoulders."

The frequency receiver is no bigger than a deck of cards and Nathan shows Clarence how to route and connect the blasting caps—explaining the dangers of the mercury fulminate switch and cyclonite base charges. Together, Clarence having some knowledge of explosives and Nathan recalling a publication he read, they assemble nine detonators, arranging them on the slab as far from the C-4 as possible.

Standing atop the cistern, Nathan kneads the first bar into the crevice. Clarence, whose nose has stopped bleeding, stuffs a second bar in place, forming a lengthy, deep mass. The detonator is next. Nathan embeds the receiver into the C-4, burying the blasting cap deep inside. Climbing down, he looked over at Clarence. "Not too difficult … is it?"

"P'erty much the same way me an' Uncle Will does it. 'Cept fer stickin' that blaster next to the receiver. We always use a fuse."

"Just don't drop it and everything will be fine," said Nathan, the lanky teenager then scaling the cistern, climbing on Nathan's shoulders.

A detonator in one hand while steadying Clarence with the other, the boy holding the C-4 cupping the ceiling with his free hand, inch by inch Nathan navigates the floor. The chalice now in their shadow, no longer an illuminate glow, it appears salient to Nathan nonetheless.

"Ain't gonna be much of that fountain left when we're through," said Clarence, stuffing the crevice with C-4. "We gonna take that fancy cup with us or leave it here?"

Nathan glanced at the chalice, handing the detonator up to Clarence shortly thereafter. "I think it's fitting if we leave it here," he replied. "Don't you?"

"I agree," said Clarence, his undertone giving Nathan the impression he has more to say.

Expecting what it might be, Nathan remained quiet.

"Ya did the right th'ang, Mist'a Lewis," said Clarence, looking at the chalice. "If'n it was up ta' me, I'd a done the same."

Nathan did not reply. He was pleased Clarence spoke his mind but kept the matter to himself. He did, however, thank Clarence by patting his leg.

An ideal opening for the next charge, Clarence must stretch out completely, his arm and neck tiring while packing the C-4.

"This is taking a lot longer than I thought," said Nathan. "You gonna be able to work that receiver in there okay?"

"I think so," answered Clarence, grinding his thumb into the soft putty—not an easy thing to do, tiptoeing on Nathan's clavicle.

With the receiver in place, Clarence stuck the blasting cap into the clay, his legs now wobbly and Nathan unable to control him. With nothing to grab but the looping wires, Clarence teeters and falls, his topsy-turvy body colliding with the slab.

Inadvertently knocking over the lantern, a bottle of water flips precariously in the air landing on a detonator, flinging it across the slab. The battery cover pops off in mid-flight and the blasting cap flops alongside the circuitry. Nathan cringes, expecting an explosion. There is nothing he can do but watch as the detonator travels end over end toward the C-4.

Rolling off the slab, the sound echoing throughout the cave, the detonator settled near the edge, cracking in half with the explosive cap inches from the C-4.

A sigh of relief, Nathan kneels beside Clarence. "That was a close one. Are you all right?"

"I fell on my hip p'erty hard," answered Clarence, his nose bleeding again.

Clarence held his nose grimacing in pain, Nathan grabbing him by the arm helping him to sit up. Glancing at one another, as though they forgot something, they looked up at the detonator directly above them. The blasting cap and receiver still in place, the only thing amiss are the wires swaying back and forth. "It's not going anywhere, that's for sure," said Nathan, patting Clarence on the back. "The only question now … *are you able to walk?*"

"I don't know," answered Clarence, his voice filled with discomfort.

Nathan helped him to his feet and Clarence has a slight limp testing his legs. "Nothin's broken," he said. "Gonna hurt a lot more when I crawls up that tunnel."

"You're sure you're all right?"

"I'll be okay, Mist'a Lewis. I just needs ta' sit a spell 'till my nose stops bleedin'."

"Go ahead. I can manage what's left," said Nathan.

Clarence found a spot on the slab and Nathan sat next to him disconnecting the faulty detonator. "We'll have to double up on our last charge," he said. "I'll put the next one in that opening back there. It'll be dark for a while," Nathan grabbed the lantern, "… so don't go wandering off."

"Don't worry 'bout me," Clarence picked up a book of matches, "I'll manage just fine."

Nathan disappeared into the deep hollow, leaving Clarence alone for a short time. Upon his return, Clarence basically in the same spot, Nathan wonders if Laurian and Margaret are okay. "How's the hip," he asked Clarence, concerned as much, if not more, for the boy's well-being.

"Still p'erty sore. Gonna take some time gettin' up that tunnel."

"You may as well get started. I'll finish up down here and meet you at the top."

Nathan found a commodious spot inside the tunnel for the first of two charges, laying on his back packing a narrow cavity with C-4. Finishing the task, he returned to the cave, mulling in front of the cistern as to whether or not he made the right decision. *We'll see how it all plays out,* he thought.

Checking all the charges, he set the timer, placing the transmitter on the slab. One last look around, satisfied he did everything right, Nathan grabbed the lantern, dragging his feet on his way to that loathsome tunnel. Passing in front of the cistern, he ponders his decision one last time… the chalice empty and the light in the cave going out.

A honeycomb of silver and burnt-orange bursting through the trees, the sun evokes a feeling of hope in Margaret—clearly, after the darkest of times life goes on.

Out of breath and faltering along the path, Laurian has no forethought as to why the sky chose this moment to peek through the trees. "Can we rest for a bit," she asked, clutching her side in the damp undergrowth.

"We're almost there," answered Margaret, vanishing into the fervent, brighter side of day; her voice slicing through the blinding light.

Same old Margaret, thought Laurian, *immortal or not*, *she remains stringent*.

Using all her strength to keep up, Laurian recalls how she and Margaret first met. A chance encounter on a hot summer day, their vehicles next to each other in one of the parking lots at Tulane University, Margaret was gulping a bottle of Evian next to her BMW as Laurian approached her minivan.

Margaret had an appointment with Dr. Wainwright that day. Commenting on the weather, it led to a conversation with Laurian. Margaret was surprised to learn that Laurian was on Wainwright's staff. Laurian, a true redhead back then, was aware that Margaret provided most of the funding for Wainwright's research—his laboratory a state of the art facility at Tulane. Their paths had never crossed until that day and it was the last time Margaret saw Wainwright alive.

Recalling her talk with the redhead from Tulane, Margaret set up a private meeting with Laurian at the university. Apprehensive at first, Margaret unsure if she could trust Laurian, with no one else to turn to, she took a chance, divulging the secret of the fountain.

Laurian thought Margaret was crazy when she said Wainwright was acting on a theory to reverse the process. Knowing only one way to convince her, Margaret took a scalpel slicing her arm. The cut healed almost instantly and it was more than enough evidence for the incredulous doctor. Margaret kept copies of Wainwright's research, persuading Laurian to continue his work.

Early on, Laurian told Margaret about her adoption. Her parents had no recollection of her ever being sick or injured. "You, Doctor Webster," Margaret then explained, "…are the child of an immortal."

Somewhat of a shock, your parents living forever, for the longest time Laurian thought Margaret was her biological mother. One day Margaret explained that she wasn't. Laurian's relationship with Wainwright, moreover his research on immortals, cast Laurian into the limelight. Her real mother, for some reason needing to hide Laurian, Margaret thought it best that Laurian leave Tulane and finish her research in a private facility—one with resources Margaret could well afford.

A new life style, and hair color as well, it took some time for Laurian to adjust. She had many questions about her biological parents and what it was like to be an immortal. A mother-daughter relationship soon developed, and now, approaching the wreckage of the plane, Laurian understands why Nathan is so appealing to her. Not only is she attracted to him physically, *saving her life part of the equation*, Laurian shares with Nathan something no one else can. *How do I tell him who my real father is? And moreover*, thought Laurian, *explain to Margaret what the serum is doing to her body.*

Her legs aching and stomach cramping, Laurian made it to the edge of the crash site, Margaret well out in front. Shadwell is against the tree where they left him and Margaret scurries the rest of the way. The last few meters Laurian is overcome with fatigue. Bending down, gasping for air, she happened to look over at Margaret, now crouching beside Shadwell's lifeless body.

Continuing forward, the crackling of brush at her feet, Laurian can hear nothing but her own craggy breath. What seems to be taking forever, *approaching Shadwell and Margaret with a heavy heart*, soft, whisper-like voices cloud the air.

Propped against the tree, his face filled with determination, Shadwell draws an anxious breath, gazing at Margaret while poignantly drawing another. His cloths look as though they've shrunk two sizes and Margaret begins to weep, committed not to let the tears take what precious time is left.

Laurian maintains her distance, but not too far, taking in every word as Margaret fluffed the old fedora, placing it nobly upon Shadwell's head.

"How do I look," asked Shadwell, his voice reminding Margaret every mortal shares the same fate.

An encouraging smile, more for herself than her beloved William, Margaret said he looked rather smart.

"A fitting end," said Shadwell. "When I was a boy I saw myself mingling with all the highbrows of modern society."

"And what became of that," Margaret took his hand. "Did you mingle?"

"No," replied Shadwell, her hand giving him the strength to continue. "I've kept to myself all these years. The cultured, as it turned out, had nothing to offer. Most of them were running the same rails as *Paradise Lost*."

"I wish things could have been different between us," said Margaret. "And I am truly sorry I left you with no more than a cowardly note. I regret that, each and every day. But how else was I to keep you away from Marcus? And now," her lips curl inward, "... now that he's gone, I am afraid once more. Afraid of losing you again."

"It's all right, Margaret," gasped Shadwell, struggling with each breath. "I made a promise to myself when you and I first spoke. That night an old friend named Jean Claude emphasized the importance of living a good life. I took his advice to heart and ventured forth to fulfill my dreams. But those dreams, like broken promises, changed course. I ended up so far from where I started, life didn't turn out like it was supposed to. It wasn't my lack of effort, I assure you. It was my willingness to accept the fact that some dreams were never meant to be. Poverty and racism, even the lack of a good education I was able to overcome. That never would have happened if not for you, Margaret. When you left it didn't matter anymore. Looking at you now, I managed to keep that promise. It's what Jean Claude said to be the most important thing in life. I found my fortune," he squeezed Margaret's hand. "It has taken me a lifetime and here you are, *my Lady Bird* … a comfort to me at the very end."

"No, William, *do not say that*."

Her tears flow uncontrollably and Margaret extends her hand, caressing Shadwell's weathered cheek.

"Promise me, Margaret," said Shadwell, his voice fading, "… that you will watch over Clarence. He needs someone like you … a caring hand to guide him along. And please … don't leave me on this wretched island."

"I won't. And I'll take good care of Clarence. Where is it," asked Margaret, taking a moment to wipe away the tears, "… that you wish to be buried? With your aunt and sister?"

"I would rather be close to you."

"Home then, dear William. I shall take you home. I love you so much. I always have—" said Margaret, pausing as Shadwell, slipping fast, squeezed her hand to let her know he loves her too.

"You've always been close to me," said Margaret. "And it doesn't matter where you're buried. The home I speak of isn't a plot of earth somewhere … it's here," Margaret placed his hand above her heart, "… where I shall lay you to rest. And forever— if such a time exists… this part of me will remain whole."

A glimmering smile appeared between Shadwell's pallid cheeks and Margaret is teary eyed once more. Shadwell's head drooped in silence and the old fedora fell aptly to the ground, landing prophetically at Margaret's side rather than rolling away.

Picking up the old fedora, Margaret kissed Shadwell on the top of the head. It was at this point that Laurian stepped forward—two somber faces embracing one another.

"You must tell Nathan the truth about your past," said

Margaret. "And waste no time in doing so."

"I don't know how to break it to him."

"Don't wait too long," exclaimed Margaret, "… I believe it's fair to say I know how it can tear two lives apart. Tell him. *Tell him the minute he arrives!* I see the way you look at one another. Both wanting to take the next step."

"And what of my true parents? If they find out who I am they'll come for me. They'll come for us both. Oh my God, Amy! They'll come for her too!"

"No. No they won't," Margaret assured her. "Not if you did as we planned. The fake copies of your research … you switched everything, right?"

"All but one disk."

"And you made it look as though you were using the begonias instead of the ivy to produce the serum?"

"The purple ones, yes."

"Destroy the disk and it will all be over. It will take some time to figure everything out, and by then you'll be long gone. You can go anywhere in the world, Laurian. I'll keep a close eye on everyone … even Ariel. As long as I'm alive none of them will ever find you. Take your parents and your brother with you if you want. Everything I own will be passed on to you and Nathan in due time."

"There's something you must know about that," said Laurian, no reason to keep the truth from her any longer. "About your life expectancy… it's not—"

"Shh!" exclaimed Margaret, gesturing to a rustling in the trees. "Someone's coming!"

"I hear it too," said Laurian, moving back as the surging footsteps crackle through the woods. The two women look at each other, nervous, but neither one cringing nor retreating from the wreckage.

Stepping from the trees, the tallest of men, Tantur casts an inadvertent eye upon them. His painted face, the white stripes of war, the Cariban warrior is more concerned over Shadwell's body than the presence of Margaret and Laurian.

Easing between the two women, his hands caked with topsoil, Tantur took Shadwell in his arms, transporting him to the cockpit and not one word while doing so.

"What's going on," asked Margaret.

"We can't leave him in the open. He'll be safe in here," Tantur replied, " … away from any animal that may come along."

"I understand," said Margaret.

"Good. Try not to leave him here too long."

"I'm taking him off this island tomorrow. He and Stuart both."

"Then you are ready to go?"

"Yes. I've said my goodbyes."

Tantur felt odd leading the way instead of prodding Margaret from behind. Gazing at Shadwell, his eyes no longer admiring her, Margaret turned away, grasping the old fedora as an ardent memory of Old San Juan comforts her.

Searching the treetops, an opening in the canopy, Tantur is the first to spot what everyone can hear; Rachel's seaplane having taken off. A sleek fuselage with bullet pontoons, Tantur focused on a spot between the cockpit and propeller. There, as he suspected, is a logo of a medieval sword piercing a heart-shaped leaf.

"That plane was on the beach," he said, "… a woman with red hair climbing inside with Ariel."

"*Red hair*," exclaimed Margaret, she and Laurian gazing at one another.

"What's that over there," asked Ariel, pointing to a clearing in the trees.

Rachel's middle-aged son, Daniel, seated behind the

controls, removed his headgear. He has long red hair, the same vivid color as his mother, and Ariel, who thinks the color is unattractive for his rugged features, glares emphatically having to repeat what she said.

"I didn't see anything," replied Daniel, banking toward the mainland. His fortieth birthday around the corner, a man with broad shoulders and tapered chest, Daniel sits high in the cockpit insisting that Ariel stay calm.

"There were two men outside the cave, I tell you."

"*So?*" shouted Daniel.

"So they're up to something," Ariel shouted back. "Turn this noisy heap of metal around so we can get a better look!"

Daniel glanced at his mother, his eyes wanting to know what she thought.

"Go ahead," she shouted. "I wasn't paying much attention; otherwise I would have seen what they were up to."

"The two of you are making a big deal out of nothing," said Daniel, slipping on his headset before circling back.

At the entrance to the cave, Nathan bonds together the last of the C-4, inserting a blasting cap and Clarence handing over the matchbook. "You best get back now, Clarence. Behind those trees like we talked about."

Clarence reacted quickly but he's moving sluggishly, passing Takara's altar as Nathan, *finding it difficult using a match*, lit the wax coated fuse. In a superfluous dash, he caught up with Clarence and they crouch behind a stack of fallen trees. "You're sure that was a two-minute fuse," asked Nathan, checking his watch.

"Yep. Takes 'bout a minute ta' burn two feet."

"We're good then," said Nathan. "I figure a fifteen second gap between the timer and fuse. If the transmitter fails, that last charge will stir things up."

Tantur listened to the spirit of the woods, identifying every noise in the aftermath of the storm. He can hear the ruffling of leaves and pine needles, tiny feet forging through Andrew's damage as acorns and berries, *a movable feast*, are now on the ground.

A familiar noise, much like sizzling bacon, Tantur extends his arm, stopping Margaret and Laurian dead in their tracks.

"What is it," asked Margaret.

"Get down!" exclaimed Tantur.

A deafening blast jolts the air and no one, including Tantur, can hear the seaplane soaring blindly into a cloud of dust.

Chunks of earth and a barrage of sandstone cudgel the plane—reverberating like pellets from a shotgun.

"What the hell!?" cried Daniel, a momentary loss of direction and the seaplane skimming the treetops. Glancing at the altimeter, Daniel secured the column with both hands, a sudden jolt on the way up as the pontoons shatter a heavy branch.

Bursting through the murk, an obstructed view of what lie below, Ariel shed her seatbelt scrambling to the aft window. The dust is settling and a great number of fallen trees appear around a deep crater. The Sandcat, its castle and dungeon destroyed, Ariel hammered the glass portal with an angry fist, wailing at the top of her lungs, "*No-o-o-o-o-o!*"

Forty

SEATED AT THE back of the plane, Ariel can see the mainland through the cockpit window. A reckless state of mind, she grabbed the hunting rifle, making her way forward. Peering over Daniel's shoulder, she emphatically tells him to turn the plane around. "Head for that stretch of beach where you picked us up," she exclaimed. "I'm going to take care of Margaret Lewis once and for all."

"We're not going back," shouted Daniel. "We'll take care of her later. I'm not landing this plane 'til we reach Miami."

"Who said anything about landing? All I want is one good shot. I'll take her out in the air."

"What are you crazy?! You know how difficult that is? It's damn near impossible to hit a tree from up here."

"Just get me as close as you can," said Ariel, taking a seat at the cargo hatch. "*You should have thrown the map away,*" she grumbled, blaming Margaret for everything that's happened. She then cradled the rifle in the palm of her hand, figuring the best way to steady her aim.

Furious at having to turn the plane around, Ariel such a pain in the ass, Daniel turned to his mother, his eyes pleading that she side with him.

"You mustn't upset her," urged Rachel. "She's the only one that can help you. Besides, she may get lucky."

Judging by the airborne particles around them, the edge of the woods less than a hundred yards away, Tantur can sense Nathan and Clarence heading their way. Blocking the middle of the path, he beckoned to Margaret and Laurian that they stop and turn around.

"What is it," asked Margaret, "… what's out there?"

"Look," answered Tantur, pointing to a specific spot.

Nathan and Clarence wander out of the trees—Clarence with a slight limp, motioning to Nathan that he's okay.

Margaret and Laurian rush down the narrow path to greet them, Laurian embracing Nathan and Margaret squeezing the life out of Clarence. In a bittersweet round of affection, Margaret knowing she'll have to tell Clarence of his uncle's death, and Laurian the news of her biological parents to Nathan, the two women cast a silent plea that the other be the one to speak first.

A subtle smile, Laurian intends to tell Nathan everything, but she compliments him on his demolition work instead. *This isn't going to be easy*, she thought.

Nathan flashed a boastful grin, immediately changing the subject as he is concerned about Shadwell. "How's the old man," he asked. "Is he okay?"

Laurian shook her head, wanting to spare Clarence the bad news.

Suddenly, Clarence let go of Margaret, standing eye to eye with her. "Yeah, Miss Margaret," he took an anxious breath, "… how's my Uncle Will. Is he all right? We gonna be able to cart 'em out 'a these woods?"

A deplorable silence, Margaret not speaking, Clarence

feared the worst. With great remorse, Margaret told him his uncle died peacefully beside her. Clarence, abound with tears, Margaret wrapped her arms around the boy and he buried his face in her neck, sobbing briefly then stepping back.

"What 'em I gonna do, Miss Margaret. I ain't never been on my own b'fore."

Margaret reached out to his rueful chin, lifting it gently upon her fingertips. "You can stay with me," she said.

Clarence managed a smile. "Can I say good-bye 'fore we go?"

Margaret did not argue, nor Tantur, knowing the boy may be up to more than just saying good-bye. "Five minutes," said Margaret, giving Clarence directions on where to rendezvous, explicit that five minutes means he can spend no more than that at the crash site.

Nathan offered to go with him, but as Clarence thought it over, a discerning look toward Tantur, he told Nathan he wanted to be alone with his uncle.

A sign is posted at the edge of the lagoon, one that should never be ignored: No Swimming – Alligators. Tantur, however, disregards the warning, treading knee deep into the water. Washing the war paint from his face, most every day the lagoon is crystal clear, but with Hurricane Andrew stirring things up, Tantur can barely see his feet.

"What's he doing," asked Laurian, she and Nathan just now crossing the beach—relieved to be out of the trees.

"I don't know," answered Nathan.

"He's getting ready to bring his brother to the boat," said Margaret, catching up from behind. "When they leave for South America he'll paint his face again. Red for the anger in his heart and white to mourn his brother's death."

His face rid of the ritual paint, Tantur returned to the woods. Stopping at a mound of palm fronds, he dropped to one knee pulling the top-most frond from his brother's face. Wahota's head is on top of the doctors bag—sides bulging and the top mottled with dirt. Tantur's emotions rise to an implacable fury. He can do nothing to bring his brother back. He can, in spite of everything, *his fury subsiding knowing what's in the doctors bag*, do something to preserve the lineage of his people. A lineage that will last forever.

Sitting between Nathan and Laurian, everyone's feet dangling from the dock, Margaret can't wait to get home. "The first thing I'm going to do is have a drink," she said, listing the ingredients of her favorite rum cocktail. "A wonderful combination … is it not? And I'll enjoy it so much more this time around."

"Look at that!" cried Nathan, jumping up to a penumbrous halo coruscating above the trees. An eye of wonderment, he scrambled to end of the dock, taking in the affordable pleasure.

Laurian sighed. "About that second time around," she said to Margaret, proceeding to forewarn her as before. "I've done some tests on the validity of the serum. I don't know what went wrong … but—"

"*But what?*"

Disappointment soddened Laurian's face. "Your white blood cells are out of control," she said to Margaret. Then, looking her in the eye, "Twenty years, Margaret … you'll be an old woman for sure."

"I best not waste it then," said Margaret, undaunted. "I suggest you do the same," she concluded, caressing the old fedora while motioning to Nathan. "Now would be a good time to tell him."

"I tried telling him in the woods but he changed the subject every time. Almost as if he knew I had something bad to say. I like him, Margaret. I really do. I'd hate to scare him away right now."

"You won't. Trust me, he'll understand."

"You're probably right," answered Laurian, rising to her feet.

"I know it's not the easiest thing to do," said Margaret, "... putting your heart out there with everything on the line. But you're expecting the worst. If you convince yourself otherwise, it will be a lot easier."

Laurian ambled up to Nathan, a gray speck on the horizon moving toward them. "It's beautiful," she said, admiring the sky—the fleshy color of ripe apricots laced hazily above the trees.

"Funny how the day can change," said Nathan. "One minute you're caught up in a vicious storm and the next everything turns to gold." Consumed by silence, the urge to kiss Laurian takes hold and Nathan drew close to her. "It's hard to believe," he said, feeling Laurian's breath upon his, "... everything we've been through in the last two days."

"Nathan," Laurian put a hand on his chest, "... there's something I must tell you."

Pressed softly against his body, a remote look in her eye, Nathan had a feeling something is troubling Laurian. Over her shoulder, before he can speak, he noticed Margaret scrambling to her feet. The gray speck on the horizon, now an aircraft hugging the water, everyone can see it's heading straight for them, gaining altitude at an alarming rate.

"That's the same plane that flew over the island earlier," said Laurian.

Above the treetops, Rachel's seaplane sweeping to the left, the top portion of the cargo hatch pops open and the aircraft wavers a bit before leveling off.

"Nathan!" screamed Laurian, grabbing his arm, "... is that

what I think it is!?"

Nathan saw it too, a rifle barrel protruding from the hatch. "Get down!" he yelled to Margaret, flailing his arms.

The seaplane now parallel to the beach, the hatch reveals a face at the end of the rifle—Ariel's cheek plastered against the walnut stock. Peering into the scope, no one on the dock can see the anguish in her eyes.

Margaret dropped to her knees, a bullet whizzing past her head and splashing into the lagoon.

The seaplane's 300hp engine blaring to his right, Nathan ran as fast as he can toward Margaret, trampling the astatic dock when out of the blue another gunshot erupts. The high caliber round piercing the air, his back shielding Margaret, an unexpected jolt spun Nathan around. A sharp pain surging in his left lung, he saw where the bullet came through; his shirt soaking up the blood.

Margaret dropped the old fedora reaching out to him. Nathan stumbled back and Margaret grasped a handful of air, nothing she can do as Nathan toppled off the dock, plummeting into the cloudy water; his punctured lung collapsing on impact.

Tantur heard the first shot while tending to his brother's body. He heard the second while darting through the trees.

Reaching the edge of the woods, Tantur saw Nathan in the lagoon, struggling to stay afloat. Giving into the pain, his arms and legs nothing but dead weight, Nathan can no longer move them, his body suddenly going under.

Blood now tainting the water, Laurian ran across the dock, diving into the ripples encompassing Nathan's body.

Treading the quaggy sand, Tantur flew past the no swimming sign. He can see Laurian coming up for air, franticly drawing a deep breath and going back under.

Ankle deep in the lagoon, Tantur dove into the shallow water, an uncanny trail of suds in his wake.

Laurian then popped up a third time, Tantur watching as she takes another frantic breath before knuckling into the water.

In seconds, seemingly forever to Margaret, Tantur is a few meters away and she called out to him, "It's not that deep. She should have found him by now!"

Eyeing the shades of gray and light-blue sky over her shoulder, Tantur descending into the murky water, Margaret saw the seaplane heading back for another run. Watching both the lagoon and the poisoned sky behind her, bubbles ascend to the surface and the thought of alligators come to mind.

Too long. They've been under far too long, thought Margaret, an exploding gush of water then rising from the lagoon and Tantur surging through the middle with Laurian on his back, her arms wrapped around his neck gasping for air.

Nathan is nowhere in sight and Margaret is beside herself, clasping her hands in front of her mouth overcome with grief.

Twisting his neck, Tantur broke free from Laurian's chokehold, drawing a quick breath. Tipping his head to the left, dead weight at the end of his arm, he pulled Nathan out of the water, calling to Margaret that her grandson is alive.

"Get him out of there," screamed Margaret. "The plane is on its way back!"

"Come in at an angle this time," yelled Ariel. "That way I'll have an extra shot or two."

"You said you only needed one."

"Just do it, Daniel! She'd be dead if not for Nathan."

The rifle on her lap, Ariel is fraught with anger ejecting the previous shell, jamming another in the chamber and slamming the bolt forward. Her knee on the cabin seat, the lower hatch to steady her aim, accounting for her last shot she peered into the scope—the crosshair centered precisely above Margaret's head.

The seaplane steady at 65 knots, Margaret scrambled across the dock.

Tantur exerts a one-handed backstroke with Nathan on his chest, Laurian managing to keep up, fearful of whether or not Nathan will be all right.

What was I thinking, thought Margaret, gazing reprehensibly at Nathan, … *talking him out of it like that.*

Another gunshot roused the air and the bullet hit a post in front of Margaret, splinters flying out like shrapnel from a bomb.

Ariel loads another round and Daniel is quick with a wise remark that she missed. Rachel, not one to scold her son, turned to do so but her hand is quivering and she froze in her seat. Displeased with Ariel, Daniel shook his head, turning to his mother whose hand is now trembling. "Oh no!" cried Daniel, gazing into his mother's eyes. "Not now!"

Judging the distance from the rifle to Margaret's head, unaware of the situation in the cockpit, with a gentle finger Ariel cradled the trigger. The seaplane, at that very moment, dipped unexpectedly and her finger inadvertently pulled the trigger.

Another miss, the round penetrates a nearby tree, Margaret rushing off the dock, looking up in time to see the expression on Ariel's face.

"What the hell are you doing?" screamed Ariel, loud enough to penetrate Daniel's headset.

"That wasn't me," he shouted back, another jolt and the rifle flying out of the plane. Rising from her position, Ariel looked at Rachel whose head is thrashing back and forth against her seat.

"Get out of there, Rachel. You'll kill us all if you don't."

"I can't! *I'm trying*," she screamed, her fingers unable to unlatch the seatbelt.

Ariel stormed the cockpit, straddling Rachel's armrest while reaching for the latch. Rachel's rabid hand, however, found Ariel's wrist and now both are anchored to the seat.

Reaching the shore, Tantur put Nathan on his back. "He's

not breathing," said Laurian, administering CPR.

A wary eye on the sky, the seaplane fast approaching, Margaret quickly made her way across the beach.

"LET GO!," screamed Ariel, twisting her arm in an effort to break free.

Daniel jabbed his elbow in Ariel's stomach, unaware there is nothing she can do to get away. "Get your ass out of here," he screamed, Rachel then kicking the auxiliary column and Daniel losing control.

Emitting a burst of speed, the seaplane veered left on a collision course for Nathan and the others.

"What's going on up there," exclaimed Laurian, "…four … five … six…" she cried, pumping Nathan's chest.

"I don't know," answered Margaret, appearing over Laurian's shoulder, "… but it doesn't look good."

Her persistent hands in rhythm with Nathan's crepitating breastplate, Laurian glanced at the seaplane, "…twenty-eight … twenty-nine … thirty," she concludes, her hands pumping hard … hard … harder.

Fresh air to Nathan's lungs, *two quick bursts*, Laurian continues… one … two … three …the seaplane sinking faster and faster. Unremitting, she accelerates the rhythmic beat, the pontoons then scraping the treetops and the engine drowning.

Hard … hard … harder… Laurian extrudes an aberrant amount of energy. Suddenly, an explosion rattles the air and Nathan is choking concomitantly.

Laurian promptly flipped him over, an adverse mixture of blood and water discharging from Nathan's mouth—equivocally, a plume of smoke from the seaplane tarnishing the dusky sky.

Unconscious, blood spurting from Nathan's chest, Margaret can see that death is but a heartbeat away. "This is all my fault," she inexpiably said to herself. "I should have listened to you, Nathan. Who was I to keep you from doing what you thought was right. You knew this would happen… and there's nothing we can do to save you."

Clarence stood at the wreckage, an enisled feeling as he stepped under the plane's wing into a new light. The day coming to a close he cannot avoid the shadows; the path before him littered with gloom. Traversing bright spots to dark, the length and breadth of the fuselage buried in a canopy of shade amid a multitude of marred branches, there is a lucent ray of light penetrating the cockpit.

Deliberating if he should go through with it or not, Clarence having to muscle open the cockpit door, he recalls Tantur's encouraging news of a body still warm. Taking his uncle's hand, far from being warm, or icy cold for that matter, Clarence believes he can save him.

Yesterday, with Wahota lying on the porch, Clarence thought he was looking upon death for the first time. His uncle now in front of him, Clarence can't believe how callous he was. Pulling a bottle of water from the small of his back, *the one he smuggled from the cave*, the air around the plastic cylinder is a purple, gleaming haze; Clarence pouring the strange water into his uncle's mouth… most of it bubbling out on the cockpit floor.

"No, Uncle Will! Ya can't leave me like this."

Clarence gave him a little more, but the water, though he closed his uncle's mouth, trickled through his lips. The bottle half-empty, *far too bleak to be half-full*, Clarence pulled his uncle out of the cockpit, dragging him to a patch of dim light.

"Please, Uncle Will, this 'ill save ya. Ya just needs a little ta' go down." Clarence took a deep breath, filling his uncle's mouth full of water. Reversing the process of a drowning victim, time running out and Shadwell lying on his back,

Clarence gave him mouth to mouth with a desperate blast of air. The water finally made its way down, and over and over, a small amount each time, Clarence infused what little there is in the bottle down his uncle's throat.

Margaret said five minutes. Fifteen had gone by and Clarence, a heart so weary he feels nothing but emptiness, laments over the fact that it's time to leave his uncle's sallow body behind. Embracing him one last time, Clarence cast an angry eye toward heaven, blaming God for his loss. The woodland then scatters what is left of the day between the branches and filtering leaves, a glaring light upon the face of William Shadwell and darkness on that of Clarence Brooks.

Sitting beside Nathan, tears from Margaret's cheek fall upon the white sand. She recalls when he was a young boy, watching him in the schoolyard from her car. No one knew of this, and as Nathan lay before her, Margaret sees him not as a dying man but as the little boy in the schoolyard. It was the one day, his seventh birthday, she failed to stay away. Margaret gave him a gift that day and Bourbon the scar over his brow.

"There must be something we can do," exclaimed Margaret, taking Nathan's hand.

"There's not much we can do," said Laurian, suppressing his wound. "His lung is collapsed and he's bleeding internally."

"Cape Coral! We'll take him to the hospital there."

"It's too far, Margaret. He'll either suffocate or drown in his own blood."

"Tantur," Margaret appealed to him, "… if you know of anything that can save him … tell us. *Tell us now.*"

"There is a way," said Tantur, kneeling beside his sworn enemy—a direct descendant of Benjamin Lewis. A merciful change of heart, Tantur is cognizant of the real enemy. He could not do in two hundred years what Margaret did in two days. The Fountain, keeper of lost souls and minister of deceit, she knew all along it was the real enemy, purging this world of its destructive nature.

Removing the compress from Nathan's chest, Tantur dribbled a mouthful of saliva into the bullet-hole. Nathan's blood, coagulating at an alarming rate, Tantur rolled him over brushing the sand from his backside.

In the time it took for Tantur's unique cells to flow throughout Nathan's body, the wound in his back recedes. His wheezing, short spurts of damaged breath, Nathan aspirates a lengthy gasp followed by a loud, horrid squelch … his eyes then springing open and the squelch coming to an abrupt end.

"What just happened," Nathan grabbed his chest.

"We almost lost you," said Margaret.

By the look on Tantur's face, Nathan sensed he should be dead.

"How do you feel, Nathan Lewis," asked Tantur, "… good?"

"No. I feel like I've been hit in the chest with a sledge hammer."

Assisting Nathan to the dock, Tantur is unsure if what he did will last, advising Margaret that they leave as soon as possible. Margaret, however, paid no attention to Tantur, turning away from everyone staring into the woods.

"What's wrong," asked Laurian.

"Clarence should have been back by now."

"We can't wait for him," said Laurian. "Nathan needs medical attention right away."

"You go on ahead. I'll find him and we'll meet up with you later."

"I can handle the boat," said Laurian. "Why don't you

take Tantur with you?"

"Don't worry about me," Margaret lowered her voice, "I'll be all right. Just bear in mind what we talked about before you go. Anywhere in the world, Laurian … he'll understand."

Sprawled out in the back of the boat, Nathan is holding his chest while Tantur helps Laurian to the railing. "Where's she going," asked Tantur; Margaret slipping into the woods.

"She's worried about Clarence. I told her we couldn't wait and she said to go on ahead… that she'd be all right."

"Yes," said Nathan, "I'm sure she will. But we can wait. Give her a few minutes, Tantur."

Laurian kneels beside Nathan, persistent that they don't wait any longer. "*Nathan*," Laurian spoke in a comforting tone, "… we need to get you to a hospital right—"

"I'm fine," said Nathan, sitting up to prove it. "We're not leaving without Clarence."

"What Tantur did back there, you heard what he said. It may not last."

Nathan put a finger to Laurian's lips. "It's okay," he said. "Whatever he did, I don't think it's going away anytime soon."

Having one last thing to mention, that she's the doctor and he's the patient, Laurian is distracted by someone shouting in the woods. Emerging from the trees, Margaret yelled at Tantur to hold the boat. Clarence is with her, Bourbon fidgeting in his arms as they rush across the dock.

Handing the cat over to Margaret, Clarence unties the mooring line giving the boat a gentle push before jumping in.

Tantur cranks the engine, eyeing Clarence while backing the Lady Bird from the dock.

Clarence doesn't say anything and Tantur can't tell if the water worked or not. If it did, it would be nice to know the old man is alive. Whatever the case, Tantur can see Clarence tucked it away for now, something else on his mind by the look of it.

Alone in her grief, an empty seat beside her and the Lady Bird creating a deep furrow in the water, Margaret takes to heart both the memory of her beloved William and the propitious old fedora.

Sitting quietly in the back, Laurian can tell by the look on Margaret's face how distraught she is losing William a second time. Drawing close to Nathan, with everything on the line, Laurian put a firm hand on his chest as before. "I have something to tell you," she said, glancing over at Margaret.

"Go ahead," said Nathan, "… I'm listening."

Edward P. Cummings resides in North Texas. A journeyman welder for more than thirty years, *Behind the Ivy* took over a decade to complete and is the first accomplished work of fiction by the author.

www.ingramcontent.com/pod-product-compliance
Lightning Source LLC
Chambersburg PA
CBHW020931310726
48980CB00007B/726/J

* 9 7 8 0 6 1 5 6 6 3 5 5 5 *